THE COUPLE'S SECRET

BOOKS BY LISA REGAN

Detective Josie Quinn series

Vanishing Girls

The Girl With No Name

Her Mother's Grave

Her Final Confession

The Bones She Buried

Her Silent Cry

Cold Heart Creek

Find Her Alive

Save Her Soul

Breathe Your Last

Hush Little Girl

Her Deadly Touch

The Drowning Girls

Watch Her Disappear

Local Girl Missing

The Innocent Wife

Close Her Eyes

My Child is Missing

Face Her Fear

Her Dying Secret

Remember Her Name

Husband Missing

THE COUPLE'S SECRET

LISA REGAN

bookouture

Published by Bookouture in 2025

An imprint of Storyfire Ltd.
Carmelite House
50 Victoria Embankment
London EC4Y 0DZ

www.bookouture.com

The authorised representative in the EEA is Hachette Ireland
8 Castlecourt Centre
Dublin 15 D15 XTP3
Ireland
(email: info@hbgi.ie)

ISBN: 978-1-80550-142-8
eBook ISBN: 978-1-80550-141-1

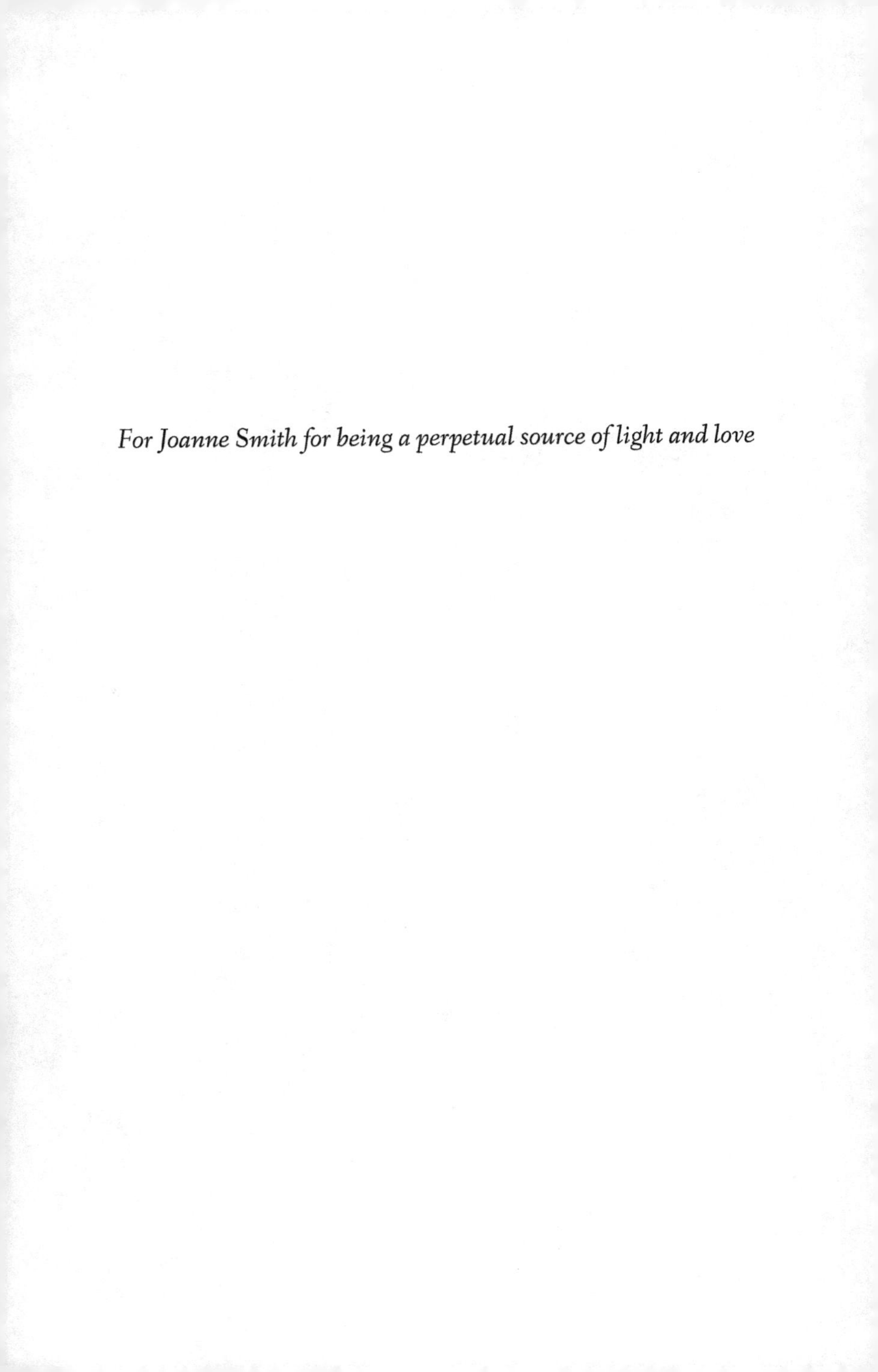

For Joanne Smith for being a perpetual source of light and love

PROLOGUE

Leave while you still can.

She ran her fingers over the words. Someone had carved them into the wood at the bottom of her underwear drawer. A splinter caught in the pad of her index finger. With a hiss, she drew her hand back. Pain stung her skin. A surprising amount of hurt for such a small injury. Her brain latched onto it though, in a desperate attempt to distract her from the uneasiness that coiled around her spine, slithering upward until it set the hair at the nape of her neck to standing.

Leave while you still can.

For almost two years, the words—the warning—had lain hidden beneath her underwear and lingerie. Under the plastic liner that had been there when she arrived. All the drawers had liners, checkered in black and white, more suited to a kitchen than a bedroom. She'd never liked them, but it wasn't as if they were visible all the time. Not unless she hadn't done her wash in a long while. If it wasn't for her leaving her coffee too close to the edge of the dresser while yanking the drawer open too vigorously, she never would have pulled the liner up, never would have seen the message.

The creak of a door opening somewhere in the house startled her. Her skin went clammy. Uneasiness turned to trepidation, settling heavily on her shoulders, like a yoke. Cocking her head, she strained to hear any movement or footsteps. A year ago, she would have called out, hoping it was him. A year ago, she would have shown him the words. He would have reassured her that they weren't meant for her. How could they be? He would have told her how he picked up the dresser from some estate sale or how some customer had given it to him as a gift. Then they'd worry about who had written them.

Now, as she heard the heavy tread of boots approaching, she scrambled to put all her wet, coffee-stained underthings back into the drawer. Her fist curled around the crumpled liner, lukewarm brown liquid dribbling down her wrist. It was too big to put in her jeans pocket, so she stuffed it into the back of the drawer.

There was just enough time to slam the drawer home before the knob on the bedroom door rattled. Cool sweat dampened her nape. She realized her breath had become quick and labored. The words were alive now, a whisper escaping through the seams of the wood.

Leave while you still can.

Hoping she looked far calmer than she felt, she faced the door as it swung open, discreetly brushing her wrist over her hip, wiping away the sticky streak of coffee. Shock made it impossible to force a smile onto her face.

Breathless, she said, "Wh-what are you doing here?"

He smiled, closing the door softly behind him and stepping closer. "You know exactly why I'm here."

"You can't be here. Please. It's not—" Breaking off, she realized she'd been about to say "safe."

It's not safe. There it was, the thing she hadn't wanted to face, hadn't even wanted to think. She didn't want to breathe life into it because if she did, then what?

"Hey." He prowled closer, too close. "Are you okay?"

"Don't."

When he gripped her wrist, she jumped. The cold sweat spread rapidly, forming a sheen over her face. He turned her arm, running his thumb over what was left of the coffee residue. Paralyzed, she wondered if he could hear the words carved into the bottom of the drawer running on a loop in her head now.

Leave while you still can.

She had to stop this. Before it was too late, she had to find a way out.

Squeezing her eyes shut, she spoke, not sure if the word was meant for him or for some deity who had abandoned her long ago.

"Please."

ONE

Detective Josie Quinn let out a stream of curses under her breath as she held up one of her work shirts. Fresh out of the dryer, heat radiated from the fabric. It was the fourth polo she'd pulled out and the fourth one that had small, dark stains peppering its tan material. Some were round, others were in irregular shapes. All of them were permanent. A domestic goddess she was not, but she understood that stains set in the dryer. Tossing the offending shirt into the basket at her feet, she squatted and riffled through the clothes still inside the drum until she found the source of the stains. A lip gloss.

"Son of a—" She swore another streak.

She must have missed it when she checked her pockets. That meant all of her work shirts and almost all of her pants were ruined and she was due on shift in an hour. At least none of her husband's work clothes had been in the load. Both of them worked for the Denton Police Department as part of its four-person investigative team, Noah Fraley as a lieutenant, and she as a detective. The city was small and nestled among the mountains of Central Pennsylvania, along a branch of the Susquehanna River, but it kept them busy.

Josie didn't have time to order a whole new work wardrobe, and she didn't even want to think about how much it would cost. Turning the small, pink cylinder over in her hand, she realized it didn't belong to her. She kept her makeup to a minimum while on duty. Mostly she worried about covering up the ever-present circles under her eyes. On occasion, she wore lip gloss but nearly every tube she owned was upstairs in a bathroom drawer. Another search of the remaining clothes in the dryer revealed a pair of shorts that didn't belong to her. They must have been left in the washer, the lip gloss snug in one of the pockets, and she'd unknowingly mixed them in with her own laundry.

A high-pitched squeal of delight cut through her thoughts, followed by waves of feminine laughter.

"I won again!" eight-year-old Harris Quinn declared triumphantly.

From the laundry room, Josie had a view of most of the kitchen. She had only been half paying attention to the activity while she finished her wash. Everyone seemed to be getting along just perfectly without her anyway. Even their Boston terrier, Trout, was in on the fun, though Josie knew he was only there for any food that might fall to the floor. For a moment, she watched, transfixed. Some muted part of her brain marveled at how life could change so quickly, sometimes in the time it took to answer the door.

Her palm closed around the tube. She didn't need to read the label to know the color. Cosmic Primrose.

Other times, life changed so slowly you didn't even realize it was happening until your home was filled with warmth and laughter and delicious smells and a found family so strange it sounded like the premise of a trashy nineties talk show.

"Don't gloat." Misty Derossi turned away from the counter, pointing a whisk in the direction of the table, where Harris was ensconced on the lap of one of their other guests. "It's not polite."

Trout was seated near Misty's feet, his ears two perfect steeples. His soulful brown eyes tracked every minute movement of the whisk like his life depended on it.

"Mo-om," Harris complained, hopping down. "It's not gloating if I won seventeen times."

What seemed like twenty lifetimes ago, Josie had been married to her high school sweetheart, Ray Quinn. After their marriage fell apart, he'd started seeing Misty. Initially, Josie had been so consumed with jealousy and hurt that she'd treated Misty horribly.

Then Ray died and it turned out Misty was pregnant with his child. A set of bizarre and dangerous circumstances forced the two women together, and the moment Josie held little Harris in her arms, she knew she would give her own life to protect him.

Harris snatched a piece of paper from the kitchen table and brandished it at his mother. "I'm the tic-tac-toe champion!"

Now, Misty was one of Josie and her husband Noah's best friends and Harris called them Aunt JoJo and Uncle Noah.

"It was fifteen times." Erica Slater shifted in her chair, arching a brow at her little rival. "We played seventeen times, and I beat you twice."

Tic-tac-toe was his new obsession. Every person Harris encountered was coerced into playing. Josie and Noah had found dozens of scraps of paper around the house, filled with completed tic-tac-toe games. She'd just cleaned the remnants of several of them out of the dryer filter.

"So the *score* is fifteen to two," said another female voice. The owner of the Cosmic Primrose lip gloss that had just ruined all of Josie's work attire. The girl stood next to Misty, her gaze on the pile of dough she was kneading. Misty was teaching her how to make homemade pasta, and she was a far better student than Josie or Noah had ever been. "This seems like a tournament situation to me. Better keep playing."

Trout looked back and forth between her and Misty. When no scraps dropped at his feet, he whined softly.

Erica snickered as Harris heaved a sigh and climbed back onto her lap. She handed him the pen and they started a new game. His blond head bent in concentration, making the little whorl at the crown of his head visible. Ray had had one exactly like that.

Erica leaned closer to him as their game moved faster, the pen being passed back and forth with lightning speed. Nine months earlier, Josie and Noah had met the twenty-year-old during a case so harrowing that they both still had nightmares about it. Erica had been instrumental in solving it—and in saving Noah's life. Not to mention that she'd turned out to have a shocking connection to Josie's past.

"That's one for me!" she said excitedly, much to Harris's disappointment. "Fifteen to three!"

Erica had quickly and seamlessly become part of Josie and Noah's inner circle. Once a college drop-out, she was now enrolled at Denton University where she could have a fresh start and Josie and Noah could act as part of her support system. Her first semester was under her belt and she was waiting to start summer classes. She stopped by their house often. Her dad, Alec, still lived in Williamsport but he was looking for a job in Denton so he could relocate. Erica's newly discovered maternal grandmother had just moved into a skilled nursing facility nearby. Erica wanted as much time with her as she could get. Josie couldn't blame her. She hadn't had nearly enough time with her own grandmother and Lisette had been present her entire life.

"I won again!" Harris crowed triumphantly, pumping his fist into the air.

"That still doesn't give you permission to gloat." Erica

flicked her long blonde hair over her shoulder, feigning supreme confidence. "I could totally catch up, you know."

He scoffed. "No, you can't! Me and Aunt JoJo played like a hundred times last week. She tried to catch up with me and she couldn't do it and she's the best tic-tac-toe player in the world, besides me!"

Warmth stirred in Josie's chest. At least Harris still adored her. He probably always would. He didn't remember a time when she wasn't in his life, unlike fourteen-year-old Wren McMann, who had shown up on their doorstep on New Year's Eve to declare that her father had died of pancreatic cancer and left custody of her to them.

Abandoning the wash, Josie stepped into the doorway just as Wren turned and aimed a dazzling smile at Harris. "Haven't you ever heard the saying, 'Girls rule, boys drool?'"

Misty laughed, her blonde ponytail swishing across her shoulders as she shook her head. Wren handed her the ball of dough, and she started wrapping it in cellophane. It had to "rest," whatever the hell that meant. Trout watched carefully, whimpering when none of the dough was offered to him.

"Nuh-uh," Harris protested.

"It's true," Wren said solemnly. "Just ask Erica and your mom."

The banter continued. Josie watched Wren. As she teased Harris, her smile reached her eyes. That didn't happen often. She was still very pale, and she'd lost weight since moving in with them. Josie and Noah were legendary for their poor culinary skills but with Misty's help, they'd gotten much better. It wasn't lack of food that kept Wren thin. It was grief. Josie remembered after losing her grandmother—who had been the most important person in her life—that the first few months or so were a blur of raw feelings and utter shock, filled with crushing fatigue and zero appetite. All things considered, Wren was handling it quite well. Her black hair had grown well past her shoulders since she'd arrived, but its tips were still dyed a bright red. If her dad had allowed it, Josie and Noah certainly couldn't tell her to stop—not that it did any harm. Besides, as every parent they knew had told them when they finalized guardianship of Wren—they would need to pick their battles wisely.

"You used to drool in your sleep, honey," Misty teased her son.

Harris's cheeks turned bright red. "No, no. I didn't. I never did!"

Wren and Erica exchanged a conspiratorial smile. Wren had often wondered aloud whether he had a crush on Erica.

"Your Uncle Noah also drools in his sleep," Wren told him. "I saw it just a couple of days ago when he was napping on the couch."

Josie opened her palm and looked at the Cosmic Primrose tube. Wren's therapist had told them that when it came to setting and enforcing house rules, they should not take her grief into account. Children needed structure. It gave them certainty and Wren needed that now more than ever. All Josie had to do was tell her to please check her pockets when she did her wash from now on.

Except that Wren hated Josie. Or at the very least, disliked her intensely. Josie had tried everything to get the girl to open up only to be met again and again with an emotional wall so high that Josie didn't know if it could ever be breached. Whenever Josie had to do or say anything remotely parent- or guardian-like, Wren shut her out for days. Staring at the stupid lip gloss, Josie wondered if this was a hill she wanted to die on.

"Boys do not drool!" Harris insisted.

"Uncle Noah drools all the time," Josie said, pocketing the lip gloss as she walked to the table to ruffle Harris's hair.

She smiled at Wren but all she got in return was a blank stare. Then the girl turned away, busying herself by cleaning up the leftover flour on the countertop. Only Misty seemed to notice the slight, giving Josie a sympathetic smile. Erica was already challenging Harris to another game.

"I've got to get ready for work," Josie said awkwardly. No one responded. Trout, who was normally attuned to every small shift in Josie's mood, didn't even glance at her. Instead, he followed Misty to the fridge, still hopeful that he might receive an unexpected treat.

Josie waited until she got upstairs to the primary bedroom to let out a heavy sigh.

TWO

In their bedroom, Josie dropped the lip gloss on top of her dresser and checked Noah's closet for one of his clean work shirts. No luck. With a sigh, she fished one from the rest of the dirty laundry. She pressed her face into it, reveling in his scent. It had always brought her comfort but more so since he'd been returned to her. Every time she caught the scent of his after-shave or touched him or woke before he did to find him sleeping peacefully beside her, butterflies took flight in her stomach. It was impossible to forget how close she'd come to losing him. At least a dozen times a week, she was assaulted by terrifying memories of the days he'd been missing followed by waves of gratitude that he had survived. Her body could barely contain the emotions, even all these months later.

Pausing, she took a couple of deep breaths and examined the shirt more closely. It was wrinkled but stain-free. It would be huge on her but she didn't have any other options. Luckily, she had one pair of work pants that had escaped the Cosmic Primrose massacre. She changed quickly.

More laughter floated up from the kitchen. Harris loudly declared something, but Josie couldn't make out the words.

She sat on the edge of the bed and pulled her boots on. Her cell phone chirped from its place next to her on the bed. It was a message reminding her that the final payment was due for the venue she and Noah had chosen for their vow renewal ceremony in three weeks. It was an old barn that a nearby farm had converted into a beautiful, rustic event space. They'd only been married for five years but their wedding had been hijacked by a homicide investigation. When the ceremony didn't happen, their guests had danced the night away in the reception hall while the two of them worked against the clock to prevent more carnage.

Unfortunately, they'd been too late to keep Josie's grandmother out of the crossfire. Lisette had been shot. After undergoing extensive surgery, she continued to bleed internally. Knowing that she had days, possibly only hours left, Lisette had insisted that Josie and Noah get married at her bedside. She'd known that if Josie didn't get married before her death, she wouldn't ever do it. It had been a somber occasion. The best and worst day of her life. Just before his abduction, Noah had suggested renewing their vows for their fifth anniversary. It was a way to give themselves the wedding they'd had to skip. Josie had been elated and once Noah was safely home and recovered from his injuries, she'd thrown herself into planning it.

Now, with Wren in their care, it seemed so unimportant.

She stared at the message for a long moment. They had already postponed it once so they could prioritize Wren, moving the ceremony from late April to late June. Maybe they should call it off altogether. They could get their deposit back if they canceled within the next week. Josie had already missed the last two fittings for the dress that her mother and sister had helped her pick out a few weeks before Wren came into their lives. They'd lose a bit of money at this stage, but nothing compared to what their original wedding had cost them. Their home life felt so precarious, so fragile. Perhaps she and Noah should continue to focus solely on their new family unit instead of renewing their vows.

She'd have to talk to him about it.

As she set her phone down, she saw that her nightstand drawer was open. No more than an inch but noticeable. Had she failed to close it properly the last time she was digging around in there? Or had someone been searching the contents? She had her answer when she took a good look inside. The mess of random items she kept there—a flashlight, a pen and notepad, a small bottle of lotion, a bottle of ibuprofen, and some cough drops—had all been rearranged. Josie knew this because normally, they hid the anniversary card Noah had given her last year. It was suggestive to say the least, but the sweet and very private handwritten note he'd scrawled inside had made it impossible to part with, which was why it lived hidden in the recesses of her nightstand drawer.

Beneath that was where she'd been keeping the letter that Wren's father left for her. Now, she saw the corner of it peeking out from under Noah's card. Josie had read it dozens of times. Apparently, Wren had found it and read it as well.

With a sigh, Josie pulled it free. For the second time in the last half hour, she asked herself was this a hill she wanted to die on? Wren had invaded her privacy. Last week, Josie had sat in this exact spot and read the letter twice before wiping her tears and putting it back in its hiding spot. When she'd turned toward the open doorway, Wren had scurried away. Josie had followed her to the living room, asked if everything was okay, if she needed anything, and received a quick "yes" and "no" before Wren bent her head to the sketchpad she carried everywhere and ignored Josie for the rest of the day.

Then, instead of asking to read the letter, she went behind Josie's back and rummaged through her things.

All Josie had to do was go downstairs, take her aside and tell her: "Remember to check the pockets of your clothes before you wash them," and, "Don't go through my personal things. If there's something you want to know about, just ask."

Grief doesn't cancel out accountability. That's what the therapist had said. In other words, Josie needed to parent.

But could she really blame Wren for wanting access to this small piece of her father? Of course not. Josie would gladly have handed it over, if only she'd asked.

"Shit."

Josie unfolded the letter. Its creases were well-worn. Her fingers grazed Dex's neat, blocky handwriting. The letter was addressed to her, but she had always intended to pass it on to Wren at some point. It belonged to her as much as it belonged to Josie. It contained her father's words, his handwriting, his intentions, his reasoning, and shining through it all, his lovely soul.

More excited shrieks came from the kitchen. Trout barked in that way he did when all the humans were excited, and he felt like he needed to be part of it even though he didn't know what was happening. Either that, or no one had given him a treat in a really long time, meaning ten to fifteen minutes.

Dear JoJo,

I wish I didn't have to write this. Like I told you, I was only with Wren's mother once. She never told me I had a daughter. I found out after she died. My beautiful Wren was already nine years old by the time I met her. Imagine that. A little girl who just lost her mom learning that a beast like me is her dad.

A tear rolled down Josie's cheek, off her chin, and landed on the page. Quickly, she blotted it with her shirttail. She hated crying. There wasn't much that could slice through her mental defenses and inspire tears and even when there was, she rarely let them fall. For Dex though, she let them flow. He'd earned it.

He had only looked like a beast. In reality, he was one of the best men Josie had ever known.

When she was three weeks old, she'd been abducted by a woman named Lila Jensen, who passed Josie off as her own in a ploy to get back together with her ex-boyfriend, Eli Matson. By the time Josie was six, Eli was dead and Lila—who had always been careless and neglectful—was free to inflict all manner of abuse on Josie. It had been hell. She had the scars to prove it, on the outside and the inside.

Then, when Josie was thirteen, Lila bewitched Dexter McMann and he moved in with them. Dex had parented Josie more in one year than Lila had her entire life. He had been kind and compassionate, making sure she never went hungry, caring for her when she was sick, taking her to get stitches when she cut herself, helping her with school projects, buying her books she was interested in, and even making sure she was able to go to the freshman dance with Ray.

The problem with being kind to Josie was that it made Lila homicidal.

What did he get for his efforts? Lila set his pillow on fire while he slept, causing catastrophic burns to his face and scalp. Disfiguring him for life. Josie could still smell his flesh and hair burning as she threw a blanket over his head, trying to douse the flames. She could still see the smug smile on Lila's evil face as she guided Dex out of the burning trailer.

Josie had spent her life feeling guilty—and responsible—for what happened to him. She'd only seen him twice since that horrible day and both times he'd tried to convince her that she'd done nothing wrong. The last time she saw him, three months before he died, he'd finally gotten through. It wasn't so much his words that helped her finally let go of the guilt. It was seeing him so genuinely happy, and that happiness had everything to do with his daughter.

Josie wiped another tear away and kept reading even though she had the words memorized by now.

The worst part of all of this is that Wren and I didn't get enough time together. This poor kid is really getting the short end of the stick. Losing everything she ever knew with her mom and now with me. She's at a difficult age, too. Vulnerable and sassy and fragile and mouthy all at the same time. But JoJo, she's spectacular. The brightest star in the whole sky. She's way smarter than me, stubborn as hell, a million times more talented than me, and under all her attitude, she's got a soul that's pure and true and worthy of so much more than what this shitty life has dealt her. She reminds me a lot of you.

"Oh Dex," she choked. Never once had she gotten through the letter without breaking at those words. This was a very sadistic form of self-torture, but she couldn't stop herself.

You think you trust the people in your life. Then you become a parent, and you realize that there's a hell of a long way between leaving your kid with someone for a few hours and entrusting them with your kid's emotional well-being—with their soul. That's what this comes down to, JoJo. My daughter's beautiful, tender heart and her wonderful soul. It's going to be shredded. Destroyed. When I thought about the best person to pick up the pieces, there was only you.

Josie wiped some snot from her nose with the back of her hand. Good God. How had Wren felt reading this? Reading all the incredible things her father said about her? Being reminded just how fiercely he'd loved her? Had it been a comfort? Had it felt like a small gift among days of endless mourning? Or had it made her miss him worse than she already did? Had it made her furious at the unfairness of life? Grief was different for everyone. Something that might buoy one person could crush another. Although Wren spent a lot of time in her room, Josie hadn't seen her upset recently. Noah hadn't said anything either.

According to the clock on Josie's nightstand, she had fifteen minutes to get to work. Quickly, she read the rest of the letter.

You've been through a lot and come out stronger for it. You also know what it's like to lose people you love. Wren's going to need someone who's been there to get her through all this. There's no one better suited than you. I know you'll put Wren first because that's the kind of person you are. You have a good heart, a big heart, and I know it's big enough for my little girl (even if she's not so little anymore). If you're reading this, then it means I went faster than expected and didn't have a chance to ask you to take Wren or a chance to introduce the two of you —to get you both used to the idea. To meet and talk with your husband and ask him to be part of this, too. For that, I'm sorry. What I'm not sorry about is having been in your life. That was my honor. I should have told you this a long time ago, but I love you, kiddo.

Tell Wren not to be too sad. I'll always be right here, even if it's just in spirit.

Dex

Josie wiped away more tears. Cheers erupted from downstairs. Trout barked again. Were they still having a tic-tac-toe tournament or had they moved on to something else? Whenever Harris came over, Wren indulged his every request. Tic-tac-toe, Mario Kart, tag, hide-and-seek. She even played catch with him out front. If he wanted to watch a show or a movie, she made popcorn and curled up on the couch with him. Sometimes he brought books and asked her to read with him. Erica was just as game. When all three of them were there, it tended to get loud.

Regardless of what they were doing, they'd be having fun the better part of the afternoon and evening. Misty would oversee their activities until Noah got home. Josie tucked the letter back into the bottom of the drawer and then retrieved her service weapon from its lockbox on the top shelf of their closet. Downstairs, everyone had moved into the living room. Wren, Harris, and Erica were so intensely focused on the video game they were playing that none of them heard or acknowledged Josie's goodbye. Trout, at least, gave her a head tilt. From the couch, Misty smiled and mouthed, *I got this*.

That was probably for the best because Josie certainly didn't.

THREE

Denton Police headquarters was located in the most densely packed part of the city, its historic central district. The building towered over the others along its main thoroughfare, as imposing as a castle with its gray stone façade, bell tower, and arched double-casement windows. Seventy years ago, it had been converted from the town hall into the police station. Josie loved the old building. Each time she pulled into the municipal parking lot behind it and entered on the ground floor, a sense of calm washed over her.

Everything always made sense at work.

Even while investigating the most difficult and unpredictable cases, there were always rules and procedures to rely on. They lent a consistency that Josie had never found in any other place in her life. Except, perhaps, with Noah.

She trudged up the stairs to the second-floor great room. It was a large, open area filled with desks, filing cabinets, and a printer that was arguably as old as her. Most of the workstations were used by uniformed officers for completing paperwork or making phone calls. Only five of the others were permanently assigned. One belonged to their press liaison, Amber Watts.

Josie, Noah, and the other two members of their investigative team, Detectives Gretchen Palmer and Kyle Turner, held the remaining desks. They had all been pushed together in the center of the room, forming a rectangle. It was supposed to make them feel as though they were sitting around a table together while they discussed open cases and gave change-of-shift reports, but with Turner now directly across from her, Josie hated the idea more and more.

"Hey." Noah turned from his computer and smiled at her.

All the anxiety and sadness from earlier, at the house, drained away. He'd always had a calming effect on her. She didn't remember needing it as much as she had since Wren came into their lives. Then again, she'd never been so afraid of screwing something up as she was with Dex's daughter.

"You lose some weight since yesterday, Quinn?" said Turner.

As usual, he was dressed in a suit like he was headed to court for testimony. Leaning back in his chair, he clutched his cell phone in one hand while his thumb scrolled endlessly. With the other hand he squeezed a small foam basketball. The day he started, he'd affixed a tiny net to his desktop. Josie rarely saw him make a basket. It had been more than two years since their colleague, Detective Finn Mettner, was killed in the line of duty. Just over a year since Turner joined their team. Whereas Mettner had been fastidious, prompt, and respectful, Turner was a mess. His reports were subpar and usually late. He tended to disappear for long stretches of time during shifts with no explanation. There was also the matter of his sexist and inappropriate remarks, though he was learning to behave himself there.

To say working with Turner had been an adjustment was the understatement of the century.

Josie ignored him.

"Oh, what? You're not talking to me today?" Turner goaded.

Noah's brow furrowed as she walked toward him and leaned a hip against the edge of his desk. He touched the fabric of the shirt where she'd tucked as much of it in as possible. "Is this mine?"

"Yes," she said. Lowering her voice, she filled him in on the lip gloss catastrophe.

"Did you talk to her?"

Josie didn't respond.

Noah grimaced. "It's going to be expensive to replace all those clothes. I understand she didn't do it on purpose, but this is definitely something that needs to be addressed."

Josie looked away from him. At her back, she could hear Turner's chair creak. She almost wished he'd throw his stupid basketball and miss so she didn't have to have this conversation.

"Josie," Noah said softly. "This is uncharted territory for all of us. Wren's loss is pretty raw right now. She'll come around."

"Will she?"

The unspoken questions swirled at the front of her mind. What if they couldn't do this? What if they couldn't give Wren what she needed? What if they were never meant to be parents —of any kind? What if they just weren't cut out for it?

Noah didn't answer.

"She hates us," Josie said. "Me more than you but still, she hates us."

For the longest time, Josie hadn't even wanted children. After working through some of her past traumas, she'd changed her mind only to find out that she had fertility issues that would make it extremely difficult for her to get pregnant. The fertility treatment options open to them were far too costly given their salaries, and were not guaranteed to work. They'd spent the better part of last year getting approved to adopt a baby. They'd even started painting the nursery. Then their lives were turned upside down. Noah was abducted and their approval was revoked. They hadn't even had a chance to fully process the news when Wren came into their lives. They'd been preparing for an infant, not a grieving teenager.

Josie wasn't sure why, but the stakes felt so much higher with Wren. It seemed like the potential to fail her was so much bigger than it might have been with a baby, though she wasn't exactly sure why. More than Josie wanted anything else in the world, she wanted to be the guardian that Wren needed.

"That's not true," said Noah. "She doesn't hate us."

"Come on, Noah. She barely speaks to either of us and yet, she literally gets along with everyone else in our lives like they're her family."

It was true. Wren was a completely different person when she was around other people. Open, kind, good-humored, interested, funny, talkative. She absolutely adored Josie's twin sister, Trinity Payne, a famous television journalist, and her FBI agent fiancé, Drake Nally. Josie's parents had finally moved to Denton back in March, and watching the three of them together, it would be easy to assume that Wren was *their* daughter. Even the Chief of Police, Bob Chitwood, and his much younger sister, Daisy, who was college-age now, got to experience Wren at her most relaxed. So did Gretchen and her adult daughter, Paula.

Noah frowned.

"You know I'm right," said Josie. "She responds to everyone except us."

Something soft hit the back of Josie's neck. The foam basketball fell and bounced along Noah's desk. Turner said, "Of course she hates you."

Josie turned her body, staring at him in disbelief. "Are you kidding me right now? Eavesdropping?"

Turner held one of his large palms up, signaling for one of them to return the ball. "You're not that quiet, lovebirds."

Noah snatched it from the desk and scowled at Turner. "Stay out of this."

Turner never had learned to follow instructions. Rocking in

his chair, he shrugged. "It's not a criticism, LT. I'm just saying. This kid lost her mom, right? Then she spends a few years with Dad, finally gets settled in and starts to feel all happy again and then bam! Dad dies, too, and he leaves her with two people she's never met and now she has to start over."

Josie glanced at Noah to see that the shock in his expression matched her own.

When neither of them spoke, Turner kept going. "Listen, the one thing this kid knows for sure, with one hundred percent certainty based on her experience, is that the people who are supposed to take care of her die. That's a fact. Why would she want to get close to the third parent or parents in line? You'll probably die, right? In her mind, anyway. Plus, you're law enforcement, so you've got that inherent risk of death and all that shit. Just be glad she wasn't here for the whole home invasion and abduction thing. You would have never gained her trust after that."

Studying him, Josie wondered if she'd slipped into some alternate universe when she walked through the stairwell door. Turner looked the same with his unruly brown curls threaded with gray, deep-set blue eyes, neatly trimmed beard and perpetual smirk, but this guy was definitely not the crass, thoughtless, irritating douchebag she'd come to know and want to throat-punch. He was almost... insightful. Even the therapist Wren saw hadn't mentioned this.

"Okay." Noah tossed the ball across the desks. "What should we do?"

Turner laughed, aiming for and missing another basket. "How the hell should I know? Do I seem like the kind of guy who knows how to handle an emotionally scarred teenager?"

He definitely didn't. Then again, Josie knew absolutely nothing about Turner outside of work. She knew he'd come from a department a little larger than Denton and that he'd solved a very famous case involving high-end escorts that had garnered a lot of press coverage. That was it. They had never discussed each other's personal lives. The only reason he knew so much about theirs was because of his eavesdropping and his work on Noah's abduction case last year. He didn't wear a wedding band, but she had no idea whether he'd ever been married or if he had a girlfriend or even children.

Did he have children? The thought made her stomach turn. "How do you know this stuff?" she asked.

Turner stood and walked around until he was standing in front of her. He towered over her. Amusement danced in his eyes but now, having worked together for a year, Josie noted the tiny flicker of something else. It lasted the span of a heartbeat. Pain? Vulnerability? She couldn't tell.

"Seriously," she said. "How do you know this stuff?"

He pulled out a crumpled dollar bill from his jacket pocket. "After-school special, sweetheart."

With that, he stepped to the side and stuffed the dollar into a money-packed jar on Josie's desk. Noah had instituted the jar system shortly after Turner joined the team. It was a form of operant conditioning, he'd explained. Behavior that was punished was less likely to occur in the future. Well, that was the hope. Every time Turner called Josie "sweetheart" or "honey," he had to place a dollar in her jar. Any time he made an inappropriate comment, he owed her a dollar. He owed Gretchen a dollar whenever he called her "Parker" instead of her actual name, Palmer. It worked both ways. If Josie called him a douchebag to his face, she put a dollar in his jar. Same with Gretchen, though her preferred name for him was "jackass."

These days, the dollars were far more likely to find their way into a jar when one of them intentionally broke the rules, like Turner just had.

Like Gretchen did as she sailed through the door, a cupholder in one hand and a dollar in the other. As she passed

Turner, she slapped it into his waiting hand. "Afternoon, jackass."

He grinned at her back. "Detective Palmer, you're in a fine mood today."

Gretchen didn't spare him a glance as she settled behind her desk, handing a coffee across to Josie. "I'll be in a better mood when you get out of here. Let the real police handle shit."

It was the most pleasant these two had ever been to one another.

Turner studied the bill thoughtfully and Josie knew he was weighing his options. Poke the bear or stand down?

Noah cleared his throat, drawing Turner's attention. "Take the money, Detective."

Gretchen didn't acknowledge any of it. She booted up her computer and took her reading glasses from the top of her head where they were frequently nestled in her short, spiked brown and gray hair.

Josie folded her arms across her chest. "Or tell us where all this insight into the hearts of teenagers really came from."

Turner stuffed the bill into his pocket and gave her a blinding smile, followed by a wink. "Nah. I've got to maintain my air of mystery. How else am I gonna get you to hang on my every word, Quinn?"

Before she could respond, he turned and sauntered off, disappearing into the stairwell.

"Good riddance," Gretchen muttered.

"Well," said Noah. "I guess I'm giving the report myself."

He gave them a rundown of all pertinent information, then handed Josie a file. "I didn't have a chance to go speak with this woman, so if you can get out to her place and take down her statement, grab any documents or anything else she's got, that'd be great."

Josie cracked it open, immediately recognizing the name. The poor woman had a stalker—one savvy enough to be untraceable thanks to modern technology. She'd been contacting police and documenting everything for the past year.

"We'll go see her first thing," Josie said.

Noah stood and took her hand, squeezing it. He was headed home now that she was on duty. They'd been working a lot of opposite shifts to ensure that one of them was almost always at the house. "Want me to talk to Wren?"

What Josie wanted was to wrap her arms around his waist and bury her head in his chest. It was hard not to touch him whenever they were in the same room after what had happened last year, but they'd always been discreet at work. Still, with only Gretchen in the room, neither of them was worried about a little hand-holding and possibly a chaste kiss.

"No," said Josie. "I need to be the one to do it. Just try to get a read on her, will you? She's more likely to talk to you than me. I'm pretty positive she snuck into our room and went through my nightstand to read Dex's letter. That also needs to be addressed."

"I can do that," he said. "It's my room, too."

"No. I need practice doing this whole guardian thing. Let me handle it. I'll figure out how to talk to her but for now, can you just check in with her? I just want her to be okay."

"I'll do my best." Noah pressed a kiss to her forehead. "Josie, we can do this, you know."

She smiled, trying to look as though she believed him, but he saw right through that. Chuckling, he gave her one last, light kiss and whispered, "Just wait. Everything will work out."

She wished she could be as optimistic as him.

FOUR

Josie pumped the brakes of her SUV in time to avoid running over a groundhog sauntering across the road. The stalking victim lived in northeast Denton, in a secluded development near the top of a mountain. Josie and Gretchen had finished taking her latest statement and headed back to the stationhouse, passing through a remote area of forest. With the rodent out of the way, she sped up, rounding a corner only to be confronted by the mother of all sun glare.

"Shit."

She slowed again and flipped down the visor, blocking out some of the blinding June sunshine. She'd forgotten her sunglasses, because apparently she was too frazzled to handle even the smallest task that wasn't work-related. Wren had turned her entire world upside down in the best and worst ways. The best because Josie was honored that Dex had chosen her to care for his daughter and she genuinely liked Wren. The worst because watching the girl wade through the devastation of losing her father ripped Josie's heart out every single day.

"What do you think?" asked Gretchen, interrupting her thoughts.

Josie glanced over to the passenger's side where Gretchen was adjusting the air-conditioning vent so that the air blew directly on her. She hadn't forgotten her sunglasses.

"About the stalking victim," Gretchen clarified, knowing with uncanny accuracy that Josie's thoughts were at home.

Ever since she decided she wanted to have children, Josie had worried that she'd be terrible at caring for a child because she'd be too consumed with work to be present when that child needed her, but as it turned out, it was quite the opposite.

Who knew?

"I think—"

Josie was interrupted by the sound of her portable radio squawking. In the dispassionate tone that all their police dispatchers used, a male voice announced that a car had gone into the Susquehanna River and asked all nearby units to respond. Josie noted the location. Her pulse ticked upward. She slammed on the brakes and did a U-turn in the middle of the two-lane road, glad there was no one else around.

Although Gretchen had been with the Denton PD for nearly ten years after having worked for Philadelphia PD's Homicide squad, she wasn't as familiar with Denton as Josie, who had grown up there. "I don't— Where is that?"

Josie punched the gas. "We just passed the turnoff about a mile back. It'll take us five minutes to get there. There's a road that leads down to an abandoned state mental hospital. Past that is another road that runs along the riverbank."

Gretchen advised dispatch that they were on their way with an ETA of five minutes. Then she turned to Josie, voice incredulous. "There's an abandoned state mental hospital in Denton?"

Josie laughed as she took the turn with screeching tires and barreled toward the old hospital campus. "It's more like the ruins of it. None of the buildings are even standing anymore. No one lives around here—as you could see from the drive—and hardly anyone uses these roads. There's an old boat ramp though, so sometimes fishermen launch from there."

It was the beginning of June, which meant that it was open season for most fishing. It was possible that someone had been fishing in the area and their vehicle rolled into the water, from the boat ramp—especially if it was in poor condition.

The grounds of the defunct mental hospital appeared. On either side of the road were grassy areas overgrown with brush and weeds that sprang up among the heaps of rubble that used to be buildings. Straight ahead, at the bottom of the hill, was the road that ran perpendicular to the one they were now on. It was lined with trees but through gaps in the foliage, the Susquehanna was visible. Josie took a left, hoping she remembered the location of the boat ramp correctly. It had been years since she'd been here.

"There," said Gretchen.

A woman stepped out from the trees and into the road, waving her arms over her head. Josie stopped the vehicle in front of her. She and Gretchen hopped out.

Searching behind the woman, Josie asked, "Where's the car?"

"I'll show you." The woman smiled serenely and turned back in the direction of the bank. She didn't seem to be in much of a hurry.

As they followed her through a break in the trees, Josie noted her khaki pants, short-sleeved button-down white blouse, and black galoshes. Her brown curls were tied into a ponytail that stretched almost to her waist.

Gretchen said, "What's your name?"

"Heather Slack. Dr. Heather Slack. I'm a paleontologist at Denton University."

"You saw a car go into the river?" Josie asked. There would be time for other questions later. Right now, the priority was getting to the vehicle.

As it was, Josie didn't feel as though the doctor was moving fast enough. The urge to push ahead of Dr. Slack and race toward the water was almost too great to resist. Then again, the path they were taking was covered in uneven rocks. One wrong move could cause a bad fall or a sprained ankle.

"Oh, I didn't see a car go in," Dr. Slack said over her shoulder. "I just saw it under the water. I mean, I think that's what it is."

Gretchen glanced back at Josie, one eyebrow arched. Had dispatch gotten the call wrong?

"You're not sure if it's a car?" Josie asked.

Dr. Slack held a branch out of the way so they could pass in front of her. "I don't know what else it could be."

Now in front, Gretchen stepped aside to let Josie take the lead. She moved swiftly, surefooted even in her boots, this kind of terrain familiar after having traversed it since childhood. Seconds later, they emerged onto a stony ledge. The river basin stretched out before them. At their feet brittle husks of underwater river grass poked from between bone-dry rocks. The river used to be at this height, but the county had been in a near-constant state of moderate to severe drought for the past two years. There was a four-foot drop from the ledge into the expanse of sunbaked river stones and cracked mud. The water's edge was at least twenty-five feet away.

Dr. Slack joined Josie and Gretchen along the edge and pointed across the water. "I've been coming down here for the past several days—this area, I mean. The water must have receded even more because now there's a weird kind of ripple over there."

The current was almost non-existent and for the most part, aided by the sunlight, they could see to the bottom in the shallowest parts of the water, even though it was brown. Near the center of the river, at its deepest point, there was a tinge of blue-green. Josie saw the ripple Dr. Slack had indicated immediately.

Something under the otherwise smooth surface of the water caused a break in the lazy current, forming tiny swells.

"I see it," said Gretchen. "How do you know it's a car?"

"Over here," Heather instructed, leading them along the bank to a more elevated position. It was then that Josie saw the shadow of what looked like a big hulking box, the long rectangular shape of a roof, its angles too sharp to be a large rock or pile of organic debris.

Quickly, Josie took off her belt, dropping it, along with her holster and pistol, onto the ground. Next came the contents of her pockets—credentials and phone—and then she tore off her boots and socks.

"What are you doing?" Dr. Slack asked.

"Checking to see if anyone is alive," Gretchen told her.

Between the two of them, Josie was the stronger swimmer. She ran barefoot along the ledge until she found the lowest spot and dropped into the basin. Skipping from rock to rock, she raced toward the water, keeping the ripple in sight. It was cold, even at ankle and calf level. Goosebumps erupted along her skin as she waded deeper. This time of year, the water temperature hovered between seventy and seventy-five degrees. It wasn't ideal but as long as she limited her exposure and entered gradually, she should be able to avoid cold water shock, cold water incapacitation, hypothermia and circum-rescue collapse. Despite wanting to dive right under the water, Josie took her time immersing herself, breathing carefully. At waist level, she splashed water on her face and the back of her neck. Once she got to shoulder level, she gritted her teeth, sucked in a deep breath and dove under.

Even with the sunlight piercing the surface and the calm current, this deeper part of the river was murky. As Josie swam toward the object, her movements kicked up silt and dirt from the rocks and underwater plants, making her surroundings cloudier. It didn't take long to reach the object but even up close, it was difficult to tell whether it was a car or not. Touching its surface, her hand slid over a slimy film. She pushed through it, feeling something hard beneath. The dislodged particles of the grime spread like a dust, filling the water all around her, obstructing more of her view.

Josie's lungs started to burn but she kept going, using her hands to map the shape of the object. The flat edge of a roof, the seam along the tops of doors, then a crack a few inches wide, big enough for Josie to put her arm through, feeling only empty space. Beneath that was the solid surface of what must be a window and under it, a metal lip. Then a door handle. She didn't attempt to open it. With a coating of muck this thick, the car must have been in the water for some time. If anyone was inside, they were long dead. Josie kicked back to the surface, gulping air as soon as she broke through. Treading water, she turned and saw that Gretchen and Dr. Slack had been joined on the bank by a uniformed officer.

Her nose caught a whiff of something rotten and putrid, something beyond the usual pungent, earthy smell of the river. Decomposition. It hovered over the top of the water, churned up by her exploration, there and gone in an instant. A familiar feeling of dread settled in her stomach.

"Shit."

The car would need to be removed from the river, cleaned up and processed. It could take hours, days even, before they could begin to piece together where it had come from, how it ended up submerged and who had been inside it.

Josie glanced at the shore again where more officers gathered along with a pair of EMS workers and a couple of firefighters. The press wouldn't be far behind, particularly if it was a slow news day. Years ago, any member of the public in the Commonwealth of Pennsylvania could purchase a police scanner and tune in to their local department's radio communications. Now, anyone could livestream that same audio via a website called Broadcastify. Like many departments across the country, Denton PD used a timed encryption with a fifteen-minute delay. Someone from their local news station was always listening for calls that might lead to a big story. With Denton's police, fire department and EMS deployed, there was no way reporters would pass up a call like this one.

Josie sucked in a few more breaths and plunged back under. Visibility was worse. Again, she used her hands, disturbing more of the sludge until she found the slope of what she hoped was the back windshield. It was still intact. Then came the square expanse of a trunk. With nothing to grab onto, her body slipped, buoyancy sending her upward until she slid across the roof. Before the current carried her too far, she kicked away from the car, diving deeper, and swam around to the rear until she touched something that felt like the hollow under the wheel well.

She gripped the edge. More thick biofilm oozed in and around her fingers. Her hands ached with the cold and the effort of keeping hold of the slippery car. She worked her way around to the rear bumper until her fingertips brushed the slight depression in the center of it where the license plate was affixed. There were too many layers of filth to claw away for her to get a look at the number, especially in the hazy brown all around her. Instead, she slipped her fingertips underneath it, grabbing both sides, and started to bend and yank at it. A pressure spread through her chest, lungs searing from lack of oxygen. She brought her legs up to brace her feet against the bumper for leverage. Muck squeezed between her toes as she struggled to find purchase.

Just as she reached her limit, needing more air, the license plate snapped off. Clutching it in one hand, she pushed off the back of the car, bursting out of the water. She swam toward the bank. By the time she was able to stand, Gretchen and two uniformed officers were wading into the water.

Officer Brennan held out his arm for her to take. Josie waved it away. "I'm fine," she breathed. "There is a car. Been there a while."

"What the hell is that?" asked Brennan, pointing at the bent license plate in her hand.

It was still covered in filth, reddish-brown mud and organic matter with an extra-special coating of something that felt jelly-like.

"The tag," Josie explained. "We'll have to find something to scrape all this off."

Officer Dougherty reached them, shading his eyes with one hand. "Maybe a stick or something."

Gretchen fell in beside Josie as they came to the dry part of the basin. "The ambulance will have something we can use."

"I'll go find out," said Dougherty.

Noah's shirt was long and heavy on Josie's body. Without her belt, it had come loose from her waist, swinging as she walked, the hem slapping against her pants. Locks of her black hair stuck to her cheeks. The scent of the river clung to her and under it, that hint of decomposition again.

Josie scanned the ledge. At least a dozen people waited for them. "Gretchen," she said. "Once we figure out how to bring the car up, this entire area will need to be cleared. If there's anyone inside that car, I don't want their loved ones finding out on the news."

With a nod, Gretchen hoisted herself back up onto the ledge and then held the license plate while Josie did the same. Dougherty appeared at her side and draped a blanket over her shoulders.

"Ambulance had it," he explained. "They've got some stuff we can use to clean up the tag."

"Thanks. Take this. I want to see if we can get the number and run it."

Dougherty grimaced but took the slimy license plate and

disappeared along the same rocky path they'd used to get to the bank. Through the trees, Josie caught glimpses of emergency vehicles and what she guessed was a van from their local news station, WYEP.

"Let's go," said Gretchen, gesturing toward the spot where Josie had left her pile of belongings. Dr. Slack was still there as well, watching all the activity with curiosity.

Josie hugged the blanket tightly around her shoulders, grateful they'd been having an unusually warm June.

"I was right, wasn't I?" asked Dr. Slack when they reached her.

Josie nodded and found the widest, flattest rock she could, sinking onto it and trying to get her socks over her damp feet. "Yeah. I'm not sure how long it's been under there, but you might not have seen it if the water levels weren't so low."

A notepad and pen appeared in Gretchen's hands. She put on her reading glasses. "What were you doing down here?"

Dr. Slack waved a slender arm in the direction of the basin. "Looking for fossils."

Gretchen dipped her chin, looking over the top of her glasses, brows raised skeptically. "Fossils? In the Susquehanna?"

"Oh yes." Dr. Slack clapped her hands together. "You'd be surprised. With the water levels down for so long, I was hoping to get a better look in areas that are normally submerged. There's an old boat ramp upriver, not far from here at all. That's where I'm parked. I could show you what I've already found, if you'd like."

"Maybe some other time," Gretchen said. She shot Josie a look, her unspoken question loud and clear in the air between them. *Is this a real thing?*

Josie fussed with her socks, trying to smooth the fabric over her feet but they just wouldn't sit right on her moist skin. "There are fossils in the Susquehanna," she told Gretchen. "In fact, back in the nineties, paleontologists discovered a 360-some million-year-old fossil up in Renovo. First of its kind. A 'fish with fingers' I think they called it."

"That was exciting," Dr. Slack said enthusiastically, her eyes widening. "The most I've ever found around here were trilobites and crinoid fragments."

"Right," Gretchen said. "Until today."

"Oh, well, yes."

Josie yanked her boots over the top of her crinkled socks while Gretchen took down the paleontologist's personal information and sent her on her way. Moments later, Dougherty reappeared, hurrying toward them, phone in hand.

"You got something?" Gretchen asked.

"Yeah," he said. "The tag is dead. Hasn't been renewed since 2018."

The dread in Josie's stomach solidified into a hard mass. She buckled her belt and made sure her holster was securely in place. "What else?"

With the back of his hand, Dougherty rubbed at his forehead. "The license plate is from a 2015 Hyundai Accent. Owner was a man named Tobias Lachlan."

"That sounds familiar," said Gretchen.

"Yeah," Dougherty replied. "I thought so, too, so I did a quick internet search. Seven years ago, Lachlan and his fiancée, Cora Stevens, went missing from Brighton Springs. No trace of them has ever been found."

FIVE

Josie's eyes were drawn to the ripple in the middle of the river, marking the location of the Lachlan vehicle. A prickling sensation spread over her scalp. She tugged her fingers through her matted hair but it was no use. There wasn't any physical cause for the uncomfortable feeling. She'd been on the job a long time and had worked enough cases to know when something big and ugly was on the horizon.

"We'll need Hummel and his team," she said.

Officer Hummel was the head of Denton's Evidence Response Team. They were a big enough department with a big enough budget to support their own evidence techs and some basic forensic equipment. Anything they couldn't handle went to the state police crime lab.

Dougherty blinked. "For an underwater... crime scene?"

Josie had no idea how a situation like this would or could be handled. If the car had been under there for seven years, that was seven years of seasons changing, rising and falling water levels, growth and decomposition of marine life and underwater vegetation, and shifting accumulation of chemical substances. The car alone would likely be a nightmare to remove and process. The odds of finding anything in the riverbed around it were slim to none but, as always, they only got one chance to properly process a scene.

"Just call him," Josie said.

"If we have to call in resources from elsewhere, we will," Gretchen added.

Dougherty nodded.

Josie used the blanket to pat her clothes dry. Well, as dry as she could get them. Normally, she had a set of backup clothes in her vehicle for situations like this one, but she'd changed into those two days ago after she'd had to interview a witness living in a flea-infested apartment. Those had been double-bagged and deposited into the garbage. "See if you can get rid of any press that showed up. Erect a perimeter from the boat ramp all the way down to here."

He looked over his shoulder, in the direction of the boat ramp. It couldn't be seen from where they stood but they had to consider the possibility that the car had gone into the water from there. With the windows cracked, the air inside the tires would have given it buoyancy for a short time. From the ramp, it could have floated, slowly sinking, until it reached its final resting place.

"Yes," Josie said. "The boat ramp, and Dougherty, whatever happens, do not let this get out. We still don't know what we're dealing with here."

Gretchen said, "Once the car is removed, we'll need to match the VIN to the license plate."

"Right," said Dougherty, scratching at his forehead again.

Josie strongly doubted that someone had swapped license plates and affixed Tobias Lachlan's to some other vehicle before it ended up in the river, but they had to be sure.

The moment he walked off, both of them took out their phones. It would be a half hour or more until Hummel arrived, and Josie was certain that the job at hand far exceeded the capabilities of his team. Rounding up the necessary people and equipment to remove and process the car would take even longer.

They had nothing but time.

"Brighton Springs," Gretchen murmured as she scrolled. "Isn't that where Chief Chitwood is from?"

"Yep."

The Chief hadn't worked in that area in decades, but his father, Harlan Chitwood, had been a decorated and celebrated detective on the Brighton Springs police force for almost fifty years before his retirement. He'd also been one of the dirtiest police officers that Josie had ever known. His time with Brighton Springs PD was up long before Tobias Lachlan and Cora Stevens disappeared, but the corruption lingered.

"That's how far from here?" Gretchen asked. "Two hours?"

"Three," Josie answered as a photo of the couple came up on her search.

At a glance, they appeared to be in their early to mid-forties. Perhaps Cora was younger. The photo showed them at a concert of some kind. Evening had been setting in. Bright lights in the background illuminated a raised stage. All around them people were packed together, faces turned up toward a musician—leather pants and a mic stand the only thing visible from the angle of the photo. Bright orange bracelets circled Tobias and Cora's wrists. Each of them raised a red solo cup in a toast. Wide smiles split their flushed faces. Tobias's hair had receded from his forehead, leaving a dark fuzz around his crown and over his ears. He had a friendly, open smile and the bulky build of someone whose athleticism had waned with age. Cora was tucked under his arm. She was short and curvy with strawberry-blonde hair that barely brushed her shoulders. Her brown eyes were bright and sparkling.

Gretchen peered down at her own phone, obviously perusing one of the thousands of articles about the couple that had popped up online in the past seven years. She read off the pertinent facts. "They lived in Brighton Springs. Went out to dinner. Left in Tobias's car. Somewhere between the restaurant and their home—a twenty-minute drive—they vanished into thin air. Their car was never even found—now we know why."

How had they ended up in Denton?

"Any chance Trinity did a show on this couple?" asked Gretchen. "Seems like a case she would take on."

Josie's twin sister had her own television show called *Unsolved Crimes with Trinity Payne.* Every week she took on a cold case, laying out the facts, offering theories, and asking viewers for help bringing new information to light.

"It's possible," Josie said. "But I don't want to call her just yet. I'm not tipping my hand unless I have to. She's brutal when she smells a story, especially if it's a follow-up to something she's already investigated, even though she knows I can't tell her any details."

"Fair."

Josie skimmed article after article, clicking through photo after photo of the couple. The Lachlan/Stevens case had been the subject of intense public scrutiny, locally and nationally. People were intrigued. They couldn't get enough. Clicking on a couple of true-crime forums, Josie saw seemingly endless threads about it. It had become an obsession for Brighton Springs residents and cold case buffs nationwide. At the time of the disappearance, several national media outlets ran stories about the couple. Even *Dateline* did an episode about them.

Josie wondered what it was that had sparked such widespread fascination. Was it the fact that the couple looked so normal? Like they could be any couple in any city enjoying a dinner out before vanishing into thin air. By all accounts, they were a fairly average middle-class couple. Tobias Lachlan had been co-owner of a junk removal company and Cora Stevens had been a waitress. He had two sons and she had a daughter.

They were two single parents getting a second chance at love. A couple trying to blend their families and start a new life together. A lot of people would be able to relate to their situation. A lot of people would see themselves reflected back when they saw photos of Tobias and Cora.

As Trinity would say, the couple was television gold.

Maybe the obsession was just due to them seemingly vanishing into thin air. After all, it wasn't often that an entire car went missing along with its occupants, especially with so many developments in technology.

Gretchen looked up from her phone and waved, getting the attention of Hummel as he stepped out of the trees. "Why doesn't this seem like a tragic accident?"

Cars accidentally went into waterways all the time. Rivers, lakes, ponds, creeks, the ocean. There were nonprofit organizations that traveled the country in attempts to locate people who'd been missing for years. Decades, even. People who'd gone missing along with their vehicles. An astonishing number of them were located still in their cars, not far from where they were last seen. Last year, a New Jersey man who'd gone missing forty-two years ago had been recovered inside a sedan that had been submerged in a local creek. Near where he was last seen.

"Because everything we know about these types of cases tells us that if they were going to be found in a waterway, it should be in Brighton Springs," said Josie. "Denton's not even close to the last place they were seen."

"If they'd had some strong connections here, Brighton Springs PD would have shown up poking around," Gretchen said. "You remember anyone from there calling to say they'd be questioning people? Searching for the couple in our jurisdiction?"

"Nope."

"Me either."

Given the thousands of online articles on the couple's disappearance, the press would have been stalking Brighton Springs PD investigators. Had there been some sort of search here in Denton, their local news station would have been all over it.

"If Brighton Springs PD thought they were here, there would have been public pleas for information circulated in Denton," Josie said.

Gretchen didn't say what they were both thinking. The odds of foul play in this situation were high. That was assuming they found the remains of Tobias Lachlan and Cora Stevens in the car and that there was enough evidence to suggest that their deaths weren't accidental.

"We'll need to request a copy of the case file from Brighton Springs PD," Gretchen said.

"We are not equipped for this," Hummel blurted as he reached them. It was odd seeing him in regular work clothes and not a white Tyvek suit.

"I figured," said Josie. "I was hoping you'd know where to start, who we need to call."

Hummel ran a hand through his hair and glanced out toward the water, eyes catching on the ripple. "We need divers and a heavy-duty rotator truck, neither of which we have."

Gretchen tucked her phone into her back pocket. "What's a rotator truck?"

Josie patted her hair, now stiffening as it dried. "It's kind of like the mother of all tow trucks. They've got rotating booms—like giant cranes—that can spin 360 degrees. Outriggers to stabilize the trucks themselves so they don't tip. Hydraulic systems. They can usually handle lifting tens of thousands of pounds."

"You know this how?" asked Gretchen.

Josie shrugged. "Whenever there's some big pile-up on the interstate with overturned semis or buses and cars in ditches, rotators are used to get things cleaned up."

"The state police don't have their own tow trucks," said Gretchen. "They contract with outside towing companies."

"Yeah," said Hummel. "But a single rotator costs over a million dollars. Not something your average towing company has on hand. It might take me a while to find a company that has one and can get it here in a reasonable amount of time."

Josie sighed. "That car's been under there for seven years—a few more hours isn't going to make a difference. Find one and I'll contact the state police about getting divers out here to help, as well."

While Denton had its own marine unit, its primary purpose was swiftwater rescues. Only one of the members had diving qualifications.

"What are we looking at in terms of processing the vehicle?" asked Gretchen.

Hummel looked out at the water again. "It's probably pointless, but I'd set up some grids around the car where it's currently sitting. Fifty feet in each direction. The divers can use metal detectors to see if there's anything around it."

"Like a gun?" Josie said.

"Yeah. Anything, really. Like I said, the odds of finding something important in the area around the car are pretty nonexistent given how long it's been and especially if the windows are closed."

"The passenger's side front window is cracked a few inches," Josie said. "Not sure about the others."

"Okay. Well, even so, seven years in a river? I doubt we'll find anything outside of it but it's best to search anyway. Once those grids have been searched, the marine unit can work with the towing company to get the car out of the water and onto the bank somewhere. That's when the real hard work begins."

"What do you mean?" Gretchen said.

Hummel tugged at the hair on the back of his head. "A car under water for that long? One window, possibly more, partially open? It's going to be filled with crud from the floor probably up to the dash. At least to the seat cushions. Silt, debris, biofilm, algae, all kinds of delightful shit."

"That sounds like it will be a bitch to process," said Josie.

"I did a couple of these before I started working here," Hummel explained. "The first issue is that in the water, all that stuff is light, almost like dust. As soon as you bring the car up onto dry land, it will start to harden. If you don't process the car fast enough, it will turn into a block of cement and that makes preserving anything that's still inside a hell of a lot more difficult."

"You won't have time to transfer the car to the impound lot," said Gretchen. "Is that what you're telling us?"

"It's a risk," Hummel replied. "It's certainly possible to get it to the impound lot before it hardens but there's no guarantee. The best thing to do would be to process it right here. Cover the vehicle with tents to keep it out of view of the press or any nosy civilians who might try to get a look. We get a bunch of tarps, lay them out on the ground, and then we empty the car out bucket by bucket. Filter the mud through screens so that any objects or remains are separated out."

Josie scanned the area again. The sun was sliding lower toward the horizon. The job ahead would take hours. Into the morning and the next day. "Then we'll do it here," she told him. "Gather whatever we need now so it's ready for when the vehicle comes out of the water. Better get some lights, too. It's getting dark."

SIX

Under her thin vinyl gloves, Josie's hands had gone numb with the cold. While the daytime temperatures were warm, hovering near eighty-five degrees, at night, they dropped significantly. Wind whistled through the valley, skating over the dark ribbon of the Susquehanna and spilling over onto its banks. The state police divers had left hours ago, after their underwater grid search turned up nothing. The sides of the tent the ERT had erected over Tobias Lachlan's sedan flapped and fluttered loudly, the soundtrack to their gruesome task. With each gust, the sickening smell from inside the car assaulted her. It was rotten, a mixture of decay, marine life, motor oil and rust.

Josie took a tainted breath and dumped another bucket of mud into the screen she'd been using for hours. Then she picked up the fire hose next to the tarp and ran the water over both mud and screen. Denton's fire department had provided two trucks to assist them. The hoses were set to a trickle—enough to clean the grime from any objects embedded in the mud but not so much that the force of the water would destroy fragile evidence. With five of them working, processing the inside of the car moved more quickly than expected, but it was still a tedious job. Both the front windows had been cracked a few inches. Hummel had been right. The muck had accumulated well over the seat cushions. The first twenty or so buckets they'd removed had turned up nothing.

Josie's lower back screamed for her to take a break. At her feet, reddish-brown sludge gathered, covering the blue of the tarp almost entirely. The white Tyvek suit she'd donned early in the evening was now almost entirely dirt-colored. As the last of the mud drained away, a long, thin object emerged. It was black, just like most of the other remains they'd found so far. Given its size and shape, Josie guessed it was part of a forearm. The radius, maybe. There were a few smaller bones. Probably parts of fingers.

Sorrow pushed at the edges of her professional veneer. The entire lives of two vibrant, well-loved people had been reduced to this. A sad collection of bones caked with mud, collected in buckets on a riverbank in the middle of the night. Tobias and Cora had been *parents.* Before the rotator truck arrived to remove the car from the water, Josie had had time to gather more information about the couple. At the time they disappeared, Tobias's sons had been twenty-three and seventeen. Cora's daughter had been sixteen. The two youngest were very nearly adults but there was never a good age to lose a parent.

Josie was living with the fallout at this very moment. Now with Wren at home, it was more difficult to stay mentally removed from cases like this. It was impossible to stop the thoughts from creeping out of the dark corners of her brain. The girl had already lost so much. What if something like this happened to Josie and Noah? What if Wren was left behind, never knowing what had happened to them?

Turner's little monologue from the day before came back to her.

The one thing this kid knows for sure, with one hundred

percent certainty based on her experience, is that the people who are supposed to take care of her die. That's a fact.

Wren hadn't been with them that long and their relationship was rocky, but from the moment Josie had seen the resemblance to Dex, she had felt a protectiveness toward the girl that very nearly matched what she'd felt toward Harris the first time she'd held him. It didn't matter if Wren liked her. It only mattered that Josie kept her safe. It only mattered that Wren didn't have to endure any more staggering losses in the wake of her father's death. It only mattered that she wasn't left alone in the world again.

"What've you got?" Gretchen jarred her from her thoughts.

Josie glanced over to see her colleague looking every bit as tired, disheveled, and filthy as herself. Plucking the blackened bones from the screen, she deposited them into an empty bucket nearby. "Part of a forearm and some fingers, I think."

All items and remains found were placed into buckets and loaded into the back of SUVs that belonged to the ERT. Later, they would be separated. The bones would go to the morgue and the other objects would be cataloged by Hummel at his small lab. Despite the layers of silt and other organic materials, they were able to determine that there had been two people inside the car when it went into the water—a driver and front seat passenger. Both had been wearing seat belts which were now hard as steel and embedded in the remains of the torsos left behind. Josie guessed that was due to the fact that during the decomposition process, bodies underwent bloating. Bacteria in the gastrointestinal system produced gases that had nowhere to escape, causing the body to inflate.

The occupants' jackets, and presumably the shirts beneath them, had managed to contain most of their rib cages and spinal columns. The rest of the remains—what hadn't escaped through the windows and been washed away—seemed to be dispersed throughout the layers of mud. The closer they got to the floor of the car, the more bones they excavated.

Still no skulls.

Hummel had assured them that this was due to the advanced decomposition. They were dealing with skeletal remains. There was no longer skin or fascia to hold the skulls in place. Given the upright position of the bodies, and seven seasons of changing water currents, some likely jostling the car, it was unsurprising that the skulls had separated from the cervical spines.

Gretchen said, "I found boots on the driver's side floor. They've still got socks in them. Looks like all the small bones of the feet stayed inside those."

Josie tried not to grimace at the imagery. She'd seen her share of gory and disturbing crime scenes over the years, and she could confidently say she hadn't yet encountered socks filled with foot bones.

"I'm getting close to the floor of the passenger's side," Josie replied. "What kind of boots?"

Gretchen tugged her skull cap down, leaving smudges of dirt along its edges. "Dressy. Ankle-length. Possibly leather. They're pretty badly degraded but I'd guess a man's boots."

The car belonged to Tobias. It wasn't unreasonable to think he'd been driving. Josie's stomach turned. What kind of shoes had Cora Stevens been wearing the day they'd gone into the water?

"Detectives?" Hummel called. "You're going to want to see this."

After securing the bucket in the back of an SUV, Josie and Gretchen followed the row of tarps to where Hummel was rinsing his own mound of mud through a screen. Except this wasn't just a densely packed ball of dirt. Josie knew exactly what it was even before the stream of water from the firehose washed enough grime away to reveal two deep eye sockets.

"Where did you find it?" she asked.

"Back seat," said Hummel, working to expose more of the skull's surface. "Driver's side."

Josie and Gretchen watched him carefully rinse away more grime. Like the other bones they'd found, its surface was almost black. Given the sloped forehead and the prominence of the brow ridge, it had likely belonged to a male.

"No lower jaw," Gretchen said.

"We might still be able to get a dental record match based on the upper teeth," Josie pointed out.

"There's also a chance we'll find the mandible in the back seat as well," said Hummel. "But with the windows cracked, probably not. We've still got quite a few layers of shit to wade through."

Josie had no idea what time it was but it had to be close to dawn. The Chief had authorized overtime. Turner had returned to work overnight but in the warm, dry, good-smelling confines of the stationhouse. Someone had to handle other calls, he'd argued. In reality, he just didn't want to get his hands or his expensive suit dirty. Noah would relieve them after dawn. Josie had a feeling he'd be taking her place right here.

"Would you look at that?" Hummel paused and let the hose drop to the ground. One of his gloved fingers pointed to the forehead.

"Shit," said Gretchen.

Josie stared at the ovoid-shaped hole punched through the bony surface of the skull. Their medical examiner, Dr. Feist, would have to confirm who the remains belonged to, but Josie's gut instinct told her that her prediction would be correct.

Tobias Lachlan had been shot in the head.

SEVEN

The sun was coming up as Josie let herself into her backyard. Once she had removed her Tyvek suit, the full effect of her stench had nearly knocked her off her feet, not to mention everyone around her. Hummel had joked that Noah might ask for a divorce once he got a whiff of her. Then Noah had shown up to relieve her and Gretchen and pretended to go along with Hummel's suggestion. Josie had let her colleagues have a good laugh at her expense because after the night they'd had, they sorely needed it. Still, none of them had dived into the river and disturbed the thick, slimy film enveloping Tobias Lachlan's sedan. She hadn't gone home to change mostly because she had nothing to change into. Instead, she'd air-dried before slipping on her crime scene gear. Then she'd sweated for hours while hauling buckets of mud and remains before night fell and the air turned cold.

Now, she latched the fence behind her and started toward the back door, wondering if she'd be able to get the odor out of the upholstery in her car. A few shafts of sunlight slanted into the yard, landing directly on one of the large wooden sculptures lined up in what used to be a flowerbed. Josie paused to admire the way the morning light illuminated every small detail of the intricate carving. It was one of her favorites, a dragon. Dexter McMann had made his living as an artist, sculpting animals and mythical creatures out of cut tree trunks, although to Josie it always looked more like he'd simply set free what lay trapped beneath the bark. All of his creations were startlingly lifelike.

It had taken Josie a full month before she could come into the yard without feeling watched. After Dex's death, his house had been sold. The proceeds were put into a trust for Wren. They could have sold his sculptures, but Wren had wanted to keep them. Every person Josie and Noah knew had balked at this idea. Their yard was a decent size, but it wasn't huge. Plus, moving the ten pieces from Dex's property to theirs had been costly and difficult, requiring heavy equipment and city permits. The sculptures took up nearly half the yard and Noah had had to put up wire fencing to keep Trout from relieving himself on them. All of it was worth it to see the look of joy and relief on Wren's face when she came home from her new school and saw them out back.

Josie had no regrets.

"Oh wow, you stink." Dressed in pajama pants and one of her dad's old T-shirts, Wren sat at the outdoor table on their patio, knees drawn to her chest. She wrinkled her nose as Josie got closer. "I'm sorry. That was so rude. But... wow."

Josie laughed and tried to run her fingers through her hair, but it was stiff and matted. "I'm aware."

Wren studied her and Josie's breath caught in her throat when she realized the girl's guard was down—at least for a moment.

"I'm not trying to be mean, but did you fall into a dumpster or something?"

It was the most she'd said to Josie in weeks, and she could tell by Wren's wide, curious gaze and her interested tone that she really wasn't trying to be impolite.

"A dumpster might have smelled better," Josie said, looking down at Noah's long, wrinkled shirt, now streaked with dirt.

Wren laughed and Josie's chest felt full, expanding with nervousness and a weird kind of hope. Was this progress, or had she just caught Wren at a weak moment? Josie mentally prepared herself for the inevitable shutdown.

"Hey, is that Noah's shirt?"

"Uh, yeah." This was the perfect opportunity to discuss the lip gloss massacre and yet, it would ruin this light moment between them. This glorious glimpse of what things could be like if Wren would just open up. Every fiber of Josie's being screamed at her to forget about her ruined work attire and lean into this fleeting feeling that Wren might actually let her in one day.

But she couldn't.

Dex hadn't given her custody of Wren so she could silently stand on the sidelines hoping that one day the girl would like her. Josie didn't know much about parenting, but she knew it shouldn't look like that.

Why was doing the right thing always so damn uncomfortable?

"Wren," said Josie, keeping her voice firm and even. "I had to wear Noah's shirt because when I took my work clothes out of the dryer, they were all stained. You accidentally left your lip gloss inside a pair of your shorts in the washer from the last time you did your laundry. They got mixed in with my stuff when I switched my clothes to the dryer. Unfortunately, the shorts couldn't be saved either. I can get you a new pair. Also, I—I'd appreciate it if, in the future, you could take a little extra time to check your pockets."

Waiting for a response felt like cranking the arm on one of those jack-in-the-box toys and wondering if the stupid thing was going to pop out every time you made a complete rotation.

Wren bit her lower lip. Her eyes drifted down to the surface of the table where her closed sketchbook rested. She touched the pencil on top of it, rolling it under her fingertips. "Okay," she said.

The tension in Josie's shoulders loosened just a bit. "Great."

"I'm really sorry," Wren added.

"No need to apologize," Josie said in a lighter tone. "It was an accident. Just be mindful of it in the future. That's all."

She was probably pressing her luck, asking to be punched in the face by the imaginary jack-in-the-box, but she forged ahead anyway. "Also, we need to talk about privacy. Did you go through my nightstand?"

Josie waited for a denial because that seemed like exactly what a teenager in this situation would do. She couldn't remember the last time she'd interviewed or interrogated a teenage suspect who owned up to what they'd done—at least not the first five times they were asked. Instead, Wren remained silent. She picked up her pencil, squeezing it in her palm. Drawing her knees closer to her chest, she curled in on herself, ducking her face behind her knees.

"Wren?"

She tucked the pencil in the space between her legs and her torso, then picked up the sketchbook and did the same. This wasn't just shutting down. This was something else altogether.

From the back door came Trout's mournful whine. When neither of them walked over and opened the door right away, he began scratching frantically at the screen. It wasn't his typical I-have-to-go-to-the-bathroom scratching. He was upset. Needing to get to them. No, not to them. To Wren.

She was afraid.

Josie went to the door and let Trout out. Just as she suspected, he made a beeline for Wren, pacing around the legs of her chair, whimpering. When he jumped up, bracing one paw on the edge of the seat and hitting her with his other paw, she petted his head. It didn't help. He'd always been uncannily in tune with Josie's emotions, growing agitated or distraught at the smallest shift, often signaling her turmoil before it was ever noticeable to anyone else. Since Wren arrived, he'd bonded to her in the same way. With a small bark, he looked at Josie pointedly, as if to tell her to do something about this.

"Wren." Josie softened her tone and pulled out the nearest chair. "You don't have to— I just wanted to talk about the rules."

No response.

Had she screwed this up? Was mentioning the lip gloss and the privacy thing in the same conversation too much for their fragile dynamic? The snooping was intentional whereas leaving a lip gloss in the washer was an accident. Maybe she should have prioritized discussing the snooping and mentioned the lip gloss another time. Or maybe she should have waited until she wasn't exhausted and malodorous to talk about them altogether. How the hell did parents know what to do in these situations?

Trout pawed at Josie's thigh, grunting noisily. She wasn't fixing this fast enough for him.

The one thing this kid knows for sure, with one hundred percent certainty based on her experience, is that the people who are supposed to take care of her die.

Josie had no doubt that Turner was correct, but she thought of the bones she'd just collected from inside Tobias Lachlan's car and knew she and Noah dying wasn't the worst thing that could happen to Wren. Even a mysterious disappearance wasn't at the top of that list. All of their family and friends adored the girl. They'd chosen Trinity and Drake to assume guardianship in the event of a common disaster. That was legal speak for Josie and Noah dying at the same time.

None of that would matter, however, if Josie and Noah decided they didn't want to be parents, after all. The worst thing that could happen to Wren was them deciding they didn't want her anymore.

The full feeling in Josie's chest transformed into a viselike grip.

All this time, Josie thought that Wren hated them. Maybe she hated the idea of being passed off to strangers. That was fair. Her grief likely accounted for a lot of her sour moods and monosyllabic responses to their questions. Briefly, Josie wondered at the logic of staying closed off to her and Noah because she was afraid they'd dump her into the foster care system. Then again, she was fourteen. Her entire life had just been shattered. Again. She'd lost the only person left in the world who loved her. Then every single thing about her life had changed. Drastically. Logic had no chance against that trauma.

"Wren," Josie said again. "I know it's not by choice and I know it's not what you want, but you're family now. Our family. All families have rules."

Wren's face rose just a fraction, but it was enough for Josie to see her wary eyes.

"Your mom had rules, right? And later, when you moved in with your dad, I'm sure he had them, too. Although, knowing Dex, they were probably more like gentle suggestions."

A muffled snort came from behind Wren's knees. Trout finally stopped whining and scratching Josie's leg.

"When I was thirteen, your dad moved in with us." Josie had no idea how much Dex had told her about their history. They hadn't talked about it much since Wren arrived, mostly because Wren never wanted to talk.

Now, she lifted her head, straightening her spine, and said, "He told me everything. What—um—what the woman you lived with then was like. Gorgeous and charming at first and then cruel and horrible."

Both Josie and Dex had the scars to prove that.

"He said he didn't realize just how vicious and heartless she was until it was too late."

"No one ever did." Josie sighed and scratched her neck.

Flecks of dried mud fell onto her lap. "Anyway, he moved in and it took me a long time to trust him, but I figured out that he genuinely cared for me. He took care of me. Looked out for me. He wasn't the kind of guy who would get all stern and start barking orders."

Wren laughed and Josie's heart gave a little flutter.

"I guess that never changed," Josie said.

A barely noticeable smile curled Wren's lips. "Nope."

Josie pulled at the collar of Noah's shirt, unleashing a small whiff of death and brackish water. "You might have noticed that Noah and I aren't the types to bark orders either, but we do need to establish rules. Boundaries. That means respecting each other's privacy, okay?"

Slowly, Wren nodded. The humor in her eyes fled, replaced by that old wariness, though it wasn't as strong as before.

"If there's something you want to know," Josie added, "just ask. I would never keep anything that has to do with your dad from you, not even a letter specifically addressed to me."

"I'm sorry I went through your things," Wren said, voice small.

"I accept your apology." Josie stood up and walked to the back door. "Now, I've got to put these clothes in the washer, take a shower, and get some sleep. You're hanging out with Erica today, right?"

"Yes. Can I still go?"

Josie paused, fingers wrapped around the door handle. She opened her mouth to ask why Wren wouldn't be able to go and then realized it was because she expected to be grounded for what she'd done.

Josie really was shit at this parenting thing.

Trying to make her voice sound more confident and authoritative than she felt, she said, "This time, yes, but if you go through my things—or Noah's—without asking again, there will be consequences."

"I won't. I promise," Wren said quickly.

With a nod, Josie opened the back door.

"Wait," Wren called. "Why *do* you stink so bad?"

Josie weighed her possible answers. Wren knew that she and Noah were police detectives, but they'd never discussed their jobs with her. She'd never been interested. Even if she had been, there were things they couldn't tell her. Things Josie wouldn't want to tell her like how three people, two of whom had been teenagers when their parents vanished, were about to get the worst news of their lives. Then again, the discovery of the remains of Tobias Lachlan and Cora Stevens wouldn't stay secret for long. Wren would be able to find all the details if she looked for them. For now, though, Josie kept it simple.

"I had to jump into the river to check something out."

EIGHT

Josie woke in the afternoon, eyes gritty, lower back aching. She stretched, her feet flexing. She expected to feel Trout's warm, soft body against her toes but there was only empty space. Sitting up, she blinked until the room came into focus. There were no sounds coming from downstairs. Wren was still out with Erica and would be for another two hours. Swinging her legs over the side of the bed, Josie stood and walked out into the hall. From the top of the steps, she saw Trout lying in the foyer, head pointed toward the front door. Ever since Noah's abduction, he often lay there when Noah wasn't home, quietly awaiting his return.

Josie knew trying to distract him would be futile, so she went back to their bedroom. After brushing her teeth in the en suite bathroom, she returned to the bed and checked her phone. There was a new text message from the boutique where she'd purchased the dress for their vow renewal ceremony reminding her that if she wanted it to fit properly for said ceremony, she needed to come in for a fitting, stat. Ignoring it, she scrolled through the rest of her messages, checking for any updates on the Tobias Lachlan/Cora Stevens case. There were none. Not surprising since it had only been a few hours since she left the riverbank. For all she knew, her colleagues could still be out there, sifting through what remained of the rapidly hardening mud inside the sedan. Gretchen had put in a call to the Brighton Springs Police Department. No response yet. Josie wondered if they would have difficulty getting the case file from them. She hoped the widespread corruption didn't extend to the Lachlan/Stevens case.

With a sigh, she pulled up her internet browser and started perusing articles about the case. She clicked on what looked like a comprehensive piece in the *Brighton Springs Herald,* written by a reporter named Carmen Hernandez.

FIVE YEARS LATER, THE DISAPPEARANCE OF A BRIGHTON SPRINGS COUPLE CONTINUES TO STUMP POLICE

Riley Stevens was sixteen years old when her mother and soon-to-be stepfather went out to dinner and never came back. What she remembers most from that night is that she didn't speak to her mom at all. She came home from school and went directly to her room without saying a word to her mother. "I was angry with her," Riley told me as we sat down for a meal at the diner Cora Stevens waitressed at for over a decade. "She'd grounded me—and rightfully so—because I'd stolen vodka from Tobias's liquor cabinet and gotten drunk at a friend's house. I was young and stupid, and she was the easiest target for my irrational teen rage."

Cora had rarely had reason to ground Riley in the past. The two had an easy and loving relationship. For most of Riley's life, it was just her and her mother. "She was a great mom. The best. Losing her was like having a piece of my soul ripped away. Even now, five years later, I miss her so much it physically hurts."

Josie stopped to take a couple of deep breaths, alarmed at how quickly Riley Stevens' words brought long-buried emotions to the surface. Ever since Noah's abduction, it was more and more difficult to ignore and compartmentalize messy feelings. The fact that she'd spent a lifetime trying not to process them—despite ongoing therapy—likely didn't help either. When Josie's grandmother, Lisette, died, it felt like her soul had splintered, and she had been over thirty years old with plenty of family to support her as well as blessed, painful closure.

Cora Stevens' sixteen-year-old daughter had had none of that.

"Every single day since she disappeared, I wish I'd put aside my stupid, misplaced anger and at least spoken to her before they left the house."

Instead, Riley was woken in the early morning hours of April 9th by Tobias's son, Zane Lachlan, who was seventeen at the time. He routinely got up at seven a.m. on weekdays and took the Hyundai Accent to school so he could use the weight room before classes. That day, the Accent wasn't in the driveway. His dad's work truck and Cora's old, beat-up Buick were exactly where they left them before going out to dinner.

"Zane tried calling them both. Then I tried calling Mom. No answer. It was totally unlike them to not come home and not take our calls. We started to freak out."

The teens looked to Zane's older brother for direction. Jackson Wright was twenty-three and had long ago moved out of the Lachlan home. The night the couple disappeared, he was at a party to celebrate the retirement of a family friend. The party went well into the night and Jackson was hungover.

"He got over that real quick," Riley said, "and came over right away. Jackson was always the cool head in the room. He called the police immediately."

The article was momentarily blocked out by a notification from their security system. A thumbnail video popped up, showing Noah pushing his key into the lock. A tiny knot of apprehension that she didn't even know was present unfurled in her stomach. Relief. She wondered if she'd ever stop feeling relieved seeing him again after they'd been apart, even if only for a few hours. Trout greeted him noisily and enthusiastically. Josie knew it would be several moments before the coming home ritual was completed. She turned her focus back to the article.

The rest of the day and the weeks and months that followed were a blur to Tobias and Cora's children. An exhaustive search followed, ranging a hundred miles in every direction. Community members joined. Fliers were created and hung all over the town and beyond. Reward money was offered for any information about the couple. A tip line was set up. The Brighton Springs Police Department spent well over a year investigating nearly a thousand leads that came in through that line. None of them panned out. The couple seemed to have literally disappeared into thin air.

"We had them on camera leaving the restaurant," said Brighton Springs detective John Fanning. "They were smiling and holding hands. A couple of people saw them in the parking lot getting into their car and driving off. No problems."

Josie took a minute to text John Fanning's name to Gretchen. She'd be on shift soon and she could try to get in touch with him. Noah's heavy footsteps climbed the stairs. Seconds later, he appeared in the doorway to their bedroom. His dark hair was tousled like he hadn't bothered to smooth it down after removing his skull cap at the crime scene. A slow grin spread across his face as he took in her bare legs and sleep-mussed hair.

"So, you're just helping yourself to all my shirts now?"

Josie glanced down at the Cherry Springs State Park T-shirt she'd slept in. Then she arched a brow at him in a pretend scowl. "You came home. I thought you were leaving me for a woman who sweats perfume and farts lavender incense."

Noah laughed and stripped off his shirt, dropping it into the laundry basket. "I didn't know that was an option. Where is this woman? I want to meet her."

"Over my dead body," Josie grumbled, unable to look away as he stripped down to his boxer briefs.

"Hmmm, that might be an improvement over the way you smelled this morning."

She grabbed Noah's pillow and threw it at him, hitting him square in the chest. He looked delighted as he took off his last item of clothing and strolled into the bathroom. Her skin felt hot as she watched him go, not tearing her attention away until he was out of view, and the water in the shower came on.

Trout sauntered in, glanced toward the bathroom, and hopped up on the bed, snuggling against Josie's leg. She stroked his soft back. Then she returned to the article and Brighton Springs Detective John Fanning's statement about the missing couple.

"We got the car on camera a few more times on what looked like their route home. They weren't being followed at that point. Weren't speeding. Tobias Lachlan wasn't driving erratically. They just... POOF! Vanished into thin air."

When I read this quote to Riley, she agrees. "That is certainly how it feels but whatever happened, someone somewhere knows the truth. At this point, I've made my peace with the fact that my mom isn't coming back. I just want to know what happened."

Tobias's sons want the same thing for their father. "We just want answers," Zane told me by phone a few days before I interviewed Riley. "We pretty much know at this point that they're dead. You hate to even think it, but the truth is that if our dad was alive, he would have found a way back to us by now. He was our world. Losing him was like having everything we knew ripped out from under us. He deserves to rest in peace. They both do."

Despite having realistic expectations about what happened to their parents, neither Tobias's sons nor Cora's daughter have given up hope that one day, they'll get closure.

"It would be wrong to lose hope," said Jackson Wright in response to an email I'd sent him regarding the case. "After all this time, we've come to grips with the fact that they're likely dead, but we can't give up on finding them. They would never give up on us. We still want to bring them home."

Josie's chest constricted. The bone-deep sadness, weariness borne of years of not knowing, was palpable, oozing out of the phone screen and trying to crawl under her skin. Next to her, Trout sighed.

"Hey." Noah's large, warm hand curled around her ankle. She hadn't even noticed him come out of the bathroom. Stark naked, he tugged her toward the foot of the bed until she was flat on her back and then climbed over her. Drops of water from his wet hair showered her.

With an unhappy grunt, Trout sprang up and jumped from the bed, finding a sunspot to bask in.

"You're dripping," Josie said, looking up into Noah's hazel eyes, alight with that particular kind of mischief that set every cell in her body on fire.

He took the phone from her hand and tossed it aside. "I prefer glistening."

Josie laughed, gliding her hands up his arms. Her fingers brushed over the puckered scar on his right shoulder where she'd shot him ten years ago. It was before they were together.

She'd been trying to save the life of a teenage girl. At the time, Denton PD had its own issues with corruption. As far as she was concerned, no one could be trusted. Desperation made her pull the trigger. Noah had covered for her and proven his loyalty time and again over the years.

Lowering himself, Noah kissed the hollow of her throat. "Wren?"

"Not home for another ninety minutes." He smelled like soap and fresh linen and home. Her heart thumped wildly in her chest.

"What were you reading?" he asked against her skin.

"What do you think?"

He knew her well enough by now to know that she obsessed about big cases even when she wasn't at work. Her collar was tugged down. Noah's mouth found its way lower. "I'm going to give you an update. Not because I like talking shop in bed—as you know—but because I don't want you thinking about anything else but us for the next ten minutes."

"Ten minutes!" Josie protested, wrapping her arms around him. "I just told you we had ninety! Surely, you can do better than ten."

"Maybe if you sweat perfume and fart incense..."

Smiling, she swatted at his back. "I will leave this bed right now."

"No, you won't." His lips traveled up to her neck and he was right. Short of a fire, nothing was getting her out of this bed anytime soon. "'Cause then you won't get to hear my update."

"Fine," she said. "Let's hear it."

Hot breath cascaded over her skin as he spoke. "Everything is wrapped up at the river. From what Hummel could tell, the gear shift was in neutral."

Which meant someone had rolled the car into the river.

Noah continued, "The driver's seat was back far enough to accommodate someone Tobias's height—which we got from his driver's license. Another skull was recovered. Likely belonging to Cora Stevens but that will have to be confirmed."

"Gunshot wound?" Josie asked, breathless with anticipation as his hand slid under her shirt.

"Probably. That needs to be confirmed. Also, Hummel found some personal items. The remains have been transported to the morgue. Dr. Feist should have something by tomorrow." He lifted his head and planted a soft kiss on her mouth. "Now, stop wasting minutes."

NINE

"Not a single return call?" Josie asked. "Not even one?"

Gretchen punched the down button on the hospital elevator. "Nope. I even made sure to tell the desk sergeant that this was one of Brighton Springs PD's most famous unsolved cases. Three times."

A soft ding sounded, and the elevator doors swished open. They stepped inside and Josie pressed the button for the basement. "Did you try Fanning?"

Gretchen adjusted her reading glasses on the top of her head. "Retired last year."

A year after he was interviewed by the *Brighton Springs Herald*.

"I tracked down his personal cell phone number and left a message," Gretchen added. "Nothing back yet."

Josie took her cell phone from her back pocket and the tail of Noah's shirt came loose, hanging down to the backs of her thighs. She'd ordered more shirts in her own size, but they wouldn't arrive for a few more days. With an irritated sigh, she tucked it back in and then scrolled through her contacts until she found the number for Meredith Dorton, a young officer on the Brighton Springs PD. "I don't know why I didn't think of this before."

The doors opened to a dimly lit hallway with cracked, yellowing floor tiles and white walls that were now a dull gray. They stepped out of the elevator as Josie placed the call. A few years back, she and Chief Chitwood had traveled to Brighton Springs while looking into the murder of his younger sister. Meredith had helped them find the case file. At that time, she'd been so determined to expose the corruption in the department that the brass had punished her by exiling her to a trailer in the back lot of their headquarters to digitize old files.

Meredith answered on the third ring. After exchanging pleasantries, Josie asked, "Are you still stuck in the annex?"

Meredith laughed. "No, believe it or not. We've got new leadership who are actually interested in doing things the right way. I'm inside the main building now. I've been promoted to Detective. Even have my own desk."

"I'm glad to hear it. You certainly deserve it."

"Thank you," Meredith said with a smile in her voice. "What can I do for you?"

Josie told her. She wasn't even finished speaking when she heard Meredith's nimble fingers flying over a keyboard. "It looks like the case was reassigned to Detective Thomas Chaney after Fanning retired last year. Both of them are clean, by the way, in case you're worried. Chaney is on vacation right now, but I can email you what we've got. You can touch base with Chaney when he gets back."

"Great." As they drew closer to the small suite of rooms that comprised the city morgue, the unpleasant smell of decomposition and stringent chemicals assaulted Josie's senses. "Thanks, Meredith."

Pushing inside the examination room, the odor only got worse. In the center of the room, two autopsy tables were illuminated by harsh mobile examination lights. On each one, skeletal remains had been arranged in anatomical order from head to toe. The bones were cleaner than they had been on the riverbank. Neither of their mandibles had been found. Some of the smaller bones of the wrists, hands and fingers were also missing. One body had fewer ankle and foot bones than the other—that had to be Cora's.

Displayed side by side, Josie could see the clear difference in size between the male and female remains. The male skull was larger, its forehead sloped with a prominent brow ridge. The male femur was bigger as was the width of its condyles and epicondyles—or the bony protuberances at the ends. If you knew what to look for, the pelvic bones were reliable indicators of whether the remains were male or female. On females, the pelvic girdle was broader and rounder to allow for childbirth. The pubic arch was more U-shaped whereas in males, it formed more of a V.

"I can't tell you how happy I am to see you two," said Dr. Anya Feist as she stepped out of her adjoining office. She wore navy-blue scrubs. Her silver-blonde hair hung loose around her shoulders. A laptop was tucked beneath one arm.

Gretchen said, "You mean as opposed to jackass?"

Turner was strangely intrigued by their long-time medical examiner, though Josie was sure it was harmless.

Anya set the laptop on the stainless-steel countertop lining the back wall of the room and opened it. "Yes. I'm tired of the twenty questions every time he comes in. I feel like I'm being interviewed for something."

"What did he want to know this time?" asked Josie.

"A food I've tried that I'd never eat again."

Gretchen groaned. "Is this his idea of flirting, do you think?"

"Assuming he's as inept at flirting as he is at everything else, then probably," Josie said. "We'll talk to him. Get him to back off."

Anya waved a dismissive hand in the air before punching in

the passcode for her laptop. "No need. I'm perfectly capable of telling him to piss off myself, and I have, but he's still irritating."

Gretchen laughed. "Welcome to our world."

A set of dental X-rays popped up on Anya's computer screen. With a heavy sigh, she got down to business. "I was able to get a partial match from the dental records of both subjects using the upper teeth. These are the remains of Tobias Lachlan and Cora Stevens."

The three of them were silent for a long moment, letting the weight of the couple's tragic end sink in.

"That's what we expected," said Josie. "What else can you tell us?"

Anya walked over toward the examination table that held Tobias Lachlan's remains and pointed to the hole in the skull's forehead that they'd seen on the riverbank. "This is consistent with a gunshot wound. As you can see, the bone looks punched out where the bullet entered. You can see the beveling where the projectile penetrated."

Josie leaned forward and studied the inside of the entry wound where the forward motion of the bullet had penetrated through layers of bone, pushing the fragments inward. The hole on the outer surface of the skull was small and almost neat whereas on the inner surface, it was wider due to the force and impact of the projectile. It had made a funnel shape—narrow on the outside and wide on the inside.

"Beveling typically indicates whether we're looking at an entrance or exit wound," Anya continued. "This is obviously an entrance wound, but if that cone-shaped defect in the bone was reversed with the narrow part on the inside of the skull and the wider area on the outside, that would be an exit wound. Anyway, you can also see these sunburst fractures extending out from the area that the bullet penetrated. There is no exit wound."

Gretchen took her glasses from the top of her head and slid

them on, nudging Josie aside so she could get a better look. "Any way to guess the caliber?"

"I'm afraid not," Anya replied.

As far as Josie knew, no projectiles had been recovered from the car. The bullet casing would have ejected from the gun and landed somewhere in the vicinity of where Tobias had been shot but the bullet itself—the projectile—would have remained inside his head and, like his bones, inside the car. However, if the mandibles and some of the smaller bones had escaped, it was reasonable to think a bullet had as well.

Anya moved to the other table. Snapping on a pair of gloves, she lifted Cora Stevens' skull and turned it so they could see the back. On the upper right side was a wound different from the one Tobias had sustained but unmistakably from a bullet.

"A keyhole defect," Josie murmured.

Anya smiled. "Yes, that's right. We see this when a bullet strikes at a shallow or tangential angle."

"It's a graze wound that fractured the skull," Gretchen said.

"Pretty much, yeah," Anya said. "In the simplest terms, the projectile glanced off the skull. See this round part? It's got the same clean, punched-out appearance as the wound on Tobias's skull—same type of beveling as well. That's where the initial impact occurred. Then the wound elongates into a sort of wedge shape with the type of external beveling we'd expect to see in an exit wound. Since the force behind the bullet isn't focused on one direct point at a perpendicular angle, its power is dispersed where the skull curves. It glances off the bone, causing the initial fracture, and then it continues glancing, making this triangle shape. Entry and exit."

Josie did her best to suppress the shiver that racked her body at the thought of what had happened to her husband last year after he was abducted. While being held captive, he'd received a gruesome graze wound to the head. Luckily the angle had been such that the bullet had broken skin instead of bone.

Gretchen arched a brow. "Not that a skull fracture isn't serious, but are these keyhole defects normally fatal?"

Anya's finger traced the contours of the back of Cora's skull. "No, not always, but they do have a high fatality rate. There are several factors that determine whether this kind of wound is fatal."

"Like what?" Gretchen pressed.

Josie knew this because of what had happened to Noah, though she wished she didn't. "Whether the bullet breaches the dura—the membrane that covers and protects the brain."

"That's right," Anya said.

"The location of the injury," Josie continued. She didn't even have to close her eyes to imagine the feel of the thick scar tissue along the side of Noah's head as she ran her fingertips over it. The left temporal lobe was responsible for language comprehension, semantic and auditory processing, verbal memory and the mechanism that allowed you to discern the emotion context in language.

"And how fast you can get proper emergency care," Josie finished.

"Yes," Anya agreed. "As you can see, the location of Cora's injury was to the lower occipital area which is responsible for autonomic processes, two of which are heart rate and respiration. If those were disrupted, she could have gone into cardiac or respiratory arrest. A serious injury in this region could also cause major brain hemorrhaging or even herniation."

Frowning, Gretchen looked back toward Tobias's remains. "Someone shot Tobias straight-on in the forehead."

Anya nodded. "Given the appearance and angle of the wound, it's more likely that he was standing rather than kneeling. I would estimate that the perpetrator was his height or slightly taller. Or, if he was seated in the vehicle, the perpetrator managed to be level enough to shoot straight-on."

"And Cora?" Josie asked.

"There are several possibilities." Anya placed Cora's skull gently back onto the table. "I'm not sure I can testify in court to any of them without more information, but perhaps she turned or she had started to run away or the perpetrator's aim was disturbed at the moment the gun was fired."

Josie didn't bring up the possibility of murder-suicide. She supposed it was feasible that Tobias had shot Cora, then driven the car into the water and shot himself in the head before the car sank, but it didn't make sense to her. For one thing, the gear shift had been in neutral, not drive. Second, the angle at which he'd been shot would have been difficult to pull off, especially if he'd been in a vehicle bobbing as it sank into the river. Most people who died by suicide using a firearm put the barrel into their mouths, under their chin, or aimed for their temple. Third, had Tobias meant to kill his fiancée before turning the gun on himself, why go to the trouble of driving into the river? Finally, if that was the case, the probability of Denton PD finding the gun inside the car would have been moderate, at least. Had one been found, Noah definitely would have mentioned it to her.

This was the work of someone else.

"They were both shot in the head," said Josie. "Murdered in cold blood."

TEN

It was a flawless crime. Every loose end tied up. Tobias and Cora had been shot execution-style and then the entire car, with them strapped inside, had been pushed into the river three hours from the last place they'd been seen. No traces left behind. In seven years, no one had been able to locate them. Had the drought not been so bad, they would probably still be entombed on the bottom of the Susquehanna. Who knows if they would have been found at all?

Across the exam table that held Cora's remains, Gretchen met Josie's eyes. "You thinking what I'm thinking?"

"Based on this alone?" Josie glanced back toward the other table. "Without having seen the Brighton Springs case file? One or both of them were involved with organized crime. Or they saw something they weren't supposed to."

"The other possibility is murder for hire."

"Yes," said Josie. "This looks a lot like a professional hit."

Professional killers or people who killed on behalf of a gang or the mafia often used close-range head shots because they were fast and efficient. Very precise. No chance of the victims surviving. That kind of killing was cold and unemotional. Unlike most murders that came from personal disputes.

"Yeah," Gretchen agreed. "I saw a lot of those when I worked in Philly. Very different from homicides where the killer and victim had a personal connection. Those were usually pretty messy. No organization."

That was because perpetrators who had a personal connection to their victims acted on impulse, in the heat of the moment, or they were provoked.

"Instrumental violence versus expressive violence," Josie murmured.

The former was deliberate and goal-oriented whereas the latter was usually spontaneous and driven by highly charged emotions.

There was something else bothering her. "We don't know whether they were killed outside the vehicle and placed inside after or if they were killed while they were still trapped inside."

Gretchen said, "But if they were shot outside the vehicle, blood evidence would have been left behind at the scene. Maybe the boat ramp? They could have been led, lured, or forced there, made to get out of the vehicle, killed, and then placed back inside before the perpetrators pushed the car into the river. There had to be at least two perpetrators."

"One person with a gun and a lot of upper body strength may have been able to pull it off," Josie said. "But I agree with you, we're looking at more than one person."

"Regardless," Anya said as she draped a sheet over Cora's bones. "In terms of blood evidence, it's been seven years. Outdoors. The river level rises and falls. It would be washed away by now, if there was any."

She was right. That particular boat ramp was rarely used, having been in disrepair for as long as Josie could remember. Plenty of citizens of Denton—particularly teenagers and petty criminals—liked to congregate in abandoned places but that whole area was more remote than most and difficult to reach. That was likely why the couple had been killed there. The gunshots would have gone unheard. There were no residences or businesses close enough to have registered them. Still, Tobias and Cora had gone missing in April when trout season opened. It was always a busy time for fishing. Was it possible that in the days and weeks after Tobias and Cora were murdered, no one had gone there? Or if they had, they hadn't seen anything suspicious?

Although if they had, it would never have been connected to Tobias and Cora's case because they had gone missing three hours from Denton.

Anya said, "Keep in mind that in Tobias's case, the projectile didn't go through and through. There would have been less blood at the scene than if it had. Plus, if the bodies fell with the wounds facing upward, gravity wouldn't be pulling even more blood from the wounds."

"So there might not have been a significant amount of blood evidence at all if they were killed outside the vehicle," said Gretchen. "Still, I suppose we can always search old reports to see if anyone saw anything and called it in."

Even if someone had found blood and reported it to police, Josie doubted such a report would yield anything useful after all this time. On the other hand, perhaps the couple had been killed closer to the place they were last seen and then been driven to Denton.

Anya removed her gloves and went back to her laptop. "There's something else you should know."

Moments later, a series of X-rays appeared on the screen. Anya clicked through them, pausing when she came to the ghostly image of two eye sockets. "This is an X-ray of Cora Stevens' face taken using the remains you found yesterday. See these cloudy spots?"

Josie counted three of them around the edges of Cora's eye sockets.

"Calluses?" Gretchen asked.

Anya nodded. "You've probably heard this from me a hundred times but when someone sustains a fracture, a blood clot forms at the site. Then it's replaced by what we call a 'soft callus' which is just fibrous tissue and cartilage. Over time, it hardens and becomes bone. Eventually the hard callus matures and remodels into the bone's original structure."

"But you can still see the calluses on X-rays," Josie said. "We're looking at old orbital fractures."

"Yes." Anya clicked through more images, stopping to point out more old fractures. "Cora Stevens had several old fractures. Clavicle, ribs, ulna, some on the finger bones that were recovered."

Face, collarbones, ribs, forearm, fingers. Those types of breaks were hallmarks of intimate partner violence.

"Someone abused her," said Gretchen. "Regularly."

"These old fractures are consistent with that, yes," Anya replied.

"Can you tell how old those injuries were?" Josie asked.

"Months or years," Anya answered. "Healing time varies from person to person but once the bone remodels, even with the appearance of the callus on the X-ray, it's impossible to pinpoint any specific time frame for when the fracture occurred. If I had Cora Stevens' medical records, I could potentially determine the age of some of them."

"We'll keep that in mind," Gretchen said.

"I wish I had more," Anya said. "Now that we've confirmed their identities, I'll need to call the ME's office in Brighton Springs so they can notify the family."

Josie had already looked up all three of the couple's children. "Only Tobias Lachlan's youngest son still lives there.

Zane Lachlan. His oldest son, Jackson Wright, and Cora Stevens' daughter, Riley, live right here in Denton."

ELEVEN

Saliva gathered in Josie's mouth as the waitress at the Denton Diner set a mug of steaming coffee in front of her. The place had recently undergone renovations, transforming it from a rundown eatery that hadn't seen a single modernization since it opened in the seventies to a gleaming, chrome and vinyl facsimile of a diner from the fifties. The tile was checkered in black and white, and everything from the booths to the counter and its stools were red with white accents. Erica had brought Wren here twice already. Both of them loved it.

Across the table, Gretchen fixed her own coffee and pushed the sugar toward Josie. "Let's have the highlights."

Josie dumped four half and halfs into her coffee and then a spoonful of sugar. With one hand she stirred it, while the other used her phone to scroll through countless reports and interviews from the case file about the Lachlan/Stevens disappearance. True to her word, Meredith had emailed it over within an hour.

"Let's see." The coffee scalded Josie's tongue but she ignored it. There was something that had stoked her curiosity since the moment she read about the couple. "Pings from their cell phones placed them near a clearing along Geerling Road which apparently is not a residential area."

"How far from the restaurant?"

"About four miles. No blood evidence, no tire tracks. No sign of them."

Gretchen took a long sip from her cup. "That answers the question of where they were killed."

"Here," Josie said. "Someone was waiting for them in Brighton Springs, though. On their way home from the restaurant. Got Tobias to stop somehow. Or they were driving along and saw something they weren't meant to see."

From there, the couple and their car were transported to Denton. Whoever they'd encountered had managed to do it without leaving one iota of evidence. A gun was an easy way to control people. Had Tobias and Cora been restrained for the long drive to Denton? If there had been abrasions or bruising on their wrists or ankles, the evidence was long gone. Or had they been beaten into submission and then restrained?

"I'm assuming the phones were never found," said Gretchen.

"They were not."

She wondered if they'd been recovered from the sedan. They'd find out from Hummel later. If so, that meant whoever had murdered the couple had either destroyed them or made sure to turn them off before leaving Brighton Springs.

As if reading her thoughts, Gretchen said, "Whoever did this knew enough to make sure the phones couldn't be tracked to Denton—or linked to any location that would lead back to them."

Even seven years ago, it wouldn't have taken a genius to realize the police would be able to track the couple through their phones, but Josie was continually surprised by how many criminals were caught because they were too stupid, too lazy, or too careless to make sure that their electronic devices didn't give them away.

"Phones were a dead end," Gretchen said. "What about the car? GPS? Infotainment system?"

Josie searched through several more reports. "The 2015 Hyundai Accent had neither."

Gretchen made a noise of acknowledgment and slugged down more of her coffee. "And since the vehicle just spent seven years in the river, any DNA the killers might have left behind is gone by now. Does that file say anything about potential suspects?"

"Here's something. Tobias was co-owner of At Your Disposal Junk Removal Company. It was doing well. So well that his business partner, Hollis Merritt, wanted to expand, move east, and set up a second location in Denton."

Gretchen lifted a brow. "That's certainly interesting considering Tobias and Cora were here in Denton all along."

"Very interesting," Josie agreed. "Tobias and Hollis disagreed on the cost and location of the expansion. Several employees reported hearing them argue over it. Hollis had an alibi for the night of the disappearance—he was... get this: in Denton spending the night with a woman. She corroborated his story. He got there at nine, which was around the time Tobias and Cora left the restaurant in Brighton Springs."

"That's pretty convenient if you've hired someone to take out your business partner," Gretchen noted.

"True. Except now that Tobias and Cora have been found in Denton, it doesn't look very good at all. Maybe it wasn't a murder-for-hire thing. Maybe Hollis did the deed himself. The woman he was seeing could have lied. Hell, she could have helped him for all we know."

"That's possible," Gretchen said. "Although how much money are we talking here? Does a junk removal company really bring in that much?"

Josie shrugged. "Plenty of people have killed for less."

They quieted as the waitress returned with their food. Gretchen thanked her and then regarded her pile of pecan pancakes with something akin to lust in her eyes. "Don't tell Paula."

Josie shook her head but smiled. "How long do you think you can keep this little affair with sugary pecan treats from her?"

After giving her twins up for adoption as a young woman, Gretchen had been reunited with them eight years ago. They had both been college students by that time but Paula, Gretchen's daughter, was hell-bent on making up for lost time. She'd moved in with Gretchen a few years earlier and now had her mother on a very strict diet and exercise regimen so that she'd be around as long as possible. Gretchen was in her late forties, hardly at death's door, but she couldn't deny Paula anything.

Except a promise to swear off pecan pastries and pancakes.

Gretchen stuffed a forkful into her mouth and spoke around it. "Tell her and they'll never find your body."

Josie laughed. "If she finds out I knew and didn't stop you, they'll never find my body!"

"Less focus on my dietary transgressions and more focus on the case, my friend."

Snickering, Josie took a few bites of her omelet and went back to reading through the file. "This says that Fanning didn't rule Hollis Merritt out but couldn't find any evidence that his alibi wasn't solid or that he hired someone to kill them."

"Where is Hollis Merritt now?" asked Gretchen.

Josie clicked out of the case file and onto the JNET database. "Looks like he got his expansion after all. He lives right here in Denton."

Was that why Riley and Jackson had moved to Denton? Were they connected to the company?

"We'll pay him a visit after we talk to the kids. How about the woman who gave Merritt his alibi? Does she still live here?"

Josie searched her name in JNET. "She's dead. Hit-and-run. Two and a half years after Tobias and Cora went missing."

Gretchen took another huge bite of her pancakes, eating them like they might escape if she didn't go fast enough. "Isn't that convenient?"

TWELVE

According to their drivers' licenses, Riley Stevens and Jackson Wright lived at the same address. It was a brick, ranch-style home with a two-car garage located in a quiet development north of Denton University's campus. Most of its residents were working-class people like nurses, tradespeople, and teachers. Its quaint, tree-lined streets were also home to several city patrol officers.

"What do you think?" Gretchen asked, parking in the empty driveway. "Former almost-step-siblings turned roommates?"

"Maybe," said Josie as they got out and approached the front door.

Riley was now twenty-three and Jackson thirty. While Tobias's oldest son had already moved out at the time the couple disappeared, Riley had still been in high school, financially dependent on her mother. Since Cora hadn't been found, in the eyes of the law, she was still alive. If her body hadn't been discovered, she would still be considered alive. That status wouldn't change unless her daughter petitioned the court to have her declared legally dead. That was only possible after a person had been missing without a trace for over seven years. Since her mother disappeared, Riley would not have had the benefit of a life insurance policy—if Cora had one—or even any assets available through her mother's estate. Since the age of sixteen, she had been alone and broke. Josie didn't know if she'd had other family to step in or whether her father was in the picture, but in the *Herald* article, Riley had said it had always been just her and her mother.

They hadn't had time to comb through the Brighton Springs case file as carefully as Josie would have liked at this point, but she wanted to give the death notifications before anything was leaked to the press. They'd just have to play catch-up later.

Gretchen lifted her hand to knock but before she could, the door swung open. Riley Stevens stood there, tears streaking her face and a cell phone pressed to her ear. Josie had seen the resemblance to Cora Stevens when she pulled up Riley's driver's license photo but in person, it was even more pronounced. Riley had the same strawberry-blonde hair—piled loosely on top of her head—and the same vibrant brown eyes. From the many police reports Josie had skimmed at the diner, she knew that Cora had been five foot three. Riley was about the same height. A pair of leggings and a fitted T-shirt with the words *I'm Not Short, I'm Fun-Sized* emblazoned across it showed off her soft curves—another feature she shared with her mother.

Her eyes flitted back and forth between them, zeroing in on the guns at their waists. Into her phone, she said, "I'll call you back."

"Miss Stevens..." Gretchen began.

Riley used the palm of her hand to wipe away her tears. On her left hand, a dainty pear-cut engagement ring flashed. Below it was a thin diamond wedding band. Perhaps she and her former almost-step-sibling weren't simply roommates after all.

"It's definitely true then?" Riley croaked. "You found them?"

Josie made introductions. She and Gretchen presented their credentials, but Riley barely looked at them. Holding her cell phone to her chest, she said, "That was Zane. Um, Tobias's son. He said... he said someone was just at the house and—" A sob shook her body. Her free hand clutched the doorframe.

"We're very sorry, Miss Stevens," Gretchen said gently. "It's true. Your mother and Tobias Lachlan have been located."

"Would you mind if we came in?" Josie asked. "We can answer any questions you have."

Riley sniffled and nodded, shoring herself up. Her phone chirped. Wiping away more tears, she glanced at the screen. "Yeah, you can come in. My husband is on his way home now."

Josie and Gretchen followed her over the threshold and into a small living room filled with random objects. One box of vinyl records and two boxes of old books sat on the couch. Atop the coffee table was a large marble bust of what appeared to be a Victorian-era woman. Beside that was an eight-track machine. Along the opposite wall was a church pew with a rolled-up carpet standing beside it. There were three red industrial bar stools clustered together and a tall cherry cabinet of some kind with a crank on its side—an antique phonograph cabinet maybe. Beyond that was a gorgeous Chinese rosewood table. Three Corningware bowls were stacked on its surface.

"Sorry about the chaos," Riley said over her shoulder, leading them into a dining room. At the center of it was a table covered in piles of paperwork. Near one end was an open laptop. "I work from home selling antiques and collectibles online."

Josie paused in front of a credenza, taking a quick inventory of the framed photographs displayed. There was one of Tobias and Cora dressed up—at a wedding perhaps. Just like most of the other photos Josie had seen of the couple, Cora's face glowed, eyes sparkling, and Tobias looked as though he couldn't believe she was on his arm. Other pictures showed a younger Cora—sometimes alone and sometimes with Riley when she was just a gap-toothed elementary schooler. In another, Tobias appeared, thinner and with less weight around his middle, crouched between two pre-teen boys. Then there were wedding pictures, just as Josie had expected.

Riley had married her older, would-be stepbrother, Jackson Wright.

Josie recognized his face from the driver's license photo she had pulled up while searching for his current address. Thick dark hair contrasted with midnight-blue eyes. His sharp jaw was covered in stubble, giving him a rugged look. In his driver's license picture, he'd stared at the camera, unsmiling, giving off an air of menace but on his wedding day, he was transformed, gazing at his bride with adoration that was so palpable, it was difficult to look away. He was considerably taller than Riley. She had to angle her head back sharply to beam at him. Former potential step-siblings or not, they were clearly deeply in love.

"Please, sit," said Riley, taking her place at the head of the table and snapping her laptop shut.

Josie took one last look at the frames, noting several of an infant and then a toddler boy with a young woman who strongly resembled Jackson. His mother, most likely. In one she held an infant bundled in a blue blanket and stared lovingly at his tiny face. The others showed him as a toddler. The woman held him or hugged him. They played with wooden trains and building blocks. In another picture Jackson held a record while she tapped against a keyboard. Without fail, her eyes twinkled when she looked at the camera.

The last photo showed Riley as a teen, flanked by a younger Jackson and a teenage boy whose smile was very similar to Tobias's. It had to be Zane Lachlan.

"Anywhere is fine," Riley added. "Don't mind all the paperwork."

Josie tore her gaze from the credenza and took a seat at the table. Gretchen settled next to her. They exchanged a look that told Josie that she, too, had mentally cataloged all of the photos, and taken note of the nuptials.

On the table, Riley's cell phone rang. The grizzled face of an older man with rust-colored hair and a patchy beard flashed across the screen. "Hey," Riley answered. "I can't talk right now. The police are here... Yeah, I know. I just talked to him... Hol! Seriously, I'll call you later."

She punched the end call icon and dropped the phone back onto the table. Covering her face with her hands, she took several deep breaths.

Hol had to be Hollis Merritt, which meant that Riley had kept in contact with Tobias's business partner.

"Tell me," Riley said finally, putting her palms on the table as if physically bracing herself for what she knew was coming.

Gretchen said, "Miss Stevens—"

"Riley. Just call me Riley."

"Riley," Gretchen went on. "Should we wait for your husband?"

"No, please," Riley said, face beginning to crumple again. "I can't—just tell me. I don't care if you have to say it again. Please tell me."

Sensing her rising hysteria, Josie said, "I'm very sorry but your mother and Tobias Lachlan were found inside Tobias's vehicle. It was submerged under several feet of water in the Susquehanna River, near the site of the old state hospital."

Riley let out a long, shuddery breath. "Oh God. Are you sure—are you sure it was them?"

"The license plate matched up," said Gretchen. "We were also able to match the VIN on the vehicle with the VIN assigned to Tobias's car. In addition to that, the medical examiner made a positive ID on both your mother and Tobias using dental records. I'm so sorry, but yes, it's definitely them."

As the reality hit, passing through Riley's body like a barely perceptible shiver, Josie could feel the strain she'd been under for the last seven years. The crushing weight of not knowing. The mental precariousness that came with constantly skirting around the crater that Cora's loss had left in her emotional landscape. The agonizing push and pull of logically knowing her mother must be dead but still clinging to the infinitesimal chance that she wasn't.

Hope could be a cruel, vicious thing.

Riley said, "So they crashed or something? Drowned in the river? They got stuck inside the car? Oh God."

Her palm closed over her mouth. Josie knew she was imagining her mother and Tobias fighting to free themselves from the car as it sank. Fighting to breathe as water filled it.

Gretchen said, "They didn't exactly crash—"

Riley removed her hand from her mouth. Her words tumbled out in a rush. "But the police in Brighton Springs checked all the nearby waterways. They even looked at lakes and rivers within a fifty-mile radius. We got an independent dive team to... Wait. What were they doing in Denton?"

"We were hoping you could help us figure that out," said Gretchen. "There's something else you should know."

Josie could sense Riley's dread, see the flash of terror in her brown eyes followed by a horrifying realization. After years of not knowing, she didn't want to know what they were about to tell her. Not this.

It was one of the more painful death notifications Josie had had to make. "Your mother and Mr. Lachlan were murdered before their vehicle went into the river."

"Murdered?" Riley croaked, all the color draining from her face. "How? What are you even talking about? Who would do that? Why?"

"The medical examiner found injuries on both your mother and Tobias Lachlan that are consistent with gunshot wounds to the head," Josie said.

There was a brief, tense moment where Riley stared at them in disbelief. Then she sagged in the chair. Her hands went to her hair, yanking locks from the bun. Grief and rage burst from her in long, keening wails that made Josie's teeth hurt.

Before she or Gretchen could react, a vibration shook the house, followed by a gust of cool air. Jackson rushed into the room, striding toward Riley with singular purpose. Heavy brown work boots clomped across the hardwood floor. A gray T-shirt clung to his muscular frame. Blotches and streaks of several different substances streaked his jeans. Pain was etched across his handsome face. He snatched Riley from the chair like he was saving her from toppling over the edge of a cliff, bundling her in his arms.

"Hey," he whispered, pressing her head to his chest. "I'm here, Ri. I'm here."

She shook violently in his embrace. Patiently, not even sparing Gretchen and Josie a glance, he stroked a hand up and down her spine and planted kisses against the top of her head. Her bun was in disarray. Half the hair was loose. Jackson tugged at her scrunchie and tossed it onto the table. He ran his fingers through her locks, smoothing them until they hung halfway down her back.

When Riley's cries slowed to whimpers, he looked over at Josie and Gretchen. Tears gleamed in his eyes, but he blinked them back. "I'm sorry," he said. "Jackson Wright. My dad was—"

"We know," said Josie.

"My brother called me. I wanted to get home before you found out but—"

Riley lifted her head. "He called me right after he got off the phone with you and then they showed up. They wanted to wait for you, but I made them tell me and... and... oh God, Jacks."

Jackson's lips pressed into a thin line. He closed his eyes briefly, taking a deep breath before opening them again. "So it's true."

"We're very sorry for your loss," Gretchen said.

"Jacks," Riley said in a shaky voice. "It's so bad."

Before he could say another word, Riley blurted out everything Josie and Gretchen had just told her, growing more hysterical with each fact that fell from her lips. Jackson kept her tucked firmly against his broad chest, listening. The higher-pitched her voice became and the more agitated she got, the less Josie could understand her words. Jackson, however, had no such trouble.

"Wait," he said, cutting her off. "Denton? Did you say they were found here?"

"Not the point, Jacks!" Riley said.

He locked eyes with Josie's and she confirmed it, giving him the location where the vehicle had been found.

Riley fisted his shirt. Her face was red and blotchy, tears still falling freely. "Jacks, I can't. I can't. I need—"

"I know," he said. "I know. I'll go get it. Just sit. Can you sit at the table for me? I'll be right back."

Without waiting for her answer, he guided her back to her chair and helped lower her into it. Dropping a kiss on her forehead, he disappeared deeper into the house. Every few seconds, he called out to his wife. "Be right there, Ri."

Beneath the table, Gretchen nudged Josie's leg with her own. Riley slumped in her chair, unmoving, eyes vacant. Was she going into shock? Having a medical event? Did she have a condition? Had Jackson gone to retrieve medication of some kind? Just as urgency began to pound through Josie's veins, he returned.

With a sweater.

It was a yellow cable-knit cardigan that had seen better days. Jackson knelt next to Riley, murmuring words of instruction and comfort as he manipulated her upper body and wrapped the sweater around her. "Come on, Ri," he encouraged her gently, picking up her arms one by one so she could slide them into the sleeves.

She only seemed to come back to life when he finished, swiveling her head to say, "I need a drink."

"Yeah," he said huskily. "You and me both. Later, though. I need your head clear right now, okay? How about coffee?"

She nodded weakly.

With a pained smile at Josie and Gretchen, he disappeared into the kitchen.

THIRTEEN

Jackson didn't ask whether Josie and Gretchen wanted coffee. Instead, he emerged from the kitchen ten agonizing minutes later carrying a tray with four steaming mugs on it. The scent of it made Josie's mouth water even though she'd already had three cups so far today. She certainly didn't need more but her body always reacted to coffee like Pavlov's dog. Jackson lowered the tray right over the top of a pile of paperwork and motioned for them to help themselves. Out of courtesy, they both took a cup but left them untouched, despite the milk and sugar offered. Josie was too busy monitoring Riley for any signs that she needed medical attention. She hadn't spoken a word while her husband was in the kitchen.

"It was Cora's," Jackson said as he drew a chair up beside Riley and tapped the sleeve of the yellow cardigan. "It helps when she's really anxious."

Josie fought against the twinge of sadness that writhed deep in her stomach.

Gretchen smiled gently. "I get it. My husband died when we were young, and I've still got a flannel shirt he wore all the time."

Riley's eyes flickered to life. "Does it still smell like him?"

"I don't know. I've tried to only handle it when I couldn't stand not to so that the scent would last longer. Sometimes I think there's something left but other times I wonder if it's just my brain playing tricks on me. Either way, it helps to have it."

In all the years that Josie had known Gretchen, she'd rarely talked about her late husband. The circumstances of his death were traumatic. She'd been so young when he passed, not even old enough to drink, but Josie knew they'd loved one another deeply. In fact, to her knowledge, Gretchen hadn't dated anyone seriously since.

Riley pulled Cora's sweater more tightly around her, giving Gretchen the ghost of a smile. Jackson stirred two sugars and a splash of milk into a mug and slid it in front of her.

Josie said, "Riley, if this is too difficult, we can come back later to speak with you."

Resting a large hand on the back of Riley's neck, Jackson said, "It's up to you."

"I want to talk now," she said, drawing herself up straighter, as if her mother's cardigan gave her a jolt of inner strength.

Josie asked, "Do either of you know why Cora and Tobias were in Denton the night they disappeared?"

Riley and Jackson shook their heads.

A notebook and pen appeared in Gretchen's hands. Moving her coffee cup aside, she set them on the table. "Did either of them have any connections here? Friends? Colleagues? Family?"

"No," Riley said.

"None that I know about," Jackson replied.

Gretchen lowered her reading glasses onto the bridge of her nose and picked up her pen. "If you had to guess as to why they ended up in Denton, what would you say?"

The answer was that their killer—or killers—had brought them here to dispose of them far from home but Josie wanted to see what Riley and Jackson would say, to expose any connections their parents might have had to Denton.

There was a long moment of silence. Riley's fingers peeked out from the sleeves of the sweater and curled around her coffee mug. "I couldn't even guess."

"Someone brought them here," Jackson said. "Why else would they leave dinner at nine at night and drive all the way here? It makes no sense. Back when they disappeared, the police told us that the last place their phones pinged was near the restaurant."

"We always thought it was weird," Riley sniffled. "They wouldn't have just turned them off. I think all three of us knew what that meant but we just didn't want to face it. As long as they were missing, there was a chance they might still be alive. Now that we know they were in Denton all this time, I think Jacks is right. Whoever killed them brought them here."

Josie nodded. "That is the most likely explanation but we still need to look at any connections they might have had to Denton. Any idea who might have brought them here?"

"My mom didn't know anyone here." Riley clutched her mug until her knuckles blanched. "I don't think she'd ever been here before. What about your dad, Jacks?"

Jackson rubbed at the stubble along his jaw. "I can't think of anyone Dad knew who lived here. I don't know. Maybe it had nothing to do with knowing someone here. Isn't it possible that whoever killed them brought them to Denton because no one would think to look for them this far from home?"

"Yes," Josie said. "But is it possible they drove here to see Hollis Merritt?"

Riley's brow furrowed. "What? Oh—Hollis was with that woman. No, I don't think they would have driven all the way here late at night just to see Hollis. Why? They could have just called him."

Which meant that there had been no calls from Tobias or

Cora to Hollis that night. At least, none that the Brighton Springs police had released. Josie still needed to go through the file with a fine-toothed comb.

"Hollis was due back in Brighton Springs the next day anyway," Jackson added.

"No family or friends here. No business associates," Josie said. "What about ex-spouses or ex-intimate partners? Anyone from the past they might have been feuding with?"

Jackson glanced at Riley. "Your dad?"

She shook her head. "My dad never lived in Denton. I don't think he's ever been here."

"We hadn't had any contact with my mother since I was three years old," Jackson said. "And Zane's mom died of cardiac arrest."

Riley leaned toward him. "Did your dad have any girlfriends before he met my mom?"

"None that I know about. Zane and I kept him pretty busy. He always said he didn't have time to date."

Changing the direction of the questions, Josie asked, "Did either of your parents own a gun?"

"Not my mom," Riley said. "She hated guns. Your dad had some though, right?"

"Yeah. A couple of rifles, a shotgun. Pistol, too, I think." Jackson lifted his chin in Josie's direction. "Zane would have those. Still in Dad's gun safe, probably. We didn't mess with them. He got the long guns for hunting and then never went hunting."

"What was the pistol for?" Gretchen asked.

"Home defense."

"Did he carry it with him?"

"Nah. It was always in the gun safe."

"How about you?" Gretchen continued. "Did you own a gun?"

Riley's lips twisted. There was an edge to her voice as she

answered for her husband. "Jackson wouldn't bring a gun into our home. I don't like them anymore than my mom did."

"It's okay, Ri," he said softly, brushing the hair from the back of her neck. "They mean back then."

"What? Why?" She turned her narrowed eyes toward them. "Why do you need to ask that?"

"They need to ask everything, Ri," Jackson soothed. "They need to investigate everyone, even me. They're just doing their jobs. It's fine."

Riley didn't look convinced, but she didn't protest. Addressing Josie and Gretchen, Jackson said, "The answer is no. I've never owned a gun. No need."

Josie decided to change the direction of questioning. "Did Hollis Merritt have business associates here?"

Riley seemed momentarily confused by the abrupt shift. "What?"

"We know that at the time of your parents' disappearance, Hollis wanted to expand the business and open a new location here in Denton," Gretchen said. "Was there someone here Hollis was connected to that Tobias might have wanted to speak with? Maybe without Hollis being present?"

Riley looked at Jackson again. "Was there?"

Jackson shook his head. "I don't know. You'd have to ask Hol."

"According to the Brighton Springs police file," Josie leaned forward in her chair, "before the disappearance, Tobias and Hollis had been seen by several employees arguing about the expansion plans. Do either of you know how serious the expansion disagreement was, or if there were other issues they fought about?"

Jackson answered, "They didn't have other issues that I knew about. The expansion thing wasn't that serious. I mean they got heated sometimes but they were still friends. Dad was worried about overextending themselves. He didn't think they were ready to expand. He thought they should wait. Hol said he'd do all the work himself, but Dad said that wasn't the point."

"Jacks started working for them before he even turned eighteen," Riley explained. "So he was with them a lot."

Jackson took a long sip of coffee. "I don't remember them ever disagreeing about anything besides that. I mean small, dumb shit, sure, but nothing that would have led to violence."

Gretchen lowered her chin, looking over her reading glasses at Jackson. "What *did* happen in terms of expansion?"

"Hollis went ahead with it," he said. "When Dad didn't come back after two years, he asked me and Zane if we'd be opposed to it. Dad and Hol had an operating agreement for the company that if Dad ever became incapacitated, his interest would go to me and Zane. If Hol ever became incapacitated, his would go to his sister. Dad vanishing wasn't in the agreement, but Hol treated it as though he was incapacitated which meant that he needed mine and Zane's approval to move forward with the expansion. We were fine with it. We have a place here, and we just opened a new one in Allentown."

"You came with Hollis to Denton?" Josie said.

Jackson grimaced. "Yeah. Too many memories in Brighton Springs. I moved as soon as Hollis got a place here. Zane was old enough by that time to take over at home. He'd been tagging along with Dad since he was fourteen. He knew how the place ran."

Gretchen jotted something down. "Who's in Allentown?"

"Some guy Hollis hired about five years ago."

Josie asked, "Riley, did you move here to be with Jackson?"

FOURTEEN

"I know what you're thinking." Riley fidgeted with a thread on the sleeve of Cora's sweater. "That it's weird that we're married because we were almost step-siblings, and if you don't think that's weird, you think it's gross because Jackson is seven years older than me."

Gretchen's face softened. It wasn't something she showed other people often. "My husband was twelve years older than me when we got married. I followed him all the way across the country."

Riley's eyes lit up. She shot her husband a loving smile which he returned. "Well, I didn't follow him. Nothing ever happened between us in Brighton Springs. I decided to go to college in Denton for art history. Jacks was already here working with Hollis. They were the only people I knew here so I hung out with them a lot and, over time, we fell in love."

"You're still Riley Stevens," Josie pointed out.

"I never changed my name because we were afraid the press would have a field day. I mean we're not trying to hide or anything, but I had planned to keep doing interviews about the disappearance, keep spreading awareness of the case so that maybe someone would come forward. Someone must know something, right? Anyway, we thought it might be awkward explaining why I'm Riley Wright."

Jackson squeezed her shoulder. "We just didn't want people to get so caught up in the 'former almost-step-siblings get married' thing that they stopped paying attention to the case."

Gretchen asked the question Josie had been wondering about all day. "Wright. Not Lachlan?"

"Tobias isn't my biological father." Jackson's fingers tapped lightly against the side of Riley's neck. "He was engaged to my mom. She left us for some other guy. Tobias raised me. My grandparents wanted to, but my grandmom had MS and needed full-time care. They couldn't take on a three-year-old. They were happy when Tobias took me in."

"Your mother gave him guardianship?" asked Josie.

"No," Jackson answered. "My biological dad was in and out of prison since I was born so my mom had my grandparents designated as standby guardians in case something happened to her while he was incarcerated. He consented to it. Once she left, that stayed in place. Gram and Grandad technically had guardianship of me, but Tobias was the one who raised me. My bio dad didn't give a shit. He would have gladly signed away his parental rights."

"You're lucky," Riley grumbled, pinching the thread on her sleeve. "I wish my dad had just given up."

"The medical examiner found that Cora had several old, healed fractures," Josie said. "Eye sockets, collarbones, ribs, forearms. Do you know how she got those?"

Riley's lips twisted like she'd tasted something sour. "My shitty father, that's how. He used to hit her all the time. Even after she left, he was always stalking her. She made police reports but that never stopped him."

Josie made a mental note to check the Brighton Springs file for any investigation into Riley's father. Surely Detective

Fanning had suspected him of being involved, whether on his own or in a murder-for-hire scheme.

Gretchen scrawled something on her pad. "Had he been stalking her up until she and Tobias went missing?"

Riley rolled her eyes. "When was he not stalking her? Yes and yes, he was a suspect. The police could never find any evidence he was involved."

"What do you think?"

"As far as suspects go, he had the most motivation." Riley clutched her mug tightly again. "But I don't know, he's too dumb and too impulsive to have avoided getting caught for seven years. Plus, he wouldn't be able to resist gloating about it to someone."

"Was Tobias ever violent with Cora?"

Jackson shook his head. "No, never. He wasn't like that. He could get moody but usually if he was upset or mad about something, he'd get quiet, avoid you—avoid Cora."

"Did they fight a lot?" asked Josie.

Again, husband and wife looked at one another, some sort of silent communication passing between them. Then Riley said, "The chair."

They both started laughing, keeping it up until they had tears in their eyes.

Finally, Jackson swiped a hand down his face and turned his attention back to Josie. "My dad had this recliner that was ancient. I mean, it seemed like it was older than him. It was worn and creaky."

"And it smelled, no matter how much Febreze he used," Riley added. "He would not get rid of it."

"'Cause his ass-print was just right," Jackson said. They both chuckled. "They fought over that a lot."

Riley's voice was thick but filled with a sweet sort of nostalgia. "Mom hated that stupid chair. Actually, we all did. Zane, too."

Jackson surreptitiously wiped away a tear as it fell from his eye and curled his arm around Riley, hugging her close to his side.

"Where is the chair now?" asked Gretchen.

Riley said, "It's Zane's year."

Jackson grinned. "Yeah, my brother and I pass it back and forth every year. At Christmas. Zane's got it now. It's a silly tradition but..." He drifted off, face going slack. Grief raged in his eyes. He blinked back more tears.

In the silence that followed, their pain—and now their defeat—was a living, breathing thing.

"Traditions help," Gretchen offered.

Riley looked down at her sweater and then back at Jackson. "You got joint custody of the chair, and I got the cat."

Jackson dragged a hand down his face again, wrestling some of his composure back. "Stupid cat."

"She's around here somewhere. Probably in our bedroom. Captain Whiskers. That was the last thing—" Riley's voice cracked. "The cat was the last thing she texted anyone about that night."

Not for the first time, Josie wished there had been time to review all the phone records. "What do you mean?"

"Mom and Tobias were on their way home," Riley explained. "Mom sent Jacks a text right after they left the restaurant."

"That was meant for Zane," Jackson said. "But yeah, I mean that was on the news a few times. The last message either of them sent before vanishing was about the damn cat. The police told us both their phones either went dead or were turned off about twenty minutes after that."

Tapping her pen against the notepad, Gretchen asked, "What did Cora's message say?"

"To make sure I let her in. Something about how Captain

would be wound up and give Cora hell when she got home if she wasn't let in right away."

"Zane and I found this stray cat," Riley explained. "It was right after Mom and I moved in with him and Tobias. They let us keep her but insisted that we take care of her."

"Which they didn't," Jackson said. "Naturally."

Riley gave a sad smile. "We tried, but yeah, Mom ended up doing all the work. That stupid cat loved her the most. Every afternoon she'd let her out and then in the evening before bed, she'd be at the back door, scratching to come in for the night."

"When I got Cora's text," Jackson said, "I replied that she had the wrong son. She said she was sorry. I told her not to worry and that I'd just call Zane because he was supposed to help me paint my apartment that weekend. She said thanks. That was it."

"Did you call Zane?" Gretchen asked.

"Well, yeah."

Josie frowned. "Cora texted Zane but not you, Riley?"

Riley's lower lip quivered. "We were fighting. I, um, had stolen some liquor from Tobias and gotten drunk at a friend's house. She punished me and because I was a dumb sixteen-year-old, I got angry with her. I think she didn't trust me to respond or to let Captain Whiskers in just to spite her."

This lined up with what Josie had read in the *Herald* article. "They had just left the restaurant to go home but she wanted someone to let the cat in. Wouldn't that have been an indicator that they intended to stay out later?"

Riley and Jackson looked at one another, their faces lined with consternation. "I never thought of it that way," Riley whispered.

"Me either." Jackson squeezed her shoulder. "I didn't know what their routines were at that time. I was already living on my own. Did Captain Whiskers have to be in at nine sharp, or could she have waited for your mom to get home?"

"I'm not sure. I don't remember. I never gave it much thought."

It could very well be one of those mundane details in an investigation that took on more weight than it warranted and, in the end, meant nothing at all. Maybe the couple had intended to stay out later or go somewhere else before heading home. Josie could check the witness statements from people who saw them at the restaurant. Perhaps someone had overheard them making post-dinner plans.

"We won't take up much more of your time," Gretchen said. "One last thing. Was either of them acting strangely before that day?"

"In what way?" asked Jackson.

"In any way," Josie said. "Unusually withdrawn? Jittery? Anxious? Depressed? Paranoid?"

"No." Jackson shook his head. "Dad seemed the same as always to me whenever I saw him at work. What about your mom, Ri?"

"Other than being furious with me, she seemed fine."

FIFTEEN

Denton PD's evidence processing site was part of their impound lot. It was located in a remote area of North Denton that didn't see much traffic. Fencing surrounded the premises. In the booth by the entrance gate, an officer was always on duty, ensuring that only authorized personnel entered. He waved Josie and Gretchen through without a word and they found a parking spot near the squat cinderblock building at the back of the lot. It always looked inhospitable. No windows. A single blue door. Even the tiny windows on the garage bay doors were covered with white laminate so no one could peek inside.

Josie and Gretchen made their way through the small, empty front office and into a more spacious room that was used to process and catalog evidence. Hummel sat at the large stainless-steel table in the center of the room. At least a dozen old, dirty items were arrayed before him. His head was bent toward his open laptop, fingers flying across it. The scowl on his face when he looked up at them made Josie regret their decision not to stop and get him a coffee. Hummel was almost as much of a control freak as Josie, which meant that he probably hadn't slept very much since Tobias Lachlan's car was recovered from the river. He had a good team but the only person he really trusted to do things right was himself. Plus, out of the entire ERT, he had the most certifications for in-house evidence processing.

Gretchen must have had the same thought. She pursed her lips for a moment before addressing him. "You look miserable. We can go get you caffeine or food or both, come back, and try this again."

Hummel pushed his laptop aside and rubbed at the nape of his neck. "Forget it. I don't have anything here that would make that trip worth it."

"We're not expecting much," Josie admitted. "The car was submerged under water for seven years. I'm surprised anything survived."

He stood and stretched his arms over his head. "You'd be surprised what stays intact underwater over long periods of time. Depends on the body of water, of course. A buddy of mine once found a woman's purse at the bottom of a pond. It was under water for seventeen years. All her stuff was still inside. Everything. Not in great shape, obviously, but there."

"Not much of a current in a pond," Gretchen said.

"True. I wouldn't have bet on finding much in Lachlan's car because it was in the river but since the windows weren't open all the way, it looks like a lot of what was in there when they went into the water was still there." He motioned toward the objects spread across the table. "This is what I've got. Everything is still drying out. Once it does, I'll seal it in evidence bags."

Josie stepped forward, scanning his findings. A rusted car jack. A handheld air compressor, crusted with dirt, its hose rotted. Two men's dress boots. Remnants of reddish-brown mud clung to them. Another set of shoes were nearby. Ballet flats, from what Josie could tell. The soles had peeled away. They looked one minor jostle away from total disintegration. Faded, threadbare pieces of fabric, stiff from having air-dried, took up almost half the table. Pieces of the clothing that Tobias and Cora were wearing the night they were killed. A set of keys. A cell phone. Despite the ERT's efforts to wash away all traces of the river from each object, they were still streaked with grime.

"Would you look at that." Gretchen pointed to a wallet that had fared well beneath the water. Hummel had removed Tobias Lachlan's driver's license, credit cards, and health insurance card. All of them appeared remarkably unscathed.

"Weird, right? What survives years of submersion and what doesn't."

Gretchen put her reading glasses on and leaned over the table, peering closely at each object. "No projectiles?"

"Nope."

Josie sighed. "What else do you have?"

Hummel walked around the table to a countertop along the wall. "This is the rest. Cora Stevens' things. No jewelry."

"Not even her engagement ring?" Josie asked.

Hummel shook his head. "Either she wasn't wearing it or it somehow slipped through a crevice or out the window."

"Or the killer took it before rolling the car into the water," Gretchen suggested. "It should be easy enough to figure out if she was wearing it the night they were killed. What else did you recover?"

Hummel waved a hand over another array of items spread across the countertop. "Her purse was on the passenger's side floor. Zipped up so everything was still inside."

It was a medium-sized black purse with one long strap that was now broken. Its polyester shell was cracked in places. Just like everything else they'd recovered from the car, a coating of dried mud adhered to it. Its inner liner had started to disintegrate. Cora's ID, insurance card and credit cards were as near pristine as Tobias's. Her other possessions still bore the river's imprint, crusted with dried muck. A lipstick, compact, mascara, hairbrush, a change purse, a pen, a keychain that said "#1 Mom" with four keys on it and a cell phone. All pretty standard things one would expect to find in a woman's purse.

Except one thing.

Josie pointed to it. "Is that a skeleton key?"

Hummel sighed. "Yeah, looks like it. I can't figure out what else it would be."

It was small, not much bigger than a soda bottle cap, and made of some sort of metal. The head appeared to be circular, but it was badly corroded, obscuring any details or design that might have hinted at what it was meant to unlock. Josie guessed there were probably thousands, if not more, of those sorts of keys in the world.

"I assume you've got a lecture on skeleton keys prepared for us," Gretchen said, barely suppressing a smirk.

Hummel narrowed his eyes, glaring at her. "I have a lecture on Google and how you guys can use it, too."

Gretchen said nothing. Silently, Josie counted off the seconds. When she got to thirty-seven, Hummel shook his head. Blowing out a breath, he said, "It's not a lecture. More like a bullet point list."

"Let's hear it." Gretchen was full-on grinning now, satisfaction written all over her face.

"Fine," he huffed, evidently put out by his own thoroughness. "Skeleton keys have been around since ancient Rome, believe it or not. They were originally used on doors, chests, trunks, stuff like that. In the Middle Ages they were used to open a variety of different locks."

"Kind of like a master key?" asked Josie.

Hummel nodded. "More or less, yeah. There's a hell of a lot more to their history, but you get the gist. By today's standards, the locks they opened were pretty low-quality. Skeleton keys are still used today, mostly on antique locks, from what I gathered. Also, replica skeleton keys are a thing now. For decorative purposes."

Gretchen leaned over the table to get a closer look. "Isn't it a bit small to be a skeleton key?"

Despite how tiny it was, it had the hallmark features of one with its straight blade and rectangular tip.

"They come in all different sizes."

"Any way to tell whether it's from some kind of antique or if it's more recent?" asked Josie.

Hummel shrugged. "Not sure. I tried doing a reverse image search on the internet, but this thing is too corroded for that. I'm reluctant to try to remove some of the corrosion in case it just disintegrates. That's above my pay grade. I'm going to send it to the state police lab to see if they can figure out what kind of metal it's made of and whether it can be cleaned up."

Josie said, "The real question is why this was in Cora's purse and how important is it?"

"It's important until we know it's not," Gretchen sighed. "Which means we'll need to find out if she owned anything that required a skeleton key to unlock it. We know the kids kept Tobias's recliner, but we don't know what Riley kept of her mother's things—aside from her sweater."

Josie wondered if Zane Lachlan still lived in Tobias and Cora's old home. No one would have been able to sell it while they were missing because legally, the couple had been considered alive for the past seven years. The torturous state of limbo their children had lived in all this time wasn't merely emotional. There were practical and physical considerations. The couple had left behind a house, vehicles, half of a business, bank accounts, credit card accounts, retirement funds. All adult things that their children would have been restricted from using or benefiting from.

The only thing they would have had control over were their parents' personal possessions, which included anything inside the house. If Cora had had a trunk or some small piece of furniture that could only be unlocked with the skeleton key, Josie was certain that Riley would have broken into it at some point.

Lots of parents kept items they didn't want their kids to see or touch under lock and key. Josie and Noah had lockboxes for their service weapons. They'd always had them but after Wren moved in, they upgraded to newer ones that required a passcode as well as a key. Despite the redundancy, they'd started carrying the keys with them rather than leaving them hidden in the bedroom. After realizing that Wren had gone through her nightstand, Josie felt validated in taking the extra precautions. The girl hadn't been looking for a gun, but she had invaded Josie's privacy. If they hadn't taken such great pains to secure their weapons, Wren might have come across the key, might have figured out what it was for. Maybe she wouldn't have ever tried to access the gun, but she would have known that she could.

Josie trusted no one but herself and Noah with their firearms. Securing them was a safety issue. She believed Riley when she said Cora hadn't owned a gun. Looking at the small, corroded skeleton key, she was certain that whatever Cora had been trying to keep private had less to do with safety and more to do with keeping secrets.

The question was: what secrets?

SIXTEEN

The Denton location of At Your Disposal Junk Removal was located in the flat, industrial area of South Denton. Josie had driven past it hundreds of times in the last five years. The property previously belonged to a used car dealership. Josie knew that beyond the two-story, glass-front building was a huge asphalt lot. Perfect for housing trucks, dumpsters and any other equipment needed for junk removal.

Gretchen parked in front of the building. They walked into a cavernous, tiled lobby that used to be a showroom. Instead of a car taking up the center space there was a long, L-shaped desk. Behind it sat a woman in her forties. Long auburn hair fell to her shoulders. Manicured nails tapped against a mug that said, *Secretary: Because Badass Miracle Worker isn't an Official Job Title.* She spoke into a headset, discussing the sizes of dumpsters and how much it would cost to rent one. Her nameplate read Ellyn Mann. Eyeing the logos on their Denton PD polo shirts, she said, "I've got to put you on hold, hon."

She smiled, a hint of sadness in the depths of her blue eyes. "Mr. Merritt thought you'd stop by. He's in his office. Up the steps, first door on your right."

The door to Hollis Merritt's office was cracked but Gretchen knocked anyway.

A gruff voice called, "Come on in!"

Hollis Merritt's office was the opposite of the pristine, perfectly ordered lobby in every way. The desk was metal. Piles of documents covered nearly every inch of it. More papers burst from the filing cabinets along the walls. Scattered along the floor were random objects, much like the ones in Riley and Jackson's living room. A large blue flambé-glazed vase, a pair of elephant table lamps, an old painting of a clipper ship, and an antique birdcage.

"The kids called me. Told me you found Tobias and Cora." Hollis stepped out from behind his desk, giving them an unobstructed view from the only window in the room.

The old car lot stretched into the distance, filled with dumpsters, trucks, and heavy machinery just as Josie had suspected. There was also a large area that resembled a junkyard, with piles of refuse everywhere. Looking more closely, she realized there was some sort of system. Things had been separated into piles. Electronics. Furniture. Paint and aerosol cans. Metal. Hazardous materials handled by employees dressed in hazmat suits very similar to what Denton PD wore to crime scenes. A separate building with large garage bays sat near the back, the dealership's "Auto Service" sign still hanging proudly on its face. Beside it, two workers threw plastic bags and other debris into a commercial-sized trash compactor. There were three in all.

Standing only a couple of feet away, Hollis hulked over them. Not as tall as Jackson Wright but wide and heavyset. His hair was the color of faded rust. Broken blood vessels webbed across his ruddy cheeks and bulbous nose. Josie estimated him to be in his mid- to late fifties. He was dressed in an At Your Disposal T-shirt and cargo shorts. His boots were similar to those Jackson was wearing when he arrived home.

Josie and Gretchen introduced themselves. Hollis gave their credentials a cursory glance. "Riley just called me back and told me they were murdered. That true?"

There were no guest chairs so the three of them stood in the center of the crowded room. A combination of smells wafted from Hollis. Must, mothballs, WD-40, and wet wood. Must be a hazard of working in this field.

"Unfortunately, yes," said Josie.

Hollis sighed. One of his large paws reached for the sleeve of his shirt, absently pulling it down over a device attached to his tricep. It was a continuous glucose monitor, Josie realized. He must be diabetic.

"Guess that was always the news we were going to get. Horrible. Well, I know you're not here to give your condolences. So let's get on with it." Folding his arms across his chest, he backed up and perched on the edge of his desk. "You want to know if I killed them? The answer's the same as it was seven years ago. No, I didn't. I know what you're gonna say. 'Mr. Merritt, they were found in Denton, which is where you were the night they went missing.' Shit. That looks bad. Real bad, but my answer's the same. I didn't kill them. You talk to Fanning yet?"

Josie knew that Gretchen was just as bemused as she was but kept her expression impassive. "Detective John Fanning?"

"That's right," Hollis said. "Surprised he ain't here himself."

"This isn't his jurisdiction," Josie said. "But we will speak to him soon."

Gretchen arched a brow. "You seem to remember him well."

Hollis laughed mirthlessly. "When someone accuses you of killing your best friend and his fiancée, or of hiring someone else to do it, yeah, you tend to remember his name. He even know about this yet?"

"He's retired," Josie said. "We've left several messages for him."

Hollis shifted, peering over his shoulder at the lot. "Surprised he's not lurking around outside. He was on my ass for years. God. Murdered. You know, I knew they were gone. There was no reason for them to run off together and leave their lives behind. Police said their bank accounts and credit cards, phones and all that, were never touched again. But I kind of hoped it was just an accident. I mean, I guess that's not a better way to go. I don't know."

A thunderous boom sounded from outside followed by metal screeching against metal. Another came shortly after. Hollis was unfazed. The heavy equipment probably kept up a cacophony all day.

"How long had you known Tobias before you opened the company with him?" asked Gretchen.

Turning back to them, Hollis scrubbed a hand down his face. "We gotta do this all over again? All the questions?"

Josie said, "This is a double homicide. Officially. In our jurisdiction, so yeah, we're going to do this again."

"Fine. But let's go somewhere we can sit. Downstairs we have some rooms where the car salesmen used to do paperwork. One of those should work."

Hollis labored to get down the steps, lowering his left leg to each step so he didn't have to bend it. Knee problems, he explained. As they passed by the front desk, he called out, "Ellyn, how about some coffee?"

"Coming up," she replied.

As promised, a hall off the main lobby led to five doors, each one filled with more stuff. Hollis chose the room that was easiest to navigate. A sleek black conference table sat among clusters of cleaning supplies. Josie and Gretchen edged past a row of mops and took their seats. Hollis lowered himself into a chair across from them.

"All right, then. You wanna know how we knew each other? Tobias stole my girlfriend."

He let those words hang in the air between them. The gleam in his eyes told Josie he was waiting for some sort of reaction. When they gave none, he laughed. "Nah, just kidding. I used to rib him about it, but she wasn't really my girlfriend. It was Jackson's mom, Rachel."

"Rachel Wright?" Josie asked.

"Yeah. I took her out a couple of times. Everyone in our neighborhood used to go to the same bar—that was where I met her in the first place. One night we went there after dinner and Tobias charmed her right off her bar stool. That was the end of that."

Gretchen said, "Had you known him before that?"

"Of course. He was always around. We went to the same high school, but he was a few years behind me."

More concussive booms came from the back lot although here in this room they were somewhat muted.

"Were you angry with him when he started dating Rachel?" asked Josie.

Hollis waved a hand in the air. "No, not really. We weren't serious. Never did more than go to the movies or dinner. Plus, she already had a kid from her last relationship. She was a looker, but I wasn't interested in being a stepdad. Course, I didn't know Jackson yet or I probably would have changed my mind."

"Somehow Tobias stealing your date led to the two of you opening a company together?" Gretchen said skeptically.

"No. Rachel did. She knew I had this inheritance from my dad passing and she also knew that Tobias didn't have a steady job. Landscaping in the summer, snow removal in the winter. It was unreliable, particularly if the snowfall was low during any given year. Then as a side hustle, he started helping people by cleaning out their places for extra cash. Word got around that he was quick and wouldn't charge an arm and a leg, so he kept getting more requests. Rachel suggested he bring me in on it."

"Tobias was okay with that?" asked Josie. "Given the romantic rivalry?"

Hollis chuckled. "It was hardly a rivalry. Women always liked him better. He wasn't the best-looking guy in town but he was sweet and liked to spoil his girlfriends. Gifts, dinners, flowers, romantic gestures. When Rachel told him it was her idea for him to partner up with me, he went for it. We made decent money so I kept helping him out. Eventually we became real friends. One night we were out drinking away the day's wages and had this crazy idea to start an actual company. I had the funds to start it up, so we did."

"It was successful," Josie said.

Hollis nodded. Ellyn swept into the room, carrying a tray which she set in the center of the table. It held a carafe, three coffee mugs with At Your Disposal's logo on them, creamers, sugar packets, and wooden stirrers. She waited as Hollis took a mug and poured himself some coffee. When he reached for the sugar packets, she slid the tray out of reach, toward Josie and Gretchen.

"Aww, come on," he complained.

"You know the rules," she told him. "You need to be compliant keeping your blood sugar under control or you won't be eligible for that pump. No cheating!"

"You know, if I wanted to get bossed around all the time, I would have gotten married again."

Ellyn rolled her eyes. "Please. Like any woman would have your sorry ass."

He took a sip of the black coffee and winced. "I'm sorry I hired you."

"No, you're not," she said. "Family takes care of family."

Josie watched the two of them bicker. Seeing them side by side, she noticed the resemblance. Russet hair, blue eyes, soft chins. Siblings, most likely.

Hollis grumbled something under his breath, which Ellyn ignored. She turned to Josie and Gretchen. "Help yourself. It's really not that bad."

With that, she left the room. Josie's energy was flagging so she gave in and poured herself a mug. "We heard that you and Tobias had a disagreement over the expansion plans around the time he and Cora were killed."

"Yeah, we fought over the expansion, sure. Tobias didn't think we were ready. He was afraid we'd bite off more than we could chew, which was fair. But the real reason we were fighting was that he didn't think I was serious."

Gretchen had her notebook out, sitting on the table in front of her. "Why not?"

"He said I was just chasing a woman and that's the only reason I wanted to expand—to Denton."

"Were you just chasing a woman?" asked Josie, stirring some cream and sugar into her coffee.

Hollis shrugged. "Yeah."

"So Tobias was right, but you fought him on it anyway," Gretchen said.

"Just because he was right doesn't mean the expansion was a bad idea. Look around you. It was a smart decision."

Josie assumed the woman in question was the one who'd given him an alibi the night Tobias and Cora went missing. The one who passed away two and a half years after the couple disappeared. "How did it go with the woman?"

Hollis's face reddened. "It lasted a week. I'm not great at relationships. Stopped getting married after my third divorce."

"When was the last time you saw Tobias and Cora before the night they were killed?" asked Gretchen.

"This is all in Fanning's file, you know."

"Now it will be in our file," Gretchen replied simply. "Answer the question."

He regarded her for a moment, a spark in his eyes. "I like you, you know that?"

SEVENTEEN

If Gretchen was surprised by this turn in the conversation, she didn't show it. "Answer the question, Mr. Merritt."

He kept staring at her appreciatively. Gretchen held eye contact, unblinking, her face a mask of total disinterest. Suspects, persons of interest, witnesses—there was always a handful who tried to flirt as a way to deflect from the subject at hand, but Josie didn't think that's what Hollis was doing. Regardless, it was inappropriate and a waste of time.

Josie gave a dramatic sigh and made a show of taking her phone from her pocket and studying the screen as though she was reading messages. "Mr. Merritt, we've got a lot more people to talk to after you and a very long day ahead of us trying to figure out who killed your business partner, not to mention his fiancée. You can talk to us now or you can come with us to the stationhouse for a more formal interview."

His gaze dropped to his mug. "Fine. I saw him at work that day. We'd both been out on jobs. When I got back to the office around three, he was there doing some paperwork. He usually stayed later but he said he was taking Cora to dinner."

Gretchen made a note on her pad. "Any particular reason?"

"Don't know. Things between them had been strained. I think he was trying to pay her a little extra attention, try to get them back on track."

More muffled sounds penetrated the walls of the building. Loud bangs, metal grinding, and the shrill, high-pitched rhythmic beeps of a truck reversing.

"Do you have any idea why things were strained between them?" Josie asked.

Hollis spun his mug around a few times. "It was a little bit my fault, probably. Cora was a waitress at this diner. She'd been working there forever. It was tough raising Riley herself, but she did it. After she and Tobias got engaged, he wanted her to stop working. She didn't. It was this whole thing about maintaining her independence, but Tobias didn't see it that way. He felt insulted, like she didn't trust him to take care of her. After what she went through with her piece-of-shit ex-husband, he really wanted to take care of her."

"How was that your fault?" Gretchen asked.

"Cora came to me and asked me to talk to him. Convince him that he was being... what did she say? 'Ridiculous.' Tell him if he really loved her, he would understand."

"You and Cora were friends?" asked Josie. "Before she and Tobias met?"

"Nah, not friends. I knew her from the diner. Had been going there and sitting in her section for years before Tobias set his sights on her. I liked her, too. She was real pretty. Sweet as could be, but she never saw me that way. One smile from Tobias, though and—" He gave a low whistle. "Forget it. That woman was off the market. Once they got together, I saw her all the time 'cause Tobias and I were good friends and running the business together. Anyway, I guess she figured if we were best friends, I could talk some sense into him."

"He didn't see it that way," Gretchen said.

"Sure didn't. Told me I was meddling. Said a bunch of other

shit, too, but the gist of it was 'butt out.' Didn't hear a peep from either of them on the subject after that."

"How long before they were killed did these conversations with Cora and then with Tobias take place?" asked Josie.

"About two months beforehand. Something like that. For a while, when they were together, it seemed like there was tension. Things were getting better, though. I mean, Tobias loved her. That was the bottom line. He would have given her anything she asked for. He'd bought her some necklace or something the week before they went missing. The evening out was supposed to be part of him making shit up to her for being so stubborn."

Josie made a mental note to look into the necklace. Had she been wearing it out to dinner? Had it been washed away by the river? Or had the killer stolen her jewelry? She didn't believe the couple's deaths were a result of a robbery gone wrong, but it wasn't outside the realm of possibility that their killer had stolen their valuables at the last minute. Hummel hadn't found any cash but perhaps it hadn't survived seven years of immersion. She wondered if Fanning had ever looked into the possibility of Cora's jewelry showing up at a pawn shop.

"They went to dinner," said Josie. "You had your own date here in Denton. Did Tobias know you were coming here?"

"That night, specifically? No. I didn't mention it because I didn't want to fight over the expansion when he was about to take Cora out. Even talking about the woman I was seeing here got him fired up."

"When was the last time you saw Cora before that night?" Gretchen asked.

Hollis reached across the table for the carafe, pouring himself another coffee. "A few days before. She stopped by the office to bring Tobias lunch before she went to work."

"Had either of them been acting strangely in the weeks or days before they were killed?" Josie asked.

"You're asking me if something was up. Like if they were having problems with somebody or something. No. Shit was normal. I mean the kids were getting in trouble. Dumb teenage shit. Zane was a bit of a hellion. Always getting into some kind of trouble. Underage drinking, mostly. When the girls moved in, he got Riley into a heap of trouble. Tobias caught her drinking with Zane and his friends a few times. Gave her a talking-to but never told Cora."

Gretchen frowned. "Why not?"

"Cora had already caught him and Riley sneaking back into the house after curfew totally plastered. It was only that one time but boy, she was fit to be tied. Told Tobias that Zane was a bad influence. Said Tobias wasn't strict enough—which was probably true—but he didn't want to hear it. So yeah, the kids were a bit of a handful together. Tobias and Cora fought over it on the regular though. It was nothing new. That was the only thing that I remember going on between them that week."

Josie remembered the *Herald* article she had read and Riley's admission earlier today about her drinking and how it had caused a rift with Cora. She hadn't mentioned Zane. Had he also been involved with that particular incident or had Riley gone solo?

Gretchen scribbled on her notepad. "You and Tobias weren't having any problems or disagreements other than over the expansion of the business?"

"Is this like a 'gotcha' thing?" he asked. "Like if you keep asking me the same question, eventually I'll slip up and give a different answer? No. We weren't having any problems. No fights other than the expansion."

"You didn't hire someone to kill them?" Josie asked pointedly.

"This again." Slouching in his chair, he sighed heavily. "Of course not. You really need to talk to Fanning. He went through all my financials. I know I seem like the most obvious choice here. Tobias was my business partner, and he was standing in the way of my big plans. But look, if I was gonna hire someone to kill him, I sure as shit wouldn't want Cora to be collateral damage. She was a good woman. Zane and Jackson loved her, and it was real hard for those boys to warm up to anyone after losing their own moms. Plus, she had Riley, and those two were real close."

Josie had wondered after reading about the case if the perpetrators had intended to kill both Tobias and Cora, or if only one of them had been the intended target and the other had simply been an unfortunate casualty. If that was the case, and they could determine which of them was the target, they could narrow the suspect pool considerably. Throw all their resources into investigating people associated with one person instead of both. Surely, Detective Fanning had had the same thought and already followed that line of inquiry.

Hollis went on, "Also, if I was going to hire someone to kill him, it would have been better for me if he'd actually turned up dead back then. Trying to run this place and make decisions without his input when we didn't know if he was alive or dead was worse than fighting with him over every little decision. Our operating agreement allowed Jackson to take over for Tobias until Zane came of age and they could split the responsibilities, but those boys were messed up after their dad vanished. For a long time. It was a lot on me to hold the company together on my own till they got to a place where they could start filling Tobias's shoes."

Hollis made good points, but Josie had the feeling that they hadn't even begun to scratch the surface of the lives of Cora Stevens and Tobias Lachlan.

"Okay," Gretchen said. "If not you, then who would have wanted to kill Tobias and Cora?"

"That's easy," Hollis said. "I've been telling Fanning this for years. The number one suspect should have been Dalton

Stevens, Cora's ex-husband. Riley's dad. First of all, he routinely kicked the shit out of her when they were married. She barely got out of that marriage alive. After she left him, he was completely obsessed with her. Wouldn't leave her alone. He was always showing up at the diner, sitting in a corner booth for hours, all creepy and shit. He'd send her anniversary cards on their wedding date even though they were divorced. Send her flowers and shit on Valentine's Day and her birthday. Like he was trying to get her back or something, and whenever she didn't fall all over his sorry ass, he'd get mad and slash her tires or scratch the word 'slut' into the side of her car. He used to come to their house when Tobias wasn't home and threaten her. One of us would have to leave work and get over there, drag him off."

Josie said, "You and Tobias?"

"Or Jackson, if Tobias was on a job and couldn't get there in time. He was old enough by then to take on a jerk-off like Dalton. You've seen the kid, right? He's huge. Moved a hell of a lot faster than me or Tobias, that's for sure. That wimpy-ass bastard was afraid of him."

"Did Cora ever call the police?"

"Sure. Every time. She had one of those PFAs or whatever. Restraining order?"

"Protection from Abuse orders," Gretchen said.

"Right, right. But those things are worth less than the paper they're printed on."

Josie and Gretchen knew that better than anyone. If they had a dollar for every call police responded to for partners violating their PFAs in the last ten years alone, they'd never have to work again.

"Plus," Hollis went on, "Dalton hated Tobias. Despised him. Cora didn't date anyone after her divorce. No one, and it wasn't because men weren't lining up. You've seen her pictures. She wasn't short on offers, that's for sure. It just seemed like

Dalton ruined all that for her. Not just because she couldn't trust men but also because she knew any guy she dated was going to get harassed by that prick. She went years without going on a single date. Then Tobias came on the scene and suddenly, she was moving in with him and wearing his ring. Dalton damn near lost his mind. For as many times as he threatened Cora, he said he was gonna kill Tobias double that amount. Check the police reports and see how often our place was vandalized. Could never prove it was Dalton, but everyone knew he did it."

"Tobias didn't have a problem with Dalton stalking him and Cora?" Josie asked.

"I told you, Tobias loved Cora. He would have put up with a thousand Daltons if it meant being with her. He wasn't a little bitch like Dalton either. Tobias wasn't afraid of him. I guess he should have been. Honestly, I was surprised nothing happened to Tobias before that night 'cause Dalton had it out for him bigtime. You know how those types are."

"Yeah," Josie and Gretchen said in unison.

The abusive husband who got off on terrorizing his wife, controlling her with violence. If she managed to get away—if she lived—it became his sole mission to continue making her life hell. He made sure that she spent the rest of her days looking over her shoulder, waiting for the proverbial axe to fall, wondering what would be next. He made sure that she never had a peaceful night of rest again, sleeping with a bat or a gun or a knife next to her bed, starting at every unusual noise. His constant harassment ensured that she wouldn't be able to form new friendships or relationships. No one wanted to deal with their new friend or girlfriend's crazy ex-husband. No one wanted to get caught in the crossfire. He isolated her just as sure as he had while they were married. Only now he used psychological guerilla warfare instead of broken bones. For as long as he was alive, she would spend every moment wondering if this was the day he finally came after her for good.

Men like Dalton Stevens were dangerous. Their need for control usually outweighed their own self-preservation. They were ticking time bombs and often, they didn't care if they took themselves out in the process of destroying their ex-wives.

But men like Dalton Stevens could also be impulsive. They were more likely to kill in a fit of rage than with some well-thought-out and carefully executed plan. The demise of Tobias and Cora smacked of meticulous planning. That didn't mean Dalton Stevens wasn't behind it but Hollis seemed a much more likely suspect. He was clearly smart, even-tempered, and strategic and he had both resources and motivation. Not to mention that he was strangely calm and glib after just having learned that his close friends had been murdered.

"Hollis." Gretchen twirled her pen in her hand. "Do you own any firearms?"

He went still. For the first time, his easy bravado slipped, and he looked older than his age and scared. "Doesn't everyone around here?"

"What kind?"

"A Sig Sauer .45 and a Glock 17."

"How long have you owned them?" Gretchen jotted down more notes.

"I don't know. Ten years? What are you getting at? You think I shot them, right? The kids told me they were shot. Here we go again. What do you want? You got some fancy test you want to do on my guns? Some forensic shit? Go for it."

"We'll let you know," Gretchen said coolly.

He had no idea that they hadn't found any bullets inside the car. Without the projectile, there wasn't any forensic testing that could be done. They didn't even know what type of rounds had killed Tobias and Cora. Neither Josie nor Gretchen was going to tell him that.

Before they could continue questioning him, the sound of shouting drew their attention. Hollis hefted himself out of his chair, maneuvering around a floor polisher. He was almost at the door when it flew open. Standing on the threshold was a younger, fitter version of Tobias Lachlan. Unlike his father, he had a full head of thick, sandy hair. His hands were fisted at his sides and his chest heaved. Tears rolled down his cheeks.

Ellyn ran up behind him, peeking around his solid frame. "Sorry, Hol. He's a little worked up."

"It's fine," Hollis said softly. Then he beckoned the man toward him. "Come here, kid."

EIGHTEEN

Zane Lachlan stepped into Hollis's arms. Sobs shook his entire body. He was the shorter of the two so his forehead rested naturally against Hollis's shoulder. Great, gulping cries spilled from deep in his chest, filling the air. Josie had heard the sound of this kind of raw grief countless times in her line of work—had experienced it personally—yet it never failed to pierce her professional armor. That kind of deep, visceral pain hit true every time, like an arrow finding its mark in an instant.

Hollis gripped the back of Zane's neck, kneading the skin. "I'm sorry, kid," he murmured. "Real sorry."

Josie and Gretchen stood, moving toward them, trying not to knock over the stack of industrial-sized toilet paper rolls near the door. "We'll give you a few minutes," Josie murmured.

Hollis nodded at them and moved Zane aside so they could pass. In the lobby, Ellyn was speaking into her headset again, this time giving a spiel about how the company handled hazardous chemicals. Josie and Gretchen stood near the mouth of the hallway, out of the secretary's earshot but close enough to eavesdrop on the two men.

"Hollis is pretty close with the kids," Gretchen said.

"He stepped right up," Josie agreed.

"Both of Tobias's sons are part of the company. Jackson was already working for them when his dad disappeared. Zane's running the show in Brighton Springs now. Did he step in because of his friendship with Tobias or because it would be easier to implement his expansion plans with Tobias's sons on board? Easy to control them?"

"He says he was never interested in having children," Josie said. "But he was obviously interested in at least two of Tobias's girlfriends—both of whom already had children."

"True."

Had Hollis grown jealous of Tobias? Always getting the girl while he stood on the sidelines, being asked to intercede in his friend's relationship by the woman he'd been admiring for years? He certainly knew a lot of personal details about Cora's life. More than Josie would expect from the friend of her fiancé. Even if he'd regularly eaten at the diner where she worked, would Cora have divulged so much to him in that setting? According to Hollis, they hadn't been friends at that point. He'd been a patron and she'd been a waitress.

Hollis was trying too hard to get ahead of the investigation. He offered too much honesty, too many explanations before they'd even had a chance to ask their questions. Most people in his position who had spent seven years under police scrutiny and now faced the prospect of that scrutiny becoming more intense would be somewhat apprehensive, guilty or not. They'd be tight-lipped, evasive, perhaps even retain a lawyer in anticipation of being investigated as a murder suspect. If he wasn't behind Tobias and Cora's deaths, he was certainly hiding something.

"Step-siblings—well, almost—living in the same house," Gretchen said. "Both parents go missing. Who's stepping in to take care of them? Keep the household going? Pay the mortgage, utilities, car insurance? Make sure they're eating and going to school? Sure, they were sixteen and seventeen, but they were still kids."

Josie had had the same thought. In the online articles she'd combed through so far, there hadn't been any mention of grandparents or aunts and uncles. Jackson's mother, Rachel Wright, was out of the picture. Zane's mother, Gabrielle Lachlan, had died. Riley's father clearly wasn't fit to care for her. Dalton Stevens may not have been interested in regaining custody of his daughter after Cora disappeared. From what they'd learned about him thus far, Josie would bet a week's pay that Riley was nothing more to him than an effective way to manipulate and control his ex-wife. With Cora out of the picture, he had no use for her.

"Jackson was twenty-three," Josie said. "He'd taken over Tobias's position in the company. It was probably him. Though I'm sure he was unprepared to become a guardian, co-owner of a company, and head of a household all at once, in the blink of an eye."

The sound of another soft sob came from the hallway.

Gretchen nodded. "Lucky for him, his dad's best friend could swoop in and keep things running smoothly."

Hollis and Zane emerged from the conference room, walking slowly toward the lobby. Wiping at his eyes, Zane said something Josie couldn't make out.

"Yeah, sure," Hollis replied. "You can stay with me. Long as you want. You talk to Riley and Jackson yet?"

"Riley," Zane said in a pointed tone.

A sigh. "You know you're gonna have to talk to him to plan the funeral."

"Whatever."

"Son, don't you dare put Riley in the middle of this again."

Josie and Gretchen exchanged puzzled looks. What did Hollis mean by "this"? There was obviously some long-standing issue between the brothers and yet, Jackson had acted like they were on good terms, passing their dad's old, cherished recliner back and forth every Christmas.

"She was always in the damn middle," Zane muttered.

They stopped walking. Hollis's voice was low and angry. "You shut your mouth. That girl didn't do a thing but lose her mother. Just like you and Jackson lost your father. You boys work your shit out or don't but leave her out of it. She's already fragile. This is liable to break her."

Hollis wasn't wrong. Josie knew a person hanging onto their sanity by a thread when she saw one and Riley was certainly that. She'd probably been standing on the emotional precipice for the past seven years.

Once they reached the lobby, Hollis gave Josie and Gretchen a strained smile. Zane studied them with curious, bloodshot eyes. Slapping a hand on the back of Zane's neck, Hollis said, "These are the detectives here to talk about your dad and Cora. Their, um, murders."

Zane winced.

Josie and Gretchen introduced themselves and presented their credentials. Zane spent several seconds studying each one of their IDs before looking up at Josie with an expression that was childlike in its hopefulness. "Do you have any suspects?"

"Not yet."

"Me," said Hollis.

Zane's head snapped toward him. "What?"

"We don't currently have any suspects," Gretchen said calmly, sensing, as Josie did, that Zane's grief was as raw as Riley's had been earlier. His eyes were glossy with unshed tears. His lower lip quivered, giving away his vulnerability. Jackson had been better at containing his pain, but he had had years of experience as the older brother, the cool head, the caretaker. Clearly, he continued to be that for his wife.

"We're in the very early stages of the investigation," Josie added. "We're gathering information."

"What information?"

Hollis squeezed Zane's neck. "All the same shit we told Fanning in the beginning."

"No," Zane cried, gaze flickering frantically back and forth between Josie and Gretchen. "There has to be more. Fanning never figured out what happened to them. You have the car now, right? That means more evidence. It has to mean more evidence."

"Kid," Hollis whispered as Zane's voice grew higher-pitched.

"You have to have something. You just have to." He was teetering on the edge of hysteria. "I can't—we can't do this. Ending one nightmare just to start another. It's too much. You have something to go on now, right? If you're just repeating what Fanning did, you'll never find out who killed them."

"Hey," Hollis said. "Calm down. Maybe with a new set of eyes on the case—two sets—things will be different this time."

Josie hoped Hollis was right. Neither she nor Gretchen tried to convince Zane of that, however. Ultimately, their actions would speak louder than their words. Instead of starting with the same types of questions they'd asked Riley and Jackson, Josie said, "After your dad and Cora disappeared, did you and Riley continue to live in their house?"

Zane sniffled. "Um, yeah, it was our home, and we thought they'd come back. Maybe it was stupid, but we were kids. Plus, where else would we go?"

"I offered to take them in after about six months," said Hollis.

"Into your tiny-ass house?" Zane joked weakly. "I don't think so. Jackson got rid of his apartment and moved back home to look after us until I turned eighteen. Then he moved here to help with the expansion."

Gretchen said, "You and Riley kept living there alone?"

"Yeah." Zane jammed a hand into his pants pocket and

came up with a tissue. "It was weird and freaky but technically, I was an adult so it was legal."

"Riley was a minor," Josie pointed out. "Did any of her relatives or her father try to get her to move in with them?"

"The only person Riley had left was her piece-of-shit dad." Zane paused to blow his nose. "Since we didn't know if Cora was coming home or not, and she wasn't dead, he would have had to petition the court to get custody of her and he wasn't interested in spending a bunch of money and showing up at hearings, so he didn't bother."

As Josie suspected, Dalton had only ever been interested in Cora. Poor Riley had grown up with a father who not only abused her mother but didn't care about her at all. A sudden flash of Dex's face burst across Josie's mind. How he had smiled with such pride when he told her that he had a daughter. Wren had been nine when her mom died and they first met. He could have reacted with horror—a perpetual bachelor having a nine-year-old dumped on him—but instead, Dex was happier than Josie had ever seen him. Dalton Stevens had had the opportunity to be a father all of Riley's life, and he'd pissed it away.

"Then Riley came to Denton for college," Gretchen said, pulling Josie from her thoughts. "Do you still live in your father's house?"

"Yeah. Couldn't sell it 'cause he was still technically alive."

"I helped them out whenever they needed," said Hollis.

"Was Cora's name on the house?" asked Josie.

Zane looked momentarily confused but Hollis knew what she was getting at. "No. Cora didn't have any assets beyond what was in her bank account, which wasn't much. But there was never any talk of making Riley leave. That's not what Cora or Tobias would have wanted."

"No way was I letting her go to her dad's," Zane said. "None of us wanted that."

No wonder Cora had wanted to keep working. If her assets

hadn't amounted to much, it was likely she hadn't owned her own house before meeting Tobias. Not surprising given that she was a single mother waiting tables to make ends meet. It was doubtful that Dalton Stevens had ever paid child support. Cora probably hadn't had the funds to take him to court.

Cora and Riley had been absorbed into Tobias's household. Without keeping her job, Cora would be left with nothing should the relationship end. Even if they'd been married, she would only have been entitled to assets accrued during the marriage. She'd been smart to insist on maintaining some independence. As it was, now that the couple were dead, Riley would only be entitled to whatever was left in Cora's bank account, if anything. Zane and Jackson would split everything Tobias had left behind—the house, bank accounts, vehicles, and all personal property. They already split interest in the business.

"Did you help her out with college tuition?" Gretchen asked Hollis.

He chuckled. "Hell, no. She wouldn't let me. Wouldn't let anyone. She put herself through college with scholarships and loans."

"Cora's old boss from the diner started a GoFundMe for us," Zane said. "Ri could have used that money for school, but she hired a private investigator instead to look for Dad and Cora."

Josie wasn't surprised. Many families did the same when their loved ones' murders or disappearances became cold cases. "What was the PI's name?"

Hollis and Zane looked at one another, brows furrowed. Then Zane said, "I don't remember. You have to ask Riley. Doesn't matter though. He didn't find anything."

"Did Cora bring any furniture with her when she moved in with your dad?" Gretchen asked.

Zane looked surprised by the change in the direction of

questioning. "Um, I'm not sure. Maybe? I was fifteen. I wasn't really paying attention."

"What happened to her personal effects?" Josie said. "Did Riley take them with her when she moved?"

"Yeah. When she married Jackson. Once they got their own place."

"Do you recall if Cora owned anything that required a skeleton key to open it?" Josie pressed.

Both men were silent. The moment stretched on, becoming awkward. Finally, Hollis said, "What are you talking about?"

"Are you familiar with skeleton keys?" Gretchen asked as though he hadn't spoken.

"Yeah," Hollis and Zane answered in unison.

"Did Cora own anything that required one?" Josie repeated.

"I don't—I don't know." Zane's voice dripped with exhaustion, but he took a moment to think about it, eyes narrowed in concentration. "I'm sorry, but I really don't remember. I can ask Riley next time I talk to her."

"How about anyone else in the household?" Gretchen followed up.

Zane took another pause to consider the question. "Um, no, I don't think so."

Hollis threw his hands up, palms out. "I don't have anything that needs a skeleton key if that's where you're headed with this."

"I know this has been a long day." Josie addressed Zane. "We're very sorry for your loss. I appreciate your taking the time to speak with us. We can talk again another time. Just one last question. Do you know of anyone who would have wanted your dad and Cora dead?"

Zane used the tissue to dab at a rogue tear sliding down his cheek. "Other than Riley's dad? No."

NINETEEN

Noah's hand drifted down Josie's spine. His lips pressed against the top of her head. With a sigh, she nestled her cheek against his chest. The sound of his heartbeat, sure and steady, made her drowsy. They were sprawled across their couch, Josie on top of him. Normally, Trout would be sitting on the floor nearby, whining about them not leaving him any room to lie with them. But after dinner, Wren had retreated to her room, and he'd gone with her. It was a rare night when all three of them were home for more than fifteen minutes. There was a movie that Josie and Noah had wanted to watch. They'd tried to entice Wren to join them, but she had politely refused. They put it on anyway, but it hadn't held their attention.

Cuddling was way better.

"I got a call today from the vow renewal venue," Noah said. "They need the final deposit. I thought you were going to take care of that."

Josie buried her face in his chest, muffling her words. "I'm not sure we should do it."

"What? Why?"

Lifting her head, she grimaced at the fleeting look of hurt in his eyes. "We should be prioritizing Wren, not our vow renewal."

"We can do both, you know." He tucked a strand of her hair behind her ear. "We already postponed it once. I thought you wanted this."

There was a note of disappointment—no, defeat—in his voice which made her feel terrible. It had been his idea. She hadn't realized how important it was to him until this moment. She thought he'd mainly suggested it to make her happy.

"I'm sorry," she whispered. "I did want it. I do. But I wonder if this is the right time for it. I'm worried about how it will impact Wren. After talking with her the other day, I think she doesn't really feel secure with us. Not yet. I'm worried that she thinks we'll decide caring for her is too difficult and kick her out. We should be focused on making her feel like she really has a home with us. I want her to know that we're not going anywhere, no matter what. I want her to feel like a priority."

He nodded along with her words, a pensive expression on his face. "I hadn't thought of it that way."

Josie snuggled deeper into his arms. "We have a few days before we lose our deposit. Just think about it."

They fell silent, neither of them bothering to watch the movie playing on the television. Josie's limbs relaxed in a way that they hardly ever did. This was as close to inner peace as she ever got. Noah holding her. His warm body beneath her. His strong, steady heartbeat against her cheek. Easy silence.

She dozed off and when she opened her eyes again, the credits were rolling on the television screen.

"We should get up," Noah murmured. "You have to pack."

Josie groaned. "I don't want to go."

The news was out that Tobias Lachlan and Cora Stevens had finally been found. The moment Riley started calling funeral homes in Brighton Springs, Denton PD was flooded with calls from reporters. Josie had hosted a press conference earlier that day confirming that they'd been located in the Susquehanna River in Denton and that their deaths had been ruled homicides. After she and Gretchen met with the Chief and their press liaison, they chose to leave it at that for the time being. Josie knew this was only the beginning of the furor.

Dalton Stevens had hung up on her three times, but she had managed to get in touch with John Fanning. He lived in Florida now, but he was flying in for the funerals which were being held in Brighton Springs two days from now. Josie and Gretchen planned to attend as well. Sometimes it was instructive to see who came to the funerals of murder victims. They'd meet with Fanning, track down Dalton Stevens, and trace the path Tobias and Cora had taken the night they were killed. Plus, Zane had offered to speak to them again at his home and Josie really wanted a look inside. She wasn't even sure why since they had confirmed that Riley had taken all of Cora's personal things.

Josie had insisted they could squeeze everything into one day but Chief Chitwood, Gretchen and Noah had told her she was crazy.

"Wait," Noah said. "You're telling me that *you*—Josie Quinn—don't want to do something work-related?"

He was mocking her. She swatted his bicep and then got distracted by how hard the muscle felt under her touch. "It's not just because of Wren. You and I haven't been apart since... you know."

"I'll miss you, too," he said, reaching up to stroke her hair. "We can have phone sex."

Josie lifted her upper body so she could look into his hazel eyes. "Be serious."

"I am serious." He grinned. "We've never had phone sex."

"Noah."

"Josie."

She tried to disentangle herself, but he didn't let her. Apparently, they'd entered an alternate dimension. Some realm where everything was reversed because now she was the one who wanted to talk about their feelings while he wanted to pretend they didn't exist. If this was what personal growth felt like, she'd rather have a root canal. Still, she pressed on because this was important.

"You're still having nightmares," she said, watching the playfulness in his eyes drain away and hating it. The abduction—more specifically, the savage beatings he'd taken while being held against his will—affected him far more deeply than he was willing to admit.

"I sleep without you all the time," he said, voice low and tense. "When we work opposite shifts."

"That's not the same," Josie said. "I'm never more than a half hour away."

"I don't—" His jaw tightened. She wondered if she should have left it alone, but she owed him this after all the times he'd been there for her. The times he'd patiently pushed her to deal with her trauma head-on. In the last nine months, her sweet, easygoing, good-humored husband had become frayed around the edges. He'd seen a therapist as a condition of returning to work but the moment his required sessions were finished, he stopped attending. Josie had hoped the nightmares would wane with time, but they hadn't. Noah slept so poorly at night that she'd found him napping on this very couch during the day so many times that it was starting to bear the imprint of his body—and it was a new couch.

He swallowed, hand drifting down to her ass. With a light squeeze, he said, "I'm fine. I just need you."

"Right."

They'd had more sex in the last nine months, even after Wren arrived, than in the entire two years before that. At first, it was life-affirming. Them needing physical intimacy to reassure themselves that the hell they'd endured was truly over. That they had one another and no one was going to tear them apart again. But now, she suspected he was using sex as a way to avoid dealing with his feelings. He was insatiable. Part of her knew she'd want to kick her own ass later for trying to put a stop to it, but Noah's mental health took priority.

"It's one night, Josie." His hand slipped under the hem of her shirt, tracing circles over the skin of her lower back.

Fighting her body's response to his touch, she said, "You need to see someone, Noah. Please."

Again, he tried to blow her off with a teasing smile. "What are you saying? We should see other people?"

With an angry huff, Josie pushed herself off him, untangling her legs from his so she could stand. Her cheeks heated with anger. "Don't!" she snapped. "You almost died. It's a miracle you don't have permanent injuries! It was traumatic. Stop acting like it wasn't. Your nightmares are not getting better. It's been almost a year! You need help, Noah."

He sat up. Anger flashed through his eyes. Josie was so unaccustomed to seeing it that it set her back on her heels. Maybe this was good, though. She had to get through to him somehow.

"I need help?" he said.

She put her hands on her hips. "You know you do."

"That's rich, coming from you."

A few years ago, that remark would have leveled her. Not only was it completely out of character for him, it was a low blow. The cruel, casual way he tossed it out at her made it worse. The traumas Josie had endured in her childhood alone had left her emotionally raw. They'd been mortal wounds to her innocence and sense of self. Battles she had to fight each and every day well into adulthood. She'd had no idea how to deal with the aftermath. She'd had to learn to accept help. It had been painful, but she'd done it. She'd worked on herself because her actions affected the people she loved—Noah most of all.

Now, she was strong. She'd gotten better at having these

messy, unpredictable conversations about feelings. Well, feelings that weren't her own. Instead of retreating and licking yet another wound, Josie glared at him. "Go ahead, lash out at me. It won't help. All it's going to do is make you feel like shit later when you realize what an asshole you're being."

She saw the surprise on his face and the moment he tried to shutter it.

"If you don't want to go back to the person the Chief made you talk with, we'll find someone else," she continued. "Or... or talk to Luke! He went through the same thing."

Noah stood up. A muscle in his jaw ticked furiously. Through gritted teeth, he said, "Let me get this straight. You want me to talk to your ex-fiancé about how it feels to be tortured for information you don't have? What? Over a couple of beers? How would that go? 'Hey, I know you almost married my wife, but wanna swap stories of how it feels to be beaten so badly you piss yourself?' Really, Josie? Oh, I know, we'll invite him over to the house that he almost moved into when the two of you were engaged and throw some steaks on the grill. Maybe over dinner, I can casually ask him how *he* felt when he was in so much pain that he couldn't figure out whether dying would be better or worse. Or what it was like for him lying in a puddle of his own blood and filth, wondering if he did make it back to you, whether he'd be permanently disfigured? Yeah, that would be fun. Let's do it. We can compare notes."

Her heart was beating too fast in her chest. It was the most he'd said about what had happened to him since he gave his statement to the state police after he was rescued. "Noah, I—"

"I'm not discussing this with you right now."

"Okay," she said softly. Part of her wanted to push him. Try gently coaxing more details from him. Not because she needed to hear them—she had her own nightmares about what had been done to him—but because he was as close as he'd ever been to opening up. At the same time, she didn't want to leave town with tension or anger between them. Reaching out, she placed her hand over his heart, relieved when he didn't recoil. "But promise me we'll discuss it after I get back."

Before he could answer, they both heard the distinct click of Wren's door closing upstairs. Josie's body went rigid. Dread passed over her like a cold gust of air.

Noah tipped his head back, closing his eyes. "Shit."

Wren had been listening. How much had she heard? Did it matter? Josie recalled all the articles she'd read about parenting last year when they were preparing to adopt an infant. Adults fought all the time. Modeling healthy conflict resolution was an important part of parenting. Sharing stories of your past traumas with your child, when done using age-appropriate language and maintaining boundaries, could strengthen your bond and inspire trust.

Blah, blah, blah.

They weren't Wren's parents, and she was already afraid, unsure of her place with them.

"How much do you think she heard?" Noah whispered.

"Enough," Josie said. It was probably shitty of her to play this card, but she needed Noah to get help. She needed them to work—the three of them. "If you won't talk to someone for my sake, do it for Wren. She lost everything. She needs us to be at our best right now."

TWENTY

John Fanning's rental car was small and uncomfortable. Josie was pretty sure it also lacked shocks. Entirely. Every time they went over the smallest bump, it felt like she was about to wear her pelvic bone as a neck pillow. She had wanted to drive but for the purposes of their tour of Brighton Springs, it made more sense for him to do it. He had met them at the Brighton Springs PD headquarters. Now, they were in Fanning's tiny, temporary ride. Gretchen sat in the front seat. Josie had chosen the back so that it wouldn't be obvious that she was checking her cell phone every five minutes to see if Wren had responded to her flurry of text messages from earlier that morning.

After hearing Wren's door close the night before, Josie and Noah had gone upstairs and knocked, hoping to speak to her immediately to clear the air. She didn't answer. They could only conclude that she was pretending to be asleep so she wouldn't have to talk to them. Josie had had to leave before she woke up. According to Noah, they'd had a brief and very awkward exchange over breakfast during which Wren had responded to his apology and reassurances with a grunt.

"All right, here's Tobias's house." Fanning pulled onto the

shoulder of the two-lane road they'd just turned down. It was on the fringe of Brighton Springs, where the small city gave way to more rural areas. There were no sidewalks here, only mailboxes marking gravel driveways. The homes were spread well apart, each one occupying three or more acres, most of them separated by small groves of trees rather than fencing.

The two-story Lachlan house was big, but it needed work. The brick façade crumbled in some places and spalled in others. One of its gutters hung loose. A handful of roof shingles was missing.

Gretchen rolled down her window. "Guess the kids didn't use any of the money they were earning from Tobias's share of the business to maintain the house."

Fanning laughed. He wasn't at all the hard-nosed pain in the ass that Hollis had described. At least, not to them. He was warm and chatty. Energy practically fizzed from his tall, lanky frame as they discussed the case. Josie could tell that it bothered him that he hadn't been the one to find Tobias and Cora, but his relief that they'd finally been located was palpable.

"They spent the money on that," he said, pointing to a large freestanding garage to the right of the house. It looked brand new, bay doors and clean tan siding gleaming in the sun.

The scent of cut grass and honeysuckle drifted along the warm air. It was another cloudless day. Josie watched two small white butterflies dance across lavender milkweed flowers near the back of the structure. "What's it for?"

"How much do you know about junk removal companies?"

Gretchen answered, "Once they clean out a place, they typically do three things: recycle anything they're able to, donate gently used goods, and dispose of the rest."

Fanning nodded. "Except that Tobias kept finding valuable stuff in a lot of the houses they cleaned out. Antiques and such. When he and Hollis first started out, they got hired by this woman from California to clean out her recently deceased mother's home. They found this weird sculpture. Looked really old. They didn't know what to do with it. Tobias started contacting universities and art museums and came to find out it was some kind of ancient Mayan artifact. Worth twenty grand."

"No shit," Gretchen blurted.

"Yeah, it made the papers here." Fanning eyed his side mirror, watching a car approaching from behind. "That's how I know about it. Anyway, legally they can't sell something they found in someone's house."

Josie thought about all the antiques and collectible items littering Jackson and Riley's home as well as the ones in Hollis's office. "But they can sell it on behalf of the owner and take a small commission."

Fanning put his own window down so he could wave the other vehicle around him. "Exactly. Zane started collecting things and storing them in the new, climate-controlled garage while he found buyers."

Gretchen shifted in her seat, turning to face him. "Then Riley took over."

"Yeah." Fanning let his arm dangle from the driver's side window. "They worked something out with her. She's good at it, from what I've heard."

Next to the garage sat two older-model vehicles. Their tires were flat. Weeds sprouted from the gravel under and around them. They had been there a while. "What about the cars?" Josie asked.

"One of them's Cora's old car," Fanning explained. "The other was registered to Tobias, but Zane was the one who drove it. After the disappearance, Zane started using his dad's work truck."

"Multiple vehicles in and out all the time," Josie noted, watching as the twin butterflies circled one another while flitting from the back of the garage across the front lawn of the house.

"You're wondering if Tobias and Cora were mistakenly targeted because of the car they were in?" Fanning said as he made a U-turn and headed back toward the more populated area of the city. "Sure. Maybe some asshole was looking for some other asshole driving a Hyundai Accent and got the wrong one. They confronted Tobias and Cora, and things went wrong."

"That seems like a distinct possibility," Gretchen said.

"Yep," Fanning agreed. He motioned toward the road ahead. "I'm driving the route we believe they took to the restaurant based on where their cell phones pinged before they reached it."

"Tell us what you really think." Josie watched as the homes became smaller and grew closer together, their lawns shrinking. "Murder for hire? Organized crime? Wrong place, wrong time?"

"Yep," Fanning said.

Gretchen chuckled. "That's an answer, all right."

"Listen." He continued dangling his hand out the window, letting air slide through his parted fingers as he drove. "I went through all of Tobias and Cora's phone records, emails, and social media accounts. Hell, I even went through their kids' phones, emails, and social media accounts. Then I talked to everyone who knew Tobias and Cora. Their coworkers, customers, neighbors, people they went to school with, cashiers at the stores they frequented, their doctors, their damn dentists! There was no beef with anyone other than Hollis and Dalton and those two have alibis. The pings from their phones as well as GPS from their vehicles put them exactly where they claimed to be when Cora and Tobias disappeared. Dalton was at a pub across town. According to the bartender, he left when the place closed. Hollis was chasing some woman in Denton although as far as I'm concerned, she could have helped him kill them and dump the car in Denton."

"You didn't eliminate murder for hire," Josie pointed out.

"But I couldn't find any proof," Fanning replied. "Believe me, I tried. If that's what happened, my money's on Hollis."

"Really?" asked Gretchen. "Dalton has a history of violence."

"Dalton Stevens is a dumbass with the patience of a rabid dog. His financials checked out, too. Besides, what did he stand to gain by paying someone to murder his ex-wife and her new man?"

"Satisfaction," Josie said drily.

He shot her a wide smile in the rearview mirror. "Exactly. They had a kid. Financially, he gained nothing from her death—or disappearance. In fact, he should have ended up with custody of Riley and trust me, this guy did not want that."

Josie discreetly checked her phone but there were no new messages.

"Fanning," said Gretchen. "With all due respect, men like Dalton Stevens don't typically kill their ex-wives and their new partners for financial security. It's more of an if-I-can't-have-you-then-no-one-can situation. Maybe he didn't have the money to pay someone to do it, but he could have compensated them in other ways."

"Like what?"

"Favors," Josie filled in, pocketing her phone.

"Well, shit," Fanning blew out a sigh. "Okay, so I didn't really consider that, but I did a deep dive into everyone Dalton was associated with. His neighbors, friends, coworkers from the steel plant and the barflies. Brought them all in for questioning. There was nothing that sent up any red flags. I mean, pretty much half the people he hangs around with are scumbags but there wasn't any evidence connecting any of them to the disappearance."

Josie looked out the window again, watching as they drove

down a street filled with twin homes and turned onto a commercial block. "Any of them own guns?"

"A lot of them, I'm sure," he mumbled. "Firearms weren't exactly on my radar, but I did make a list of which witnesses had purchased handguns or admitted to owning any type of gun. Due diligence and all that. Should be in the file."

By law, Pennsylvania was restricted from creating or maintaining a gun ownership registry. The commonwealth and federal government did, however, keep records of legal gun transactions. Those records were created every time a citizen bought a handgun since they had to fill out forms for the state police and the Bureau of Alcohol, Tobacco, and Firearms in order to do so. The two organizations weren't prohibited from keeping records, only from creating a database with them. Local police departments could contact the state police and ATF to request a check for handgun purchases from a specific person.

"Dalton had two pistols but he had to relinquish those when Cora took out the first PFA against him," Fanning added.

"That wouldn't keep him from getting his hands on one, I'm sure," Gretchen muttered.

Fanning slowed in front of an Italian restaurant called Ecco Domani. It was a squat, glass-front building in one of Brighton Springs' older commercial districts. The rest of the street was filled with quaint shops offering everything from old vinyl records to chocolate and coffee. The restaurant had made an effort to ditch its strip mall look and match the welcoming small-town vibe of its neighbors. The exterior walls were painted to look like faux stone, the effect almost 3-D. The tops of each window were adorned with overflowing flowerpots. Along the bottoms, matching flowerpots stood like little sentries, bursting with color. Josie wondered what they did during the winter.

"Nice place, right?" Fanning said. "Food's great. Anyway, they were parked back here. This spot, actually."

He pulled into a parking lot between the restaurant and a small bookstore and took one of the half-dozen spots. The three of them got out. Josie massaged her lower back and scanned the tops of the buildings. Two cameras, one on each side.

"There's a camera at the front door of the restaurant, same as seven years ago. Caught them walking out—hand in hand."

Josie had found the footage and viewed it before they left Denton. Tobias and Cora had been the picture of a happy couple indulging in a date night. The film quality wasn't ideal but it looked as though Cora had worn a necklace and her engagement ring.

"Fanning," she said. "Did you check local pawn shops for the jewelry that Cora was wearing?"

He closed the car door. "Yeah. Here and in several other places, too. Nothing ever turned up. Then again, I didn't look as far as Denton."

Gretchen put her hands on her hips and eyed the camera pointed down at them. "When Tobias and Cora left the restaurant, they weren't fighting."

"Wait staff said they had a great time. They were laughing and joking. Cora complimented the food. They shared a dessert." Fanning shaded his eyes from the sun. "Tobias didn't have anything to drink. Cora had one glass of wine. Next, we had them on camera here, getting into the car. A witness who had just parked also saw them and said nothing about them seemed off. No tension."

This was important. They hadn't rushed out of the restaurant before their meals were finished. There was no emergency. Nothing out of the ordinary. At that point, around nine p.m., everything had been completely normal for the couple.

Gretchen asked, "Did any witnesses overhear them talking about going anywhere after the restaurant? A bar, maybe?"

"Nothing," Fanning answered. "Come on. I'll give you the rest of the tour."

Back in the car, he cruised through the streets so slowly that several drivers beeped angrily and swerved to go around him. Fanning was oblivious, pointing out all the businesses with exterior security cameras on which Tobias's sedan had been captured.

"Was he speeding?" Josie asked. "Driving erratically?"

"Nope." He took a left onto a residential street. "In fact, we have them driving past one of these houses around the time that Cora sent the text to Jackson about letting the cat in."

At this point during their drive home, everything had still been normal. Tobias was driving safely. Cora's mind was already at home, focused on Captain Whiskers.

Fanning turned right at the next stop sign. "This is where the camera trail ends. A few folks had cameras on their properties, but none caught the car. Two people walking their dogs along here saw it though, so we know they came this way."

He wove through several more residential streets. Josie wasn't very familiar with the city, but this didn't look like the way they'd come. "He took a different way home."

"Yep." It seemed to be Fanning's catchphrase.

"Any idea why?" asked Gretchen.

"None at all."

TWENTY-ONE

The homes flashing past got further apart. Streets narrowed and sidewalks were replaced with gravel. They passed by a mile or two of woods on both sides. Geerling Road. This was the area in which Tobias and Cora's phones last pinged. Josie searched for breaks in the trees where cars could pull over. There didn't appear to be any but then Fanning found one and drove into a dirt clearing large enough to accommodate at least two cars, maybe three. Josie had no idea what it had looked like seven years ago but now, the foliage concealed most of it from passersby.

"This is what I figure," Fanning said quietly. His long fingers curled around the steering wheel as he stared straight ahead. "They stopped here. Tobias's house is about four miles away. This is all overgrown now and with the drought, everything's dried up but there used to be a creek straight ahead. With the whole car missing, you gotta think waterways."

"If you'd assumed there was no foul play," Gretchen said.

Cool air drifted through Fanning's open window. The remote area was preternaturally still, the only sounds coming from birds chirping overhead. Josie felt like they were a million miles from civilization. Through the windshield, she saw where new vegetation had sprouted and flourished between tall trees. It spanned the width of a car. An old path to the now-barren creek.

"Yeah, but Tobias and Cora didn't have any issues with anyone," Fanning said. "Hell, everyone loved Tobias like he was their own son or brother, and people knew Cora from the diner as a nice, hard-working woman who was always in a good mood, even when Dalton knocked her around. Of course we thought it was an accident. One of the first things we did was call the state police and ask for their marine unit. They searched the creek and every other pond, lake, and river in and around Brighton Springs. It was when nothing turned up that I started thinking it was something else."

"I read through your file, Fanning." Josie watched a cardinal flit from the branches of one tree to another. "There were no shell casings, no blood evidence or tire tracks that matched Tobias's car here or anywhere nearby."

"Now we know why," he said. "But back then, we still had to search the waterways. I was grasping at straws. It really was like they up and vanished into thin air." In the reflection of the rearview mirror, he rolled his lips together and then let out a "Poof!"

He'd had no reason to believe they'd ended up in Denton.

Gretchen's stomach growled. "Keep talking. Why are we here?"

"Two scenarios." He lifted his hand, curling his fingers into his palm and sticking his thumb out. "One is that they were driving past and there was something happening here, something that made them stop but when they did, it became clear they were getting into the middle of some kind of crime. Whoever they stumbled on took them to Denton and killed them. It would have been dark so it's possible Tobias slowed down when he saw headlights." His index finger popped up.

"Second scenario is that they were ambushed. Someone waited for them along their route home. This would be the perfect spot. Put your car close to the road. Make it look like you broke down. Hood up, tire jack out, something that telegraphs that you need help."

"Because Tobias was the kind of person who would stop to help someone," Gretchen said.

"Yep. I have no way to prove it, but I've always believed that whatever happened—it started here, in this place. Their phones put them within half a mile of here. I've combed the area a thousand times. This place right here is the only one that makes sense."

Regardless of where things had started, no physical evidence had been found in seven years, no witnesses had come forward to report that they'd seen the couple in this area.

"This kind of crime," Josie said. "Killing two people in cold blood, disposing of their bodies along with their car, knowing to turn their phones off, transporting them to a place three hours away, doing it so efficiently that there's not a single trace of them left... it's ruthless and meticulous. If we're looking at your first scenario, where they happened onto a crime in progress, then we're not talking about some low-level drug deals or anything like that."

"I know," Fanning said. "No one has thought about this more than me. We've got some neighborhood gangs running drugs and illegal firearms. They get pretty violent, especially when it comes to protecting their territory. They've been known to kill informants before or witnesses planning to testify against them."

"Did Tobias or Cora have any connections to them?" asked Josie.

"None that I could find. They never ran in the same circles."

"What about the kids?" Gretchen said. "Zane? Jackson?"

"No association," Fanning answered. "I even looked into Riley but nothing there either. Hollis and Dalton? Same thing. Anyway, about four years back, Brighton Springs put together a task force to deal with these little shits. The Feds were part of it and everything. Before I retired there was a big bust. About a dozen gang members were rounded up, charged with a whole bunch of nasty stuff. I got to talk to them, see if there'd ever been any chatter about Tobias and Cora. None of them even knew what I was talking about. They could have been lying, of course, but regardless, it was a dead end."

There was nothing but dead ends in this case.

The sound of a car passing by the clearing seemed far away even though it wasn't. A tingle worked its way up Josie's spine to the nape of her neck. Even in broad daylight, there was something creepy about this place, as though it held the residual energy from whatever had happened here. The beginning of Tobias and Cora's demise. The beginning of their children's nightmare.

"Scenario two, then," she said. "The ambush. Tobias took a different way home than he did to the restaurant. How did the killers know he'd come this way?"

"No idea. Maybe they didn't. Maybe they just took a chance that Tobias would take this road home, and it worked out."

"Which would mean, in the second scenario, that whoever killed them was biding their time, waiting for an opportunity to do it."

Gretchen's head swiveled, taking in their surroundings for at least the fourth time since they'd parked. "Which brings us back to murder for hire."

"I always figured that Hollis was behind it and that he'd somehow managed to get the car—with them in it—to one of the junkyards where they dump their stuff. He's got access to a couple of them. I checked them all, interviewed the staff, reviewed camera footage and all that but got nowhere. Then again, I always figured that if Hollis paid some guys to do it—let's say guys who worked at one of the junkyards—then I definitely wouldn't find anything. They would have made sure of that. Of course, now I know they were in the river in Denton."

"It's always been Hollis then," Josie said. "In your mind."

Fanning turned the car around and pulled back onto the road. "He had the motivation, the means, and an alibi. I checked his financials. Everything was clean. I looked into his employees, old friends, even the woman he was seeing in Denton. None of them made any big purchases, even years later."

"You think Hollis paid the killers cash," Gretchen said.

"Hollis is a little rough around the edges, disorganized as hell, but he's not stupid. Not by a mile. He could have easily paid someone cash, and no one would be the wiser. As co-owner of the company, he had access to plenty of it. For all we know, he sold something valuable like that artifact Tobias found years ago and didn't report it. Who knows how much unreported cash he had laying around?"

Josie saw his logic. She and Gretchen considered Hollis their main suspect, but she wondered if Fanning had overlooked something in his relentless pursuit of the man. His investigation had been thorough and dogged, but the absence of other suspects didn't mean there weren't any.

Moments later, they pulled up in front of the Lachlan home again. While Fanning turned the car around again, Josie said, "You searched the house."

It was standard procedure. Police would have wanted to make sure that there hadn't been any domestic issues or anything in the home that might help them locate the couple. Fanning hadn't needed a warrant. According to the file, Jackson had given permission.

"Sure did," Fanning confirmed.

"Do you recall if there was anything—some piece of furniture, a trunk or box of some kind—that required a skeleton key to open it?"

Fanning caught her gaze in the rearview again, one bushy brow arched high. "No, not that I recall, although I wasn't really looking for that sort of thing. Why do you ask?"

Gretchen said, "Cora had a small skeleton key in her purse. It's too corroded for us to figure out what it was from."

"A skeleton key?"

"I'll show you a photo when we stop," Gretchen said.

"I know what that is," Fanning said, sounding mystified. "But why would she be carrying one around with her?"

"That's what we're trying to figure out," said Josie. "It could be nothing, but—"

"It could be something," Fanning finished for her.

TWENTY-TWO

The chime of Josie's cell phone woke her. Sunlight streamed through the hotel windows. She'd left the curtains open because she couldn't stand waking up in a completely darkened room. It made her feel too disoriented, brought memories of childhood traumas too close to the surface. A steady pounding in her head worsened as she sat up. She hadn't had a drink after Fanning dropped them off the evening before. Hadn't had a drink in years, but it sure felt like she'd spent last night with a bottle of Wild Turkey. Sleep hadn't come easy. She'd spoken to both Noah and Wren before bed. Things seemed normal at home. Or whatever passed for normal these days. But her anxiety raged on, coupled with the myriad nagging questions about the Tobias Lachlan/Cora Stevens case. It felt like an endless loop. All questions and no answers.

Her phone went quiet. The sheets were like sandpaper across her bare legs as she tossed them aside. Nothing in the room was conducive to sleep. The mattress was so soft she practically needed a ladder to climb out of it, and the pillow was some kind of medieval torture device.

"Should've had the phone sex," she muttered to herself,

reaching for the bedside table. Maybe then she would have been too relaxed to care about the shitty accommodations.

The missed call was from her sister. It was inevitable. Trinity was the queen of cold cases, and this case was most definitely a crowning jewel. She'd never done an episode on it, though, and there was only one reason Josie could think of as to why. Tobias and Cora's kids hadn't agreed to be interviewed. Presenting the facts of a case and the police response was part of her show's format, but Trinity's aim was always to elicit tips that hadn't been offered before, and for that she needed a more emotionally compelling element—grieving loved ones.

Somebody always knew something.

The kids had been interviewed for the *Dateline* episode but at that time, only two years had passed since the disappearance. Riley was about to go off to college. Trinity's show had started a few years later. Assuming she'd approached them, had they avoided it because of Riley's fragile emotional state? The bad blood between the brothers? Or Riley and Jackson's marriage? Josie had no doubt that Riley was right. Their relationship would become a point of morbid fascination, eclipsing the details of their parents' cold case altogether.

She tried to run her fingers through her sleep-matted hair, without success. Her phone buzzed again. The thought of dealing with her sister later was laughable. Trinity was more persistent than Trout when he knew one of them had food. With a sigh, Josie swiped answer and grumbled, "I can't talk about the case."

There was a beat of silence. Then Trinity scoffed. "Please. I know that. Although it should go without saying that if there comes a point when you can discuss it, I want dibs."

"Dibs?" Josie rubbed tiredly at her temple. "What are we? Ten?"

"You need coffee."

"No shit." She needed a shower, too, and some ibuprofen. Then more coffee.

There was a huff. "I'm calling because Noah told Drake that you want to cancel the vow renewal."

Josie groaned. "Ugh. We really are in middle school."

Ignoring the barb, Trinity softened her tone. "I think you should go through with it. You deserve it. Both of you."

"It's just that Wren—"

"I'm going to stop you right there," Trinity cut in, voice still gentle. "This isn't about Wren. You were right to postpone it before because she'd just arrived. She's a bit more settled now. Sure, the three of you have a lot of work to do but I know you, Josie. You don't think you deserve this."

She had no response to that. It was far too early, and she was far too uncaffeinated for an impromptu therapy session.

The twin telepathy must have stretched across the miles because Trinity didn't bother to dive into psychoanalysis. Instead, she said, "Just know that if you cancel this, you're going to break Mom's heart. She's pretty much made this her entire identity."

Josie laughed. It was true. Noah had worried that Trinity would be the one trying to take over the planning but instead, it was her mother, Shannon, who had been treating it as if it was her own vow renewal—no, her own wedding. What had started out as a small, simple ceremony was now an affair nearly as big as their ill-fated wedding had been. After Josie and Noah announced they were going to do it, Shannon bombarded them with calls and texts and a zillion ideas for everything from the venue to the font they should use on their invitations.

Invitations. Shit. They had already gone out. Trinity and Drake lived in New York City. They'd both already requested time off from their very busy jobs to attend. Noah's brother had probably already booked his flight from Arizona. Surely, they would all understand if the ceremony was canceled.

"Mom missed so much of your life," Trinity said, breaking into her thoughts. "Then your wedding was ruined. Don't get me wrong. She's overjoyed that Wren has come into our lives, her first grandchild and everything. But seeing you two celebrate your marriage properly, with all the trappings and everyone you love in attendance? Josie, she needs that."

"If you're going to guilt me like this, you could at least DoorDash me a latte and a dozen cheese Danishes," Josie complained.

She *did* feel guilty. Lila Jensen had worked for Shannon and Christian Payne's cleaning service when Josie and Trinity were three weeks old. She'd set their home on fire and kidnapped Josie. Authorities believed Josie had perished in the blaze. They had no idea that Lila had spirited her away to Denton. Thirty years later, a cold case knocked Josie's world off its axis and fate set it to rights, reuniting her with her parents, twin sister, and little brother.

But there was no getting back the time they'd lost or the milestones they'd missed.

"It's not just Wren," Josie mumbled. "It's—"

She couldn't bring herself to tell her sister how much Noah was struggling. It felt like a betrayal. He wouldn't even talk to her about his trauma or his nightmares. Was he even in the right frame of mind for something like this? Just the other night he'd gone from being sweet to cruel in the span of a few minutes.

"You don't have to tell me," Trinity said, again practically reading her mind. "Just please, think it over, okay?"

Josie made a half-hearted noise of agreement before hanging up. She'd think about it. Just not right now.

There were funerals to attend.

TWENTY-THREE

The services for Tobias Lachlan and Cora Stevens were held entirely outdoors at Brighton Springs' biggest cemetery. At first, Josie thought their children had chosen a graveside service to keep things simple and expedient but when she and Gretchen showed up, joined by Detective Fanning, there were already hundreds of people everywhere. News vans and parked cars clogged every lane of the cemetery, their owners all heading in the same direction—to the top of a hill. Josie, Gretchen, and Fanning followed, trying not to draw attention to themselves. They'd worn proper funeral attire, but Josie was sure all three of them screamed law enforcement with or without the trappings, just like the few plainclothes Brighton Springs police officers she'd noticed nodding at Fanning as they passed. Detective Thomas Chaney, the current lead on the case, was still on vacation.

On the crest of the hill, several reporters and their camera crews waited, eagerly approaching attendees, hoping for a juicy soundbite. Spread out below were dozens of headstones and even more people filling the gaps among them. Fanning took the lead, waving Josie and Gretchen toward the bottom of the hill where a large tent had been erected. As they drew closer, two coffins came into view, mounted on a casket-lowering device. Surrounding them were massive floral arrangements and enlarged photos of Tobias and Cora in the prime of their lives, smiling brightly.

A pastor stood nearby, slowly flipping pages in his bible. Along the ground, artificial turf had been rolled out. A dozen empty chairs were lined up, awaiting family and close friends. Smartly dressed representatives from the cemetery and funeral home strode about purposefully, corralling reporters and keeping everyone several feet away from the seating area. Josie didn't see Riley, Jackson, or Zane yet.

"Why not have a private service?" Gretchen asked Fanning. "The majority of these people probably didn't even know Tobias and Cora."

None of them said what Gretchen actually meant, which was that it was likely that most of the people in attendance were here out of morbid curiosity, here to get a bit of gossip they could share when they went back to their homes or jobs.

Fanning scratched his scalp, dislodging a lock of thick white hair. "Yeah, some of these people definitely didn't know them but a lot of folks remember Tobias. This is just one in a long line of tragedies. They stood by him before, they'll stand by to see him to his final resting place. That's what community is about."

They drew closer to the tent. A plainclothes officer raised a hand to stop them from getting near until he saw John Fanning. "Sir," he said in acknowledgment before letting them pass. They found a spot a few feet away from the side of the tent, facing the hill. From this position, they were close enough to observe the family and the crowd.

Josie slipped on a pair of sunglasses. "The community stood by Tobias when his wife died? Zane's mother?"

"Gabrielle, yes. She was quite young."

"She died of a heart attack, right?" asked Gretchen from his other side.

Fanning nodded. "Cardiac arrest. It was horrible. Unbelievably tragic. But even before that, Jackson's mom, Rachel, up and left Tobias with a three-year-old that wasn't even his own blood. She took off with some guy. Victor something. Tobias kissed her goodbye that morning and when he got home from work, she was gone. Left a note asking him to take care of little Jackson. Never saw or heard from her again."

Poor Jackson. His start in life was almost as tragic as Tobias's relationship history. A mother who'd abandoned him. A biological father who had been incarcerated and from what Jackson told them, only too happy to give up any claim on his son. Tobias had been the only stable adult he'd ever known, and he was dead now, too. Josie's heart ached for the happy little boy in the photos she'd seen at his and Riley's home. "That's awful."

"Sure was," Fanning agreed. "Folks took pity on Tobias. Bringing him meals and babysitting Jackson until he got on his feet. In fact, that's how he met Zane's mom. Gabrielle was a teacher's aide at the preschool Jackson went to and she'd babysit him after hours whenever Tobias needed. They started dating. Got married. She was a good mom to Jackson. Then Zane came along. They were happy. When Gabrielle passed, Tobias was even more devastated. People rallied around him just the same as when Rachel left. A lot of those people are here today."

As if on cue, more people appeared on the crest of the hill. Some stopped to talk with the press before trying to find a place in the crowd nearest the tent.

Josie mentally reviewed what she could remember from the massive case file. This level of Tobias's personal history wasn't detailed in Fanning's notes. "How do you know all this?"

Fanning shot her a grim smile. "I was friends with Tobias's dad before he passed away. He was a volunteer firefighter. We crossed paths often. Him and his crew hung out in the same bar as me and a bunch of other officers."

"Is that why you took the case?"

He turned back toward the caskets, smoothing his tie. "It's why I wanted the case but no, it was just my turn."

No wonder it had become an obsession for him.

Gretchen watched the people milling around the hillside, many of them craning their necks over the shoulders of those in front of them, trying to get a glimpse of one of the kids, no doubt. "Tobias was one unlucky guy."

"Cora was quite unlucky herself," Josie said.

Tobias had experienced more tragedy than anyone should and then he'd met a horrific end. Now, his children would bear the weight of his loss their entire lives. Cora hadn't fared much better, escaping an abusive marriage only to die beside her new fiancé.

So much loss. Josie saw it on the job on a daily basis. If she didn't maintain a strong professional armor around her heart, it would be too much to take. She now had a teenage girl at home who was living through it. Wren was hurting badly and all Josie wanted to do was be a positive force in her life, try to put some light back in her eyes. Gain her trust and squash the ever-present fear that her place in Josie and Noah's home wasn't secure.

She resisted the urge to quickly text Wren to see how her day was going. Phones were supposed to be used sparingly at school, even in the last two weeks before summer break. Besides, the only response would be the word "fine" or worse, "okay." Josie and Noah had been surprised that Wren had been so willing to leave her old school in the middle of the year to start at a new one in Denton. They'd offered to make arrangements to get her back and forth from Fairfield so she could finish the school year before transferring. The transition from her father's loving home to that of strangers was difficult enough. Their intention was to do everything in their power to make it as smooth as possible. Although Wren kept in touch with two friends from her old school, she had insisted on leaving mid-year and as far as they could tell, she'd adjusted.

The crowd stilled as Tobias and Cora's children appeared on the top of the hill. Jackson and Zane flanked Riley, each of them holding one of her hands. Both brothers were dressed in dark suits that matched Riley's plain black dress. Her strawberry-blonde hair cascaded over her shoulders, bouncing softly with her steps. She kept her head down. Zane and Jackson pressed in closer to her, shielding her from the crowd. Whatever beef they had with one another, they were united in their feelings for Riley.

People murmured condolences as they passed. Hollis shuffled behind, wearing charcoal-gray slacks and a white button-down shirt that was only half tucked in. Red suffused his face. The early summer air still had a cool bite in the morning hours, but a sheen of sweat covered his forehead. He was the one to respond to the condolences, pausing to shake hands with people or give quick hugs.

Josie felt Fanning tense beside her. Once the children and Hollis were seated, he whispered, "Did I mention that Hollis had a thing for all of Tobias's women?"

"No," Gretchen replied just as quietly. "But Hollis mentioned he dated Jackson's mom, Rachel."

"And the way he spoke about Cora, it was clear he felt something for her," Josie added.

"I think he had his eye on her for a long time before Tobias came into the picture," Fanning said. "He was also sweet on Gabrielle. Sometimes he'd pick up Jackson from the preschool when Tobias was working late. Before she started dating Tobias, he asked her out, but she said no."

Riley, Jackson and Zane took their seats, Riley nestled

firmly between the brothers. Hollis sat next to Zane, mopping his brow with his sleeve.

Josie looked over at Fanning. "You know all this from your association with Tobias?"

"Most of it," he said, laser-focused on Hollis. "But I also worked this case for six years. That's a long time. Long enough to find out every possible thing about every person ever associated with Tobias and Cora."

The pastor urged the crowd to move closer to the tent. Reporters and camera crews began to descend the hill, edging their way around people to get as close as they dared.

"Hollis told us he's been divorced three times," Gretchen said. "It seems he's a known womanizer and a flirt. Hell, he tried to flirt with me while we were questioning him about a double murder."

It definitely gave credence to the theory that Hollis had either committed the killings or orchestrated them, given that he'd shown interest in every woman with whom Tobias had had a serious relationship.

Fanning opened his mouth to respond but the pastor cleared his throat, quieting the crowd. Josie watched the faces of the people gathered as he began the service. They were solemn. Some people wept silently. Others couldn't hold back their whimpers. One woman plucked a packet of tissues from her purse and began handing them out to those around her. Many of the men remained stoic, the only evidence of their grief the pain in their eyes and the clenching of their jaws.

Only one man looked out of place, and given the smirk on his face, Josie knew it was Dalton Stevens. He stood alone on the other side of the tent. Short and stocky, with the build of a wrestler, his frame bulged under his navy suit. Shocks of dirty-blond hair threaded with gray fell across his forehead. His hands were tucked into his pockets. Despite the way he was dressed and the palpable grief in the air, his posture was relaxed and casual. The barely concealed satisfaction on his stubbled face made Josie's skin crawl.

TWENTY-FOUR

Riley wept as the pastor read several bible passages. She leaned into her husband and Jackson slipped an arm around her protectively. Pain was etched across his face, but he kept his emotions tightly controlled. Zane held one of Riley's hands and stared straight ahead. Tears rolled down his cheeks, but he was as still as a statue. The pastor asked if the family wanted to say a few words. Riley shook her head and sobbed into Jackson's chest. An awkward silence stretched on, filled only with the happy chirping of birds. The sound was perverse given the circumstances. Finally, Hollis raised a hand. "I'll say a few words."

"Thanks, man," Jackson said huskily, eyes glassy with unshed tears.

Zane nodded his approval.

Hollis lumbered toward the pastor. Tucking the loose tail of his dress shirt into his pants, he began speaking. It was clear he hadn't prepared anything. He rambled on for ten minutes, talking about how he knew the couple and their children. While his impromptu eulogy was meandering, the stories he told about Tobias and Cora painted a vivid picture of how good-hearted and kind they'd been. Many people in the crowd murmured their agreement.

Finally, he finished with a nod to Jackson, Riley, and Zane. They mumbled thank-yous as he returned to his seat. As he wiped more sweat from his face, the pastor concluded the service. Zane and Jackson helped Riley stand. A cemetery worker handed them each two carnations—one red and one white—for them to place atop the caskets. Hollis lingered, waiting his turn.

Then Dalton strode forward, drawing up next to Jackson and holding his palm out for flowers. Riley slowly swiveled her head in his direction. Her mouth dropped open, and her legs wobbled. Hollis moved toward him, but Jackson got there first, pressing a large palm flat against Dalton's chest.

"You have some fucking nerve, asshole," he said, voice low and menacing. "How dare you show up here?"

"I have every right to be at my wife's funeral," Dalton sneered.

They were out of earshot of the rest of the mourners but a few people in the front of the crowd caught on to the tension, craning their necks and shuffling closer to try to hear the exchange.

"Charming," Gretchen said under her breath and Josie knew she was remembering all the fractures Dalton had given Cora in the years they were married.

It was a miracle that she'd survived his abuse—and leaving him.

With his free hand, Jackson tucked Riley behind him. Zane stepped forward, hugging her to his chest and guiding her to the opposite side of the tent, closer to where Josie stood with Gretchen and Fanning.

"Cora wasn't your wife," Jackson said. "She was engaged to our father and let's face it, even when you were married to her, you weren't a husband. You barely qualify as a human being."

"Gentlemen." The pastor moved closer until he was nearly between them. A strained smile was plastered across his face.

"Jacks," Hollis said.

Dalton puffed his chest out, pushing against Jackson's palm. "I have a right to see my daughter."

"No, you don't."

"You can't stop me."

"This guy never did know when to quit," Fanning muttered under his breath.

Jackson's face hardened. His fury was like a thundercloud, rolling off him, enveloping everyone under the tent.

Hollis clamped a hand down on his shoulder. "He's not worth it, son."

There was a rustling in the crowd as several of the reporters and their crews muscled their way through the throngs of people, trying to get closer. A couple of the plainclothes officers began weaving their way toward the front with far more finesse than the journalists.

"What's going on?" someone on the hill said. "What's happening?"

The people near the front surged forward, almost touching the backs of the chairs, despite the cemetery workers trying to maintain some space.

"Sir," the pastor said to Dalton. "This is not the time or the place."

A slow smile spread across Dalton's face. Ignoring the pastor, he told Jackson, "Last time I checked, my daughter was an adult and not your prisoner. You can't keep me away from her."

Jackson's fingers curled, clutching a handful of Dalton's shirt. "I can and I will. Riley doesn't want anything to do with you. Ever. So do yourself a favor and leave. Don't contact her. Don't come near her. Don't even think about her. Forget she exists."

"Or what?"

Hollis tightened his hand on Jackson's shoulder. "That's enough. Dalton, don't make a scene. If you want to—"

His words were cut off by Riley's ear-piercing shrieks. "Stop it! Just stop it! I don't want you here! Nobody wants you here! Leave us alone! Just leave us alone! I hate you! I've always hated you! It should be you! It should be you in that coffin. I wish it was. Get out, get out, get out!"

The shock that tore through the crowd was a physical thing, like a groundswell. One reporter started pushing mourners roughly out of the way, snapping at her cameraman to hurry up.

"Oh shit," Fanning said.

"I hate you! I hate you!" Riley's voice was high and shrill, carrying across the cemetery with perfect clarity.

The murmurs of the crowd became a buzz. More reporters pushed through, trying to reach the bottom of the hill, with no regard to those around them. One woman stumbled and fell when a camera bumped her shoulder. People started shouting.

Finally, the plainclothes officers were there, stomping forward, taking Dalton's arms just as Jackson pushed him backward.

"It should have been you who died!" Riley screamed, twisting and flailing in Zane's arms.

"What a shitshow," Fanning said.

Hollis used his grip on Jackson's shoulder to spin him toward his wife. Zane let her go and she sprang forward, rushing toward Dalton. Jackson caught her around the waist. She pointed a finger at her father. "You should be the one in the ground! I wish it was you! I hate you!"

One reporter made it through the throng with her cameraman who was filming the entire exchange. The crowd went chillingly silent, leaving only birdsong, and the sound of Riley's angry cries.

Until Dalton laughed.

Riley glared at him with red-rimmed eyes. "How dare you."

Dalton lurched forward, managing to free one of his arms from the officers holding him. He reached for Riley. Hollis stepped between them. Dalton registered the move, fisted his hand, and punched Hollis. The blow glanced off his chin, snapping his head back.

The entire thing unfolded in a matter of seconds.

Josie and Gretchen started to move forward in tandem, their bodies reacting to the threat before their minds could catch up to the fact that this wasn't their jurisdiction. Fanning threw out his arms, barring them. It was just as well since the plainclothes officers had Dalton on his stomach, cinching his wrists with zip ties.

"He just went from disorderly conduct to simple assault," said Gretchen.

He'd be in a holding cell within the hour. If Hollis decided to press charges, Dalton would be detained, processed, and possibly arraigned.

"You think I'm shit but your mom, she had secrets, Riley," he shouted as he was dragged away. "She wasn't the saint you all make her out to be! It's time you knew."

Hollis rubbed his chin and turned back to Riley. "Sorry, Ri."

Jackson loosened his grip on her waist so she could go to Hollis. She reached up and touched his chin. "Are you okay?"

"I'm fine, kiddo. I'm just sorry he had to ruin this, and saying stupid shit like that..."

Riley shook her head. "He knows I won't have anything to do with him and he hates it. He'll say anything to get my attention."

Jackson said, "She's right. He's just trying to get under her skin."

"But Ri won't let him," Zane piped up.

"That's right," she said, lifting her chin proudly. "And I'm not letting him take another thing from my mom. Let's lay her and Tobias to rest and never think about that asshole ever again."

Hollis joined the kids around the caskets. They kept their backs to the crowd as they composed themselves before finally placing flowers on the coffins.

The press continued to push forward, cameras trained on the final farewells, invading a moment that should have been private. Except that nothing about the lives of Tobias and Cora had been private since their disappearance, since the public had become morbidly fascinated with what had happened to them. In minutes, the videos of the confrontation next to the caskets would be on the internet. They'd probably go viral. Josie was watching the hungry reporters so closely, she didn't notice Hollis ambling over until he was only a foot away from them.

"Thank you for coming," he said. "Even you, Fanning."

John smiled insincerely. "Right."

With an exasperated sigh, Hollis added, "It meant a lot to the kids. They know how hard you worked on the case, okay? So let's just call a truce for today."

Chastened, Fanning nodded. "Of course."

Hollis turned to Josie and Gretchen. "Zane told me he'd give you two a tour of the house but with the press... The kids are going to head to Denton. All of them."

"Unfortunately, the press will be there as well," Josie said.

"Yeah, but there aren't as many people there for them to cull for interviews. People who knew Tobias, Cora, the kids. All of us."

He wasn't wrong. The press would expect the kids to stick around. Heading right to Denton might buy them a precious day or two before the full onslaught of reporters descended again.

"We can tour the house another time," Josie offered.

"Oh no," Hollis said. "Zane wants to do it while you're here, but do you think you could meet us there in about an hour? We had planned to have a luncheon at the diner, but I think it's too much for them. They're going to pack and get out of town but if you come now, Zane will show you around."

Gretchen said, "Will you be pressing charges against Dalton?"

Hollis lifted a brow. "Of course."

To Josie, she said, "Then he won't be going anywhere for the next few hours."

"Perfect," Josie replied. "We'll see you at the house, Mr. Merritt."

TWENTY-FIVE

By the time they reached Tobias Lachlan's house—which had been his son Zane's home for the past seven years—the press was already camped out. Several news vans littered the road. Journalists milled about. Some gave live reports with the property in the background. Brighton Springs PD had dispatched two uniformed officers to make sure no reporters snuck onto the property. After a brief conversation with one of them, Josie and Gretchen were allowed to proceed down the driveway. Next to the freestanding garage, Josie recognized Hollis Merritt's truck from when she'd seen it outside of the Denton office of At Your Disposal. She and Gretchen parked next to it. They were going to ring the doorbell until they heard the sound of arguing from behind the house.

With a jerk of her head, Josie motioned for Gretchen to follow. As they rounded the house, a door slammed.

"I told you not to give her anything else to drink." It was Jackson's voice, gruff and annoyed.

"Baby, it's fine," Riley said.

"Yeah, *baby*," Zane said. "You know she can do whatever she wants, right?"

"Stay out of this, asshole. We have a three-hour drive home and I don't want her getting sick."

"Then she can ride with me, *asshole*," Zane shot back.

This time it was a car door that slammed.

"Come on, boys," Hollis said tiredly. "Knock it off. This day has been long enough. Nobody wants to deal with your bullshit."

"What even happened between you two, anyway?" Riley asked.

Complete silence. Josie and Gretchen reached the backyard. An SUV and a pickup truck were parked side by side in the grass only feet from the back door. Riley sat in a lawn chair beside it, wrapped in Cora's yellow sweater, a beer in her hand. Her strawberry-blonde hair, which had been loose and silky earlier, was windblown and tangled. Hollis stood behind her, a large paw on her shoulder. Zane threw a duffel bag into the bed of the truck and glared at his brother, only feet away, near the closed hatch of the SUV. It was a silent standoff.

"Oh, hey," Hollis cleared his throat. "The detectives are here."

"Sorry to interrupt," Gretchen said.

"You're not interrupting," Riley assured them. "We invited you here."

"Which we appreciate," Josie said. "We'll get out of your hair as quickly as possible. Before we see the house, we had a few questions for you, if you don't mind."

Zane said, "Ri's drunk, so—"

"Stop speaking for my wife," Jackson said irritably.

Riley slugged her bottle of beer and then rolled her eyes. "Oh my God, just stop. I'm not that drunk. Anything that's going to help find out who killed my mom and Tobias, I want to do it. What do you need to know?"

Josie stepped closer, noticing the way Zane studied Riley, his eyes filled with longing. That's what it was between the brothers. Jealousy. Zane had a thing for his would-be stepsister, too. She wondered how long this had been going on and why Jackson was so easily riled by it. Clearly, he'd won her over, if it had ever been a competition.

Had it been? Riley and Zane were only a year apart, and they'd lived together when their parents were still alive. From everything Josie and Gretchen had heard so far, the kids managed to get into trouble together more than once—hanging out, sneaking out, drinking together. Enough that Cora had found Zane to be a bad influence on her daughter. Had there been something between Riley and Zane back then? It wasn't as though they'd grown up as step-siblings. They were both teenagers already when Tobias and Cora got together.

It really didn't matter though. Not for the purposes of the case. Pushing those thoughts aside, Josie said, "I'm not sure if Zane or Hollis told you but your mother had a small skeleton key in her purse at the time of her death."

Riley nodded. "Yeah, they said. I was going to call you but then the funeral planning kind of overtook everything else. I don't know what it was for. I took all her stuff when Jacks and I got married but there's nothing that needs a skeleton key."

"A jewelry box?" Gretchen said. "Trunk? Something larger like a cabinet of some kind?"

"Nothing."

"Do you own anything like that?"

Riley shook her head.

"Jackson?" Gretchen went on.

"Nope."

"What about something Tobias owned?" asked Josie.

Riley glanced between Jackson and Zane. "You guys would know better than me."

"After the last time you asked, I took a look around but didn't see anything." Zane motioned toward the house. "You're welcome to take a walk-through. I can even give you a tour if you'd like but I don't think Dad owned anything like that. Jacks?"

"Nothing that I can remember," he replied. "Maybe it was from something that passed through? Dad was always bringing stuff home to be sold for customers."

"Not sure why Mom would take the key to something like that, but that's the only thing that makes sense." Riley looked up, patting Hollis's hand. "Hol, would you still have a record of stuff the company sold for clients going back to before... before..."

He squeezed her shoulder, silencing her. "I'm sure we do. I can get Ellyn to look that up and get that to you."

"That would be great," said Gretchen. "The other question we have for you, Riley, is the name of the private investigator you hired to look into the case."

"What for?" she hiccupped. "He didn't find anything."

"Due diligence," Josie said.

"Bruce," Jackson said. "Bruce Olsen."

The name was vaguely familiar. Josie remembered seeing it in Fanning's case file but couldn't remember the context.

Zane walked past Jackson, bumping his brother's shoulder. Stopping at the back door, he motioned Josie and Gretchen forward. "Come on, I'll show you the inside of the house."

As Zane led them through each room on the first floor, Josie was struck by a profound sense of loneliness. It filled the house, making even the brightest areas feel dark. A musty smell permeated the air. There was a stagnant energy to the place, as if time had been suspended. She supposed it had for the blended Lachlan/Stevens family.

"Have you made any changes in the past seven years?" she asked Zane as they entered the dining room. A thick layer of dust covered the table and the surface of a matching sideboard.

He jammed one hand into the pocket of his jeans and used the other to brush through his sandy hair. "No, not really. I wanted to keep everything the way it was in case they came home. It sounds stupid, I know, but even up until the day that the medical examiner showed up to tell me they were dead, a part of me genuinely believed that they were still going to walk through the front door and apologize for putting us through all those years of torture."

"That doesn't sound stupid at all," Gretchen assured him with a gentle smile.

Zane's cheeks flushed. "Thanks. I thought about changing things up so many times because realistically, I knew they weren't coming back but it just felt... I don't know."

"Wrong," Josie filled in. "Like you were giving up."

His eyes snapped to hers, wide with surprise. "Yeah, that's it."

"Preserving everything made you feel like you were still close to your dad, didn't it?" Gretchen said.

Zane chuckled but his eyes filled with tears. "Exactly. I guess this means I'm not crazy for keeping changes to the bare minimum."

"Nope," Josie said. "Not crazy at all. Just grieving."

They followed him into the living room. So far, on the first floor, there were no doors, furniture, or other items that required a skeleton key. The infamous recliner was there, pointed toward the television. Its fabric was thin in some places and pilled in others. It didn't match the rest of the furniture at all. It was no mystery as to why Cora had hated it. Zane touched the back of it reverently. Josie wondered if the sagging chair was the boys' equivalent of the sweater that Riley clung to in her most anxious moments.

Slowly, they ascended the steps to the second floor. Framed photos adorned the walls of the hallway. They told the story of Tobias's sons. Jackson's youngest moments were of him as a toddler. They were similar to the ones that Josie had seen in Riley and Jackson's home. Him playing with toys, messily eating ice cream, dressed as a superhero. In many, it was Tobias who held him, hugged him, and played with him. Josie stopped in front of a photo of the two of them sitting on the floor of the living room they'd just come from. Jackson wore a paper birthday hat with the number two emblazoned on it as he rested in Tobias's lap. His small hands clutched a brightly wrapped gift. In the upper right-hand corner of the image something caught her eye. A sliver of an object. Was that brass? All she could see of it was a small section that looked conical, narrow on one side and flaring slightly on the other before it was out of frame. Below it was a flash of bright Kelly green. Something about it plucked at her subconscious. What was it?

"This is my room." Zane's voice came from several feet away where he was opening a door to allow Gretchen entry.

Josie moved on, taking in the rest of the pictures as quickly as possible. There were none of Rachel Wright, which made sense. Seeing her face each time he walked down the hall would have been devastating for Tobias and likely very confusing for a young Jackson. The next set of images were of Tobias and a woman with sandy hair, big blue eyes, and a nose ring. She had the smooth, supple skin of a woman ten years younger than him. Everything about her was luminous and vital. Soon, Jackson joined the pictures, looking about seven or eight years old, standing between his father and this new woman. Vacations, picnics, parties. In each one, the woman's hand curled protectively around one of his thin shoulders. Then she was in a hospital bed, cradling an infant while Jackson lay next to her, peering down at his baby brother.

This was Gabrielle Lachlan, Zane's mother.

More photos of her and the two boys growing up followed. Then she was gone and it was only Jackson and Zane, both looking sullen and sad. Until Cora and Riley came along. A small ache formed in the pit of Josie's stomach. It had been a long time coming but the two women had breathed life back into this house and the lives of the three lonely souls who inhabited it.

Then everything came crashing down.

Josie was aware that Gretchen had been following Zane in and out of the rooms while she surveyed the visual history of Tobias Lachlan's life.

"This was their room," Zane said.

Josie tore herself from the last of the pictures and joined him and Gretchen at the threshold of the door at the end of the hall. He pushed it open and gestured for them to enter but stayed just outside. The layer of dust on every surface in the room was twice as thick as that in the dining room. Here, the musty scent was much stronger, the air close and thick. Daylight strained against translucent curtains browned with age. The queen-sized bed was rumpled. One nightstand had a clock, a box of tissues, and a phone charger on it. The other was barren. It must have been Cora's since Riley had removed her mother's personal items. On each side of the bed was a dresser. The closet door was shut. In the corner of the room was a laundry basket half filled with clothes. Time had stopped in this room. The entire tableau was sad and creepy in equal measure.

The only thing out of place was the glass gun cabinet. It was nearly six feet tall, made of solid oak. Its tempered glass was covered in dust but Josie could see three long guns. At the base of the cabinet was another glass enclosure the size of a small drawer where a pistol rested. From the doorway, Zane said, "The key is on the top if you want to look inside. When Dad and Cora went missing, the police went through the cabinet. Didn't take anything."

Somewhere downstairs, a door slammed. Josie straightened up and turned back to Zane. "Did you or Jackson ever use any of your dad's guns?"

"Nah, no reason to. A lot of kids we knew liked to hunt but Jacks and I were never interested in that."

There was a crash below them. Glass shattered. Zane spun on his heel and raced toward the stairs. Josie and Gretchen jogged after him. They were halfway down the steps when they heard Jackson's voice, tortured and pleading. "Ri, you've had too much."

"I haven't," she answered but her words were slurred. "It was an accident. Zane will forgive me."

Zane stopped just inside the kitchen with Josie and Gretchen at his heels. The tile floor was covered in broken plates and wine glasses. A thick ceramic mug with the At Your Disposal logo on it lay split in half. Scattered among the debris were several pieces of flatware. A dishrack was upside down at Riley's feet. She clung to the kitchen counter, legs wobbling. Jackson was at her back, an arm looped around her waist, holding her upright.

Zane stepped toward her, but Jackson stopped him with a glare. "You've done enough. Come on, Ri. Let's go home."

TWENTY-SIX

An hour later, Josie and Gretchen walked into an interview room at the Brighton Springs Police headquarters, trailed by Detective Meredith Dorton. Like the rest of the building, it was modern and new. The taupe-colored walls were pristine. The thin carpet showed no signs of wear. Even the metal table was sleek and free from stains, scars, and scratches. The smell of greasy food, body odor, and cigarette smoke wasn't yet present.

Gretchen stopped inside the door and looked around. "Swanky."

Josie sipped her much-needed fourth coffee of the day. "Now this is taxpayer money going to good use."

Meredith hid a smile behind her own cup.

"Hey." Dalton Stevens glared at them from the other side of the table. "Can I leave or what?"

"You'll have to ask Brighton Springs PD about that." Gretchen turned to Meredith. "Detective Dorton, can he leave or what?"

Meredith took a seat across the table from Dalton. Since Josie and Gretchen were in Brighton Springs' jurisdiction and in their stationhouse, one of their own was required to sit in on their interview.

"Or what," Meredith muttered.

"There you have it," said Gretchen.

Dalton rolled his eyes. "Can't ever get a straight answer out of you bitches."

Josie sauntered toward him, took a moment to study him, and then glanced at her colleagues. "Hey, bitches, this guy wants a straight answer."

Meredith sighed. "Mr. Stevens, you were booked for simple assault. You'll be arraigned by a duty judge later today so no, you can't leave yet."

Since he hadn't yet been arraigned, he was still wearing the clothes he'd had on at the funeral. Minus his jacket and tie. He had rolled up the sleeves of his white button-down shirt, revealing thick, hairy forearms covered in tattoos.

Glowering at Meredith, he said, "I didn't mean to punch that prick."

Gretchen still stood in the middle of the room, scanning it leisurely before slowly producing her credentials and flashing them at him. "We're not here to talk about Hollis Merritt or the funeral. We're from Denton PD. That's where Tobias and Cora's bodies were found." She tipped her head in Josie's direction. "My partner here has been trying to get hold of you. You hung up on her three times. Pretty rude, if you ask me."

Josie sat down in the chair closest to him, catching a whiff of cologne, sweat, and vape juice. She set her paper coffee cup out of his reach and presented her credentials. "Totally rude."

Dalton sat back in his chair, manspreading his thick legs and folding his arms across his chest. "I don't got to talk to no police."

"Nobody has to talk to the police," Gretchen said. "But they do. How about we read you your rights first? Then we'll tell you why we came all the way from Denton to talk to little old you."

He scowled.

Josie read off his Miranda rights. When she asked if he understood them, he said, "Of course I do. I'm not an idiot."

"That remains to be seen," Gretchen said, leaning against the wall next to the door, tucking one foot up against it.

"Fuck you," Dalton snarled. "I don't have to talk to you bitches."

"No," Josie took another slug of coffee. "You don't, but Mr. Stevens, I think you've got something you want to say. Information you want to share, and it might do you good because this is no longer a missing persons case. It's a double homicide and guess what? Your name has come up a lot. Every person we've interviewed so far thinks you killed Cora and Tobias."

Up close, Josie could see the deep lines scored across his forehead and the many crows' feet fanning out from the corners of his eyes. The skin at his jawline sagged. Beneath his stubble, a deep flush colored his face. "That's bullshit."

"So you say. We'd love to hear your reasoning. Like I said, it might be in your best interest. Hey, Detective Palmer."

"Yes, Detective Quinn."

"What's the minimum sentence for first-degree murder in Pennsylvania?"

"First-degree?" Gretchen echoed.

"Yeah. That's the one where you intend to kill someone and then you do."

"Right, right. Hang on. I know this one." Gretchen tilted her head toward the ceiling, squinting as if that helped her recall facts. The room went so quiet, only the ticking of the clock on the wall could be heard. When Gretchen snapped her fingers, Dalton startled. Grinning, she said, "I got it. Death, or life without the possibility of parole."

Josie held up her index and middle fingers. "Times two."

Dalton lowered his arms, fisting his hands in his lap. He

looked over at Meredith as if seeking help. She shifted in her chair, a bored expression on her face, and checked her nails.

"I didn't do nothing," he said, turning to Josie.

"Sure, sure," she replied. "But you can see why you're the first person who comes to mind when we ask people who they think killed Tobias and Cora, right?"

"What?" He looked genuinely confused.

"Detective Palmer."

"Yes, Detective Quinn?"

"When the medical examiner performed the autopsy on Cora's remains, how many healed fractures did she find?"

"Hmmm." Gretchen pursed her lips and started counting her fingers. One hand. Then the other. Back to the other hand. Finally, she blew out a breath and said, "It was over fifteen. That much I remember."

Josie arched a brow at Dalton. "Over fifteen healed fractures. Detective Dorton?"

"Yes, Detective Quinn?"

"How many reports of physical altercations, assaults resulting in injury, stalking, and harassment did Cora Stevens make with respect to her ex-husband?"

Meredith tapped her chin with an index finger. "Each or combined?"

Josie shrugged. "Let's go with combined."

The shade of Dalton's face was so red it was nearly burgundy. If he was a crayon, he'd be Apoplectic Red.

"You forgot PFA violations," Meredith informed her.

"Better add them in then," Josie said without taking her eyes from Dalton.

Meredith, too, pretended to count with her fingers.

Dalton lurched forward in his chair, slamming his palms on the table. There was no reaction from Josie or her colleagues. Like a beast baring its teeth, his head swung from side to side, as if seeking to rattle them. Gretchen took out her phone and answered a text message. Meredith kept counting, mumbling numbers under her breath.

"Just a minute, Mr. Stevens," Josie said. "Detective Dorton's almost there."

He let out a low growl but as the moments stretched on, the anger emanating from his body dissipated. "I didn't kill no one."

"How about Tobias?" Josie asked. "Did you kill him?"

"No! I told you—"

"Did you kill Cora?"

"I didn't kill no one!" Another slap against the surface of the table.

Meredith sighed loudly. "It's over thirty."

"Wow," said Gretchen. "That's a lot of wife-beating and stalking."

Dalton made a noise of exasperation in his throat. "So I knocked Cora around sometimes. She had it coming."

"Detective Palmer," Josie said.

Gretchen looked up from her phone. "Yes, Detective Quinn?"

"Remember that case we had a few years back? The one where the guy killed his ex-girlfriend?"

"You mean the guy who's serving life without parole right now?"

"That's the one. What did he say when we asked him why he killed his ex-girlfriend?"

"He said, 'She had it coming.' I remember because that seemed like a perfectly reasonable explanation for killing the mother of his child."

Josie hummed in agreement. "Pity the jury didn't agree."

Dalton gripped the edge of the table. The muscles of his forearms flexed, and Josie got her first real look at some of his tattoos. On his right forearm was the face of a leopard, inked in black and snarling. Red blood dripped from its teeth. "I told you

I didn't kill no one," he said through gritted teeth. "What. Do. You. Want?"

Josie made him wait, sipping at her coffee like she had all day, watching him gnash his teeth. "When was the last time you saw Cora alive?"

With his left hand, he reached up and squeezed the bridge of his nose. His outer forearm was swathed in an elaborate tattoo that depicted an angel battling a demon. "Hell, I don't know. It's been seven years. We were divorced."

From the other side of the room, Gretchen said, "That's weird 'cause at the funeral today, you said she was your wife. Not ex-wife. Wife."

"I just meant that we had something together. We weren't nothing, you know. I deserved to be up there with Riley and Tobias's little bastards. Way more than Hollis, that's for sure."

"Over fifteen healed fractures makes me wonder if you're wrong about that," Josie said. "Why were you really there?"

TWENTY-SEVEN

She and Gretchen had discussed Dalton's motive for disrupting the funeral on the way over. Cora had been his punching bag, literally and figuratively, for almost two decades before she disappeared. He never bothered to have a relationship with Riley, and he didn't express any interest in being a father to her even after she was alone and living with Tobias's sons. Dalton Stevens had a lot of pent-up anger and he was addicted to the high of making his ex-wife miserable. Josie didn't know how he'd survived the past seven years without an outlet, but he hadn't made any attempts to harass his daughter until today.

The day his ex-wife was laid to rest.

"Let me rephrase that." Josie picked up her cup and swished the dregs of her coffee around. "It's not unreasonable that you wanted to pay your respects to your ex-wife, who was also the mother of your child. No one can really fault you there."

"But you don't seem very good at reading social cues," Gretchen said innocently. "Because the kids did not want you there."

"You just shut the fuck up," he spat.

Gretchen pretended to think about it. "No. Don't think I will, but thanks for the suggestion."

There was Mr. Apoplectic Red again. Josie should really pitch this new color to Crayola.

"Mr. Stevens, you could have waited until the service concluded, until the kids had vacated the area, before paying your final respects. That's not what you were there to do, was it?"

"I—I just wanted Riley to know..." He drifted off and began cracking his knuckles.

"To know what?" asked Josie.

"You know, that kid turned out just like her mother. A stuck-up snob. Acting like her shit don't stink. Like marrying her stepbrother was moving up in the world. Just like her mom. Marrying a 'businessman.' It's a junk removal company. They ain't lawyers or accountants. I'm tired of being treated like I'm the problem."

Josie knew that Gretchen had a snarky comment locked and loaded that would wind Dalton up, but she restrained herself. They'd both had enough experience with assholes like Dalton Stevens to know that at some point, in order to get to the things you wanted to know, you had to listen to some bona fide horseshit. Once the ill-advised pity party was over and out of his system, he would be more amenable to answering the questions Josie really cared about.

"What's the problem, Mr. Stevens?"

He rubbed his palms on his thighs. The knuckles connecting his middle fingers to his hands were bulging and unsightly. Boxer's knuckle. It was an injury to the joint at the base of the finger—usually the middle finger—gained from repetitive impacts. Punching.

"The problem is that everyone is ready to nominate Cora for sainthood and they don't know nothing about her," Dalton began.

Josie wondered how many punches Cora had had to endure to cause Dalton to have boxer's knuckle—on both hands.

"She wasn't as good as everyone makes her out to be." He kept going, voice dripping with disdain. "Every time I turn on the TV or go to the diner, people are talking about her like she was Mother Teresa. It's all bullshit. I never said nothing before, to that other guy, Fanning or whatever his name is, but you wanna know how much of a saint she was? I'll tell you. Cora was having an affair. She was cheating on Tobias."

That's what he'd been getting at when he accosted Riley at the funeral. Josie knew he'd been holding onto something, waiting for the right moment to unleash it. The question was whether it was true. With Cora's death, there was a finality to his ability to use her as a receptacle for all his anger and inadequacy, but provoking Riley could be his new sport. It was easy to make things up about a person who wasn't here to defend herself—and was never going to return.

Gretchen now had her notepad and pen out though her posture still shouted casual indifference. "How do we know you're not just saying that to get Riley's attention?"

"Riley needs to know the truth."

"But she didn't need to know the truth for the past seven years?" Josie asked. "It never occurred to you that maybe Cora's lover killed her and Tobias?"

"You didn't think it was important enough to tell Detective Fanning? You must have known that you were a suspect," Gretchen said.

"Fanning thought Hollis did it. I didn't need to tell him."

"Cora was having an affair with Hollis?" asked Josie.

Dalton shrugged. "I think so."

"But you don't know." Gretchen's pen was poised over her notepad as she watched Dalton.

He folded his arms over his chest again, giving Josie a quick glimpse of yellow sweat stains under his armpits. "I never saw them kissing or nothing like that."

Maybe no one had seen them kiss. Maybe Dalton was full of shit and they'd never kissed at all, but Josie would bet a week's pay that Hollis had been infatuated with Cora Stevens for a long time. He had definitely wanted to kiss her. "What did you see?"

"I saw them out back at the diner where Cora worked, talking privately. A few times."

"In full view of the public," Gretchen said.

Dalton pushed strands of his dirty-blond hair out of his eyes, giving Josie another eyeful of his tattoo. The angel and demon grinned at one another, both of them looking devious.

"What do you mean?" he said.

"They were meeting in a place where anyone could see them," Gretchen pointed out.

"Yeah, but they were sneaking around."

Hollis had already told them that Cora had spoken to him privately about intervening in her relationship with Tobias to convince him that she should keep her job. Hollis hadn't mentioned where that conversation took place.

"When was this?" asked Josie. "How long before Cora and Tobias disappeared?"

"I don't know." Dalton shrugged. "Couple of weeks, I guess."

That conflicted with Hollis's timeline. He'd told them that the private conversation with Cora had taken place a couple of months before the couple went missing. The last time he had physically seen her had been at the company headquarters. Josie tucked the discrepancy away to ask Hollis about later.

"Is that the only reason you think Cora was having an affair?"

It was hardly damning evidence. John Fanning had spoken to practically every person in Brighton Springs, and no one had mentioned anything about seeing Cora with another man. Plus, Hollis had frequented the diner long before Tobias and Cora started seeing one another.

"I saw her at a motel," Dalton blurted out.

Now that wasn't in Fanning's file.

"Which motel?" Josie pressed.

"There's a shitty place over by the interstate. It's called Majesty Motel. They rent by the hour, if you know what I mean."

"You saw Cora at the Majesty Motel?" Gretchen scribbled on her notepad. "Going in or coming out?"

Dalton leaned an elbow on the surface of the table and rested his chin on his fist. He looked weary now and a little bored. "I'm not sure. I was just driving past. She was in the parking lot. By the time I looped around the block, she was gone."

"When was that?" asked Josie.

"Don't know. Five or six months before she and Tobias went missing."

"How many times did you see her at this motel?"

"Twice," Dalton replied.

"How about the second time?" Gretchen continued her notetaking. "Was she going inside or coming out?"

"She was in her car," Dalton answered. "Like, just sitting there, with her hands on the wheel."

Josie peered into her coffee cup, wishing it would magically refill itself. "Did you see anyone with her?"

"No, but come on. This is Cora. Why else would she be at a motel in the middle of the day?"

With all the documented evidence of Dalton's relentless harassment of his ex-wife, Josie found it hard to believe that he had simply walked away and never mentioned it. Never tried to use it against her.

Dregs it was. She tipped the cup as far as it would go and let the last bit of coffee drip into her mouth. Two cups would have been the smart way to go. "What did she say when you approached her?"

His eyes snapped to hers. "What? How do you know I approached her?"

Josie arched a brow. "Really? You're really going to ask me that? Detective Dorton?"

Meredith pretended to be startled out of a daydream. "Oh, yes, Detective Quinn?"

"How many times did Mr. Stevens violate the PFAs that Cora had against him?"

"Oh, well, at least—"

"Fine," Dalton cut her off. "I talked to her. Went up to the car and knocked on the window. She was crying, okay? When she saw me, she got real mad. Told me she was going to call 911 'cause I wasn't supposed to be near her and shit so I asked if she really wanted to do that considering she was sneaking around behind Tobias's back."

"What did Cora say to that?" asked Gretchen.

He laughed, shifting back in his chair, assuming a casual pose. "She said it wasn't what I thought. Yeah, right. She just didn't want me blowing up her life. So I told her. If she didn't tell Tobias, I was gonna do it."

"Classy," Gretchen said.

"Hey, that guy was an asshole."

"What did Cora say when you gave her your little ultimatum?" Josie said.

"She didn't say anything." His eyes clouded over. Confusion creased his brow. "She just started laughing. All crazy-like. Sounding like some kind of hyena or something. Then she drove away."

"When did this happen?" Josie said.

"I don't know. A few months before they went missing, I guess?"

"Did you tell Tobias about seeing her at the motel?" Gretchen asked.

Avoiding her eyes, he wiped his palms over his thighs. "Um, no."

"Why not?" Josie asked even though she already knew. As long as he didn't tell Tobias, he had something to hold over Cora's head. An ever-present threat. A measure of control.

"Listen, it doesn't matter, does it?" he groused. "He's dead. She's dead. Hollis is still here acting like he wasn't banging his best friend's woman. You should be talking to him."

"You've got no proof that Cora and Hollis were having an affair," Josie pointed out.

"No, I don't," Dalton agreed. "But I did see Hollis hanging around the Majesty a few times, too."

TWENTY-EIGHT

The Majesty Motel was not even a tiny bit majestic, but it was a lot less seedy than Josie expected. It was a two-story building with rooms on both floors. Their exterior doors were clearly numbered. The place hadn't been painted in a long while given its cream and sea-foam-green color scheme and yet, it was meticulously kept. There wasn't a single piece of litter along its walkways. Even the asphalt of the parking lot was smooth. No potholes, no cracks. Maybe the owner rented the place by the hour, but it was well cared for. Then again, a lot could change in seven years.

Like the staff. They'd spoken with the nineteen-year-old kid tasked with managing the place during the week. He was new but he'd contacted the owner who had spoken with them via speakerphone. No one who was currently employed had worked there seven years ago. In addition to that, their records only went back four years.

Back in the SUV, Josie curled her fingers around the steering wheel and scanned the area. Four other cars in the lot. Next door to the motel was a laundromat which was extremely busy. On its other side was a bar which, at two in the afternoon, was shuttered. Across the street was a worn strip mall that looked like it was one good thunderstorm away from collapsing. There were plenty of cameras, but no one kept footage from seven years ago.

"You think Dalton was bullshitting us?" Gretchen asked.

Before driving to the Majesty Motel, they'd stopped at their hotel. They had found the reports Fanning had secured from Cora's cell phone carrier with her location history going back several months. Her phone had pinged near the motel but no specific location had been pinpointed. After digging through her credit card statements, Fanning had found a transaction from a grocery store nearby.

"I'm not sure," said Josie.

"I took a quick scan of the witness reports," Gretchen said. "There was nothing to support that she was having an affair with anyone. Maybe she was just going to the grocery store."

"Maybe." Josie flexed her hands over the steering wheel. "Maybe she went to the grocery store before or after coming here. There is one thing that makes me think Dalton was telling the truth. What he said about her laughing at him. He was clearly confused. That's not a detail someone like him would think to make up."

"Agree," Gretchen replied. "Although when he first approached the car, he said she was crying. It's possible she was just letting off some steam in private. Away from her family and friends. A lot of women cry in the car. Or the shower."

"Misty cries in the shower. So does Trinity."

Gretchen ran her fingers through her short hair. "It's very efficient, isn't it?"

"Seems that way."

"You don't cry though. In the time we've known each other, I've only seen you cry twice just to let off steam and not because someone was dying. Once when we were up a tree and once in my bathroom. Maybe I should be honored that I was there for both of those instances."

"I'll make you a punch card," Josie said. "Witness five Big Cries and I'll buy you a tall stack of pecan pancakes."

"You'll buy me those anyway."

"I'm not keen on incurring Paula's wrath," Josie said but she was smiling. "You're not a crier either."

They were the same in so many ways even though Gretchen was ten years older. The steel in their souls had been forged in trauma. Processing it often felt like a full-time job that neither of them was equipped to handle, even with the help of their therapists.

"I'm getting better at it." Gretchen shrugged. "You know, we could both be more committed criers if we sat with our feelings or whatever the hell we're supposed to be doing."

"Fuck. That."

Chuckling, Gretchen looked around the parking lot. "Maybe Dalton was smart enough to make up the laughing detail. Maybe he's lying so he can distract us from the fact that he's a violent stalker piece of shit who can't let go of his ex-wife even seven years after her death. He's still a suspect as far as I'm concerned."

"I'm with you on that."

He certainly wasn't credible. The statements he'd given Fanning over the years were riddled with inconsistencies.

Josie's phone chirped. A text message from Noah. *Wren's making dinner tonight. Said she finally got Misty's homemade pasta recipe right. We're going to try it.*

Her heart soared and then sank in the same moment. The three of them had dinner together whenever their schedules allowed but Wren barely spoke. She'd never been an active participant before, despite how much she enjoyed cooking with Misty. This had to be progress. Regardless, even if Josie and Gretchen left Brighton Springs now and broke some land-speed records, she'd never make it back in time to join them. Disappointment hit her hard.

But maybe they were also having dinner with Misty and Harris. Possibly Erica. Wren was always more animated and open with them around. Josie typed back.

Who else will be there?

No one. Just us. Wish me luck.

She sent him a bunch of fingers crossed emojis before tossing her phone into the center console and swearing under her breath.

Gretchen raised a brow, a silent invitation to discuss what was bothering her, but Josie just sighed and said, "We'll need to talk with Hollis."

"I'm sure he's already back in Denton. Tomorrow we'll track him down."

TWENTY-NINE

"Tell me everything," Josie said.

From where he stood at the foot of the bed, Noah grinned at her. He tucked his polo shirt into his khakis. His hair was damp from a shower and tousled exactly the right amount to give her dirty thoughts. By the time she got home from Brighton Springs, dinner was long over and Wren had retreated to her room to study for her finals.

Noah and Wren had eaten all the pasta, so Josie ordered a pizza, which she dug into while she and Noah discussed the Lachlan/Stevens case. By tacit agreement, they didn't dare discuss Wren where she might overhear them. She made a brief appearance to tell them good night before going to bed. After that, Josie and Noah had gone to their room. Unfortunately, he was due on the overnight shift, which didn't give them much time together.

"It was interesting," Noah said. "The food was good. Much better than either of us could have made."

Josie rolled her eyes. "No shit. We suck. How was she? Did she talk? What did she say?"

"She asked me if I liked the pasta. I said yes. She gave me a long play-by-play on how to make it. I asked her about school. She said it was boring and that she hates that the only thing adults ever ask kids is 'how is school?'"

"She has a point," Josie said. Again, she had the sensation of her heart soaring and sinking almost simultaneously. This was huge progress. She was thrilled that Wren had spoken so freely, acted like a real member of the household, but sad that she hadn't been there for it. Then again, would Wren have opened up if Josie had also been there? Was it easier for her to talk with them one on one? The morning Josie had come home from finding Tobias Lachlan's sedan, stinking of rot and river, Wren had said more to her than she had in the previous month.

"She asked me what's the most annoying question that I get as an adult?"

Josie laughed. That sounded like an icebreaker question that Turner would ask Dr. Feist. "What did you say?"

"Like you don't know." He sat on the edge of the bed and started pulling on his boots.

"It's either 'Do you have any plans for the weekend?' or 'Are you ready for the holidays?'"

Noah chuckled. "The holiday one is seasonal."

"There are a lot of holidays."

"I told her it was 'Do you have any plans for the weekend?'"

Josie crawled toward him, pressing her chest against his back. She rested her hands on his shoulders and breathed in his aftershave. "Then what?"

Boots laced, he turned his head and kissed her lightly. "That was it."

"That's all?"

"Yeah. It doesn't take that long to eat. I thanked her for the meal and did the dishes. She stayed at the table awhile, drawing."

Wren was always drawing. She hadn't yet shown them any of her art. They'd both asked but she'd told them none of her stuff was ready for anyone to see. Josie suspected she just didn't want to let them in. After all, she'd shown it to Erica, Misty, and Harris.

"How long was she at the table?"

"I don't know. Ten, fifteen minutes? I didn't try to engage her at that point," Noah said. "Didn't want to push my luck."

"That's a lot though."

Josie slumped, ecstatic and disappointed at the same time. Parenting was weird. If that's what this could be called. Noah kissed her again and then stood to retrieve his phone from his nightstand. He punched in his passcode, tapped, swiped and then handed it to her. Josie's breath caught in her throat.

"Wh-what is this?"

"Wren left her sketchbook open. It was on the kitchen table. She took Trout out back for a few minutes."

"Noah!" Josie chided, even as her eyes traced every detail of the portrait Wren had lovingly drawn of her father. "That's an invasion of her privacy."

"Swipe left," he said.

In spite of herself, she did, only to gasp. This drawing was far from finished but there was enough detail to clearly identify them—Josie and Noah—in profile. They were face to face, smiling at one another. It was beautiful. Dex had been right. His daughter was far more artistically talented than he'd been, which was saying a hell of a lot.

"Noah," Josie breathed. "This is..."

"Not a drawing of us as villains."

She laughed. "That's good news, but you shouldn't have taken these pictures. I just had a talk with her about privacy. You have to delete them."

He took his phone back, gazing at the picture. "It was a plain-view search."

Josie rolled her eyes. Trust a law enforcement officer to use the plain-view doctrine to justify snooping in his own damn home. Josie would have lectured him, but she was positive she would have done the same thing in his shoes. They both wanted so badly to know more about Wren.

"I don't think Wren would see it that way," Josie told him. "Please delete them."

He turned the screen toward her so she could watch him delete the photos. "I never intended to keep them," he said. "I felt guilty as soon as I took them. I just wanted to show you."

"Thank you."

Noah put on his belt, securing his pistol in its holster. "I've got to go. See you in the morning?"

Josie nodded. It would be heaven to sleep in her own bed again, even if it was without him. "Noah," she said before he reached the door.

His shoulders tensed. Turning slowly back to her, he said, "I think we should go forward with the vow renewal. Drake suggested finding a way to incorporate Wren into the ceremony. To demonstrate our commitment to her as well as each other."

Noah knew damn well that the vow renewal was not what she wanted to discuss but she was instantly distracted by Drake's suggestion. It was brilliant. Why hadn't she thought of it herself? Probably because her anxiety over wanting Wren to open up to them consumed every moment she didn't spend obsessing over the Lachlan/Stevens case.

Still.

"Wren is pretty guarded," Josie said. "It's a great idea, but do you think she would even be open to it?"

"No way to know unless we ask."

Her stomach roiled just thinking about how to have that conversation. Would being a guardian always be like this? Second-guessing every word, every action, every thought? Spending hours, sometimes days, planning what to say so she didn't screw things up with Wren? Spiraling? Thinking about *thinking about* things instead of just acting? Josie had always been so assured in most areas of her life although to be fair, the majority of her life revolved around work. But being competent at her job relied heavily on her ability to read people correctly, to know what to say to them in any given situation. She'd interrogated serial killers with more finesse than she was capable of when it came to speaking with Wren about pretty simple stuff.

Noah's knuckles grazed her cheek. He had closed the distance between them without her even noticing. "You're overthinking this. Sleep on it. We'll talk tomorrow."

She clasped her hand over his wrist. "We need to talk about the other thing."

He went rigid, eyes darkening. "Not now, Josie. I have to go."

This time, he didn't hesitate at the door, striding into the hallway.

"Fine," Josie called after him, making her tone breezy in case Wren overheard. "We'll discuss it later."

THIRTY

"You got questions just for me?" Hollis called as he lumbered around the side of a huge dumpster behind the Denton office of At Your Disposal. It had been two days since the funerals. The press was camped out front. There weren't nearly as many reporters and camera crews as there had been at the cemetery and at the Lachlan house in Brighton Springs, but they were accumulating quickly. Multiplying by the hour, it seemed. In the time it took Josie and Gretchen to cross the parking lot, at least three dozen shouted questions had been lobbed at them. Each one went ignored. Ellyn had let them inside and then directed them out back where Hollis was rummaging through a pile of debris, tossing pieces of demolished drywall and wood panels into the dumpster.

"We have more questions," Gretchen said.

The screech of a trash compactor blared from the old service building near the back of the lot. Three dump trucks waited nearby to deposit their contents. A strange odor hung in the air. Josie detected faint notes of spoiled food, chemicals, urine, and mildew. Across from them, two At Your Disposal employees unloaded furniture and electronics from a truck, sorting them into different areas. They kept throwing curious glances over at Josie and Gretchen.

Josie smoothed her polo shirt over her stomach. Her new work shirts had finally arrived. "We spoke to Dalton Stevens before we left Brighton Springs."

Hollis took off his thick work gloves and plucked a rag from the back pocket of his cargo shorts, using it to wipe sweat from his brow. "I can't wait to hear this. Lay it on me. What did he accuse me of doing? Besides murder."

Gretchen held his gaze steadily. "He said you were having an affair with Cora before she and Tobias were killed."

His eyes widened in surprise. Clearly, he hadn't expected that. As the weight of the accusation sank in, a scowl crossed his face. "Of course he did. He'll say anything to mess with people's lives and to upset Riley now that Cora's really gone."

"So you weren't having an affair with Cora?" Josie asked.

Hollis shook his head. "Of course not. Nothing like that ever happened between us."

"Did you ever frequent the Majesty Motel?"

"Is that what Dalton told you?" Hollis laughed. "That I was meeting Cora at that dump? Never happened."

He hadn't actually answered the question but for now, Josie let it go. She wondered if Dalton had been counting on them not being able to verify any of the information he gave them. It was his word against Hollis's since Cora wasn't here to speak for herself.

"He said that he saw you and Cora speaking behind the diner where she worked on multiple occasions," Gretchen said. "Did she need multiple occasions to get you to intervene in her marriage and convince Tobias that she should keep working?"

"We were friends," he insisted.

"Friends who needed to meet behind her place of employment rather than at one of your homes or inside the diner?" Josie said.

Hollis stuffed the rag back into his pocket. "She didn't want to air her dirty laundry where people could hear it. Everyone already knew her personal business with Dalton. She hated that."

For a city, even a small one, everyone in Brighton Springs really did seem to know everyone else's business. It made Josie wonder how seven years had passed without a break in the case.

Somebody always knew something.

"In that case, the privacy of one of your homes would have been appropriate."

"Oh sure." He tried jamming his hands back into the work gloves. His fingers trembled. Was his sugar getting low or was this something else? "The privacy of one of our homes. Where Tobias or one of the kids could easily have overheard, or at my place—that wouldn't have made Tobias suspicious at all."

"Suspicious of what?" Josie said.

He gave up on the gloves, tossing them angrily at his feet. "You know what I mean! It would have looked weird if she came to my place."

The employees across the lot froze, watching the exchange. If Hollis noticed, he didn't acknowledge it.

"Dalton said he saw you and Cora behind the diner three times," said Gretchen. "Were they all related to her staying employed after the wedding?"

"I don't know," he muttered.

"According to Dalton, one of those times was a week before Cora and Tobias disappeared. That's not what you told us or Fanning," Josie pointed out.

"I don't remember every little thing from seven years ago, for Pete's sake. Cora and I talked sometimes. So what?"

"Hollis," Josie said, "this isn't a missing persons case anymore. It's a double homicide. If you really cared about Tobias and Cora the way you claim, you'll share whatever it is that you're not telling us."

He glanced around. The workers watching them scrambled back to sorting, averting their eyes. They were likely too far away to overhear the conversation, but Hollis lowered his voice anyway. "It's not—we weren't having an affair, okay? That's true. Have I ever been to the Majesty? Sure, but not with Cora. I promise you that."

"Who were you with?" asked Gretchen.

He wiped his sweaty hands on his shorts. "Aww jeez, you're really gonna make me do this, aren't you?"

Gretchen lowered her reading glasses onto her face before producing her notepad from one of her back pockets. She flipped to a blank page. Then she produced a pen from above her ear, holding its point over the paper. "We're really gonna make you do this, yeah. Unless you want to come with us now to the station where you can put whatever lies you've got ready to tell into a formal statement. I can tell you that however bad you think the truth will make you look, lying will make you look far worse. Guilty as sin, in fact. You want to help yourself? You want to help the kids? Tell the truth, Hollis. All of it. Don't leave anything out."

He looked at her from under bushy, scrunched brows. "I'm not guilty of anything except being a dumbass, probably, but I really don't want to look bad to you."

Josie could tell that Gretchen was holding back the mother of all eye-rolls.

"I'm serious," Hollis cried. "I know this is inappropriate, but I really do like you."

Face impassive, Gretchen tapped the pen impatiently against the pad. "The truth, Hollis."

More employees had gathered near the sorting area. Apparently, four of them were needed to remove a gently used office chair from the back of the truck with the excruciating slowness befitting the transfer of a great work of art.

Hollis groaned. "Fine. I was seeing a married woman back then, okay? Not Cora."

Arching a brow, Josie said, "Oh, was that in addition to the woman you were seeing in Denton?"

From under his lashes, he darted a glance at his employees before anchoring his gaze to his feet. "I'm not proud of it, okay? You're gonna want the married lady's name, aren't you?"

"What do you think?" Gretchen said.

He started pacing in front of them but mumbled her name and address. Gretchen jotted the information down so they could verify it later.

"Tell us about Cora," Josie told him.

Again, he searched around them, galvanizing the now six employees unloading a desk from the truck to move more quickly—and keep their eyes averted. "I—I really don't want the kids to know, okay? There's no reason for them to know. I never told Fanning—or anyone else—because it's not relevant. It's got nothing to do with what happened to them. Promise me you won't tell the kids."

"We won't tell them unless it becomes necessary to the investigation," Josie said.

Exhaling a frustrated sigh, he stopped pacing. "Cora was planning to leave Tobias. She wanted out. Completely."

THIRTY-ONE

"Because she was having an affair?" asked Gretchen. "If not with you, then with someone else?"

He shook his head. "No, there was never any affair. I mean, if there was, she didn't tell me about it. And hey, I know Fanning got all kinds of phone records from me and Cora and hell, everyone. Tobias. The kids. Diner employees—"

"What's your point?" Gretchen cut him off.

"If I was having an affair with Cora, there would have been evidence, don't you think?"

That's what Josie would have expected, though it would have been fairly easy for Cora to carry on an affair with Hollis without leaving any digital footprints since their lives had been so enmeshed. In fact, she could have had an affair with anyone without leaving digital evidence if she and her lover only spoke in person while she was at work. No one would have been suspicious of her being friendly with a returning customer.

Was that the reason Tobias wanted her to quit her job? Had he figured it out?

Mentally, Josie filed the theory away to be analyzed later

and tried to get Hollis back on track. "She came to you and told you she wanted to leave Tobias?"

"No. She didn't come to me. I still went to the diner a lot and one time I was there for lunch. I was waiting for her to come out of the back so I could say goodbye to her but ten, fifteen minutes went by, and she still didn't come back. I went looking for her and found her in the ladies' room, sitting on a toilet, bawling her eyes out."

"When was this?" asked Gretchen.

"A week before they disappeared."

"Why did she want to leave him?" Josie said.

"She just... she wasn't happy. It wasn't just about him not wanting her to work. Things just weren't good."

"Was he violent toward her?" Gretchen asked.

"No, no. Never. Cora just... she said he was moody all the time. Nothing she said or did was right. He'd criticize her or get all distant and not speak to her for days. She said it was like walking on eggshells. Like when she was with Dalton except without the violence. But with Dalton, she always knew what would trigger him. With Tobias, she never knew what would bring on one of his moods or how long they would last or what he'd say. She just didn't want to live like that anymore."

"Was Tobias moody?" Josie said. "You knew him longer than Cora."

"I guess so but can you blame the guy? His first fiancée ran off with some other guy and then his wife died. Yeah, he could get dark sometimes. Quiet. Irritable. No one's perfect."

The shrill alarm from a heavy-duty vehicle reversing somewhere near the rear of the lot interrupted them. Gretchen waited until it cut off before continuing the interview. "What was Cora planning?"

Hollis glanced at the nearby workers, who had lost interest in their exchange, moving far more quickly and efficiently. "At that point, she was just putting away as much money as she could to rent an apartment for her and Riley. She made me swear not to tell Tobias. I promised her that I wouldn't as long as she promised to talk things out with him before making any major decisions. Maybe something like that could be worked out if they just communicated."

"Did she agree?" asked Josie.

"Yeah. She promised she'd discuss her feelings with him."

Gretchen scrawled more notes on her pad. "Do you know if she did?"

"I don't know. I—"

The sound of a cell phone ringing cut him off. He fished in his pocket, frowning at the screen. "I gotta take this. All the kids are staying with me this week to avoid the press." He gave Gretchen a pointed smile. "I've got a much bigger house now. Lots of land around it. Hey, Zane."

Hollis listened intently. "Did you try calling her? Oh, well, it's not the first time she's forgotten her phone. What did Jacks say? Right, right. Yeah, I'll leave now."

"Everything okay?" Josie asked when he hung up.

"Riley went out this morning after I left and didn't come back. She didn't take her phone. The boys are worried. Jacks is out looking for her now. I'm gonna go and join Zane to see if we can locate her."

"How long has she been gone?" Josie said.

"About three hours. Jackson woke up around nine this morning and she wasn't in bed. Zane didn't see her leave either. I saw her right before I left for work around seven. She was coming in as I was leaving."

"Coming in?" Josie prompted.

"Yeah, she'd gone home to get Captain Whiskers' heartworm medication and some of her little toys. Said they left all that behind when they brought the cat to my house. With the press crawling all over the city, I wasn't sure how long the kids would be staying with me so I told them it was okay to bring the cat. She must have gone back out after that."

"Does she do this sort of thing often?" asked Gretchen. "Take off on her own without telling anyone where she's going?"

Hollis grimaced. "No. She's just been really upset since the funerals. Also, uh, she's been drinking a lot more than usual. Zane thinks she might have taken a bottle of vodka from my place."

"He thinks she's driving drunk," Josie clarified.

The tight expression on Hollis's face told her everything she needed to know.

Gretchen fished her phone from her pocket. "Is there a particular place she goes when she's upset?"

"I don't think so. We'll just start from my place, drive around, see if we can find her."

Josie felt a prickle along the back of her neck. Riley Stevens had gotten under her skin in a way no one associated with a case had in a long time. "Was she wearing Cora's sweater?"

Confusion lined Hollis's flushed face. "What?"

"Cora's sweater. Was she wearing it when she left the house?"

"I don't know but probably. She hasn't taken it off in two days. Listen, I gotta go, okay? I'm sure we'll find her. If you've got more questions, just call me later."

"Hollis." Gretchen waved her phone at him. "We can help. We can take a report from Zane and Jackson and start using our resources to locate her. Get us the license plate number of the vehicle Riley is driving. We'll get all available patrol units to look for it."

"I thought there was that whole twenty-four-hour waiting period before you could report someone missing to police," he said.

Josie shook her head. "That's a myth. Besides, we both

know that Riley is distressed right now. If you have a reasonable suspicion that she might be under the influence, it's extremely important for her safety and the safety of others that we find her as soon as possible."

He pulled his sleeve down where it had snagged on his glucose monitor. "Oh, wow. Great. That's great. I don't want anything to happen to her. I'll call Jackson, get that tag for you. Then I'll call Zane back and tell him to stay put until we get there. You'll come with?"

"Of course," said Gretchen, jotting down his address as he rattled it off.

Ten minutes later, Hollis pulled out of the parking lot, dodging the reporters surrounding his truck hoping for a quote or an interview. Josie followed in their SUV while Gretchen called dispatch and gave them Riley's information as well as the license plate number of the car she was driving, asking for a BOLO to be put out immediately.

After ending the call, Gretchen looked over at Josie. "You asked about the sweater."

"You know why."

"I do," Gretchen replied softly. "She's having a mental health crisis."

"She could hurt herself or someone else," Josie agreed. "Whether she means to or not."

"You think she went back to Brighton Springs?"

"No. I don't think she'd want to be that far from Jackson."

Riley had been fragile the day that Josie and Gretchen delivered the news of her mother's death—her mother's murder. The confrontation with Dalton at the funerals likely hadn't helped, not to mention the video going viral. She was hurting on a deep, elemental level that resonated with Josie. Every aspect of her life—of Cora's life—was under scrutiny now in a way it hadn't been before, despite the interest in the disappearances over the last seven years. The yellow sweater made her feel closer to her mother. Riley wanted to feel connected to Cora. But all the connections were in Brighton Springs, where they'd lived together—Tobias's house, the cemetery, the diner where Cora had worked.

There was only one place in Denton that had a connection to her mother.

"I think I know where she is," Josie said.

THIRTY-TWO

A hollow feeling settled in Josie's gut as they drove to the remote area where Tobias's sedan had been found. Somewhere between finding the car in its watery grave and their visit to Brighton Springs, her professional shield had worn thin. As the streets flashed past, bringing them closer to what she genuinely hoped was not another tragedy, that mental armor felt as if it were made of gossamer. Riley. A fragile young woman, still a teenage girl in so many ways, stunted by her mother's disappearance. A girl who'd only had one dependable parent all of her life, who'd been left at the mercy of others, veritable strangers, when her mother vanished. She'd been lucky that Tobias's sons and his best friend were kind, caring men. They'd had no obligation to her at all. Even so, their love hadn't made up for the loss of her anchor, her North Star.

Her mother.

"Shit," Josie muttered.

"You okay?" Gretchen angled her cell phone away from her mouth. She was now on the phone with Officer Brennan, giving instructions. They'd decided to bypass Hollis's home for now. If Riley was by the river, they wanted to get to her as soon as possible. In the meantime, Brennan could get statements from the men in her life.

"I'm fine," Josie lied.

The realization had hit her while they drove. She'd been equating Riley with Wren for the past week. All things led back to Wren now. Josie had never been in this position before. Having to separate the existence of a child she was responsible for in every way from the things she saw on the job. Sure, she'd been a huge part of Harris's life for almost a decade but ultimately, she wasn't his mother or his guardian. It wasn't her job to make decisions on his behalf and then watch him suffer the consequences should they be catastrophic.

This was never a mental partition she'd needed to construct before. Faced with Wren's palpable grief each day, it was so much easier for Riley Stevens to climb past her defenses, to cause her to ache in ways she didn't know were possible.

She swore again, louder this time. Everything in her brain was messy and chaotic. Weird feelings were quaking and bubbling inside her, water about to boil over. She absolutely could not let that happen. Not now. Not ever, if she could help it. Dropping into her 4-7-8 breathing, she visualized turning off the mental burner currently wreaking emotional havoc on her system. Pouring the sizzling water into a titanium thermos. It went right into her mental vault, deep in its recesses, on a shelf somewhere, obscured by a bunch of other artifacts that she didn't have time to examine. Things that had no place in her field of work.

She had a job to do. Nothing was going to stand in the way of it.

"There's a unit closer than we are," Gretchen said. "They can be at the riverbank in two minutes."

Josie glanced at the name of the crossroads at the next intersection they drove through. They were still a good twenty minutes away. "Great."

Ten minutes later, the call came over the radio. Riley Stevens had been found at the boat ramp. Unresponsive. An ambulance was dispatched. An ache bloomed in Josie's chest.

The rest of the drive passed in thick silence. Josie doubled the speed limit. By the time they flew past the remnants of the old state mental hospital and turned onto the road running parallel to the river, there were two patrol cars and an ambulance, which was slanted across the entrance to the boat ramp.

No reporters, although Josie was certain some would arrive within the hour.

Officer Dougherty stood near the entrance to the boat ramp, ensuring that no one crossed the threshold. He shook his head as they approached. Josie's heart sank.

"She's gone," he said. "When I got here, she was already showing signs of livor mortis."

"The ambulance is for transporting her to the morgue then," Gretchen said.

"Yeah. I secured the scene and called Hummel and Dr. Feist. They'll be here as soon as possible."

Josie stepped to the side, peering through a gap between Dougherty's tall frame and the ambulance where a sliver of the boat ramp was visible. The back of a red Subaru Crosstrek obscured the river beyond.

"Where is she?"

"On the ground near the front of the vehicle. From what I can tell, she parked and got out to look at the water. I'm not sure if she was sitting on the hood and slid off or if she just collapsed where she was standing."

"Signs of a struggle?" Gretchen asked. "Trauma?"

Dougherty shook his head. "None that I could see. There's a bottle of vodka next to her. Not much left in it. I found her on her stomach, turned her over so I could get a pulse, maybe do CPR, but like I said, she was already showing lividity."

Lividity, which was a sign of livor mortis, occurred when

the heart stopped pumping blood. Gravity pulled all the blood in the body to the lowest point, causing the skin to be discolored a deep reddish-purple. Once lividity became fixed, the discoloration was permanent. However, assuming that Hollis, Zane and Jackson had all told the truth, that meant that Riley had left Hollis's home sometime between seven and nine a.m. If she had come right here, she would have arrived within twenty to twenty-five minutes. They'd be able to retrace her steps via the GPS in her vehicle's infotainment center.

Lividity could begin anywhere between twenty minutes to four hours postmortem. The time at which it became fixed, or permanent, was much later and spanned a much wider range, but they already knew that Riley had died before twelve thirty, which was roughly the time that the first Denton PD units showed up. Since Dougherty had rolled her over, the discoloration would now be on the back of her body.

"It's like she just laid down and passed," Dougherty added.

Hummel's team would provide more insight, as would Dr. Feist. Without knowing Riley's cause of death—even if all signs indicated she'd had some sort of medical event—they had to operate under the assumption that there was foul play. In the event that her death was ruled a homicide after the autopsy, they had to preserve any and all evidence that might be present. Police only got one opportunity to process a crime scene properly. The fact that Dougherty had moved Riley's body was a disadvantage but not a problem. He'd been right to evaluate whether she needed medical aid or not.

A news van barreled down the road, followed by another and another. Reporters poured out of the vehicles, camera crews in tow. Josie's stomach dropped. Patrol officers moved in, waving them back and quickly setting a perimeter.

"So it begins," Officer Dougherty muttered.

Another tragedy. A legacy of death and heartache.

"We need to tell Jackson," Josie said. "He's Riley's next of kin."

Gretchen put her reading glasses on and took out her phone, thumbs tapping out a message. "Brennan's with them now. He'll handle it."

More Denton PD vehicles appeared. The ERT arrived, Hummel and his second-in-command, Officer Jenny Chan, lugging their equipment toward the cordoned-off crime scene. It would be hours before Josie and Gretchen could get onto the boat ramp to see the scene for themselves. Dr. Feist followed, setting up her equipment and waiting on the sidelines with them until they had permission to enter.

An hour later, Josie and Gretchen were still waiting for Hummel's team to finish their work when shouting erupted from behind the press vehicles. Josie turned her head to see Jackson muscle his way past the crowd of them and toward the patrol officers. He charged down the road, stark fury blanketing his features. Zane jogged behind him, followed by Hollis, moving much more slowly. His body shook and tears rolled down his ruddy cheeks. It was the most emotion Josie had seen him show.

"Jacks, Zane, wait!" he called feebly.

Officer Conlen stepped in front of Jackson. "You can't go beyond this point."

The distance between the entrance to the boat ramp, where Josie and Gretchen loitered, and the cruisers parked sideways to keep the public at bay was nearly a quarter mile. They walked toward the burgeoning confrontation, watching with rapt attention.

"Where is my wife?" Jackson yelled. His eyes were wild. "I want to see my wife."

"Sir, I'm going to need you to go back to your vehicle."

Jackson didn't look at Conlen. His gaze was focused beyond the officer, to the crime scene tape that had been erected across the entrance to the boat ramp. "What happened to her? Where is she?"

"As soon as we're able to give you information, we'll do that but for now, I need you to go back to your vehicle."

"I can't just go back to my vehicle!" he roared. "I need to know what happened to my wife!"

Zane put a hand on Jackson's shoulder. "Hey, man, you need to back down. The last thing any of us needs is you in a jail cell."

Jackson spun around, giving his brother a withering glare. "Stay out of this."

"Stay out of this?" Zane said incredulously. "Stay out of this? Have you lost your damn mind? This is Riley we're talking about."

Jackson lunged, fisting the collar of his brother's T-shirt and shaking him like a rag doll, until his feet lifted off the ground. "This is your fault! Your fucking fault!"

"Sir," Conlen snapped. "Let go of him and return to your vehicle or you will be removed."

Zane's eyes narrowed. He brought his hands up, wrapping them around Jackson's thick wrists. "How is this my fault? You were supposed to protect her!"

"I was protecting her!" Jackson thundered. "You're here for two days and now she's gone! Gone! Drinking like... she has a problem, and you just feed it and feed it and she never knows when to stop when you're around."

Zane pushed against Jackson with a surprising amount of strength given their size difference. "Screw you! Like you ever stopped her from drinking. You said you'd protect her. You promised. This is on you. Get the fuck off me!"

Conlen gripped Jackson's shoulder and gave clipped instructions that went unheeded. Jackson let go of Zane's shirt, pulled back, and delivered a punishing blow to Zane's face.

Josie sprinted forward before the younger brother had a chance to process it, joining Conlen, dragging Jackson away.

Zane didn't bother to clutch his nose, despite the blood flowing liberally down his face, his chin, his shirt. Instead, he glowered at Jackson, watching as Josie and Conlen took his still-flailing body to the ground. "You didn't deserve her," he told his brother. "You never deserved her."

THIRTY-THREE

Time crawled as the ERT worked along the boat ramp. Josie spoke briefly to Hollis. She wasn't releasing the brothers until they'd had time to cool off. She wasn't surprised by Jackson's behavior. It would take time for both brothers to process the fact that they'd lost Riley forty-eight hours after burying their father. The reality kept poking Josie with small jabs of unease. What were the odds?

"Hey," Gretchen said. "Which one do you want?"

The brothers had been moved to opposite sides of the road —Zane in the back of a second ambulance that had arrived, nursing his busted nose, and Jackson in the back seat of a cruiser, his hands zip-tied behind him. Both of them looked pale and exhausted, dazed even.

Josie pointed to the ambulance. "That one."

Zane reclined on the gurney, an ice pack pressed to his nose. His voice was slightly muffled and nasal as he answered her questions. "The last time I saw her or talked to her was last night in Hollis's living room. We stayed up late watching Netflix and, um, drinking."

He said the last word quietly, shame coloring the skin of his neck and cheeks.

"Where were Hollis and Jackson?"

"Bed."

Outside the perimeter of cruisers, several reporters began to set up for their live shots. Denton PD hadn't released any information but given Jackson's outburst, the bare bones of the situation were pretty obvious.

Another viral video.

Josie looked back at Zane. "How would you characterize Riley's mood?"

"How do you think? She was sad."

"Did she say anything to make you think she might try to harm herself?"

He lowered the ice pack, his red-rimmed eyes bulging. "Wait. Did she—is that how she—"

"We don't know what happened yet," Josie said. "But I need to know if she talked about harming herself or if she appeared to be distraught enough to do so."

"No." Zane shook his head vigorously. "No. If I thought she was going to do something like that, I would have told someone. Woke Jacks up. Or Hol. I don't know. Something. We talked about the press, about Dalton, about what the hell to do with ourselves now that finding our parents wasn't a thing anymore. She cried a little, but she's been crying on and off for days. Then we put on this show we used to watch when we were in high school and she fell asleep on the couch."

His eyes took on a faraway look, as though he was transported back to those last hours with Riley. A host of emotions flashed across his bruised face. The sorrow that finally settled over his features was so devastating that Josie felt it in the pit of her stomach. Like Riley, he had been a teenager when the only parent he had left was taken from him. All he had was Jackson and Riley. The shared trauma bonded them like nothing else could and now they were fracturing in spectacular fashion.

Josie hated the way this case cut her to the bone.

Pushing the morass of feelings down deep, she focused on the information she needed to get from Zane. "Did she wake up after that? Go to bed?"

"She had a blanket. I left her there. Things were so awful." He pressed the pack against his nose again. "You know how when something bad happens and it's like every minute that you're awake is torture and you can't stop it or get away from it? Like just breathing is hard and distractions don't work and you kind of want to die even though you would never hurt yourself just because the pain is, like, constant?"

Josie did know. "Yes," she said, keeping her voice and her expression carefully neutral.

"Right, and so the only relief is sleep. When you're asleep, you can't feel it but when you wake up, it's all there again and sometimes you're sorry you woke up because it all rushes back. Well, that's what it's been like, especially for Ri, so I didn't wake her up. I left her on the couch, figuring if she woke up on her own, she could just go to bed. That was the last time I saw her."

"How much had she had to drink?"

"I don't really know. I wasn't counting or anything. Hol and I were over at the office for a while last night. We had takeout there with Ellyn while Jacks and Riley were home. They'd already eaten when we got back around nine or nine thirty so I don't know what she drank before that. You can ask Jacks. She had a few beers that I saw and after Jacks went to bed, she opened a bottle of wine. We split it."

Josie glanced over her shoulder to see that Gretchen was still conducting her interview. "Jackson didn't join the two of you?"

"No," Zane said.

"Why not?"

He removed the ice pack and pointed to his blood-crusted nostrils. "Why do you think?"

"But he woke you up this morning when he couldn't find Riley?"

The skin beneath Zane's eyes was already starting to bruise. "Yeah, it was around ten, I guess. Hols was already at work."

"How long have you and your brother been on the outs?"

"I don't know." He shrugged. "Since I was in high school."

"Because of Riley?"

He pressed the pack against his nose again, tipping his head back so she could no longer see his eyes. "No."

"He's implied more than once that you contributed to her drinking."

"Yeah, well, he's wrong. I never made her drink or encouraged her to drink. Sure, we got busted a few times in high school, but she made her own choices. She always made her own choices."

"The two of you disagree about a lot of things when it comes to Riley, don't you?"

"What? No."

"Zane," Josie said, suppressing a sigh. "The jealousy isn't subtle. I'll ask again: is the tension between you and Jackson because of feelings you both have for Riley?"

"That's not how it started." His free hand drifted over his bloodstained T-shirt. The streaks ran from collar to hem and had even dripped onto his jeans. "You know what? It doesn't matter. Let's just say that when we were younger—before Dad met Cora—Jackson wasn't all that morally upstanding when it came to women, okay? He didn't make good choices."

"What does that mean?" Josie asked.

"What do you think it means? He was an asshole."

"I'm going to need a specific example, Zane."

With a heavy sigh, he pulled the ice pack from his face. "He was twenty, I was thirteen. Dad was working all the time, like he always did. Jackson was usually the one who picked me up from school. That's how he met my eighth grade English teacher. She was almost thirty. Really pretty. Nice, too. Patient, especially with all of us wild, hormonal boys in her class. Anyway, he started dating her."

"That made you uncomfortable?"

Zane dug a nail into one of the blood droplets on his thigh. It had dried some time ago. "She was pretty upset when he dumped her, so yeah. Made it real awkward for me for the rest of that year."

"Did you have a crush on this teacher?" Josie asked.

"Maybe," he mumbled. "Maybe I didn't like seeing them together or having a front-row seat to how hurt she was when it ended. But that's how he always was with women. Start seeing someone, get them all infatuated and starry-eyed over him and then dump them. Every single time. Our neighbor's daughter when she came home from college. The receptionist at urgent care he went to high school with. A couple of customers. Dad was pissed. When I was fourteen, he dated one of my friend's moms after her divorce. Lasted a few months. She was devastated. He was fine. My friendship was destroyed. Fast-forward to five years after Dad and Cora disappeared. After all the shit the three of us dealt with, he went after Riley."

"He pursued her?"

Zane nodded. "I didn't even know he was interested in her. It took him a while but eventually she went all starry-eyed like the rest of them. It bothered me, okay? She deserves better. I didn't want her to be hurt any more than she already was by missing her mom."

"It looks like they were happy together," Josie said. "Did he cheat on Riley?"

"I don't know. Ask him."

"Were you interested in Riley?"

"I love her like a sister, okay?"

"Were you interested in her?" Josie repeated.

Zane abandoned the ice pack on his lap and examined his cuticles, also stained with dried blood.

"Zane," Josie coaxed.

He let his head loll back against the gurney, squeezed his eyes closed and exhaled through his mouth. "When I was a teenager, yeah. Okay? Happy? Yeah, I had a crush on the girl who was supposed to be my stepsister. I never once acted on it or even thought about acting on it."

She could tell the admission cost him something and wondered if this was the first time he'd ever said it out loud. Forging ahead, she said, "Even when the two of you were out drinking together?"

Zane blinked, keeping his eyes trained on the harsh overhead lights. "I didn't bring her with me because I was trying to hook up with her. Even though we weren't blood-related, it would have been gross, okay? We lived in the same house. Our parents were getting married. It would have been too weird. I invited her to go drinking with me and my friends because she was bored. She caught me sneaking out one night and asked to come. That was it. I never even told her how I felt, much less acted on it."

But Jackson had. Well after Zane's crush started, but still. How had it felt for Zane all these years? Him being so careful never to cross any lines with Riley only to have his womanizing brother swoop in and marry her?

Before today, the rift between the brothers had been nothing more than a curiosity but now the woman both of them were in love with was dead. Josie knew what Dougherty had told her about the scene. Knew without yet viewing it that the signs pointed to a medical event. Knew that Riley had a drinking problem and had been under tremendous stress in the past week. Those things might have contributed to said medical event.

Still, deep in Josie's gut, unease swirled.

How could a family be this unlucky?

Josie asked if she could search his phone. Zane handed it over readily. It was standard procedure. She needed to know if there were inconsistencies in his statement, the timeline he had given or red flags in communications he might have had in the last twenty-four hours. She scrolled through the text messages and the call log. There was a flurry of messages on a group chain with him, Riley, and Jackson regarding the funerals. A barrage of texts from people whose names Josie didn't recognize offering condolences. A thread between him and Hollis regarding company matters. More messages from that morning between him and Jackson about whether Jackson had located her yet. There were calls to Riley between ten seventeen in the morning and when he had contacted Hollis earlier that day—the same time that Josie and Gretchen had been speaking with him at the company lot.

If there was anything remotely suspicious about Riley's death, they'd get a warrant for the contents of the phone and serve it directly on his cell carrier. It would give them access to anything he might have deleted in the past several hours. They'd do the same for Hollis and Jackson.

Josie handed the phone back to Zane. He leaned to his left a little, peering over her shoulder in Jackson's direction.

"You going to arrest him?" he asked tiredly. "'Cause I'm not pressing charges."

"Then no, we're not arresting him," she said. "But you two have to leave the scene. Stay in Denton but try not to beat the hell out of each other."

"I'm not leaving this city until I know what happened to Riley."

THIRTY-FOUR

Josie left Zane in the back of the ambulance. His eyelids were drooping, his limbs going loose with exhaustion. She watched as the rise and fall of his chest slowed into an even rhythm. The day he'd found out about Tobias and Cora being murdered, he had shown up at the Denton location of At Your Disposal in tears. As far as Josie could tell, he hadn't cried since finding out about Riley. She had no doubt that, very soon, the stress and trauma of the day would hit him like a freight train. In the few interactions she'd had with Zane Lachlan over the past week, she was struck by his vulnerability and his almost childlike sweetness. Losing the woman he'd been secretly in love with for nearly ten years immediately after burying his father was a level of devastation she wasn't sure he could handle.

Turning away from the ambulance, she found Hollis standing patiently near one of the other patrol cars.

He ambled over. "I'll keep an eye on the boys. I promise."

Brennan had already taken a statement from him at his home, but Josie asked anyway. "When you saw Riley this morning, was she alone?"

Hollis nodded. Tears welled in his eyes.

It would be easy enough for them to trace Riley's steps from this morning using the GPS in her vehicle. They could verify the timeline that Hollis had given. Josie knew there were reporters camped outside the home Riley and Jackson had shared. One or more of them should be able to confirm that she'd been alone when she went to get Captain Whiskers' medication and toys.

"How did she seem?" Josie asked.

Clearing his throat, he glanced toward the back of the ambulance where Zane rested. "I don't think she was drunk, if that's what you're asking. Well, I mean maybe she was a little. I don't know."

"How was she acting?"

"It wasn't so much how she was acting," Hollis said, "more like the way she looked. Pale. A little shaky. Maybe she was hungover? Or all the strain of the last week just made her sick? She just didn't look well. I told her to eat something and go to bed. Get some rest."

"What did she say to that?"

Hollis twisted the rag in his hands. "She said she would and that was it. I left."

"Did you speak about anything else?"

"No." The word was strangled. He lifted the rag to his face again, covering both his eyes with it. Sobs shook his large frame.

Josie gave him a few minutes to compose himself. "I'm sorry, Hollis. I just have a few more questions. Did you see Zane and Jackson this morning?"

"No. I figured they were still in bed. Both their cars were in the driveway. I didn't talk to either of them until Zane called me. You were there."

She thanked him and left him with instructions to stay in Denton and make sure Zane and Jackson didn't pummel one another.

As she turned to head back toward the boat ramp, she

spotted Gretchen across the road. Josie gave a faint shake of her head, signaling to Gretchen that they could cut Jackson loose since Zane wasn't going to press charges. Moments later, Jackson unfolded himself from the police car. Officer Conlen cut the zip ties. He rubbed at his thick wrists as he strode toward Hollis and Zane. His eyes were dark with pain and fury. Josie stiffened, half expecting him to hop into the ambulance and attack his younger brother again, but he stopped in front of Hollis instead. The two men spoke for a moment, voices too low for anyone to overhear. Then Jackson let himself be enveloped into the older man's arms and, like a dam breaking, he began to cry. His large body trembled. Irritation flared in Josie's gut as she saw a half-dozen cameras swing in his direction. Luckily, one of the paramedics noticed and herded Hollis and Jackson into the ambulance with Zane.

Josie turned away. Right now, her only concern was Riley Stevens.

Gretchen joined her and they walked toward the crime scene tape that cordoned off the boat ramp. The ERT had set up a makeshift equipment station.

"What's Jackson's story?" Josie asked as she fished out a Tyvek suit.

Dr. Feist was already in full crime scene garb, waiting patiently next to Dougherty with her equipment bag.

"He woke up sometime after nine. From what he could tell, Riley hadn't come to bed. She wasn't anywhere in the house. Her car was gone. He tried calling her, but she'd left her phone on the kitchen table. After waiting an hour, he knocked on Zane's door and woke him up to see if he knew where she went. Zane said he hadn't seen her since the night before when they were watching TV on the couch. Jackson went looking for her. Their house, the coffee shop she likes, the liquor store."

"Shit," Josie murmured.

"Yeah. After a couple of hours, he called Zane back who then called Hollis."

Josie tucked her black hair into a skull cap. "Did Jackson let you look at his phone?"

"Yeah. No arguments there." Gretchen put booties on over her shoes. "Nothing unusual."

"Did you ask him if Riley had any medical conditions?"

"None. What'd you get from Zane and Hollis?"

Josie filled her in as they zipped up their Tyvek suits and snapped on gloves. Dougherty logged their names onto the list of people who had entered the crime scene, and they slipped under the tape. The boat ramp was in poor condition. Its wide concrete slabs were cracked in several places. Weeds sprang from the fissures, reaching for the sky. Several potholes had formed. Trash collected inside them. Beer cans, food wrappers and cigarette butts. Trees and bushes crowded the edges of the area. A fishing bob had caught in one of the branches, the red and white standing out against the greenery. Riley's red Subaru was pointed toward the river where the concrete dipped, forming a ramp from which boats could be launched. With the drought, the water had receded too far for anyone to use it, leaving only dried stones and cracked patches of mud.

There, between the car and the place where the ground sloped, was Riley.

She was sprawled on her back, eyes closed, lips parted. Blowflies crawled and flitted across her exposed skin, seeking entrance to her mouth, nostrils, ears, trying to access her eyes, looking for warm, moist places to lay their eggs. They were always the first insects to arrive postmortem, usually minutes after death. More buzzed in the air and darted over her clothes. There was no evidence that her body had been disturbed by animals and no scavenger birds hovered nearby, which confirmed she hadn't been dead very long at all when she was found.

Long locks of her hair fell in disheveled piles around her head, the sun-kissed strawberry-blonde matching her mother's oversized yellow sweater in a way Josie hadn't noticed before. Her legs were straight, her arms at her sides, palms angled slightly upward. Likely the result of Dougherty having turned her over. Two bees buzzed lazily above a vodka bottle on its side a few feet from her body. It was big. Able to hold around twenty-five ounces if Josie had to guess. A small amount of clear liquid pooled inside, winking in the sunlight. There was a faint smell of alcohol, mingling with the first wisps of impending decay.

Josie stared at the bottle. Her chest felt tight. Mentally, she spun the gossamer around her heart into a more durable fabric, tightening, layering, weaving, keeping her emotions in check. She knew exactly what it was like to drown her pain in alcohol before ten in the morning. To need to do it. To have no other outlet for it, no way to contain it. No way to keep it from scratching the husk of your soul until it was raw and excoriated. Riley had been seeking numbness as a respite. Somewhere deep in the recesses of Josie's mental vault, that too-full thermos full of hot emotion jolted in recognition.

Anya let out a long sigh before sliding her camera out of her messenger bag. Josie and Gretchen waited while she photographed the scene and Riley's body. Once that task was complete, she knelt on the ground, batting at the persistent flies.

"She's in full rigor," Anya said, almost to herself.

Rigor mortis set in two to six hours after death. This also fit in with the timeline of Riley's death.

Josie and Gretchen knelt across from Anya, watching as her gloved hands worked nimbly over Riley's clothes, pushing her collar down, rolling up the cuffs of her sleeves, spreading the lapels of the sweater, folding up the hem of the T-shirt under it to check for any injuries or evidence not immediately visible. Today's shirt was hot pink with black lettering that said: *I'm*

Like 104% Tired. Anya lifted the waistband of her leggings. There were no marks along her abdomen.

Anya got on her hands and knees, lowering her face until it was inches from concrete as she tried to get a closer look at Riley's hand. The blowflies scuttled away, taking flight, before diving back toward another area of exposed flesh. Their greenish-blue backs gleamed in the sunlight as more and more attacked Riley's face.

"Hmmm," Anya murmured, sitting back on her haunches and grabbing her camera.

Josie stood and rounded the body. Once Anya finished taking additional photos, she pointed to Riley's palm. It was angled toward her thigh. Kneeling, Josie, too, had to contort her body to get a look at what had caught Anya's attention.

"I don't see anything."

Anya's index finger slid between Josie's face and Riley's palm, pointing to a small series of tiny punctures. Four of them, evenly spaced to form the four corners of a square in the fleshy skin below her index finger.

Josie huffed out a breath to discourage the blowfly that landed dangerously close to her nostrils. "What is it?"

"Some sort of patterned injury, I'd imagine," Anya said. "Though I'm not sure what from."

A patterned injury was one that reproduced a mirror image or features of the object that caused the injury. Sometimes they were easy to identify—like a belt buckle—and other times, like now, it wasn't clear.

"Nothing on the other hand besides rings," Gretchen reported before joining them. Josie shuffled aside to give her room to examine Riley's palm.

"It's too symmetrical to be from pebbles or gravel. It looks like she was clutching something in her hand hard enough to break the skin," Anya added.

"Something small," Gretchen said.

Anya continued her examination, moving down to Riley's pantlegs and finally, the tops of her socks, finding nothing. Her sneakers were snug on her feet, laces tied tightly.

Josie and Gretchen helped Anya turn Riley over so she could repeat the process—peeking under sleeves, hems, and waistbands. Nothing.

Finally, Anya hauled herself to her feet and used her forearm to wipe sweat from her brow, batting away more flies. "No visible injuries other than those punctures on her palm. Nothing to suggest foul play. Not at this point. She's twenty-three?"

"Yeah," Josie answered. "No medical issues."

Anya's gaze was locked on Riley's face. "I'll have to perform an autopsy. Sometimes young people have undiagnosed cardiac conditions. There are no signs until... well, until there are and then it's too late."

THIRTY-FIVE

Chief Bob Chitwood's voice boomed, echoing through the stairwell. Josie, Noah, Gretchen, and Turner were all at their desks when they heard him from the second-floor great room. If he was hollering before he even walked through the door, it wasn't good. Seconds later, he appeared, his acne-pitted face flushed, and his eyebrows drawn down in a dark scowl. Wisps of his thinning white hair floated over his balding pate.

"What in the hell is going on?" he said. "The couple from Brighton Springs. Now one of their kids? Is this for real? Quinn, Palmer. Tell me you've got something. The press are outside multiplying like maggots on a damn corpse. Pretty soon I'm gonna have the Mayor breathing down my neck, and I can't stand that woman."

"Pretty sure no one likes her, Chief," Gretchen muttered.

He folded his arms and looked down his nose at the four of them. "Well? What do you have?"

"On Riley Stevens?" Gretchen said. "Waiting on the autopsy, but it looks like she had a heart attack or went into cardiac arrest."

The Chief frowned. "Natural causes?"

"Possibly. Probably."

"What about the couple? What do you have on that case?"

"A big fat nothing," Josie answered honestly.

Turner gave a low whistle. "Damn, Quinn. You're not even trying to save your own ass here."

"Shut up, douch— Turner," she said without looking at him.

"Palmer?" the Chief said.

"We're still working on some leads."

All none of them. Josie kept the thought to herself.

"So nothing, then," the Chief said.

Gretchen didn't answer.

With a disgusted shake of his head, he turned his back on them, stomping toward his office. "Get something!" he shouted. "Fast!"

Once his door slammed, Noah spun in his chair to face Josie. "Let's go over it then, while we're all here."

Their collective shifts would only overlap for another half hour.

Turner threw his foam basketball at its net and missed, as usual. "You know what's missing from this investigation?"

"Leads," Gretchen said flatly.

"My exceptional detective skills," he said arrogantly.

At this point, Josie would take anything they could get, even if it came from Turner. Still, she couldn't let his remark slide. "If they're on par with your report-writing skills, then we're well and truly screwed."

Gretchen snickered.

Noah tapped a hand against his desk. "Come on. What've you got?"

Josie leaned back in her chair, rubbing her temples with her fingers. A headache was brewing. Had been since she left the boat ramp.

She and Gretchen walked them through the case, from all of Detective John Fanning's findings to what little new information they'd uncovered: both Tobias and Cora had been shot in the head; Cora had had a mysterious skeleton key in her purse; Cora's abusive ex, Dalton Stevens, now claimed Cora had been having an affair at the time the couple were killed; and Hollis had revealed that Cora had intended to leave Tobias.

Then they went over the uselessness of the new information. According to everyone closest to the couple, Cora hadn't owned anything that required a skeleton key to open it. In fact, the key might not mean anything at all. Dalton Stevens was unreliable, which meant that the assertions that Cora was having an affair and that he'd seen her in the parking lot of the Majesty Motel were questionable. Hollis denied having an affair with Cora, claiming that any conversations they had before the murders were about her intention to break up with Tobias. Whether Cora truly intended to leave him was immaterial. He had been murdered, too.

"We've still got to talk to the private investigator that Riley hired," Josie concluded. "He's agreed to meet with us tomorrow. But I'm expecting more of the same."

"Every person in their lives had an alibi," Noah said.

"Correct." Gretchen caught Turner's foam basketball as it ricocheted off the tiny net in her direction. "Also, keep in mind that to have pulled off the murders and the disposal of the bodies inside the car, there had to be more than one person."

Noah folded his hands over his stomach. "Which means you're back to murder for hire."

At this point, Josie was getting sick of hearing the words.

"We'll start looking for anyone arrested for, charged with, or convicted of murder-for-hire plots in or around that area in the past ten years," Noah suggested. "Murder for hire isn't usually a one-off and like you said, this crime doesn't seem like the work of amateurs."

Turner waved at Gretchen, trying to get her attention and

holding his palm up for her to throw back his ball. She ignored him, squeezing it in her hand like a stress toy.

"We can also start rechecking everyone's alibis." Josie yanked open the center drawer of her desk and fished around for ibuprofen. "Maybe we need to bring in associates of Dalton and Hollis, even if Fanning already interviewed them. Question witnesses again."

They'd be retracing Fanning's steps, but all they needed was one person to crack and tell them something that they hadn't revealed before. Or one person remembering a detail they hadn't when they were first interviewed. Or someone revealing something that hadn't seemed important until now.

Someone always knew something.

"The diner might be a good place to start in terms of witnesses." Without warning, Gretchen launched the basketball toward Turner, smiling smugly as it went over his head and he had to dive for it. "Cora worked there for years. Her boss organized the GoFundMe for Riley. Coworkers and patrons might have something to say that they didn't tell Fanning."

Josie kept pawing through her desk drawer for her elusive supply of painkillers. "With respect to the skeleton key, Hollis's sister sent over the company records Hollis promised. A list of antiques and collectibles At Your Disposal sold on behalf of clients in the year before Cora and Tobias were killed. Nothing there."

The sound of a can snapping open drew their attention to Turner. He guzzled some of the disgusting energy drink he loved so much. After letting out a loud belch, he said, "The skeleton key belonged to someone else."

"No shit," Gretchen said. "None of the kids or Hollis admitted to having any items that need skeleton keys."

Turner shrugged. "Then she got it from someone else. Her lover."

"We have no proof she had a lover. None." Josie said as her

hand closed over the bottle of ibuprofen. Twisting it open, she was relieved to find two tablets left. She palmed them and tossed them into her mouth, swallowing them dry.

"They could have been making arrangements at the diner," Turner said. "That way there was no evidence on her phone. You said Hollis was there all the time. If he wasn't messing around with her, maybe some other guy was."

It was the same thought Josie had had but now she was struggling with whether the damn key meant anything at all. It wasn't like Cora had been carrying around the key to a locker or a safe deposit box. Anything that needed to be opened with a skeleton key would be easy to break into. In that sense, it was more symbolic than anything else. This wasn't like a movie where they discovered what the key opened, located it, and found loads of cash and a flash drive with deep, dark secrets on it.

"We're getting nowhere with the key," Noah said. "Let's shelve that for a minute and talk about organized crime."

Gretchen shook her head. "Fanning looked into that. Neighborhood gangs. Didn't find anything. I don't think they were killed by members of some criminal organization."

Turner slugged down the rest of his drink and crumpled the can in his hand. "You're not being liberal enough in your definition of a criminal organization," he informed her.

"What's that supposed to mean?"

"The Brighton Springs Police Department counts as an organization. It has a history of corruption, right? Whether it's documented or not, it's an open secret."

Gretchen swiveled in her chair to stare at him. "You think someone on the Brighton Springs PD had something to do with this?"

"I'm just saying it's possible."

"Meredith said Fanning is clean," Josie said. "I trust her."

"I'm sure he is," Turner said. "Clearly, he kicked over every rock. But it didn't occur to him to look at his own people. Maybe Tobias and what's her name? Cora? Maybe they were on their way home, stumbled onto the officers of Brighton Springs doing some dirty deeds and got killed for it. Or maybe it's as innocent as them covering up some things."

Josie couldn't help but think about the sorts of things that the Chief's father, Harlan Chitwood, had done during his tenure with the Brighton Springs PD. His superiors had overlooked his crimes for decades. He'd long been retired but corruption was a deep rot that wasn't easily excised from any department. Josie and Noah knew that firsthand. How many others were there like Harlan in the ranks? Meredith had said things were turning around but that didn't guarantee that the Lachlan/Stevens case hadn't been tainted. She made a mental note to call Meredith about the matter, since it was delicate.

Turner shot a grin in Gretchen's direction. "You can say it, Palmer. I'm brilliant."

"I'm not complimenting you for having basic critical thinking skills that are required for your job."

"Awww, come on," he goaded. "Quinn, you know I'm right."

"About being brilliant?" she said. "Don't be ridiculous."

THIRTY-SIX

Bruce Olsen's office was located just outside the state capital of Harrisburg in a five-story brick building that overlooked the Susquehanna River. Josie had read his biography before she set up the appointment. It had seemed fairly innocuous at the time but now, standing in front of a heavy wooden door with Olsen's name stenciled across it, Turner's words looped through her head. She couldn't dismiss the possibility that someone on Brighton Springs PD had been involved in the deaths of Cora and Tobias.

Bruce Olsen was a retired Brighton Springs police officer.

He had retired long before Cora and Tobias vanished but prior to that, he'd served on the force for thirty years. The first time she'd heard his name, it had sounded familiar. After a quick search of Fanning's case file, she knew why. The night of the murders, Olsen had thrown a retirement party at his home for a different member of the Brighton Springs PD, Karl Staab, which Jackson had attended. Olsen and several guests had attested to Jackson's attendance. Fanning's extensive check of Jackson's phone records, pings from his cell phone and GPS from the infotainment center of his vehicle all confirmed his presence at the party well into the night.

But Fanning hadn't checked the alibis of any of the other party attendees—most of whom were either former or current sworn Brighton Springs PD officers. Including Bruce Olsen.

Turner was an unrepentant pain in the ass, but he had a point. Maybe they weren't being liberal enough with their definition of a criminal organization.

Gretchen rapped against the door. A muffled voice from behind it called for them to come in. The reception area was clean and welcoming. Cushy chairs formed an L around a coffee table scattered with magazines. In one corner, a water cooler hummed. In another stood a potted plant that had clearly outgrown its home, fronds spreading in every direction. An empty desk took up the rest of the area.

From the half-open door beside it, Bruce Olsen emerged. He was smaller and shorter than the photos on his website, but he still moved with the air of someone used to taking charge. The light gray suit he wore added to the impression and his thin, wire-rimmed glasses made him look studious as well as confident. Though he gave off more of a college professor vibe than that of former law enforcement.

"Detectives," he greeted them. "Glad you found the place okay. Please, step into my office."

Moments later, after making introductions, Josie and Gretchen were seated in front of his desk. The space was just as clean and warm as the reception area. The window behind Olsen was large and offered a partial view of the river. Next to that was a bookcase filled with framed photographs. Some were official—Olsen in uniform alongside colleagues or superiors. Others were clearly him with his family. By the looks of those, he was now a great-grandfather.

"I was devastated to hear about Tobias and Cora," he said,

settling into his own chair. "I don't think anyone was holding out for a happy ending, but it still hurts to know the reality. And now Riley? I saw it on the news. She was a sweet person. It's incredibly tragic. How are the boys? Have you spoken with them?"

"About as well as you'd expect," Gretchen told him.

He smoothed a hand down his light blue tie. "Right. Of course. I called but didn't get an answer. They've had their hands full, I'm sure, between the press and the funerals. Now with Riley... I didn't know Jackson had married her. I'll call again later today. Anyway, listen, I'm sorry you came all this way because I never found anything. Nothing more than John Fanning did. You're welcome to my files though. Since they relate to a double homicide, I don't see an issue with confidentiality."

"Jackson referred Riley to you," Josie said. "Is that right?"

"Correct," Olsen said. "I hosted a party the night Tobias and Cora disappeared. Friend of mine on the force retired. Karl Staab. Jackson was there."

"How did Jackson know Staab?" Gretchen asked.

Olsen laughed. "From his hell-raising days. Jackson's, that is. Karl and I went way back with that family. Before At Your Disposal was opened, Tobias helped me clean out my late mom's house. She was a bit of a hoarder so it was quite the undertaking. I paid him for the work. There were some items my mom had that were valuable and Tobias sold them to collectors for me. It was a nice little windfall. He never took a commission though. When Karl's dad died, I sent him to Tobias, too. He didn't get near as much as I did but it was still a tidy sum. So later, when it was just Tobias and the boys, Karl and I did what we could to look out for them. Those kids got into the usual type of trouble and Tobias would call one of us up, ask us to come around and scare some sense into them."

"What kind of trouble?" Josie asked.

"Underage drinking. Vandalizing school property. Taking Tobias's car for a joyride without a license and running it through a neighbor's garden. Harmless stuff. For a time after Gabrielle passed, they were a little lost. A little wild. They settled."

"You weren't at the funerals," Gretchen said.

"Karl wasn't either," Josie added.

If either Olsen or Staab had been there, surely they would have approached Zane and Jackson.

"No. Karl passed a few years ago. Cancer. I was in California, looking into something for a client. By the time I found out, it was too late for me to catch a flight home in time."

"Had you ever met Cora?" Josie asked.

He blinked. "Cora? No. By the time she came onto the scene, Tobias and I—well, we hadn't spoken for a while."

"Why not?" Gretchen said.

"I won't be violating any client confidentiality rules here since this happened before I retired from the Brighton Springs PD. When Jackson turned eighteen, he came to me and asked me to find his mom."

"Rachel Wright," Josie said.

"Yes. Did he tell you what happened?"

"Fanning mentioned it," said Gretchen. "She ran off with some guy."

Sorrow flickered in Olsen's eyes. "That was a long time ago. I was on patrol. Jackson was only about three or four. She left in the middle of the day, left little Jackson alone. Must have been hours. He was a mess. Crying hysterically. He got out of the house. A neighbor found him on the road and called 911."

Fanning had given them a more sanitized version. One in which Tobias returned home from work to find Jackson alone in the house and Rachel gone. No mention of the 911 call.

"It was awful," Olsen continued. "It was summer but that poor kid was shivering like it was below freezing and he just kept saying, 'Mommy went in Victor, Mommy went in Victor.' It was one of those things—you know how kids that age don't always get their diction or grammar right? Under different circumstances it might have been cute but it was just sad. Anyway, Rachel left a note saying she didn't want to be a wife or mother anymore, basically gave her son to Tobias. Thing was, Jackson didn't remember anything. Tobias was understandably hurt by the whole thing, and he didn't want to talk about it. When he found out that Jackson came to me, he was really upset. Told me not to help him."

"Why didn't he want you to help Jackson?" Gretchen said.

Olsen sighed. "Tobias thought that it would make things worse for him. Rachel abandoned him. Even if I found her and Jackson confronted her, it was never going to be a happy reunion. Tobias begged me to leave it alone. To just tell Jackson that I couldn't locate her. He made a good case for it. I knew how troubled those kids were with everything that had happened. Rachel leaving. Gabrielle dying. Jackson had just graduated high school. He was finally in a good place. Tobias didn't want anything to mess with his future. He said if Jackson still wanted to find her when he was older, more mature, then he wouldn't interfere."

"What did you do?" Josie asked.

Olsen shrugged and in the small motion, Josie swore she saw the mantle of guilt weighing him down. "I told Jackson I didn't find her. After that, Tobias and I drifted apart a little. I saw him around from time to time but we didn't really socialize. I felt a bit guilty for lying to Jackson and I think Tobias knew that. We weren't on bad terms. Things were just... kind of awkward after that whole thing."

A cell phone on his desk buzzed, dancing along the surface. He glanced at it, frowned, and picked it up. "I have to take this."

"We can wait in reception," Gretchen said but he waved her off.

"Stay here. I'll be back in a few minutes."

They heard him move through the lobby and then into the hall, voice low but tense.

"Well," Gretchen said, running a hand through her hair. "We're eating another juicy nothing burger."

Josie stood up, stretching her arms over her head, and walked over to the window. The river had narrowed here, too, from the drought. The rocks, mud, and grass of its bed were exposed. Dry and brittle. Her cell phone chirped, and she took it out of her pocket, releasing a groan of frustration as she read the text from Noah.

I'm going to pay the balance on the venue. We only have a few hours left to do it.

Quickly, she tapped back:

We haven't spoken to Wren about this yet.

Trinity called her yesterday and sold her on it pretty quickly.

Josie gritted her teeth. She didn't know whether to be pissed at her sister for going behind her back or relieved that she no longer had to pitch the ceremony to Wren herself. She was both, actually.

Call Shannon. She said you need to have a final fitting for your dress. Also she wants me to buy you an anniversary band to go with your engagement ring.

A laugh that made her sound positively psychotic burst from her mouth. She typed: *you have got to be fucking kidding me* but then quickly deleted it. She did a minute of box breathing, happy as hell that Bruce Olsen was taking so long. Then she prepared a different response.

An anniversary band for our five-year anniversary? To go with an engagement ring that I never get to wear?

While Noah had chosen an understated—though gorgeous—engagement ring for her, it was not appropriate for work, which was where she spent most of her time. She only got to wear it if they were going out to dinner or to a party or some other event. Now she was even more protective of it since it had been stolen during Noah's abduction and only recently returned to her by the state police.

She said it will give me something to slip onto your finger, Noah responded.

The thought of how much they'd already spent on this thing with her mother treating it like the royal wedding and not the simple, intimate ceremony she'd originally wanted made the acid in her stomach boil. They had Wren-related costs to worry about now, too. Those were far more important.

Josie's thumbs punched against her screen at furious speed. *Absolutely not. We cannot afford to spend that kind of money right now and it's not necessary. This isn't a wedding. It's a vow renewal. Just wait till I get home and we can talk about all this.*

Fine. I'll just make the payment.

Did she really want to go through with this now? Did he? Trying another tactic, she messaged: *We still haven't discussed you getting help for your nightmares.*

One has nothing to do with the other, he shot back. *We can talk about that later. I'm paying the balance so we don't lose the venue.*

She quietly released a long stream of expletives. Under any other circumstances, she would call him and argue that last point. That he wasn't in the right headspace to go through with the vow renewal. She'd guilt him into agreeing to see a therapist. Unfortunately, she couldn't do that while in the middle of an interview. She couldn't deal with any of this madness right now. Noah knew that. He'd probably waited until she was in Harrisburg for that very reason. Maybe he thought she wouldn't even see his message until it was too late.

"Trouble?" Gretchen asked.

Josie resisted the urge to throw her phone onto the floor and stomp it into a thousand pieces. "Something like that. It's fine. I'm fine."

If fine meant having absolutely no control over your life anymore.

"I'm fine," she repeated unnecessarily.

Gretchen knew her well enough not to push.

Taking a deep breath, Josie distracted herself by studying the photographs on the bookshelf. There were several of Olsen with a large family. Over fifteen people, from what looked to be his wife to several toddlers. Her eyes roved over the other frames, spotting photos of Olsen with at least three Pennsylvania governors, some taken while he was on Brighton Springs PD and one more recently. In a handful of pictures, he stood beside other men in suits, friends or business colleagues, most likely. Another showed him receiving a commendation of valor while still an officer. Then there was one of Olsen alone, several years younger, his white hair threaded with brown. Grinning broadly, he sat at a desk with a nameplate that identified him as a private investigator. Had this photo been taken to mark the occasion of him receiving his private investigator license? Hanging his shingle out? She leaned in closer. The desk he sat behind was different although like the one here, it was positioned so that a window was at Olsen's back.

The view from it wasn't all that crisp but it was enough to see part of the building beyond. Walkways. Exterior doors with numbers on them—just smudges from this distance—but everything was painted cream and sea-foam green.

Like the Majesty Motel.

THIRTY-SEVEN

Josie's fingers tingled as she picked up the photo. Studying it more closely, the details were unmistakable. She thought of the strip mall across the street from the motel. The one that had sagged like a strong wind might blow it down. A few of the storefronts were empty, abandoned. Based on this photo, Olsen's first office had been in one of them. Josie walked back to her chair, sank into it, and handed Gretchen the frame.

It took her less than thirty seconds to see what Josie had seen. "Well," she murmured. "Maybe this is a something burger after all."

Excitement thrummed through Josie's veins. This was the closest thing to a lead they'd had thus far. It could be nothing. A coincidence. But that's not what her gut told her. Moments later, Olsen returned, a sheepish smile on his flushed face. "Sorry. Dealing with some stuff at home."

Josie waited until he was seated behind his desk again before asking, "When did you move into this office?"

"Oh, I guess a few years ago."

She nodded to Gretchen, who leaned forward and planted the photo in front of him.

His brows knit with confusion. "What's this?"

"A picture of you in your first office is what I'm guessing," said Gretchen.

"Oh, yeah, you're right." He smoothed his tie again. "It was a bit of a shithole, if I'm being honest, but yeah."

"In Brighton Springs," Josie said. "In the strip mall across from the Majesty Motel."

Avoiding her gaze, he blinked slowly. "Uh, yeah, that's right."

Gretchen leaned forward in her chair, tapping her hand lightly against the desk to get his attention. "Tell us again how you never met Cora Stevens."

The color drained from his cheeks. "What are you talking about?"

"Let's try it this way," Josie told him. "When did you meet Cora Stevens for the first time?"

He met Josie's eyes but quickly looked away. "I told you, I never met her."

"When was the last time you spoke with her?"

"I don't understand what's happening right now. I told you—"

Gretchen tapped the desk again, cutting him off. "We know what you told us. Now we want the truth. Don't insult us, Mr. Olsen. You did our job for decades. You know how this works."

"But just in case you need a refresher," Josie said, standing and planting her palms on his desk so she could lean into his space. "Let me lay it out for you. We have a witness who puts Cora Stevens in the parking lot of the Majesty mere months before she and Tobias were killed. The pings from her cell phone confirm it. There are only two possibilities as to why she would have been there. The first and most obvious one is that she was having an affair."

"I didn't—" Olsen choked on his words.

Josie kept going. "We have a second witness who advises

that in the weeks leading up to the murders, she was planning to leave Tobias. She'd started putting money away so she could rent an apartment for her and Riley."

"By all accounts," Gretchen said, "Tobias was a loving, devoted partner. He liked to spoil Cora."

Olsen pursed his lips but didn't interrupt.

"Tobias offered her financial security," Gretchen added. "A big house for their blended family. In fact, he had told her she didn't need to work once they got married. He also put up with Dalton Stevens, her abusive ex-husband, who continued to stalk her relentlessly. Tobias stuck by Cora even after Dalton threatened him."

"Which makes me wonder," Josie said, leaning in even closer. "Why would Cora want to leave him?"

Olsen pushed his chair back a few inches and cleared his throat. "It wasn't—there was no affair."

"So you did meet Cora," Gretchen said.

"This isn't relevant to the murders," he said quickly. "I promise you that. If it was, I would have gone to Fanning with it first thing."

Josie stepped back and folded her arms over her chest. "Let's hear it anyway."

"It wasn't an affair, okay?" he insisted. "That's the truth."

"Forgive me if I don't believe you since you lied to our faces not even a half hour ago when you said you never met her," said Gretchen.

He groaned. "Fine. I lied about that. I'm sorry. But there was no affair. I never touched her. She came to my office."

"She hired you?" asked Josie.

He nodded. "As you know, I have to maintain my client confidentiality."

"Bullshit," Gretchen said. "Cora went missing. If you had information that was relevant to her disappearance, you should have shared it."

Olsen bristled. "I'm sure you know that there's no mandatory disclosure requirement. I don't have to offer up information about a client, no matter what happened to them. Besides, the issue Cora hired me to look into wasn't relevant to her disappearance."

Josie's hips pressed against the edge of the desk as she leaned toward him again. She was finding it difficult not to lunge across it and shake him violently. "You're splitting hairs here, Olsen. What did Cora want?"

"It's not relev—"

Gretchen shook her head, slamming her palm onto the desk much harder this time. "No. Don't even say it. This is a double homicide. We get to decide what's relevant. Now, we can all sit here awkwardly while I call my colleague in Denton and have him prepare a subpoena for those records, or you can tell us what the hell you're hiding behind all this 'no mandatory disclosure' and 'it's not relevant' bullshit."

"Either way, we're serving you with that subpoena," Josie assured him. "So you'll be obligated to hand over those records. Now or later. You choose."

He looked from Josie to Gretchen and back. Whatever he saw in their faces convinced him that he wasn't going to win this fight.

"Fine," he grumbled. "But I do want that subpoena."

"Fine," Josie echoed.

He glanced back and forth between them as if hoping one of them would let him off the hook. When neither of them did, he spoke. "Cora came to me because when she and Tobias were putting their guest list together for the wedding, my name came up. Tobias told her how we knew one another—the whole story about Rachel leaving and me being the one to respond to the call about little Jackson that day. How I used to give the boys a talking-to whenever they needed one until I retired from the force and went private. Then he asked her not to bring up

Rachel when we met. Said he didn't want to taint their wedding day by mentioning her. Anyway, Cora looked me up. She wanted me to confirm what Tobias told her about Rachel leaving, which I did. Then she asked me if I'd ever done more than just take his word for it. She wanted to know if I thought—"

He broke off, looking at the ceiling.

"If you thought what?" Gretchen prompted.

"If I thought she was dead."

"Why would Cora care if Rachel was dead or not?" Josie asked.

He closed his eyes briefly. "This is difficult for me to say. I still don't know what to think. I mean, I know what the evidence shows but..."

"What is it?" Josie pressed.

"Cora thought that Tobias might have killed her."

THIRTY-EIGHT

The air in the office suddenly felt cold. Josie could tell that even uttering the words pained Bruce Olsen. Regardless of the fact that the two men had drifted apart, he truly had held Tobias Lachlan in high regard. Josie thought back to all the photos she'd seen of the man. Round from middle age, thinning hair, always smiling. In most photos, especially with Cora, his happy eyes held a note of disbelief. A silent question: how did I get this lucky? He didn't have the dark, intimidating look of a killer, though in Josie's experience, that meant nothing.

Then there was his reputation. Unimpeachable. Was it so overwhelmingly positive as to reek of fakeness? No, she decided. The people closest to him hadn't painted him in a perfect light. All of them had admitted to his moodiness, to anger at times—not an unreasonable amount—and to him not being faultless. He'd argued with Hollis plenty over the expansion and his partner's meddling in his personal life. He'd argued with Cora over issues within their blended family. Namely, handling Riley and Zane, who'd indulged in underage drinking.

None of that guaranteed that he wasn't a killer, but Josie

could certainly understand Bruce Olsen's dismay at the very idea.

Which begged the question, why had Cora come to *him*? He'd been a lifelong friend to Tobias. Or was that the very reason she'd approached him? Because he'd known Rachel, had been the police officer to respond to the 911 call the day she left? If she was after information about Rachel Wright and her fate, Olsen was probably the best and most reliable source. She could have gone to Hollis but did she trust him not to rat her out to Tobias? Why would she trust Olsen?

There was only one explanation. "Cora hired you so that you couldn't tell Tobias anything the two of you discussed."

She hadn't been saving up for a security deposit on an apartment. Or she hadn't *only* been saving up for that. Josie was certain that Olsen's retainer, even back then, wasn't cheap. The only thing that ensured that Tobias would never find out that Cora was poking around in his past were the strict confidentiality laws between private investigators and their clients.

Olsen nodded. "I think that's why she hired me, yeah. One of the reasons, anyway. She kept asking for reassurance that I wouldn't—and couldn't—talk to Tobias behind her back. She paid in cash so there would be no record. The other reason she hired me was that I knew Rachel and I was there the day she left—or as Cora believed, the day she was killed."

"Why did Cora think Tobias killed Rachel?" Gretchen asked.

Olsen gazed at the photo in front of him for a long moment. Then he turned it on its face and stood up, fidgeting with the lapels of his jacket. "I suppose it doesn't matter now. Not after all this time. Come with me."

They rode the elevator in silence down to the basement of the building. Olsen led them through a maze of brightly lit concrete halls to a door marked Storage 5. From his pocket, he produced a set of keys, fitting one into the lock. The door swung open. Olsen flipped a light switch on the wall, revealing a windowless room with shelves and filing cabinets lined up in orderly rows. Josie and Gretchen followed him as he searched the shelving units until he found an unmarked cardboard box. It was the only unmarked box in the place as far as Josie could tell and it was buried behind two other boxes, deep in the recesses of the room. Dust motes swirled in the air as he swept a hand over its lid.

"There's a table in here somewhere," he muttered.

Moments later, he located it, against a wall, tucked between two tall filing cabinets. From the box, he took an old purse. It was medium-sized and navy blue with a gold zipper and a shoulder-length strap.

"Cora found this." He opened it and began pulling items from inside. "At their house. It was hidden under a floorboard in their bedroom, near Tobias's side of the bed."

Olsen lined up the contents in neat rows. A small pack of tissues, a compact, a tube of mascara, a lipstick, a travel-sized bottle of Tylenol, a hairbrush, a set of keys, a pen, and a maxi pad. The last thing was a woman's wallet, easily the size of his hand. He flipped it open, revealing cash, rows of credit cards tucked inside and an ID window that contained the driver's license of Rachel Wright.

Josie leaned in, studying her picture, recognizing her dark hair, so similar to Jackson's, and her heart-shaped face from the photos Jackson and Riley had on display in their home. Like most people in their driver's license photos, Rachel was unsmiling but striking. The expiration date was March 25, 1999. Josie did the math, based on Jackson's age. She had left him behind in 1998.

Gretchen said, "If she ran off with some guy, why did she leave this behind?"

"Exactly," Olsen said. "After Cora brought this to me, I started looking for Rachel. I called in some favors. Rachel never renewed her license. Never opened another credit card account. Never filed another tax return. There were no addresses listed for her after she ran off. Basically, she ceased to exist the day she left Tobias and Jackson."

"She didn't leave," Gretchen muttered.

"How many times did you meet with Cora?" asked Josie.

"Twice. The first time she gave this to me."

"The second time you gave her the news," Josie said. "That Rachel had vanished without a trace all those years ago."

He nodded.

An image of Cora Stevens behind the wheel of her parked car in the Majesty Motel assaulted Josie. Crying. Unhinged. That's how Dalton had described her laughter. He'd threatened to tell Tobias she was having an affair, and her response had been manic laughter directed at the man who'd left over fifteen fractures on her body.

Gretchen motioned toward the purse and its contents. "She left this with you?"

"Yes. I asked her if she was worried about Tobias realizing it was no longer there. She said it didn't look as though he'd checked it since the day he put it into the floor. The second time she came to me, she was so upset, I'm not sure she meant to leave it. She wanted me to go to the police, but I told her I couldn't. The purse didn't prove anything. Certainly not murder."

"It strongly suggests foul play though," Josie said.

Olsen sighed. "Yeah. There was no convincing Cora that it was anything but murder. I was going to ask her to let me keep looking into the matter, but she took off, crying. I figured I'd let her cool down. She wouldn't give me her number anyway. Said she didn't want Tobias seeing my name come up on her phone. I thought she'd be back but then, a few months later, they were both gone."

"And you were left with this purse," Josie said.

"Like I said, it doesn't prove that Tobias murdered Rachel."

It was damning though, that was for sure. While it was possible that Rachel Wright could have left her life behind without taking her identification and credit cards, the fact that she never renewed her license or did anything that left evidence of her continuing existence again was a massive red flag.

"What about the guy she supposedly ran off with?" asked Gretchen. "Victor? The note she left behind for Tobias telling him that he could raise Jackson?"

Olsen shrugged. "All I had was a first name which I got from a very distraught child. There wasn't much I could do with that. Jackson didn't make for a reliable witness. As far as the note? Tobias showed it to us that day. We had no reason to question it. No reason to look for someone who had voluntarily run off."

"The last time you saw Cora," said Gretchen, "what else did you talk about?"

Slowly, Olsen began putting Rachel Wright's personal items back into the purse. "I told her I'd known Tobias for years and he wouldn't do something like that. There had to be some other explanation for what happened to Rachel. She wouldn't listen. Like I said, she didn't even give me a chance to ask her to extend our contract so I could take a deeper look."

"She probably couldn't afford it," Josie pointed out.

"True," Olsen admitted. "Instead, she asked me about Gabrielle, Zane's mom. If I thought Tobias could have killed her, too, but the autopsy findings were pretty clear on that. Anyway, I suggested that Cora talk everything over with Tobias instead of jumping to conclusions and sneaking behind his back so she could hire me to investigate him for murder."

Gretchen huffed a laugh. "You suggested that this woman 'talk' with her husband about whether or not he killed one or more of his previous partners?"

"That's a pretty fast way to end a relationship," Josie mused.

Maybe even get yourself killed.

Olsen's face flushed slightly. "It sounds insensitive when you say it like that but I'm telling you, I knew Tobias. He wouldn't kill anyone, especially not a woman he loved."

"You never mentioned any of this to Detective Fanning," said Josie. "Why?"

"It wasn't relevant. Still isn't. First of all, Tobias wasn't a killer and if this got out—that his fiancée was having him investigated for murder only days before they disappeared—all it would do is ruin his reputation. Needlessly. If they were found alive and there was some logical explanation as to what happened to them, then Tobias would know that I betrayed him and that Cora did, too. I didn't want that. If they weren't found alive, I didn't want to ruin his kids' memory of him. It was the last thing they needed. They were already a mess. Second of all, Cora and Tobias vanished together. If it had just been her and he was swanning around playing the bereaved fiancé, then I might have approached Fanning, but they were both gone and they stayed gone. Whatever happened to them wasn't Tobias's doing or else he'd still be here."

Josie couldn't appreciate his logic, especially when it was steeped in his obvious and long-standing—possibly blinding—loyalty to Tobias, but they needed to move things forward.

"The first time Cora came to you, she said she'd found this in a hidden spot," she said. "Did she say if she found anything else?"

"No. She never said."

THIRTY-NINE

"I'm starting to think the skeleton key doesn't mean anything at all," Josie said.

Noah stuffed a bag of popcorn into the microwave and punched a few buttons until it whirred to life. "Maybe it was with Rachel Wright's purse. In a secret hiding place. Regardless, when you hide something under the floorboards, it means something. Something bad."

It had been twenty-four hours since the visit to Bruce Olsen's office. In that time, Josie had told off her sister, printed out a list of therapists and left it on Noah's pillow, scheduled the fitting for her dress, and made peace with the vow renewal ceremony going forward.

What she hadn't done was make any progress on the Lachlan/Stevens case. Gretchen had driven to Brighton Springs to execute a search warrant on the Lachlan house so she could get a look at Tobias's secret hiding spot. If there had ever been anything else under those floorboards other than what Cora found, it was long gone. Another dead end.

"Definitely something bad. We can't match that key to anything. Let's say she also found it in the floorboards." Josie fished through one of the cabinets over the sink looking for their big plastic bowls. "I don't think she got it from Rachel's purse. It would make no sense to remove it before going to Olsen. So why would Tobias be hiding just a key? A random key all on its own?"

Noah leaned his hip against the counter and folded his arms over his chest. Behind him, muffled pops came from the microwave. "Why did he keep Rachel's purse for twenty years? If he killed her but managed to convince everyone in their lives —including her own parents and the police—that she'd run off with another man, why keep it?"

Josie found a set of three large bowls in three different colors and put them on the kitchen table. "It was a trophy."

Noah nodded.

There was a calculated, petty anger in that. A lack of remorse. It was a private sort of revenge, besides the killing, of course. That could have happened in the heat of an argument. Maybe Rachel had tried to leave him just as Cora had intended to do.

"Which would make the key a trophy of some kind." She had already theorized that the key was symbolic rather than practical. "I get what you're saying but it doesn't help get us closer to whoever killed Cora and Tobias. Hell, the idea that Tobias was a murderer doesn't even help us get there. In a sense, Olsen's argument that it's irrelevant holds weight."

Noah opened his mouth to speak but clamped it shut when Wren came into the kitchen. She wore a Phoebe Bridgers T-shirt. Her cheeks were rosy and there was a brightness in her eyes that Josie longed to see more often. Trout trailed behind her.

"Are you guys coming?" she asked. "We're ready to start. One of you can be the first judge."

"We" was Wren, Erica, and Josie's parents, Shannon and Christian. They'd decided to play some party game that

Shannon picked up at a bookstore. As Josie understood from the lively discussion a half hour ago, the game provided cards with various types of odd photos. In each round, one photo was presented to the players. Each player had to write their own caption and submit it anonymously to the judge who would then decide which one was the funniest. After a number of rounds, whoever racked up the most winning captions was the champion.

Shannon had been very proud of herself when Wren and Erica enthusiastically snatched the box from her hands before she'd even made it through the front door. Then she'd taken Josie and Noah aside and ordered them to play. It would be fun, she had said. A way to engage Wren in a group setting. Low-pressure. Show her that they could be cool. Whatever the hell that meant.

From the living room, Shannon called, "We need a judge with a good sense of humor!"

Noah arched a brow. "That implies one or both of us doesn't have a good sense of humor."

The microwave beeped three times in succession. Trout's nose lifted and he sniffed the air, now fragrant with the smell of butter and salt. Wren practically skipped past them and yanked open the door. She pinched the edge of the bag between a thumb and forefinger and carried it over to the table. Trout was at her heels, craning his neck to try to see what she was doing.

"You guys are pretty serious," Wren said, prying the top of the bag apart. "Like, all the time."

Josie and Noah exchanged a puzzled glance. Were they? Didn't they have their light moments? They joked all the time with one another. Although now that she thought about it, those jokes usually centered around sexual innuendo, which wasn't something they engaged in when other people were around. Josie had never considered their fun quotient. They *were* fun, weren't they? Harris thought so. Except that he was eight.

"We're going to need more popcorn than this," Wren added, dumping the popcorn into one of the bowls. "No offense, Josie, but your dad could finish this in a minute."

"So could Erica," Noah muttered, sticking another bag into the microwave. "Two more bowls coming up. We'll be right in."

Wren hugged the bowl to her chest and without warning, flashed them a dazzling smile. Then she was gone, their dog trotting after her.

"Holy shit," Josie breathed. "Did you see that?"

"I think she forgot that we were, well, us," Noah said, but a tiny smile played at the corners of his mouth.

"Whatever," Josie said. "I'm taking the win."

She sure as shit wasn't getting any wins at work. With his usual acuity, Noah returned to their earlier conversation. "Fanning never looked into what happened to Rachel Wright?"

"Why would he?" Josie said. "It had been twenty years since she supposedly left. It probably never occurred to him to track down a woman who hadn't had contact with Tobias or his son for two decades."

"Fair," Noah said. "Didn't Olsen say that Cora thought Tobias might have also killed his wife? What was her name?"

"Gabrielle. Zane's mom," Josie said, picturing the young woman with the nose ring in the photos from the upstairs hallway in the Lachlan home, looking impossibly young—more like a college student than a mother and stepmother.

Laughter came from the living room. In the microwave, the popcorn bag slowly expanded.

"That's one missing fiancée—Rachel." Noah grabbed two bottles of water from the fridge. "And one dead wife—Gabrielle. Fanning didn't think that bore scrutiny?"

"I don't think it ever occurred to him." Josie took the water he handed her. "First of all, he knew Tobias personally. Fanning was friends with his dad. There's an inherent bias there whether Fanning would admit it or not."

"Or the possibility that Fanning's not as clean as he appears."

Josie took a long sip of her water. "True. Though I spoke with Meredith again at Brighton Springs PD and she was firm that Fanning is clean. Second, at the time that Tobias and Cora vanished—were killed—Rachel had been gone for twenty years. Gabrielle Lachlan had been dead for eleven years. Third, Gabrielle died of a cardiac arrest. Olsen said the autopsy confirmed it."

In light of everything they knew now, Tobias's unlucky romantic history begged to be investigated. Josie even had her doubts about the legitimacy of Gabrielle Lachlan's autopsy report. She'd already requested a copy from Meredith. But she was certain that seven years ago, in the search for Tobias and Cora, it had never entered John Fanning's mind to track down a woman who had left Tobias twenty years earlier or to question whether it was really cardiac arrest that had killed his wife eleven years ago.

From the living room, Josie heard the low-pitched honk of the squeaker inside Trout's hedgehog, then him barking playfully, and finally, Wren cooing over him.

"Okay, so Fanning had no reason to see the pattern, especially since Olsen withheld information," Noah said. "But now *we* know that Rachel probably didn't leave at all. Don't you think Tobias's secrets are relevant to the murder case?"

The microwave beeped again. As Noah deposited the second bag of popcorn into a bowl, Josie said, "Yeah, especially since we have nothing else to go on. I'm sure he had other secrets that no one uncovered. Maybe he'd done something more recent to piss someone off. If he killed Rachel, what else did he get up to in the twenty years before his own murder? He'd gotten away with it—maybe he got bold and did something else to set off the wrong person. What if the two of them—he and Cora—weren't the target?"

"You mean what if the killers were only after Tobias and Cora just happened to be there? Then why try to pull it off while they were together? Why not wait to get him alone?"

"Maybe they couldn't. Maybe they didn't want to be spotted lurking around him in advance. Maybe they saw an opportunity and took it, and it was just bad timing for Cora."

Noah put the last bag into the microwave. "I still think this is a murder-for-hire scheme and that Tobias was the target. Who did Cora Stevens piss off besides her ex-husband?"

"Probably just Tobias," Josie said. "Especially if he had any notion that she wanted to leave him or that she'd found his secret hiding spot. She just happened to be in the wrong place at the wrong time."

FORTY

With Gretchen in tow, Josie pushed her way through the doors to the morgue, feeling all the residual joy from the evening before drain away. Her face still hurt from laughing. Shannon's picture game had been a smashing success. By the time Josie slipped into bed next to Noah, she was high on having watched Wren laugh and smile so easily and so many times. For the first time in months, hope bubbled from somewhere deep inside her. As she spied the single occupied autopsy table, guilt smothered that burgeoning feeling of happiness. Those wonderful H feelings didn't belong here.

A sheet covered Riley Stevens' body up to her shoulders. Her strawberry-blonde hair was lank, as though death had robbed it of its sheen. A stab of sorrow pierced Josie's heart. What would Riley's life have been like if Cora hadn't been killed? If seven long years of not knowing hadn't passed, compounding her stress and sense of loss? If she'd just been a normal, carefree twenty-three-year-old? If her mother had still been in her life, would she have turned to alcohol so readily? The never-knows were endless. Wherever there was loss, they were right beside it, driving the living to the brink of insanity.

Across the room, Gretchen knocked on the door to Anya's office, calling for her. It had been three days since Riley's death. The number of reporters stationed all over the city—at Riley's home, at Hollis's office, and at the police station—had tripled. At this point, Josie was beginning to associate the outdoors with questions being shouted at her. The Mayor had made an appearance at the stationhouse just yesterday, passive-aggressively criticizing their work ethic and their intelligence and putting the Chief in such a foul mood that even Turner chose not to provoke him.

Anya sailed into the examination room, her silver-blonde hair loose around her shoulders and a frown on her face. "Sorry. I was doing some research. Had to call a colleague of mine in Philadelphia."

Gretchen said, "In connection with Riley Stevens?"

"Yes." Anya stopped near the table, glancing at Riley's face. She put her hands on her hips and blew out a breath. "God, I hate it when they're this young."

"So do we," Josie said.

"Let's get to it then." All business now, Anya slowly folded the sheet down, exposing Riley's torso, stopping just below her hip bones. "No signs of sexual assault. On autopsy there was evidence of cerebral edema—an excess of fluid in the brain tissue. However, I didn't find any areas that suggested cerebral infarcts which are basically showing tissue death, which I'd expect to see if she'd had a stroke. No evidence of an infection, traumatic brain injury. No tumors. She also had pulmonary edema."

"Fluid in her lungs," said Gretchen.

"Yes," Anya replied. "But what I didn't see was visible damage to the heart, although the lab will do a host of histological tests."

"That's when they look at tissue samples under the microscope, right?" Josie asked.

"Right. But like I said, there were no abnormalities of the pericardium, blockages in the vessels, or damage to the heart muscle. She may have had a cardiac arrest, which is different from a heart attack. Cardiac arrest occurs when there's a disruption in the heart's electrical system. It's usually the result of an arrythmia. Problems with the heart's conduction system are not something that would be visible during an autopsy. There is genetic testing that can be done for inherited cardiac conditions, but those take time."

"What about alcohol poisoning?" Josie asked.

"There were no findings consistent with that. In terms of her alcohol consumption on the day she died, we have to wait for toxicology results, which as you know, can take at least six weeks, sometimes longer. Do keep in mind though that postmortem blood alcohol concentration can be very unreliable. The rest of my findings on autopsy were unremarkable."

Gretchen sighed. "What are we dealing with here? I know you can't give a complete picture without toxicology, but do you have some initial thoughts?"

One of Anya's brows shot up. "Do I ever. I was extremely suspicious given the fact that her death came so soon after her mother and Tobias Lachlan's bodies were found, the brutality of those murders, and the lengths their killer went to to ensure they were never found at all. The final red flag was the two injection sites on her left hip I found on external exam."

Josie felt a jolt through her system like she'd just mainlined three shots of espresso. Beside her, she sensed Gretchen's body go rigid.

Neither of them spoke, instead watching with bated breath as Anya moved the sheet down a few inches more. Riley had been curvy, her hips full. Anya pointed to the fleshiest part of her left hip, just below a thick set of sutures from the autopsy. Two almost imperceptible pink dots were visible, about an inch apart from each other. They looked very different from the punctures on Riley's palm.

"Subcutaneous injections," Anya said. "Fresh, by the looks of them. Her husband said she didn't have any medical conditions. Toxicology takes weeks, months sometimes. I was reviewing what substances she could have been injected with subcutaneously. There are a lot. One of them I was able to do some initial testing for here, using immunohistochemistry staining."

"Immuno-what?" Gretchen said.

"Immunohistochemistry. It's a way to detect antigens in a tissue sample." Anya pointed to the sutures near the injection marks. "Using samples of adipose tissue—body fat—from various levels beneath the wound sites to see antigens."

"Which are?" Josie asked.

"Any substance that sets off an immune response in your body. Basically, they're possibly harmful or foreign and your immune system kicks in, creating antibodies to fight them. With immunohistochemistry, we can stain the sample using antibodies. They will only bind to very specific antigens which tell us what substance started the reaction. That's a very, very simplified explanation."

Gretchen put up a palm. "That's good enough for us."

Anya smiled. "Then I won't bore you with any more details. Like I said, I had to call a friend of mine in Philadelphia to make sure I was doing it correctly. The process takes about twenty-four hours and it will have to be repeated by the state lab for confirmation."

Moving away from the table, she waved them over to the long stainless-steel countertop at the back of the room. A slide had been preloaded onto a small, blocky white microscope. "Have a look."

Josie went first. All she could see was a film of white and a color that straddled the line between bright pink and light purple. Darker pinpricks of that same indefinable color dotted the field of vision. Then there was a blotch that looked brownish-yellow.

Straightening, Josie let Gretchen have a look. "I'm guessing the ugly splotch that doesn't match anything else is the issue? The antigen?"

Anya laughed. "Yes. Those brownish-yellow granules that you see in the cytoplasm? They're positive cells."

"Positive for what?" asked Gretchen.

"Insulin."

Josie and Gretchen stared at her. "Insulin," Gretchen repeated slowly.

"Given Riley's history of having no significant medical conditions or issues, together with the circumstances surrounding her death, the findings of cerebral and pulmonary edema and the injection sites, I decided to check. It can also be confirmed via toxicology, but this was the fastest way for me to figure out if my hunch was correct."

"That she was poisoned with insulin?" Josie felt that strange mix of adrenaline and dread spreading through her system like a bad drug.

"I believe so," Anya replied. "Although I cannot make anything official until I've got all the lab results. Everything I've just told you is consistent with that possibility though. Riley Stevens was injected with insulin twice before her death. In high doses in someone who isn't insulin-dependent, it can cause severe hypoglycemia. Her blood glucose levels would have dropped to dangerous levels. She may have experienced confusion, disorientation, nausea, slurred speech, blurred vision, loss of consciousness. There are studies that have shown that severe hypoglycemia can cause cerebral and pulmonary edema, even arrythmias and sudden death. There are a lot of variables that come into play since we don't know what type of insulin or the dosage. Two injections may or may not have been enough to kill her but combined with a high level of alcohol, it most certainly could have been fatal."

"If you're right, that means the manner of death is homicide," Josie said.

"As I said, the lab will need to confirm my findings, but I can't think of any scenario in which Riley Stevens would inject herself with insulin twice. Especially in her hip. Most diabetics give themselves injections into the abdomen, buttocks, thighs, or sometimes upper arms. The fatty tissue allows for slow and consistent absorption of the insulin."

Gretchen said, "Surely she wouldn't have injected herself as a way to take her own life."

"I can't comment on her mental state," Anya said. "The question for you two is how someone else would inject her without her knowing about it or trying to fight it off."

"She might have been drunk," Josie pointed out. "Maybe she was just too out of it to notice or care. Anya, if someone had injected her with a fatal or near-fatal level of insulin, how long would it have taken for her to die?"

"Without knowing the specific concentration of the insulin or her blood alcohol concentration, it's difficult to tell. It could have been hours or minutes."

"Minutes," Josie murmured.

Had someone joined her at the boat ramp? Denton PD had tracked the phones and vehicle infotainment centers—which gave GPS coordinates—of Hollis, Jackson, and Zane. None of them had been near the boat ramp that morning. In fact, the data from their phones and cars matched their statements. The most logical explanation was that Riley was injected at Hollis's house before she left for the boat ramp. Perhaps she hadn't started drinking until she got there and the alcohol, combined with the insulin, tipped her over the edge.

"Well, we know where the insulin came from," Gretchen said. "Hollis."

Josie nodded. "The first time we met Hollis, his sister told him he needed to keep his blood sugar under control or he wouldn't be eligible for a pump."

Anya leaned against the counter, folding her arms across her chest. "An insulin pump. He may be type 1, then, and if he doesn't have a pump, he's using insulin pens."

They'd need a warrant for Hollis's home. Possibly the At Your Disposal office. Whichever pharmacy he used to get his insulin pens. He'd have to be brought in for a formal interview. So would Jackson and Zane.

All three of them had had access to insulin and the opportunity to use it.

FORTY-ONE

Josie sighed and pressed the heels of her hands into her eyes. Exhaustion made them burn. She felt like someone had thrown sand in her face. The darkness of the CCTV room should have helped but the sense of defeat looming over her was excruciating. It magnified every irritation, big or small. Tension knotted at the base of her skull, tightening with the knowledge that they were no closer to solving Riley's murder or those of Cora and Tobias. They had theories. Solid, logical theories, but no evidence. No proof.

She needed proof.

This is what Detective John Fanning must have felt like for over half a decade. Josie watched the CCTV screen as Gretchen finished up questioning Hollis Merritt. He had been the last to sit for a formal interview. The day had started with Zane, then Jackson. Hollis was the insulin-dependent diabetic but both Zane and Jackson had also had access to his insulin pens and the needles that went with them. While Josie couldn't figure out why either brother might want to kill Riley, she certainly couldn't rule them out. If there was one irrefutable fact about the blended Lachlan/Stevens family, it was that there was no end to the secrets among them.

She hadn't really expected to get anything earth-shattering by questioning them today, like a confession, but it was important to get written statements from each of them. It locked them into their stories. Later, they'd be questioned again, their second interviews scrutinized for inconsistencies.

It had been over twenty-four hours since she and Gretchen spoke with Anya about Riley's autopsy findings. They'd gotten a warrant for Hollis's home and his office soon thereafter. While Josie and some of the patrol officers executed the search warrant at Hollis's home, Gretchen took another team to his office.

Josie groaned as she checked the time. She still had a few hours to go and there was no way in hell she was getting through them without copious amounts of coffee.

She was wondering how lazy it would be to DoorDash two blonde lattes from Komorrah's when the door swished open and Noah appeared. She smiled, despite the fatigue wearing her down.

"Hey." He took a seat beside her and slid a paper Komorrah's cup over to her.

Josie's hand seized on it. She popped the lid off and inhaled the scent of her favorite latte. "I didn't think I could love you more, but I do."

Noah chuckled. "Are you talking to me or that latte?"

"Both?"

"I'll take it," he said with a grin before turning his attention to the CCTV. "Anything?"

"Nope." She slugged down half of her drink, ignoring the way it burned her tongue, desperate for the caffeine to hit.

"What do they think happened to Riley?" he asked.

"None of them believe it's homicide. Zane and Hollis think she must have injected herself and driven to the boat ramp to die where her mom died. Jackson got extremely agitated when

Gretchen made that suggestion. He said either the medical examiner got it wrong or someone else did it to her. Someone we haven't caught yet. He's definitely in denial."

The door opened again, and Turner sauntered into the room. Just what she needed. She waited for some kind of snarky greeting but instead, he just stood behind them, his fingers drumming against his thigh as they watched Hollis read over his official statement.

"No confession then, huh?" Turner said. "Palmer must be slipping."

"Shut your mouth," Josie snapped.

He chuckled. She could feel the heat from his body at her back. Standing too close, as always. "So irritable, Quinn. Guess I would be too if I was sitting here watching a killer get away with another homicide. Look at this guy. He should give classes on how to get away with murder. What is this? His third one? Hell, there are probably more than that we don't know about. He left nothing behind. Not one damn thing. If you want to nail him, you're gonna need either a confession or an eyewitness."

Groaning, Josie dug the heels of her palms into her eyes again. "Don't remind me."

"Well, we know he didn't do it alone," Noah said.

"Good luck finding the guys he paid to take out Tobias," Turner said. "They might not even be alive. What's a couple more bodies to add on his tab? So, Quinn, what are you thinking? Why'd he do it?"

Honestly, Josie was tired of thinking about this case because so far, it hadn't gone anywhere. They just couldn't find the one thread that would unravel it all. She drank the rest of her latte so quickly, some of it dribbled down her chin. Swiping at it with her fingers, she asked, "Why do you think he did it?"

Turner's finger-tapping paused. "Is this your polite way of telling me that you're not going to do my thinking for me?"

Shifting in her chair, she glared up at him. "Why would I

bother being polite to you? Also, you're standing too close. Again."

A grin spread across Turner's face, as though they were sharing some sort of inside joke. He took a small step backward. Josie really didn't have the energy or the patience for this. Noah must have sensed her growing frustration because he said, "Let's hear it, Turner. Why do you think Hollis killed Tobias and Cora?"

Josie turned back toward the screen where Hollis was flipping another page in his statement.

Turner's finger-tapping resumed at an increased tempo. "I don't think he meant to kill Cora. I think he wanted her for himself but the asshats he hired to do the job screwed it all up. Then he was so racked with guilt that he stepped in to take care of their kids. From everything Quinn and Palmer have said, this guy is closer to them than any other person in their lives. So close that somehow Riley Stevens figured out that he was behind the murder-for-hire plot."

Noah pushed his chair out slightly so he could turn and look up at Turner. "Okay. How did she figure it out after all this time?"

"Who the hell knows?" Turner said. "But she was staying at his house for a couple of days. She must have seen something or overheard something that tipped her off. Or he slipped up somehow. Then he had to kill her so she didn't rat him out. Maybe he encouraged her to have a drink while he explained that whatever she saw or heard or found wasn't what she thought it was."

"At seven in the morning?" Josie said.

"Come on, Quinn. Don't tell me that you'd be above drinking at seven in the morning if you just buried your mom, inadvertently launched a viral video from her funeral, and then found out that the man who's been looking after you and your husband for the last seven years is a murderer."

"I concede," Josie sighed. "I would have been drunk by six."

"Well, damn," Turner said. "We agreed on something."

"Don't let it go to your head," she muttered.

Beneath the table, Noah gently squeezed Josie's thigh and good God, even that simple touch made some of her aggravation melt away.

"Anyway," Turner continued. "Hollis spun a bunch of lies while he got her good and drunk, and injected her, thinking she'd die right in the house, and it would look like she just had a heart attack or something. Instead, she took off to the boat ramp. It was dumb luck she didn't crash before she got there."

"If Riley found out that Hollis killed Tobias and her mother," Noah said, "she definitely would have told Zane and Jackson. I don't think she would have confronted Hollis on her own."

"Unless she didn't know what to do with that information right away," Turner argued. "We're talking about the guy who stepped in to be a parent to all three of them. This guy's been more of a dad to Riley than her own piece-of-shit sperm donor, and Tobias, who she only knew for a couple of years. Maybe she wanted to give him a chance to explain himself before she dropped that bomb on the other two kids. Maybe she needed to process whatever lies he told her privately before doing anything, so she went to the boat ramp to think."

Everything Turner said made sense, but hell if Josie was going to tell him that.

"I'm right," he went on. "Hollis is behind all of this, and he killed this kid to shut her up. I mean if you're only looking at Riley's murder, there were three people in the house with her. Hollis, her stepbrother, and her husband. Why would her stepbrother or husband kill her?"

Josie had been turning the same question over in her head for hours. There had been a love triangle among the three of them, though Zane's affection had been unrequited. Perhaps

Riley's death had nothing to do with Cora and Tobias and everything to do with the rivalry between the brothers. Had Zane gotten tired of being on the sidelines? Tired of watching Jackson with the girl he'd been in love with since high school? While they stayed up to talk and watch Netflix, had he made advances on Riley only to be rebuffed and decided to kill her?

Noah turned his attention back to Josie. "What did the searches of the house and office turn up?"

"Insulin pens and their needles," she said flatly. "Used and unused. Hummel is trying to pull prints from the used ones and then he'll send them to the lab to see if DNA can be pulled from the needles, but if we're trying to prove that Hollis killed Riley, that's not going to help. Even if a couple of the needles turn up with Riley's DNA on them, that won't prove Hollis's guilt. Of course his prints and DNA would be on the pens. He's a type 1 diabetic and they belonged to him."

In the interview room, Hollis finally reached the last page of his statement. Gretchen handed him a pen to sign it.

"This guy must have thought he was so smart," Turner said. "If it wasn't for the doc being so thorough and finding those injection marks, the kid's death would have been classified as a cardiac arrest or stroke or something, and no one would be the wiser."

That had been obvious from the start. It would have been one more secret in the saga of Tobias Lachlan, Cora Stevens and now Riley. Secrets upon secrets upon secrets. Zane had kept his crush on Riley from her. From everyone but Jackson, it seemed. Hollis had kept knowledge that Cora was planning to leave Tobias secret. Bruce Olsen hadn't told a soul about Cora hiring him or about Rachel Wright's purse.

Josie flashed back to the discussion she and Noah had had about Tobias's secrets. She checked her phone again, gratified to see that she'd missed a message from Meredith Dorton thirteen minutes ago.

I emailed you the report you wanted. Let me know if there's anything else.

She patted Noah's hand before standing up. Turner stumbled backward as she pushed the chair back hard enough that it nearly hit him. "Watch it, Quinn. Where's the fire?"

Tossing her empty cup into the trash bin, she said, "I got an email."

FORTY-TWO

Leaving the two of them in the CCTV room, Josie went to her desk where she opened Meredith's email and downloaded the attached file. Gabrielle Lachlan's autopsy appeared on her computer screen. She read it and then read it again, both satisfied and sickened that her instincts had been correct. The pathologist who had performed the autopsy had noted four bug bites along the top of Gabrielle's right thigh. Josie found the images and zoomed in. The bug bites looked exactly like the injection marks on Riley Stevens' hip. There were no signs of pulmonary or cerebral edema or anything else unusual but if she'd died within minutes, the autopsy results would have been unremarkable. The official cause of death was cardiac arrest.

Gabrielle Lachlan's toxicology report had come back clean. There was no mention of insulin, but autopsy toxicology didn't routinely test for insulin. The medical examiner would have had to specifically request it. Would have needed a compelling reason to request such a test. Gabrielle had been perfectly healthy at the time of her death. Why would anyone suspect that she'd been poisoned with insulin?

Why had Cora suspected that Tobias had killed Gabrielle?

Was it paranoia on her part? Or something else? She'd found Tobias's hiding spot and, assuming the key had been there as well as the purse, his trophies. If the purse was related to Rachel's demise, did that mean the key was related to Gabrielle's? Had Cora figured out how?

Did it even matter?

"Your wheels are turning."

Turner startled her. She hadn't heard him come into the great room. She thought he'd go home once he left the CCTV room.

"Where the hell did you come from?"

He perched his large frame on the edge of her desk and smirked. "Quinn, you really don't know this one? When a man and a woman love each other—"

"Shut up." She groaned. "You know what I mean."

"I work here."

She narrowed her eyes at him. "Well, I'm busy, so maybe you should catch up on your reports."

Digging into the pocket of his suit jacket, he came up with a can of his favorite energy drink and snapped it open. "You're always so concerned about my work habits. Maybe I'm concerned about yours. The bodies are piling up around here and you and Palmer don't seem like you're any closer to finding what you need to charge Hollis 'The Serial Killer' Merritt with homicide."

Anger surged through her veins. "You think you can do a better job?"

He gulped down some of his drink and then used the back of his hand to wipe his upper lip. "Of course I can do a better job. Jeez, Quinn, it's like you don't know me at all."

She didn't know him at all. For the first time, his arrogant comment didn't stoke her anger further. More and more she was convinced that his whole irritating, douchebag persona was just that—a persona. A show he put on. It was very effective in keeping people from wanting to know anything about him.

"Do you have kids?" she blurted out before she could stop herself.

Something flashed in his eyes, there and gone in an instant, and she couldn't read it because he kept too much of himself to himself. He took a slow sip of his drink, watching her over the rim of the can.

"Do you think I have kids?"

"For God's sake, Turner. It's a simple question."

"Trouble at home?" More deflecting. "With your new kid?"

"No, I—" She threw her hands in the air and let them land on her lap. Why the hell was she asking? Why did she care?

He smiled. The kind that always made her want to throat-punch him. "Quinn, are you *interested* in me? I mean, I know I'm irresistible, but I don't think the LT would appreciate you flirting with me."

"You know damn well that's not what's happening here. You know what?" She jammed a hand into her pocket and pulled out a dollar bill, holding it out to him. "Get off my desk, douchebag. I have work to do."

His grin widened. Plucking the dollar from her hand, he leaned across her desk to where his abutted hers and deposited it into his jar. "Come on, Quinn. Tell me what's got your wheels turning. What's the LT always say? Let's talk this out."

Was there even any point in talking it out?

Did she have anything better to do?

"Fine," she huffed. "I know what we need is something that we can nail Hollis with, but I keep coming back to the fact that right before Tobias and Cora were killed, Cora was convinced that Tobias was a murderer. In fact, I think Gabrielle was killed in the same way as Riley. But it doesn't matter, does it?"

He drummed his fingers against his now empty can. "It matters. That's a pattern and since Tobias is dead, the common denominator is Hollis. He cozied up to all of Tobias's women. Maybe even after the first two chose Tobias over him, he made a move on them and they rejected him again. They probably planned to tell Tobias what a creep he was, so he killed them both. Then came Cora. He had her confiding in him. Crying on his shoulder. But he made the mistake twice before of giving the woman he was after a choice between him and Tobias so this time, he wanted to make sure there was no contest. Maybe he was the one who put the idea in Cora's head that Tobias was a killer. Planted Rachel's purse. Got Cora worked up, wanting to leave. Then, like I said, he paid a couple of guys to take care of Tobias so he could swoop in and have her to himself, except shit went sideways and they killed Cora, too."

All of the pieces fit so perfectly, even if the larger puzzle made Hollis far more calculating and dangerous than Josie initially thought. Even if her gut was still telling her that she was missing something.

That damn skeleton key.

"We've still got no proof," Josie reminded him. "Like you said, we need a confession or a witness if we want to nail him. Or some kind of leverage that will get him to confess."

Apparently bored with the conversation, Turner took his phone out of his pocket and started scrolling. "True. But Quinn, somebody knows something. They always do. Even if they don't know that they know something. Figure out who it is and get them to talk. That's how you nail Hollis."

She watched him walk to his desk and plop into his chair, eyes never leaving his phone. He was right again. It was maddening. Crimes weren't committed in a vacuum but Hollis wasn't the only common denominator.

FORTY-THREE

There were still reporters camped outside the Denton location of At Your Disposal. All day, cloying humidity had been building. If the gray clouds rolling in overhead were any indication, the glorious streak of sunny days Denton had been enjoying was about to be snapped. Josie and Gretchen were bombarded by questions as they walked into the building. They ignored all of them. Ellyn frowned as they approached her desk. As Hollis's sister, she likely didn't appreciate the renewed police scrutiny of her brother.

"Mr. Merritt's not here," she said curtly.

"We're looking for Jackson Wright," Gretchen told her.

"Oh, well, I guess you can... he's out back."

"Thank you." Josie gave Ellyn a professional smile that was not returned.

They found Jackson near the very back of the lot in front of one of the bays of the old car dealership's service building. Most of the garage area was filled with massive trash compactors but this area was used for storage of what looked like valuable antiques. Jackson had parked sideways across the threshold of the bay. He stood in the bed of his pickup truck among what looked like the items that had been in his and Riley's living room the day that Josie and Gretchen were there, as well as a few things Josie hadn't seen before. A huge, blocky red Coca-Cola vending machine that looked like it had been new in the 1950s, a rosewood grandfather clock with a silver face and an intricate inlay design, and a nautical telescope wrapped in plastic.

Utility gloves covered Jackson's large hands. He wore a company hat, the brim turned backward. Dark stubble peppered his face. His eyes were glassy, almost vacant. Grief and exhaustion. Josie recognized it well. Anya had told them that he'd called a half-dozen times wanting to know when Riley's body would be released so they could plan the funeral.

Another funeral.

"If you've come to accuse Hol of more shit, he's not here," he said without looking at them.

"We'd like to talk to you," Josie said, trying not to react to the heavy odor of rotting garbage wafting over from the compactors.

Jackson lifted a rolled carpet and tossed it onto the ground next to the truck. "Already talked to you."

"Let's talk some more," Gretchen said in a tone that didn't invite argument.

He shook his head and pushed a red industrial bar stool toward the edge of the truck bed. "I'm not stupid. I know how this works. Watched Fanning do it to Hol for seven years. You're here to ask the same questions again to see if I'll slip up and say something different. When I don't, you'll come back next week or maybe the week after. Let me save you some trouble. I never witnessed Hollis committing any crimes. He didn't kill my wife. Now, are we done here?"

A cool breeze sliced through the thick warm air they'd endured all morning, portending rain and lifting the hair at Josie's neck. "We're not here to talk about Riley."

He ignored them, pushing a second stool toward the edge, then a third.

Gretchen forged ahead. "What do you remember about the day your mother left?"

Jackson had one hand on the side of the truck bed, knees bent to jump down from the tailgate. He froze. Josie counted off the beats of stillness. From other parts of the lot came the sounds of dumpsters being lowered unceremoniously to the concrete with cacophonous bangs. Employees shouting instructions at one another. Truck engines purring like cats with bronchitis. Josie swore she heard the distant rumble of thunder. Slowly, Jackson turned his head, studying Gretchen, then Josie with a wary expression. "What?"

"Your mother," Josie said. "Rachel. What do you remember about the day she left?"

He sprang back into motion, hopping down from the truck and unloading the stools, placing them one by one just inside the garage bay. "Why are you asking me about my mother?"

"We understand that there is some uncertainty about what happened to her," Josie said. "You were home that day. We'd like to know what you remember."

Back in the truck bed, he picked up a small table wrapped in plastic and positioned it near the tailgate. "I was three."

"So you don't remember anything?" Gretchen asked.

"It was a long time ago. I never... The things I remember are just flashes. I'm not even sure if they're real memories or if my mind just filled them in after hearing stories about it my whole life."

"What kinds of flashes?"

He muscled a church pew from the back of the truck bed to where the plastic-wrapped table sat. "Shit. I don't know. Her face. Being hungry. Being upset. Scared. You happy now?"

"No," Josie said. "Because it sounds like you've never been able to get a break from tragedy."

He jumped down again, lifting the table out of the truck bed and placing it next to the stools. A gust of cool air, stronger than the last, batted at them. "You think it's tragic that my mom abandoned me? It's fucked up, is what it is."

"Did she abandon you?" Josie asked. "Is that what you believe?"

"That's what happened."

"You have a lot of photos of your mom on display in your home, considering that," Josie pointed out.

"Yeah, well, what few memories I have of her are happy ones even if they're only fragments, too. Riley thought I should hold onto those. She said I might find my way to forgiveness if I saw those happy memories every day." He swiped at a tear trapped in his eyelashes. "Is this really necessary? 'Cause I've got shit to do."

Gretchen watched him carefully. "Is there a man named Victor in any of your flashes?"

His hands stilled on the end of the church pew. "I don't remember a guy. That's what everyone told me. That I said she went with some guy named Victor, but I don't remember any guy. Never have. But again, I was three."

"Do you remember Hollis being there?" Josie asked.

"What?" He shot them a look that conveyed incredulity and disgust in equal measure. "God, you people are relentless. No. I don't remember Hollis being there."

"How about Tobias?"

He dropped his chin to his chest and took a deep breath. "If my dad had been there, I wouldn't remember feeling hungry and scared."

It was hard to distinguish all the different noises produced on the junk removal lot from the sound of thunder, but Josie was positive she'd heard it this time. "That doesn't answer the question."

Jackson slid the church pew toward him and hefted it up,

placing it with the other items just inside the bay. "No, I don't remember my dad being there. I told you. I remember my mom's face. Feeling hungry and scared. That's it. Are we done here?"

"What do you remember about the day Zane's mom died?"

Avoiding their gazes, he leaned into the truck bed and pulled a cardboard box toward him. "Are we going to do this for every person I've ever known who died? Don't know if you noticed, but rain's coming. I want to get this shit inside."

"Let's just stick with Gabrielle for now," Josie said. "You were twelve years old when she passed away. We've looked at the reports. You and Zane were there when your dad got home and found her unresponsive in the kitchen. Do you remember that?"

He grabbed another box. "I remember that she picked us up from school. When we got home, we had a snack and then Zane wanted to play out back but he was only five so she told me to go with him. He had a T-ball set. We whacked balls around the yard."

"When you heard her talking with someone, did you go back to the house to check it out?" Gretchen asked.

"No, I—" He stilled again. "There is no point in bringing this shit up, you know. No point. It's done. Nothing is going to bring her back. Nothing will bring any of them back."

"Jackson," Josie said. "We reviewed Gabrielle's autopsy report. There were some findings that were overlooked back then that cast doubt on the medical examiner's conclusion that she died of cardiac arrest."

Turning toward them, he fisted his hands at his sides. "What are you saying?"

Another cold gust of air slapped them. Josie pushed her hair out of her face. "There was someone else there the day that Gabrielle died, wasn't there?"

He didn't answer but behind his eyes was a maelstrom of emotion.

Gretchen stepped closer and leaned in, forcing him to look at her. "Jackson."

"There was a man there that day, wasn't there?" Josie pressed. "You heard him, didn't you?"

Still no response other than his eyes darkening like the clouds above their heads.

"Gabrielle was arguing with him, wasn't she? Is that why you didn't go back into the house?"

His jaw worked. "Zane would have followed me," he finally said. "He was up my ass back then. Everywhere I went, he was there. Yes, there was arguing. I don't know what about. Or I don't remember. It's fuzzy. Always has been. I just knew that he'd get scared if he heard it. He hated when they argued."

"Your dad and Gabrielle?" Josie asked.

"Toward the end, yeah. It always made Zane cry and then he'd be in my bed for a week, all freaked out."

"Who was Gabrielle arguing with that day?" asked Gretchen.

He shook his head again, as if having some kind of internal argument with himself, before hoisting himself up into the truck bed again. "You think it was Hollis."

FORTY-FOUR

"We don't think anything," Josie said. "That's why we're asking you."

Grabbing a sleek wooden cabinet, he muscled it toward the tailgate. "Will you even believe me if I tell you it was my dad? 'Cause it seems like you're just looking for a reason to accuse Hollis of something from back then since you can't pin anything on him from now."

"We're not trying to pin anything on anyone," said Gretchen. "We're asking you what you heard on the day Gabrielle died."

He leaned his arm on top of the cabinet. "Fine. I heard my dad. The two of them were arguing, just like always. Then it got quiet. I waited to see if they'd start again but they didn't. Instead, Dad started yelling, freaking out. He was talking to someone else. I realized later he'd called 911. That's what I remember. What are you trying to do here? It sounds like you're trying to manufacture some drama about the past instead of dealing with what's happening in the here and now."

"We're gathering information," Gretchen said.

He scoffed. Then he was back on the ground, maneuvering

the cabinet off the tailgate. The wind picked up again, gaining force as it rushed into the garage bay and back out, nearly knocking his hat off. He put it back in place. "Well, that's all I've got for you."

"Did you ever talk to your dad about what happened that day?" Josie asked.

"Why would I?"

"Did you ever witness your dad being physically abusive to any of his partners?"

"No," Jackson answered. "I never saw him act that way. That wasn't really his style anyway."

"What was his style?"

"What are you— You do realize that my dad is a murder victim, right? You're supposed to be figuring out who killed him and Cora."

"To do that, we need to build a complete picture of who he was as a person," Josie said. "Tell us about your dad. What did you mean that physical abuse wasn't his style?"

"He was more... manipulative."

"In what way?" asked Gretchen.

He draped his arm over the top of the cabinet. It was tall and narrow with a shiny mahogany surface and a domed lid. Below that were two sets of double doors with dainty brass knobs. A crank jutted out from one side. Josie frowned at the keyhole inches below where Jackson's hand dangled from the lid.

"One of the things him and Gabby argued about was her job at the daycare. He wanted her to quit. Don't ask me why 'cause I don't know. I was twelve. All I can tell you is what I overheard. One day she accused him of purposely getting her fired from the daycare so she'd be forced to stay home. At the time, I thought maybe she was mixed-up but as an adult? It made sense. A lot of times, if he didn't get his way, he'd do something sneaky. Like one time Gabby was away on a girls' trip with some friends, and he called her and told her Zane had a really high fever that wouldn't break. Dad wouldn't let her talk to Zane. Probably 'cause he wasn't sick. When Dad told her he was taking Zane to the ER, Gabby felt so worried and so guilty, she just came home. When she got back, Dad told her the fever had broken and Zane was feeling better. She was pissed and accused him of making the whole thing up—which he had."

Gretchen asked, "Did he do things like that to Cora?"

Josie edged closer to the cabinet so she could get a better look at the keyhole.

"I don't know," Jackson said. "I wasn't living there when they got together. You'd have to ask Zane."

"Ask me what?"

A scowl darkened Jackson's face as his brother joined them. He was in khakis and an At Your Disposal polo shirt. His eyes were bloodshot. The bruising beneath them had faded to a light purplish red. His sandy hair was mussed from the wind.

"Did Dad do sneaky shit to Cora?" Jackson asked.

Zane stared at him, unmoving. Gone was the anger and irritation that had colored their previous interactions. In its place was suspicion. They held eye contact, neither of them moving or speaking. The silence grew thick and awkward.

Then Zane's eyes dropped to the cabinet. He walked over to it and ran a finger across the keyhole. Jackson's hand curled into a fist. That was when Josie realized why it kept drawing her attention.

"It takes a skeleton key," she said.

"Yeah," Jackson said tightly. "We have it. This belongs to a recent client of ours. We're selling it for them."

Zane moved around the side opposite Jackson and ran his hand along the back of the cabinet. A moment later, he held up a small envelope. Tape hung from its edges. He opened it and plucked the little key from inside before handing it to Josie. It was silver and shiny, about the same size as the one they'd found in Cora's purse. The head was a circle with a V inside of it. Josie turned it over in her palm and looked back at the cabinet. Just as she'd thought the first time she had seen it—it was an antique phonograph cabinet.

"A Victrola," she said.

Zane nodded. "Yep. Contrary to what most people probably think, the Victrola is the kind with the internal horn. Everyone thinks it's the one with the big external horn mounted to it. The one that looks like the cones they put on dogs, but that's not a Victrola. Although sometimes those external horns come as part of cabinets and other times they come separately. You get to learn a lot of cool shit like that doing this job."

An alert went off in the back of Josie's mind. Mentally, she sifted through all the information she'd gathered in the last couple of weeks, searching for why.

"Zane," Jackson said through gritted teeth. "It doesn't matter. This conversation is over."

Josie returned the key to Zane. He unlocked the cabinet, lifting the top so they could see the record player. Bright green felt.

Gretchen shot a glance at Josie before returning her attention to Zane. "Then what's the cabinet with the external horn mounted to it called?"

"It's called a Victor," Zane carried on like a museum docent. "They were first produced in 1901. Victrolas came out in 1906. This one is from the 1920s, I think. What year, Jacks? Do you remember?"

"No, I don't remember. Put the key back and help me move it. If this shit gets wet, we're going to be screwed."

Zane closed the lid.

"Are all of them so small and narrow?" asked Josie, every last one of her instincts buzzing like a hornet's nest in her stomach.

"Oh, they come in all kinds of different sizes," Zane said. "Some smaller, some larger. Different brands, too."

Green felt, the sliver of something brass but conical, flaring at one end. The photographs. The damn photos.

"Can I see the inside?" Josie asked. "Underneath?"

She could see Jackson straining to keep his composure and she had an idea why. It was a crazy idea, but it was there.

"Sure," Zane said. Using the key again, he swung the doors open. It contained several wooden slots for records.

Maybe she was wrong, but the idea pushing at the edges of her consciousness wouldn't stop. The inside of this cabinet was cluttered with its internal mechanisms, but there were other brands, presumably designed differently, perhaps in such a way that the inside could be hollowed out.

"That's enough," Jackson snapped. "I need to get all of this shit moved out of the truck right now."

Josie felt a couple of raindrops land on her forearms. "Did you have one of these when you were little?"

"No," Jackson said gruffly.

"How about one like this?" asked Gretchen. She must have figured out where Josie was headed with this line of questioning. "Maybe a different brand."

"I don't remember."

"Your dad didn't have one?"

He slammed a palm on top of the cabinet. "I don't remember!"

Zane jumped. "Calm down, man. What's your problem?"

"My problem is that someone killed my wife and all I want to do is get all this shit out of my house—get everything out so I can sell it and never have to go back there and instead, I'm standing here having the stupidest conversation of my life with a couple of police officers who are trying to pin Riley's murder on Hollis."

"You remember something else about the day your mom

died, don't you?" Josie pushed, the buzzing inside her getting stronger. "Well, maybe you don't remember precisely. Maybe you put it together later. The photos of your mom on display in your house, that's how you figured it out, isn't it?"

Jackson glared at her. Zane looked back and forth between them. "What is she talking about?"

"Or maybe you had memories of her playing records. One of the photos at your house is of the two of you and you've got a record in your hands. When you saw the cabinet in the background of old photos of her, it started to come back to you. Your dad had a cabinet like this one but with the external horn. There's a photo in the upstairs hall of his house. It's you and him on your second birthday and in the background, you can just catch a glimpse of what looks like green felt from the record player and a portion of the brass horn of a Victor."

Zane's features twisted in confusion. "Seriously, what are you talking about?"

Josie plunged ahead, keeping her focus on Jackson. "Did you remember telling Bruce Olsen that your mom went 'in Victor' when you were three? Or did he tell you that when you asked him to find your mom?"

"I didn't know what it meant," Jackson said tightly. "I don't remember saying it to Olsen but all my life, everyone else said it. 'Rachel ran off with some guy named Victor. Jackson saw them.' I don't know what I saw. I told you. I only have flashes. Fragments. I was three years old."

"And you were traumatized," Josie said. "Because you watched your father kill your mother and stuff her into the cabinet to get rid of her. She didn't run off with some guy named Victor. She left the house in an antique Victor cabinet."

FORTY-FIVE

Zane looked stricken. His mouth hung open as he went completely still. Then his lips flapped soundlessly. Finally, he swallowed. Then he found his voice. It sounded choked. "Did you say Dad killed someone? Wait, are you saying our dad is a murderer? No, it can't be. It can't. I—"

"Shut up!" Jackson snarled, cutting him off. Turning back to Josie and Gretchen, he said, "I don't know what I saw. I don't know what the fragments mean but yeah, I remember my mom playing records on this old wooden thing with that big horn. I never thought about any of it until I was a lot older. Never wanted to think about it. Dad took every opportunity he could to remind me what a worthless piece of shit Mom was, leaving her three-year-old behind in the hands of a stranger. He told me she was hooked on drugs and that she chose them over me. That was always what he said. He never mentioned another guy, not at home, not when he was talking shit about my mom. The Victor thing came from Olsen and from neighbors who overheard me saying it to him that day. It spread, took on a life of its own."

The buzzy feeling inside Josie intensified. Her cop brain

told her they were on the precipice of something important. "Jackson, Zane, you two need to come back down to the stationhouse with us. Let's finish this conversation there."

"No," Jackson snapped.

"Wait, hold on," Zane said, completely ignoring Josie's instructions. His lower lip wobbled. Sporadic raindrops landed on his face, but he didn't wipe them away.

When no more words came, Josie turned back toward Jackson. "The rain is starting. Unload the rest of this stuff and let's get down to the stationhouse."

"No."

"Why not?" Zane said. "We were already there once."

"Because I'm not going to be manipulated by a couple of cops." He used his forearm to wipe at a few beads of moisture from his cheek. Tears or rain? Josie was guessing rain. He was wound too tight, vibrating with too much anger, to be crying. "If you've got something to say, say it here. If you have questions, ask them here."

"I thought you wanted to get out of the rain," Zane said.

Jackson gave him a dirty look but didn't respond.

Gretchen sighed. "I'm going to read you both your rights before we go any further."

"Fine," the brothers said in unison but in very different tones.

Josie watched them as Gretchen recited their Miranda rights and asked them for verbal confirmation that they understood said rights. Jackson looked pissed but Zane looked curious and a little scared.

There was a moment of silence and Josie knew that Gretchen was giving them each a chance to request an attorney. When neither did, Josie attempted to get things back on track. "Jackson, I want to talk about your mom."

"No," he said. "I don't want to talk about her. She's gone. Everyone's fucking gone."

There it was—her way past his defenses—he needed to get some things off his chest. How long had he been holding his feelings in, holding back? Even with Riley, he had clearly been the strong and stoic one, keeping his emotions in check so he could tend to hers. He needed to let go, to unleash. That was the only way Josie would get what she needed from him.

"You've lost so much," she said softly. "And it must have been terrible, growing up believing that your mom left you. It must have been difficult to hear the things Tobias said about her. Regardless of what she did or didn't do. Any person could tell from the photos of the two of you that she loved you—no matter what came after—and it wasn't right that Tobias tainted that."

Jackson's posture loosened a fraction as he relented, giving in to the opportunity to release some of his long-held frustration. "I hated it. My grandparents only said good things about her. How much she loved me and how she'd just made a mistake. I think that they thought she'd come back eventually. My grandmother, before she died, made some offhand comment about how my mom loved to play records for me because her and I would dance. That Tobias had this old antique record player and I'd tell Mom, 'Play the Victor, play the Victor.'"

Zane's head swiveled toward his brother. "Jacks," he said, voice cracking.

Jackson laughed brokenly. "The cabinet itself wasn't even a Victor. I found some pictures of it. I think it was a Pooley. Dad just put the Victor with the metal horn on top. It's weird, right? The way you get stuck on details that absolutely don't matter."

Josie had seen it enough—experienced it enough herself—to know it wasn't strange. "That's more common than you think," she said.

Gretchen's pen and notepad were in her hands. A few raindrops splattered against the page she'd opened to. "When did you start to suspect that your dad had killed her?"

Horror stretched across Zane's face. "Jacks, is this for real? Do you really think that Dad killed your mom?"

Jackson ignored his brother. "Not for a long time. It was right before I moved out. I was twenty. I found all these pictures of my mom and from when I was a toddler and there was the cabinet with the Victor on top. It wasn't a... sudden thing. It was weeks of examining my fragments and things coming back to me in nightmares."

"Then you started thinking about how you heard your dad arguing with Gabrielle right before she died," Josie prompted. "Did you think that he'd killed her?"

"It was just a suspicion. I had no proof. Couldn't figure out how he'd done it. But yeah, I thought he had."

Zane was still standing on the opposite side of the cabinet from his brother, pale and stunned, hands slack at his sides. Gretchen leaned toward him, getting into his personal space. "Zane?" she asked. "Did Jackson ever share these suspicions with you?"

He flinched as more rain hit his forehead. "No, no. He never said anything. I don't understand. Jacks? Why didn't you say anything? Why didn't you tell me?"

Jackson shook his head and muscled the cabinet off to the side and into the bay on his own. Climbing back into the truck bed, he said, "What would be the point, Zane? You were just a kid still. I was an adult. I wasn't putting that kind of shit on you."

Zane watched as he stripped off his utility gloves and unstrapped a dolly from the back of the truck bed. "You weren't putting that kind of shit on me, but you left me in the house with a goddamn murderer? Cora? Jesus, you left Riley with him?"

Jackson wrenched the dolly from its tethers. It clanged against the glass of the cab and then the metal wheel cover. "Leave my wife out of this."

"I can't," Zane said, voice high. "I loved her. I was in love—"

"Shut up!" Jackson shouted at him.

"You left her there, unprotected!"

"I had no proof!" Jackson roared.

"You could have told me. You should have told me."

A dump truck approached. It was filled with trash, probably headed toward the compactors. The driver stopped when he saw them gathered there. Jackson glared at him and then shook his head. Apparently, that was all the signal the guy needed to throw the truck in reverse. The back-up alarm shrieked. As soon as it stopped and the truck began driving away, Jackson pointed at Zane.

"You loved Dad. Worshiped him. Do you honestly think if I had told you, 'Hey, I think our dad killed both of our moms,' that you would have reacted with anything but disbelief and horror? You were a kid, Zane. You would have hated me for thinking it and gone running straight to him to tattle on me."

"No," Zane choked.

Jackson laughed bitterly. Abandoning the dolly, he gripped the Coke machine on both sides and tried to shimmy it toward the center of the truck bed. His forearms, now slick with rain, strained with the effort. "You know," he said over his shoulder. "I hated you for a long time. I should have been happy for you that you never had to bear the burden of that knowledge. You didn't have to live with it. To look at the man you loved and admired your entire life, who gave you everything, and realize that every single thing you thought you knew about him was a lie."

"Jacks," Zane said but his brother didn't even look at him.

The rain started coming down harder. Jackson continued to struggle with the Coke machine, rocking it from side to side, moving it in small increments. "You never had to live with the fact that Dad was a piece of shit. Maybe he didn't hit women like Dalton did but in his own way, he was abusive. Sneaky, manipulative, ruthless. You didn't see that side of him. It was almost worse because you never knew what he'd do or what would set him off. You didn't have to smile at him and act like a loving son knowing the entire time that he had taken the one person who had truly loved you."

Josie felt a prickle along the nape of her neck that had nothing to do with the rain sluicing down into her shirt. It was that familiar goading of her subconscious, teasing her, daring her to put the pieces of the puzzle together when she still couldn't work out the larger picture.

"You should have told me," Zane repeated.

"Drop it, Zane," Jackson said flatly. "It doesn't matter now anyway."

Josie watched Zane swallow, his throat working. Water rolled down his forehead and dripped from his battered nose. His pallor was starting to look unnatural.

"I saw Hollis's insulin pens in the trash the day my mom died," he said quietly. "In our kitchen."

FORTY-SIX

Jackson froze, wet hands still gripping the sides of the Coke machine. This time, he looked directly at Zane. A flurry of emotions passed over his face. Sadness, defeat, frustration, love, and then pity. He shook his head slowly. "Dad was sloppy. Ironic, isn't it? How careless he was and he still never got caught? It doesn't matter now, Zane. Hasn't mattered for seven years."

Zane stepped forward until his stomach brushed against the tailgate. His sandy hair was soaked through. "Was he going to kill Cora?"

"How the hell should I know?"

"Well, what the hell were you planning to do with all of that information? All your suspicions?" Zane asked angrily. "There were three of us living with him and you knew—you knew for... for years! You said you were twenty when you started to remember. That means you left us in that house with him for three years. Did you ever plan to do anything?"

Jackson turned his back to them, resting his head against the face of the Coke machine. He didn't answer.

"Did you ever confront your father?" Josie asked.

The puzzle pieces were shuffling around in her mind. Common denominator. Motive. Expanding their definition of a criminal organization. Police corruption. Someone always knew something.

"Jackson," she said. "Did you ever confront Tobias?"

He lifted his head from the machine but didn't turn back toward them. "No. Why would I do that?"

Gretchen put away her notebook and pen. "What *were* you planning to do with your suspicions?"

Three years was a long time to hold onto something like that. To keep working side by side with your father. To let your anger and betrayal fester and grow. To plan.

"I don't know." Jackson wiped the moisture from his face and then turned his hat around, the brim keeping the rain from his eyes.

Zane laughed humorlessly. "Oh, so you were just going to sit on that indefinitely. Do absolutely nothing. You had to know Cora was in danger. Riley, too. Are you telling me you would have just left her—"

"Shut up, Zane!" Jackson whirled around. "I didn't have plans, okay? What was I supposed to do? I didn't have proof!"

"That's never stopped people before," Josie said carefully. "When they want to stop someone from hurting someone else or when they want revenge. You must have been pretty angry."

Jackson looked down at his hands, twisting his wedding ring around his finger.

Gretchen locked eyes with Josie briefly. They were on the same page. She said, "Plus your dad had all those law enforcement connections through his dad. John Fanning, Karl Staab, Bruce Olsen. They were all on his side. They never looked beneath the surface."

Josie didn't miss the almost imperceptible wince at the

mention of Olsen's name. "You must have felt pretty powerless."

"Zane's right," Gretchen went on. "Cora was in danger. Could you have lived with yourself if she was taken from Riley the same way that Rachel and Gabrielle were taken from you and Zane?"

Jackson said nothing.

"Did you know she was planning to leave your dad?" Josie said.

Zane shook his head. "What? Things got that far? Jacks, what about Riley? What was going to happen to her?"

Through gritted teeth, Jackson said, "It doesn't matter if she was planning to leave him. They're both gone now."

"Cora knew." Josie pushed a wet lock of hair from her forehead. "She found Rachel's purse and the skeleton key. Maybe she didn't know what the key meant but she understood the significance of the purse. It belonged to your mother. That's when Cora knew she was in trouble. Did she ever talk to you about it, Jackson?"

He kept twisting his wedding band, watching it turn around his finger. "No, and maybe that was for the best. What could I have done? What good would it have done any of us?"

None, Josie realized. Not for Jackson, anyway. It would have taken Riley away from him. Had he been in love with her back then, too?

"Jackson," Josie said. "Did you know that Cora was planning to leave?"

He didn't answer. Twisting his wedding band a final time, he grabbed the dolly and began trying to fit it beneath the edge of the Coke machine.

"You did know!" Zane accused.

It would have been easy enough information to come by given his position in the company and the family. Working with his father and Hollis. Rescuing Cora from Dalton Stevens periodically. He might have overheard something. Arguments between Cora and Tobias. Conversations between Hollis and Cora. Regardless, Josie believed Zane.

"You knew Cora was in danger," Josie said. "Knew what your dad was capable of and you let it all slide. Then you found out she was leaving and realized it would sever your connection to Riley permanently. There was no way she'd be with the son of the man who killed two of his romantic partners, who scared her mom so badly that she thought she might be next."

Jackson finally fit the dolly's edge under the machine. "This trip down memory lane has been a real drag but there's nothing left to say. I'm not sure what you're hoping to accomplish but I've got shit to do."

"You went to Karl Staab's retirement party," Josie said. "But your dad didn't."

He didn't look away from where his hands curled around the handle of the dolly. "Is there a question in there somewhere?"

"They were your dad's friends. Tobias was the only reason your family had connections to law enforcement," Gretchen pointed out. "Fanning, Staab, Olsen."

"Olsen was the one who responded to the 911 call the day your mom went missing," Josie added. "When we talked with him, he made it sound like his loyalty was firmly with Tobias but that wasn't true, was it?"

Jackson didn't answer.

"What is she talking about?" Zane asked him.

Nothing.

"Olsen had a soft spot for you, didn't he?" Gretchen said, picking up Josie's thread. "You went to him when you turned eighteen and asked him to find your mom. He lied to you and said he couldn't find her. Because Tobias asked him to. He must have felt pretty guilty about that, especially after Cora brought him Rachel's purse. Maybe guilty enough to come clean with you and tell you the truth about what he found when he actually did search for her."

"What?" Zane said. "What is this about a purse? Cora talked to Olsen? Jacks, what the hell is going on?"

"It's a little strange," Gretchen said. "You being twenty-three and going to a retirement party with a bunch of guys your dad's age and older."

"You know," Josie said, "Brighton Springs PD has a long history of police corruption. It's interesting that on the night your dad and Cora disappeared—were killed—you were at a party with a bunch of their officers. Even if they weren't dirty, you'd only need one of them to give you an alibi."

"Jacks," Zane whispered. "What did you do?"

Shaking his head, Jackson reached around the vending machine, pulling it toward him as he tilted the dolly.

"Bruce Olsen was highly decorated," Josie continued. "Revered. Everyone had been drinking at that party. They might not have remembered seeing you past nine in the evening but if Olsen told them you were there until the early hours of the morning, they wouldn't question him."

"Holy shit, Jacks," Zane said. "Did you do this? Did you kill Dad and Cora? Were you after Riley even then? Did you ever give a shit about *me*?"

The machine teetered on the edge of the dolly, its weight pulling it back toward the truck bed. With a grunt, Jackson pushed it forward a couple of halting steps.

"Fanning checked your phone," Gretchen said, "as well as the GPS in your car but it never occurred to him to check Olsen's. Why would it?"

Zane's face crumpled. "Cora, man? How could you? Holy shit. It's— This is so bad. So... disgusting. You married Riley after killing her *mom*? Do you have any idea how fucked up that is? You're so much worse than Dad!"

This earned Zane a glare from his brother. "You shut your mouth," Jackson growled.

"Oh God," Zane said, new horror washing over his face. "She knew, didn't she? Riley found out. You lied to me about the morning she died, didn't you?"

"What are you talking about, Zane?" Josie asked.

"I thought I heard them arguing that morning. It woke me up. I was hungover and it was none of my business anyway, so I went back to sleep. When he knocked on my door to ask if I knew where she was, I asked him what they were arguing about, and he said he didn't know what I was talking about. Said I must have been dreaming. That was bullshit, wasn't it, Jacks? It was you. You knew how to kill her with insulin 'cause you saw Dad do it to my mom. You saw it, didn't you? That day in the yard. You told me to wait for you, to hit some more balls, and you went back to the house."

"You don't know what you're talking about," Jackson said menacingly, pushing the dolly closer to the tailgate.

"Maybe you didn't see Dad inject her, but you saw the pens and needles in the trash, just like I did. It's true, isn't it? You knew what they were—knew how Hol was constantly telling us not to touch them, not to mess with them because an accidental dose could put us in the hospital and kill us. Even I remember that. He drilled it into our heads. Then when you started realizing he killed your mom, you remembered those pens, the needles, and the arguing—"

"Stop talking right fucking now," Jackson said.

"Nothing else makes sense," Zane insisted. "Hol wouldn't kill Riley. How did she find out? After all these years, how did she finally figure it out?"

Gretchen said, "Jackson, this stuff can wait. Let's go back to the stationhouse. Zane, too. These are things that are probably best discussed in private."

How had Riley figured it out?

Josie's brain worked to review everything she knew about the morning Riley died through the lens of Zane's revelation. Riley had gone home that morning to get medication for their cat. Hollis had seen her when she returned but she'd looked pale and shaky. Sick. He'd assumed it was because she was hungover—and she very well may have been—but what if she'd found something while she was at home that had made her that way? Something that turned her world on its head. Something that made her believe that her husband had had something to do with her mother and Tobias's murders.

But what?

"There's nothing to discuss," Jackson said. "You're all making shit up. It's like the most morbid kind of storytime. You've got some pretty wild imaginations. Zane, help me with this damn thing, would you?"

Josie thought of the punctures on Riley's palm. Four of them spaced perfectly apart to form a tiny square. She'd been squeezing something so hard in her hand that it broke the skin. Something small, its face square, but those four parts of it sharp enough to pierce the soft pad of her hand.

"We'd still like you to come down to the stationhouse so you can formally respond to these questions," Gretchen said.

What small item could Riley have found in the home she shared with Jackson that would give her the idea that he'd had something to do with the murders?

One of the only things that hadn't been in the sedan when they processed it.

Josie might not have thought of it except for the fact that Shannon kept sending her and Noah photos of anniversary bands that would match Josie's ring, despite them standing firm that they weren't buying one.

"You kept Cora's engagement ring," Josie said. "It was a princess cut. Square in a four-pronged setting."

Jackson's head lifted, his dark eyes colliding with hers, the truth of what she said plain on his face.

Zane made a noise of disgust. "Why would you keep—"

Before he could finish, Jackson shoved the dolly forward with all of his strength, its wheels bumping over the rest of the truck bed and then bowing the tailgate. Josie watched in horror as the Coke machine hurtled forward, flipping over the tailgate and straight on top of a helpless Zane.

FORTY-SEVEN

Over the pelting rain, Josie heard the crunch of bones as the behemoth fell, knocking Zane off balance and crushing his lower body beneath it. Her stomach clenched. Jackson jumped down from the truck bed, took a brief, almost regretful look at his brother's agonized face, flinched, and ran. Josie dropped into a squat and slipped her hands under the side of the soda machine. Gretchen moved to the other side, mirroring her. Jackson could wait. If he made it off the lot before they could catch up with him, they'd pick him up somewhere else. He'd fled out of panic, but he wouldn't get far. They'd put a warrant out for his arrest in connection with the assault on Zane and he'd get picked up quickly.

Rain beaded on Gretchen's eyelashes and streamed down her face. "Shit, this is heavy."

Zane made a noise that sounded more animal than human. His blackened eyes were impossibly wide, even as rain beat down on him. His hands rested against the top of the Coke machine, but they weren't moving. Josie's knees, lower back and forearms burned with the effort of trying to lift the metal hunk off him. Her grip kept slipping against the moisture and the beats of her heart felt uneven and fluttery.

It was heavy. Far heavier than she anticipated. She tried very hard not to think about the damage to Zane's body.

"Puh-puh-puh... leee..." Wherever his face wasn't bruised, it was turning from stark white to a greenish hue.

"Hold on," Gretchen told him.

The two of them counted to three and tried to lift the machine again.

"It's too slippery," Josie said, wiping her hands down her thighs even though every inch of her was soaked.

"We have to keep trying," Gretchen said. "Maybe we can roll it to the side."

Josie shook her head, water spraying everywhere. "No, no. We can't. It'll do more damage. It has to come straight up. I want to keep trying but we need to call this in."

Gretchen reached down and gently placed her hand on Zane's forehead. "Hang on," she told him. "Just hang on."

One of his hands lifted in the air and Gretchen took it, squeezing lightly. "Stay with us, Zane."

Josie stood and fished her cell phone from her pocket. The rain was torrential now and the screen was soaked instantly. It wouldn't take her thumbprint or register the numbers as she tried to punch in her passcode.

"Son of a bitch." Hurriedly, she yanked the hem of her shirt loose. "I'm getting help, Zane. Hold on. Just hold on."

She stepped into the garage bay and used her shirttail to wipe the rain from her screen. Not wasting any time with her thumbprint or the passcode, she swiped the emergency calls icon. When the 911 dispatcher answered, she shouted out details in a staccato burst before pocketing her phone and dashing out into the downpour.

She cursed when she saw that Zane's eyes were closed. In that moment, he looked so vulnerable and small and hurt, more like the teenager he'd been when his dad and Cora died than the man he was now. Like Riley, that part of him had never really grown up. For the millionth time since she became a law enforcement officer, it hit Josie just how much she hated the pain people inflicted on the ones they were supposed to love.

"He's got a pulse," Gretchen said.

Their eyes met across the macabre tableau and Josie saw her own determination reflected back at her. "Let's try again."

Gretchen gave Zane's hand one last squeeze and then she got back into position and counted down from three. Josie's brain went blank, all of her energy, her strength, her essence coalescing and channeling in answer to a single directive. Lift.

She was vaguely aware of Gretchen bellowing, face pinched with exertion and then her own grunts.

Lift. Lift. Lift.

The moment the machine gave and started to move at their hands, a surge of adrenaline rocketed through Josie's veins, so potent that she was no longer aware of the strain in her own body or the rain coursing over her.

Then the machine was standing and Zane was sprawled before them, the damage to his legs sickeningly obvious. His pelvis, at least, didn't look quite as flat and there was no blood from what Josie could see. Gretchen squatted by his side and touched his cheek. "Zane, the ambulance is coming. Stay with us. Can you open your eyes for me?"

His lids opened briefly but then closed against the rain. The damn rain. In addition to his injuries, he was likely going into shock. They couldn't move him. That was a job for the paramedics. Trying to do it themselves without the right equipment or the right technique could be catastrophic. It could be another ten or fifteen minutes before help arrived.

"He's shivering," Gretchen said, voice neutral.

Josie glanced over to where the garage bay door yawned open. "I'll be right back."

Inside the building, she dripped water everywhere, leaving a trail on the concrete and spraying every surface nearby when she twirled, scanning the items packed into the large space. Besides the ones that Jackson had set down at the entrance, each one was labeled with a bright yellow laminated card that listed an inventory number, description, and a client's name. Some things were in boxes. Others were wrapped in thick layers of plastic but some, thankfully, were draped in moving blankets.

Perfect.

She strode toward the closest thing and tore two dark blue moving blankets from it, uncovering a desk. Then she had another idea. At warp speed, she thrashed through the At Your Disposal client inventory, inadvertently breaking glass, splintering wood, and knocking over furniture that looked a hundred years old. Fleetingly, she wondered if Hollis had insurance because, right now, she was an act of God.

It didn't take long to find something suitable for what she had in mind. A table big enough to seat six people, made of a type of wood she'd never seen before—almost black with thin yellow-brown stripes throughout and a lustrous sheen that told her it probably cost more than her car. Leaving the moving blankets just inside the bay, she dragged it unceremoniously outside.

The rain came down in torrential sheets now, making her limbs feel heavy and blurring everything in sight. Water splashed with each clomp of her boots. It pooled everywhere. The table bucked and lurched as Josie yanked it toward Gretchen and Zane, just two shadowy figures in the onslaught.

"Help me!" she shouted.

Gretchen took one look at the table and jumped to her feet. They each lifted a side, guiding it up and over the top of Zane, careful to make sure none of the legs touched him. Once he was shielded from the torrent, Josie ran back for the moving blankets. She crawled under the table with him and with the care of a surgeon operating on her own child, covered him from his toes to his chin.

Gretchen appeared on his other side, scuttling close to him and placing a hand on his forehead. Josie didn't even know if he was still alive. She pressed her index and middle finger against his throat, relief crashing over her when she felt a weak pulse.

"I'm going to go up front so I can tell the ambulance where to find you," she shouted.

Gretchen gave her a thumbs up.

Then she was going after Jackson Wright.

FORTY-EIGHT

Heat blasted through the vents of Josie's SUV. Water dripped and sloshed and splashed across the upholstery, the dash, and the console. The rain still came down in sheets. Even on the highest setting, her windshield wipers barely kept up. The chatter of her portable radio filled the vehicle. The hum of the heater and the pounding of the rain nearly drowned it out.

Josie had left At Your Disposal immediately after giving the paramedics directions to the back of the lot. Zane was in good hands and Gretchen could handle the scene there. Since Jackson's truck was no longer available, he had calmly walked up to Ellyn's desk and asked to borrow the keys to her car, citing an emergency that had to do with Captain Whiskers.

Josie was about to show him the meaning of emergency. Also, someone needed to take Captain Whiskers into protective custody.

She used the hands-free feature to call dispatch and give them the tag number, make and model of Ellyn Mann's vehicle as well as Jackson Wright's name and description. Within moments, every unit in the city would be on the lookout for him although Josie was fairly certain she already knew where he was headed.

In reality there was nowhere for him to hide. Running had been a knee-jerk reaction. He hadn't been thinking clearly. Sometimes that worked in favor of the police and other times it benefited the suspect. In this case, Josie wasn't sure what the hell to think. Mentally replaying everything he'd said up until the moment he tipped the Coke machine onto his brother, she realized that he hadn't actually admitted to any criminal acts.

Not even one.

But she knew now that he was behind it all. Denton PD wouldn't be able to charge him or even hold him in connection with the murders of Tobias, Cora, and Riley but they could definitely arrest and detain him for what he'd just done to Zane. Then she would hand him his reckoning.

Traffic was backed up as she left South Denton and approached the central part of the city. The other drivers moved sluggishly, probably because they saw what she saw when they looked at the road ahead—distorted whorls of color and light, buildings that looked like melted candles, and bumpers that were nothing more than ink splotches. Pulling to a stop behind a long line of unmoving vehicles at a green light, she threw her SUV into park and got out. It took only seconds to find the emergency beacon she kept in her hatchback. Once it was affixed to her roof and flashing red, the cars in front of her began to part. She zigzagged through them until she found a cross street and turned onto it, weaving through a series of side streets at a speed that bordered on unsafe given the conditions.

Now that she was out of the rain, away from the horrific scene on the At Your Disposal lot, feeling returned to her body. A bone-deep cold from being damp through and through enveloped her. A minor shift in her seat and the chafing of the thick seams of her pants and the straps and underwires of her bra against her skin stung painfully. Her fingers ached. There were cuts and abrasions on her forearms. She had no idea where those came from. Probably from when she tore apart the storage area in her frenzy to find anything she could use to give Zane some cover. The dull throb in her lower back was the worst.

All of it would have to wait.

She powered through a deep puddle that had formed at the base of the hill she was approaching. Water gushed in waves in her wake.

Then her heart did a double-tap because in front of her, on the exact same road that she and Gretchen had been traveling along on the day they got the call for a car in the river, was Jackson Wright. Josie didn't even need to confirm the license plate number—not that she could in this weather—because she had known before she even fired up her SUV that there was only one place he was going.

Back to the scene of his crimes.

With him in her sights, she contacted dispatch again to let them know she had found him and rattle off the location so that backup units could be sent. Ahead of her, the sedan accelerated. He'd seen the beacon. He knew he was caught.

He kept going, speeding up as much as he dared, as much as Ellyn's car could handle. Josie wondered if he would still head for the boat ramp or if he'd try to outrun her. There was a sort of fatalism in choosing the boat ramp. A desperate defeat. She got her answer when he took the turn onto the road that led down to the abandoned state mental hospital so hard that he nearly spun out.

Josie's SUV handled the corner perfectly. Except that once she made the turn, it was clear that Jackson was drawing ahead of her at an alarming rate.

"Shit."

He wasn't going to the boat ramp. He was going to crash through the trees at the bottom of the road and sail straight into the river—into the same watery grave where he'd once left Tobias and Cora.

That wasn't happening.

Josie punched the gas, holding the pedal down so hard that her foot ached. The engine roared and the silky glide of the tires on the road told her she was dangerously close to hydroplaning. The muscles in her shoulder blades pulled taut. Her knuckles whitened as her fingers clenched around the steering wheel. The back of the sedan got closer, a dark red blotch strobing between the manic swipes of the windshield wipers. The trees at the bottom of the hill loomed ahead, an amorphous green blob flying toward them at terminal velocity. Jackson was going entirely too fast to make the turnoff onto the street that ran parallel to the river. If she needed more reassurance that she was doing the right thing, that was it.

Her heart fluttered, skipped a beat, then another, and finally thundered back to life, pounding so hard she heard it in her ears. This was it. She had one shot at this and if she didn't get it right, didn't pull it off before they reached the bottom, Jackson was as good as dead. Her chances didn't look that good either.

"Wren."

The name pushed past her lips, threatening to break the seal on the tornadic inner conflict she now lived with: give one hundred percent on the job, or shirk the more dangerous parts to ensure that she was alive and present for the girl whose care she'd been gifted? In this line of work, anything less than one hundred percent was a betrayal of her oath to serve and protect and yet, now, for Josie, there was a person whose needs and safety and well-being trumped every other soul in the world.

But Dex hadn't entrusted her with his daughter because she gave in to her fears.

Only a few feet away now. The sedan shimmied but quickly regained control. The wall of trees was so close now.

This was it. She had to trust herself even though she hadn't done the PIT maneuver since she was on patrol. That was Precision Immobilization Technique, a fairly safe way to stop a fleeing vehicle. Usually there was a lot more road to work with.

She ignored her galloping heart and the tightness in her chest. Ignored the frantic *thwip thwip* of the wipers, the hard drum of the rain on the roof and windows. Dismissed the shitty visibility. She could do this. She would do this.

Finally, she was almost touching Jackson's bumper. Yanking the steering wheel to the right, she gave herself enough room to pull up beside him but just until the front of her SUV overlapped with the back of his sedan by a few feet. Then she gave the wheel a jerk back to the left, hitting the rear quarter panel of his vehicle with the left-side bumper of her own. On contact, she gave her steering wheel a quarter turn toward the sedan just as it spun out in a one hundred eighty-degree turn. Josie instantly straightened out her SUV, slamming on the brakes. She passed the sedan as it slid onto the shoulder of the road and finally came to rest, facing uphill.

A film of sweat coated her forehead, her cheeks, the back of her neck. Her palms left sweaty impressions around the steering wheel as she let go and got out of her SUV. The closer she got to the sedan, the less she felt the vise squeezing her chest. As she strode toward his door, her pistol drawn, he lifted his head, the battle in his midnight-blue eyes apparent, even now.

Keep trying to run or face his fate?

Whatever he saw on Josie's face made the decision for him. Before she barked a single instruction, he lifted both hands in surrender.

FORTY-NINE

The heat coming from Noah's body was deliciously warm as he crowded into one of the second-floor stationhouse bathrooms with her. She was mostly dry but her clothes were uncomfortably stiff and chafing. The thought of looking in a mirror right now made her want to retch. When she turned to face her husband, his smile was half amused and half appreciative.

Josie put her hands on her hips. "What? Don't tell me this whole drowned rat aesthetic I'm rocking turns you on. 'Cause there might be something seriously wrong with you."

He laughed and rummaged through the tote bag he'd brought from home, coming up with one of her bras and a pair of her panties. "It's not that."

She grabbed the hem of her shirt and pulled it over her head, tossing it to the floor. His eyes roamed unapologetically over her bare skin.

"Oh," Josie said as her hands reached back for the clasp of her bra. "You knew you'd get to see me naked."

"Well, I never don't want to see you naked." He shrugged and handed her the clean bra. "It's just that I love it when you go all badass. It's hot."

Josie kicked off her boots, laughing softly, her eyes rolling. "You know I'm a sure thing, right? I'm going home with you tonight. You don't have to woo me."

He held out an arm for her to hold for balance as she peeled off her socks. "I'll never stop wooing you, Josie."

The serious note in his voice almost made her forget they were at work. Having a husband who could melt her heart and her panties was addictive in the best way. Except for when all the melting distracted her from the fact that he'd been avoiding having the discussion he'd promised her about seeing a therapist. It also didn't help that he looked so damn good.

"Noah," she said tentatively, knowing this wasn't the best time or the place for a personal conversation. "You promised you'd think about—"

"I will," he said quickly, cutting her off. "Not the guy the Chief sent me to, someone else, but I'll do it."

They stood frozen for a long moment, staring at one another. She could see the struggle in the way his hazel eyes darkened.

"Thank you," she said softly.

"I'd be a hypocrite if I didn't," he admitted. "You've dealt with trauma since you were a kid. I've been dealing with it for nine months. I can man up and get help. Plus, we've got Wren now. I know this isn't how either of us expected to become parents. Well, guardians. But I want to do it right. To get better so I can be whatever she needs. Whatever both of you need."

Emotion was thick and hot in Josie's throat, but she didn't have time for it now because as soon as she changed into clean, dry clothes, she had to walk out the door and do her job. She went for flirty instead. "Well, you are going to get very lucky later."

The full-wattage grin he gave her turned her knees to jelly, tempering the mushy feelings threatening to unfurl inside her.

"Better give me an update before you're naked, too," she muttered, shimmying out of her pants. "Any word on Zane?"

"Still in surgery," Noah said, handing her clean panties as he went back to shamelessly ogling her. "But the doctors expect he'll pull through. The prognosis is positive considering the injuries. He'll need a lot of physical therapy but hopefully he'll regain full function in his lower limbs. Hollis is with him."

Josie slid them on and then took the tote from him, digging through the contents. Thank God he'd brought her brush. Hopefully she'd be able to drag it through her tangled hair. "Has Jackson asked for an attorney?"

"No."

Why would he? Suicide attempt aside, he must have known that they had absolutely zero evidence to prove that he'd been involved in the murders of Tobias and Cora or that he'd killed Riley.

As if sensing her thoughts, Noah said, "How are you going to get to him?"

Josie slid into the pair of jeans he'd brought her. She'd been thinking about that very question since Jackson was taken into custody. They were in the same position they'd been in when Hollis was their prime suspect. Jackson had had motive and opportunity. Slotting him into the puzzle, the pieces fit but they had no way to prove it. She needed a confession and she was going to get one, whether it was from him or his co-conspirator.

"Did Bruce Olsen come in?" she asked.

"Yeah, he's in interview room two."

"Attorney?"

"Nope."

"Well," she smiled, yanking her new shirt down over her head, "it's my lucky day."

FIFTY

Chief Chitwood leaned his shoulder against the doorframe to his office, arms folded across his thin chest, flinty eyes locked on Josie. He'd been uncharacteristically quiet since watching her interview with Bruce Olsen. She sat at her desk, reviewing Detective John Fanning's case file for what felt like the hundredth time while slugging down the blonde latte Noah had left for her before he went home. Across the room, Gretchen stood by their ancient printer, collecting the documents it spit out.

"Found what I was looking for," Josie told her. "Hitting print now."

Gretchen huffed. "Which means I can expect it in four to six weeks."

Josie laughed. "Oooh, express service."

Another minute ticked by. Then another. The only sound was the printer coughing and spluttering like a three-pack-a-day smoker that swallowed a hairball.

Josie could still feel those eyes burning holes into the side of her face.

Gretchen shot her a questioning look. Josie shrugged. She

was used to the Chief's abrasive behavior, his abruptness, his tirades and the disconcerting way he dropped a compliment into what was otherwise a collection of barked commands and sharp criticisms. This silent lurking was weird.

Finally, Gretchen said, "Something on your mind, Chief?"

Ignoring her, he snapped, "Quinn, you sure about this?"

Josie sighed. "It's the only card we've got to play."

"You could be wrong."

"I'm not."

"Palmer," he said. "You on board with this little plan Quinn cooked up?"

"One hundred percent," Gretchen said without hesitation.

He made a noise in his throat. "Which one of you is going in there?"

"Josie," Gretchen answered. "That's what we agreed. She's the best option here. I'm going to bring Bruce Olsen out of room two handcuffed while Jackson's being escorted into room one."

Josie poured the last drops of her latte into her mouth. "He has to see Olsen in custody."

Before the Chief could chime in, the stairwell door whooshed open. A teenage girl strode into the room. Sixteen, maybe seventeen. She wore baggy jeans, the knees ripped out, and a black crop top that showed off the kind of flat stomach only someone under twenty-five could achieve, complete with a navel piercing. She stopped at the four conjoined desks, a familiar pair of blue eyes flashing, and flicked her long, dark hair over her shoulder.

The door opened again, slowly this time, and their desk sergeant, Dan Lamay, shuffled in, panting, cheeks flushed and sweaty. "I told her I'd call up to see—" He stopped to catch his breath. "Slipped right past me."

"I'm here to see my dad," the girl announced to the room.

The Chief didn't look even remotely surprised. Gretchen

walked up beside Josie's chair, handing her a stack of printouts while they each appraised the newcomer.

"Who's your dad?" asked Josie.

"Kyle Turner."

Josie was vaguely aware that both she and Gretchen were so stunned that they could neither speak nor move. Like deer in headlights or fainting goats.

"Did you hear me?" the girl demanded.

The eyes. She had his eyes. She was tall, too. The hair color was similar but this kid had none of his unruly curls. Unless she straightened them.

Gretchen's words came out with the speed of molasses, each word like its own complete sentence. "Kyle. Turner."

"He works here," the girl explained. "He's six four, crazy curly hair, always wears a suit. Total asshole."

Laughter burst from Gretchen's mouth and Josie knew they were thinking the same thing. Even Turner's daughter didn't like him. Was that why he never talked about her? Or was he just that private?

"Well?" the girl said. "Do you know where he is?"

"He's not due on shift for a few more hours," Josie said. "Don't you have his cell number?"

"Ugh," she moaned. "Forget it. I'll figure it out. If you see him, just tell him we need to talk. I'm Cassidy, by the way."

Josie opened her mouth to introduce herself, but Cassidy was already walking briskly toward the stairwell. She stopped when she reached Lamay. "Sorry I made you climb all those steps, but I had to see for myself."

Once they were both gone, Josie and Gretchen looked over at the Chief. "Did you know that Turner had—" Josie began.

He cut her off. "Let's get started. I want to be able to rub something in the Mayor's smug, botoxed face tomorrow when she sashays through here looking for an update on this 'high-profile' case."

FIFTY-ONE

Jackson Wright's reaction to seeing Bruce Olsen being led out of the other interview room in handcuffs was exactly what Josie had hoped for. On the way up from the holding cells, hands cuffed in front of him, Jackson had been expressionless, his body loose with defeat. Gone was his confident, purposeful swagger and in its place was the slow, sad walk of a man who now found life so pointless that every step hurt.

Josie could have worked with that but she had a feeling that the nervousness that swept over him after seeing Olsen was going to be even more to her advantage. Inside the small interview room, he hesitated, looking around as if he wasn't sure what to do next. The walls were cinderblock, painted in a depressing periwinkle blue. A scarred metal table sat along one of them with three vinyl chairs pushed under it.

"Take any seat," Josie instructed him. "Officer Conlen will take off your cuffs."

Jackson folded his large frame into the chair furthest from the door. Once Conlen removed the cuffs and left the room, Josie took the seat closest to Jackson. She placed the folder of documents she'd amassed for this interview in the center of the table.

"Can I get you anything?" she asked. "Water? Food? A coffee or soda?"

He shook his head. Since Denton transferred people to the Alcott County jail for booking and processing, Jackson was still dressed in the T-shirt and jeans he'd been wearing when he crushed his brother with a soda machine. They were stiff and wrinkled and streaked with dirt. He'd lost his hat and his dark locks were wild and unkempt.

Ignoring her offer, he said, "How's Zane?"

Josie took it as a good sign that his first concern was his brother, even if he'd been the one to harm him.

"Jackson, I'm going to read you your rights before we discuss your brother and the other things we need to talk about."

"Then you'll tell me how he is?"

"Yes."

She recited his Miranda rights. He confirmed that he understood them. When a couple of minutes passed and he didn't request an attorney, Josie forged ahead.

"Zane is in bad shape. He underwent several hours of surgery today and he'll probably need more. It will be a very long recovery."

Jackson visibly flinched. Lowering his head in shame, he said, "Did he have internal injuries?"

"No. He was very lucky. Just a lot of broken bones. Comminuted fractures. Crush injuries."

"Fuck." Jackson put his head in his hands. "Is Hollis with him?"

"Yeah," Josie said, softening her tone. "Hollis isn't leaving his side."

"I didn't mean to hurt him, I just... I don't know what happened. I..." His words were muffled by his hands.

Josie turned her chair and scooted it forward so that their knees were almost touching. "We talked about a lot of disturbing things today. Painful things. You were dealing with a lot already—burying your dad and Cora. Riley's death."

She was deliberate with her wording and careful to keep any hint of accusation from her voice.

"Then Detective Palmer and I showed up and asked you to relive your mother's death and Gabrielle's death. You were talking with us about those very traumatic memories and then Zane showed up and, being your little brother, he got upset. He had a lot of questions, didn't he?"

Jackson nodded into his hands.

"He was upset with you."

Finally, he lifted his head, grimacing. "He's always upset with me."

"Not like today. We need to talk about some of the things he said." She left out "the things that made you drop a soda machine on him."

"What the hell else is there to talk about? I figured out my dad was a lying murderer. I couldn't prove it. Then he vanished."

Josie pulled the file folder toward her, leaving her palm on top of it. "That was a tidy solution to your problem, wasn't it?"

He snuck a glance at the folder. "My problem?"

"The problem of proving that he was a killer."

"I mean, yeah, I guess. It didn't matter once he was gone."

Josie sighed and flipped the file open. "Jackson, we can dance around this all night. I have nowhere to be but there's no point. You and I both know that. So let's get down to it. Tell me about the night you killed Tobias and Cora."

An incredulous laugh bubbled up from his chest, dying when he met her unwavering gaze.

"I didn't kill them, and I didn't kill Riley. I know my brother was saying some outlandish shit earlier, but I didn't do it."

"Interesting you should say that." Josie thumbed through the documents in the file until she found the statement that Bruce Olsen had given to Fanning shortly after Tobias and Cora disappeared. "Why would Mr. Olsen need to give you an alibi for something you didn't do?"

"He didn't—that's not what happened. I—"

Josie slid the statement over to him. "This is filled with lies. We just took another statement from Mr. Olsen where he admitted to lying in this one. Pretty much the only thing he told the truth about was that you were a guest at Karl Staab's retirement party. But you didn't get drunk. You weren't there all night."

"That party started at six," Jackson said, pushing the statement back to her. "Everyone there was drunk as hell, including Olsen. How could they possibly remember anything? I was there all night."

"You make a fair point," Josie said. "And if it was just Olsen who said you left after nine p.m., I would be inclined to believe you, but we found two other men who were at the party who admitted that they saw you leave just after nine and not return."

His face paled. "Wh-what?"

"Remember what I said earlier? Olsen was a highly respected member of the law enforcement community. When he was with Brighton Springs PD he received a commendation of valor. His credibility was unimpeachable." Josie snagged another statement from the file, this time waving it in his face rather than giving it to him. It was Olsen's recent statement, but it didn't contain the things she was about to tell Jackson. "Olsen knew that you'd been seen leaving the party early by at least two of his former colleagues so as soon as Fanning started checking alibis, he took those guys aside and told them that if they were asked, you were at the party all night. They went along with it because they figured Olsen had his reasons. After a year or so went by with no sign of Tobias and Cora, they both wanted to come clean but realized that doing so would put them at risk of prosecution. Perjury. Obstructing justice."

Jackson splayed one hand over his stomach but said nothing.

"We offered not to bring charges against them if they gave us Olsen," she continued. "And Olsen, well, he's getting a reduced sentence for telling us all about you."

"So I left the party around nine or whatever," Jackson said. "That doesn't prove anything. Olsen is lying. He doesn't know anything."

That wasn't too far from the truth, but Josie wasn't going to let him know that. Instead, she pulled a pile of photos from the file and placed it in front of him. "Recognize this car?"

He stared at the top photo. "I don't... no. It's just a car."

"That is a 2017 Chevrolet Equinox that was registered to Mr. Olsen at the time that Tobias and Cora were killed. One of three vehicles registered to his household."

She spread out the other photos which she'd borrowed from a different file. They were taken while Hummel was processing the interior of a car that had almost identical upholstery for latent bloodstains.

"Mr. Olsen sold this vehicle in 2019 to a retiree in Harrisburg," Josie continued. "But she was happy to give us permission to process it for latent bloodstains and DNA."

Jackson's fingers trembled as he touched a photo of the steering wheel with three faded fingerprints on the top of it, glowing red.

"We used a selective turn-on NIR fluorescence dye. NIR is near infra-red radiation. Basically, when you've got a latent bloodstain—not visible to the naked eye—you can use this dye on it. The dye itself isn't very fluorescent but when it binds with a particular protein found in human blood, it lights right up. The great thing about this dye is that even if latent bloodstains have been cleaned up or diluted a thousand times, they can still be detected."

Jackson's fingers shook so badly that he clapped them between his knees.

"The thing is," Josie went on, "Mr. Olsen told us that the night of Karl Staab's retirement party, you asked to borrow his Equinox even though your own car was already there. That was something else he never told anyone. Until now. He said you left in it just after nine and returned it around six the next morning."

That part was true. Olsen had admitted that to Josie in his interview. He'd also given them the name and address of the woman he'd sold his Equinox to but Josie hadn't had time to contact her, much less get her car impounded and processed for blood and DNA. Those types of things required warrants and lots of time for test results to come back. Jackson had picked up a lot from Tobias's law enforcement friends over the years, but evidently he hadn't learned that processing and analyzing most evidence could take weeks or months.

She tapped a finger against the photo of the prints and then against a photo of the driver's seat where the dye had lit up red in uneven streaks. "Guess whose prints those are? Guess whose blood that is right there? Whose DNA? All of it in Mr. Olsen's old car just waiting for the police to come along with their fancy dye?"

This was her biggest bluff. Neither she nor Bruce Olsen had any idea what had actually happened after Jackson left in the Equinox. It had been returned in mint condition with a faint bleach smell on the inside.

Everything else was supposition on Josie's part. There was no actual blood. There were no actual fingerprints. No physical proof. She just needed Jackson to believe that there was.

"Jackson?"

He couldn't tear his eyes away from the pictures. The trembling in his fingers spread to his forearms.

"I understand why you did it," Josie said in her most sympathetic voice. "You were angry with your dad before Cora came along. Realizing what he'd done and knowing there was nothing you could do about it. Believe me, I get how frustrating it is to know in your bones that someone did something criminal and realize that they'll never pay for it because there is simply no proof. Nothing definitive, anyway."

"I didn't—it wasn't about revenge," he said, so quietly that Josie had to lean in to catch the words.

Inside her, a dam broke. Relief poured through her body like the sweetest drug. There it was—the first crack. She just hoped the camera had captured his words.

"Oh, I know," she said.

His blue eyes searched hers. "You do?" He sounded genuinely surprised.

"If it was simply about revenge, you would have done it a lot sooner," Josie said. "Probably a lot more impulsively, too. I have to hand it to you, Jackson. The meticulous planning that went into this is impressive. You had everyone stumped for seven years. If it wasn't for the drought, your streak might have lasted decades. You committed a flawless crime. I took in the scope of what you did, and I knew that there was only one reason you could have done it."

He watched her with a sort of hopefulness in his eyes. The desire to be seen and understood fully was powerful. Josie had leveraged it in many of these types of interrogations.

She dropped the word like a bomb. "Love."

Time stopped. She could feel it. Jackson's body was as still as the dead. She wasn't sure if he was even breathing. Then, the first tear broke free, rolling down his cheek, fat and heavy.

"I didn't think anyone would understand," he croaked. "It wasn't evil. It wasn't cold or callous. It came from the best possible place. It had to be done. He never would have stopped and he would have kept getting away with it."

"I know," Josie said. "And Jackson, I know everything that happened that night. What I don't know is whose idea it was to kill Tobias—yours or Cora's?"

FIFTY-TWO

That he didn't look surprised in the slightest told her that her crazy theory—the one the Chief didn't entirely buy—was correct. She allowed herself a quick glance at the camera, wondering if Gretchen and the Chief could sense her mental fist pump. Finally, they were unraveling the most baffling mystery of this case.

"It was Cora's idea," Jackson said.

Josie wasn't sure she believed him but blaming Cora would allow him to confess while foisting as much responsibility as he wished onto a dead woman.

"Did she find Rachel's purse herself or did you know about it already?"

He shook his head. "I didn't know about it. Dad was already acting kind of scary. In that uneasy brooding way, I mean. Other than the day he killed Gabby, I never saw him raise a hand to anyone. I'm not sure if it was her experience with Dalton or what but Cora had this sixth sense about Dad. Once the whirlwind romance wore off and she was living in his house, basically financially dependent on him, she started to get creeped out. Noticed the way he was always trying to manipulate her. Isolate her from the friends she had before him. I guess a lot of it was stuff Dalton did, too, early on in their marriage."

"How did this come up between you?" Josie inched her chair closer.

Another tear trailed down his cheek. He kept his head bent, avoiding eye contact. "Everyone was always coming and going from Dad's house. I would go for dinner or pick Zane up to do something together. There were the days Dalton came for her and Dad and Hollis weren't close enough to get rid of him. There were times I stopped over and she was the only one home. After a while I noticed something was off about her. She was jumpy, skittish. A couple of times I caught her crying alone."

Just as Hollis had found her in the diner bathroom. Just as Dalton had found her in the parking lot of the Majesty Motel. Cora's slow unraveling was a consistent detail in the narrative of the Lachlan/Stevens tragedy.

"Did she talk to you about why she was acting that way?"

He rubbed at the dark spots on his jeans where his tears fell. "Not at first, no. I mean, I was her stepson, basically. Talk about awkward. It really nagged at me though. I knew it wasn't because of Dalton and all his bullshit. She'd dealt with him for years. Even when he was at his worst, she handled him well. Cora was strong but I just... I couldn't leave it alone."

"Because you already knew what your dad was capable of."

Jackson swallowed hard. "Yeah. One day I just asked her what was going on and she blew me off. It took a long time to get her to talk to me. I had to promise not to breathe a word to Dad. Even after that, she didn't want to tell me what had her so rattled. Then, little by little, it came out. She'd started finding weird stuff in the house."

"Like the purse?"

"No, not then. More like weird messages. There was one

carved into the bottom of a dresser drawer, underneath a liner. It said, 'Leave while you still can.'"

Josie wondered where that dresser was at the moment and whether Fanning and his team had missed the message or just hadn't thought to peel up the liners. It didn't matter now. "Did you have any ideas who might have left that message?"

"It was Gabby's dresser, so probably her. Like I told you, she wanted to leave Dad too. Looking back, I wonder if she was skeptical of the story about my mom just leaving. I think Gabby was definitely afraid of him before the day it happened."

Josie felt a sense of profound sorrow mixed with deep frustration. She had no doubt that Jackson was right. Gabrielle Lachlan's instincts had been screaming that she was in danger, just as Cora's had, but in many instances, society drilled into women that those instincts couldn't be trusted, that they were overreacting. Making something out of nothing. Especially when everything was fine on the surface. Tobias wasn't violent. He hadn't hit either of them. From everything Josie had learned about him through Fanning's files and various interviews, he hadn't even been the type to lose control and trash the house, punch walls, or throw things. At his best, he was devoted, caring, and attentive. At his worst, he was manipulative and moody. Objectively, there was no reason to feel threatened by him. By all accounts, he wasn't a threat.

Until he was.

"Did Cora begin to suspect that he'd killed Rachel and Gabby on her own or did you share your suspicions?" Josie asked.

"I told her. She believed me," he said. "I'm not sure what made her look under the floorboards. Maybe the message in the dresser? That key was in there, too. I didn't realize why he had it hidden in there at first."

"But you had already put it together that he very likely killed your mother."

Jackson nodded. "I did a reverse image search and saw that it went to a Pooley phonograph cabinet and then I knew why he kept it."

Just as Noah had theorized, it was a trophy. Just like Rachel's purse. It didn't appear that he'd kept one from Gabrielle, unless you counted the creepy dresser. Had Tobias known about the words carved inside the drawer? The very thought made her queasy.

"Cora showed you the purse," Josie said, wanting to move things along.

His tears had stopped but his voice was raspy. "Right. Yeah. At first, I was just going to help her leave but then she found that stuff. I told her to take it to Bruce. On her own. I didn't know if he'd be straight with me. She thought he could help get Dad arrested but it wasn't enough."

"So you went to plan B," Josie said. "Kill Tobias. Everyone would be safe. He'd pay for his sins and he'd never be able to hurt another woman again. The relationship would be over and you'd be free to pursue Riley, eventually. Tell me, how were you two going to explain Tobias's disappearance?"

Still, he wouldn't make eye contact. "Um, we decided we would forge a letter from him."

"Like your dad did when he killed your mom."

It was poetic, really. A final and fitting *fuck you* to the man who had gotten away with murder for over twenty years. That, however, would likely have gotten them caught. They wouldn't have needed to involve the police if it appeared that Tobias had left on his own. If they somehow came under scrutiny, perhaps Jackson could have convinced Bruce Olsen to cover for them. But Josie couldn't see Zane or Hollis backing off and accepting that story. Eventually, the house of cards Jackson and Cora had built would have come crashing down.

It was ironic that Cora's death had made the crime nearly unsolvable.

Josie said, "But then everything went wrong."

Another tear slid down his face. "Yeah," he said huskily. "Everything went wrong."

"Tell me."

She waited, not moving or breathing, to see if he'd take the reins and spill everything. To confirm that all of her instincts had been correct.

"The plan was to kill him and then roll him—inside his car—into the river. Cora said it had to be really far away. Hol was going to Denton all the time so a couple of times I went with him and had a look around. Found a good spot."

"But you'd need a second car," Josie said.

"Yeah. We talked about planting one there but then the invite to Karl's party came and it just seemed like the best opportunity we were going to have. I knew that Bruce would cover for me, especially after Cora brought him my mom's purse. I knew he'd feel guilty enough to look the other way."

He had. Bruce had told her that he had no direct knowledge of the murders. There was never any discussion between him and Jackson about it. He admitted to knowing on some level that Jackson had been involved but taking care to never examine that thought too closely. Of course, Josie had no proof that Bruce hadn't played a much larger part in the whole thing, but she believed him. He hadn't even suspected that Cora was involved.

"Was Cora going to dinner with Tobias part of your plan?" asked Josie.

"No, actually. I always intended to use Karl's party as my alibi but we just figured we'd get Dad alone somehow on the night of. Then he wanted to take her out to dinner and we thought it was perfect."

Josie had known from the start that there was no way the murders were carried out by one person. Once she realized it was Jackson and not Hollis or Dalton or someone else, she thought Olsen was his partner. It made so much sense. Not only did Olsen have a soft spot for Jackson but he'd been given proof in the form of Rachel's purse that Tobias was not what he seemed. It hadn't occurred to Josie that Cora was the accomplice. Not until she read the infamous last text about Captain Whiskers. In all the news reports and interviews, the message was described simply as Cora asking Jackson to let the cat into the house.

When Josie pulled up the records from Fanning's case file, it was quite a different thing.

Hey, do you think you could let Captain Whiskers inside? If she doesn't come in right away, she'll be wound up in high gear, ready to give me hell when I get home.

"You and Cora agreed that she would send you a text when they left the restaurant," Josie said. "So you'd know when to leave the party. But it had to be something that if read by anyone else, would seem insignificant. Normal. Asking you to let Captain Whiskers inside wasn't abnormal—not if you played it off as her sending the message to the wrong brother."

"Yeah," Jackson agreed. "She was insane about that kind of stuff. I guess from being with Dalton all those years and having to be so careful so he didn't beat her."

"'If she doesn't come in right away' meant come right away, didn't it?" she asked.

"Yeah. Well, it was supposed to mean they were in the car. Once they started driving, there was a limited timeframe to get him before he went home."

"'Wound up in high gear. Gear. Like Geerling Road, just spelled differently. Had you scouted that location out beforehand?"

"I had, yeah. Cora's job was just to get him to take that way home instead of the other way."

"'Ready to give me hell' was her way of saying she was ready to kill Tobias?"

"Yeah. I got to the clearing first and stood out in the road. He stopped right away when he saw me. I told him I broke down. He never even questioned it. Pulled right into the clearing. Then I pulled the gun on him, we tied him up, threw him into the trunk of his car and drove to Denton. Cora took his car and I took Bruce's."

"Where did you get the gun?"

"It was my dad's," Jackson explained. "He never used it. Cora snuck it out and then once everything was over, I put it back in the safe after Riley and Zane called me to come to the house. They never even noticed."

The entire thing was diabolical. "Once you got to Denton, things didn't go so well, did they?"

More tears fell. "I couldn't do it. Couldn't look him in the eye and kill him."

"He came after you."

"It wasn't even this big epic struggle. He was still tied up, hands and feet, standing and trying to keep his own balance. I was pointing the gun at him. Cora was off to the side. He just kind of plowed into me hard enough for the gun to swing toward her and it just... it went off."

Josie waited as he cried quietly into his hands.

"She was dead. Bled out in my arms. After that, it wasn't hard at all to look into his eyes when I killed him. I sat there, in the dark, crying for a long time. Holding Cora. I couldn't take her back or call the police 'cause then they'd know what we did so I went with the original plan to push the car into the river, just with her in it as well."

"You took her necklace and engagement ring before you got her back into the car, didn't you?" asked Josie.

Tears gave way to violent sobs. Chest heaving, his words came out like a jagged wail. The sound of it sent an eerie prickle of disquiet, like pins and needles, over her skin. In the back of her mind, a dark curtain lifted, and the final piece of the puzzle slotted into place.

Jackson rocked in his chair, his movements fast and jerky.

"I just..."

Sob.

Cora hadn't even trusted Bruce Olsen not to run to Tobias and rat her out and Olsen wasn't a family member. She'd saved up money that could have been used to leave Tobias just to ensure that her secret would be safe.

"I needed..."

Wail.

Even if Jackson shared his suspicions, would someone as cautious as Cora really trust him not to go against his father? At age twelve, he'd witnessed Tobias murder Gabrielle and never said a word, not even as an adult. Not even to his many law enforcement friends.

"I needed..." Jackson keened, "something from her."

Would someone as careful as Cora trust Tobias's own son, who'd had ample opportunity to turn him in, to help her murder Tobias and keep it a secret?

Sob.

"I missed her. I missed her so bad. I needed..."

What had Zane told Josie about Jackson's romantic history? Yes, he was a serial womanizer but among the women he had listed, a pattern had emerged. Jackson frequently dated older women.

"Dad bought her that jewelry." More keening. His breathing was labored, face deep red. "But it was hers. It was hers."

Cora wouldn't have trusted Jackson. After everything she'd been through, trusting men was tantamount to a death sentence.

Unless.

Josie reached across and touched Jackson's shoulder, whispering for him to calm down, to breathe. Several minutes later, he quieted. Tears still streamed down his face, but his breathing was steadier.

She handed him a clump of tissues. "Jackson," she said, "how long were you and Cora lovers?"

FIFTY-THREE

Jackson lifted his chin, his watery blue eyes awash with grief and pain. His shoulders curled in. Everything about his slumped posture radiated defeat. In this moment, he looked not just harmless but pathetic. Pitiful. Yet, he'd had the size and strength to push a soda machine onto his brother. He'd loaded two bodies into a sedan and pushed that sedan into the river by himself. Jackson Wright was a contradiction in many ways, but one thing was crystal clear: he was deeply, irrevocably sick.

Using the tissues to blot his wet cheeks, he whispered, "About seven months. We didn't mean for it to happen."

Josie could practically hear Gretchen's sarcastic remark from the video room. *The slogan of adulterers everywhere.*

"There was no digital footprint," she said. "No texts or social media messages."

Jackson sniffed. "Cora was really strict about that. Everything had to be in person so Dad wouldn't find out or even suspect. I'd stop at the house to see Zane or pick something up when no one else was home. Sometimes we'd say that Dalton came by and I'd had to head him off. Or I'd go to the diner where it wouldn't be weird if we were seen talking together."

It was exactly as the team had theorized, except they'd thought that if Cora had had an affair, it was with Hollis. Dalton Stevens had been right even though the reasons he'd suspected an affair had been related to something else entirely.

"So," Josie said softly. "You and Cora were going to murder Tobias, convince everyone that he had simply left, like Rachel, and then what? You and Cora could finally be together?"

"Eventually, yeah. We were going to keep hiding it until things blew over. Then I was going to propose to her."

Josie wondered if they'd ever considered how strange and inappropriate, maybe even suspicious, it would have looked to everyone else in their lives. Jackson ending up with his dad's older fiancée whose daughter was closer in age to him than her. It didn't matter.

"She was the love of my life," Jackson muttered. "I knew I had to put her into the river with him. I hated that but she wouldn't have wanted me to go to prison. Not over him."

The urge to ask him if Cora would have wanted him to go to prison for murdering her daughter was strong but Josie suppressed it. She had one more confession she needed to get from him.

"You kept Cora's jewelry so you could feel close to her," Josie said.

He nodded. "It was stupid. I should have left it."

"Stupid because Riley found it?"

A fresh wave of sobs erupted from him. "I thought I hid it where she'd never find it but she went back to the house for the cat's meds and her toys. Those stupid fucking toys. Two of them got stuck between my dresser and the wall. We have a dozen of those dumbass fake mice but she just had to try to get to those. Never for a second did I think she would try to move the dresser herself."

"But she did," Josie said.

His chest heaved as he struggled to get his breath under

control. "She could only move it enough to fit her arm behind it, but it was enough for her sleeve to catch on the tape. I used duct tape to attach the cloth pouch with Cora's jewelry in it to the back of the dresser. She knew it was her mom's right away. When she came back to Hol's, she woke me up. She was a mess."

"You fought?"

"I didn't want to kill her but she didn't understand. She couldn't understand. Wouldn't listen to me. She was going to go to the police. I tried to tell her it was a mistake, that Cora was never supposed to be killed, but she didn't care."

"You injected her with insulin?" Josie asked.

"I had no choice. It was the only way. I asked her to sit down and try to compose herself so we could talk things over while I grabbed her a drink."

"You weren't getting her a drink."

"No, I... I knew she wasn't going to listen to reason. I sat next to her on the bed. Kept her talking. She was so upset and she'd been drinking already. She didn't even realize what I was doing. I told her I'd go to the police, confess everything if she just gave me some time. A few hours. She promised me she wouldn't tell Zane or Hol, that she'd let me do it. She wanted to get away from me and I let her go because I didn't think she'd get very far. I didn't want to do it. Didn't want to kill her. It was so bad. So bad." His voice went up two octaves. "It was like losing Cora all over again."

Josie managed to suppress a cringe as he fell apart before her eyes again. Before she knew about the true extent of his relationship with Cora, she'd wondered why he had started a relationship with Riley. He had pursued her, according to Zane. It didn't seem healthy, but it wasn't outside the realm of possibility that it had been an organic thing. That he'd fallen in love with her and just couldn't fight the pull, but this confirmed for her that the fractures in Jackson's soul that allowed him to justify the most horrific and despicable acts ran deeper than she imagined. Riley had just been a facsimile of Cora.

A replacement. A disposable replacement.

The exhilaration of coming up with theories, developing a plan to test them out, and eliciting a confession wore off quickly, replaced by bitter disappointment. One of the silver linings of her job was that sometimes, she was able to help get justice for people who were wronged. Certainly Tobias and Cora had been wronged. They definitely hadn't deserved to die but neither had they been innocent. Solving their case didn't bring the usual satisfaction. At least she'd know that she'd played a part in getting justice for Riley.

Hours later, by the time Jackson had finished writing out his statement, reviewing and signing it, Josie only cared about one thing: getting home and laying eyes on Wren.

FIFTY-FOUR

TWO WEEKS LATER

"Mom, I'm not walking down the aisle. This isn't a wedding!" Josie complained.

Shannon shoved a bouquet of flowers into Josie's hand and circled her, fussing with her dress and her hair. "You have to get to the front somehow."

"I know that," Josie said. "But I don't have to do it in a bridal procession. I wanted small and intimate."

Shannon tucked a loose tendril of hair behind Josie's ear. "You look stunning."

From the other side of the French doors that separated the lobby from the main room, Josie heard talking and laughing and somehow, above it all, her husband's deep, rich voice, like her own personal siren song. She couldn't see him now because Shannon wouldn't let her peek through the doors but they'd gotten dressed at home so she already knew he looked gorgeous in a light brown suit that went perfectly with his hazel eyes.

From behind her came a loud snort, then Wren's amused voice. "You are totally walking down the aisle."

Josie turned around and her breath caught in her throat. As much as she enjoyed looking at Noah, there was nothing more beautiful than one of Wren's genuine smiles. Josie mentally hoarded them like the little Wren addict she was, counting each one as a win in the battle against Wren's grief. The battle for her soul. That was the weighty responsibility that Dex had given her.

Things had improved a bit in the last two weeks. The two of them had had an actual moment. One evening after dinner, Wren presented Josie with a wad of cash. "To pay for your new work shirts," she had said nervously. When Josie asked where she'd gotten it, Wren explained that she'd drawn several kids at school as superheroes and charged them a couple of dollars each. Her peers had been far more excited about the idea than she anticipated so she'd earned quite a bit. Wren still wouldn't share her work with Josie, but she had allowed a brief hug. Josie had floated around on a giant cloud of euphoria for days.

"Hey, you okay?" Wren said.

Josie blinked. Shannon was assessing Misty now and shoving another bouquet into Erica's arms, and there was Erica's grandmother, Miranda, sprung from her assisted living facility for the day, looking positively radiant in a beautiful, flowing lavender dress with her long white hair cascading down her back. She kept her hand tucked in the crook of Erica's elbow. Miranda lived with aphasia which meant that she couldn't speak. With therapy and assistive devices, she'd come a long way, but whenever they took her out—which they did as often as possible—she stuck close to Erica. Honestly, the two of them couldn't get enough of one another.

Miranda saw Josie staring and gave her a bright smile. Then she winked.

Dammit all to hell.

The tears came so hot and fast, Josie had no chance of stopping them. She spun back around but not before Wren said, in an awestruck voice, "Oh my God. Are you crying?"

"She doesn't cry." Gretchen sauntered in from outside,

wearing a dress that fell just above her knees, which was one of the oddest things that Josie had ever seen. The bridesmaid dress Gretchen had worn at their first wedding—attempted wedding—had been floor-length.

Tears forgotten, she stared stupidly at her friend.

"What?" Gretchen said. "What is it?"

"I don't—you just—you have nice legs."

Wren laughed. "Was that a compliment? 'Cause you said it in the same tone of voice Trinity uses when she tells someone they have something in their teeth."

Gretchen smirked, her eyes sparkling as she held Josie's gaze. "Yeah, that was a compliment. We have a weird dynamic."

Shannon flitted over and thrust a bouquet at Gretchen. Then she stopped and looked her over. "Wow, Gretchen. You have great legs."

"Thanks." She sidled up to Josie. "This wedding is good for my self-esteem."

Josie wiped her tears away, hoping her makeup wasn't ruined. "It's not a wedding."

The ambient noise from the other room got louder as the doors opened just far enough for Trinity to squeeze through them. "They're just about ready for us and oh, look! You all look fabulous."

Josie turned again to survey the scene. Everyone's dress was different but each of them was a shade of lavender. "Why do I have bridesmaids? Mom, did you make my friends bridesmaids? I hope you know I'm not walking down the aisle."

Shannon ignored her, waving everyone else into a line and putting them one by one in front of Josie.

Wren said, "It's cute how you think Shannon's not the boss of you."

"She's not," Josie mumbled but not loud enough for her mother to hear.

Then the doors were opening and all the best women she

knew were walking in a line to a song she didn't recognize. Christian was there with his arm extended for her to take. Her actual father walking her down an actual aisle toward a husband she'd gladly marry every day of the week, even if it meant tolerating Shannon as wedding planner.

At the front of the room, the Chief waited with a little black notebook in hand. He was officiating. Little Harris bounced on the balls of his feet between Noah and Drake. Noah's brother, Theo, laughed at something that Patrick whispered in his ear. There was an energy filling up the vast space that was improbably happy considering the hardship and heartbreak it had taken them all to get to this place. Not just Josie and Noah but the Paynes, Erica, Miranda, and Wren.

Josie could get high on this feeling.

Christian gave her a kiss on the cheek before leaving her standing across from Noah. He grinned at her. "Nice bridesmaids."

She laughed, long and loud, and not even a little bit elegant. "You bought an anniversary band, didn't you?"

"No comment."

"Right. We're returning it after this... whatever this is!"

Noah leaned in, his lips brushing against her ear. Drake said, "We're not at that part yet, you two. Break it up."

"We can't return it," Noah whispered. "Wren picked it out."

Josie gasped. Spinning, she found Wren right behind her. Without thinking, she took her hand, encouraged that Wren didn't recoil or pull away. "You picked out the band?"

"Oh my God. It was supposed to be a surprise." Craning to see Noah over Josie's shoulder, Wren added, "You're, like, the worst secret-keeper ever."

"Thank you," Josie told her. "Come on. Let's do this together."

Without letting go of Wren's hand, Josie guided her until

she was standing between her and Noah. Shannon appeared behind them like some kind of wedding ninja and took their bouquets.

Noah looked down at Wren and extended his palm. Josie knew that the playful look on his face was meant to reassure her that he wouldn't be offended if she refused his offer. After a few seconds of consideration, Wren slid her hand into his, completing their circle.

"All right, all right," the Chief said. "Everyone be quiet. Let's get this wed—"

Josie gave him a pointed look which he returned with a barely noticeable smile.

"Let's get this renewal ceremony started."

A LETTER FROM LISA

Thank you so much for choosing to read *The Couple's Secret*. If you enjoyed the book and want to keep up to date with all my latest releases, just sign up at the following link. Your email address will never be shared, and you can unsubscribe at any time.

www.bookouture.com/lisa-regan

If you're familiar with me and my books, you know that I do a lot of research to try to ensure that what I write about is represented as accurately and as authentically as possible. There are sacrifices that sometimes have to be made for the sake of entertainment because this is fiction, after all. My primary job is to transport you from your daily life to the world of Denton for a few hours and keep you enthralled. For this book, I had the pleasure of speaking with Doug Bishop of United Search Corps, a non-profit organization committed to bringing closure to families of missing and murdered people all over the United States by searching waterways for submerged vehicles. Speaking with Doug was hands-down one of the most fascinating conversations I've ever had. The work that he and his team do is necessary, selfless and inspiring. If you'd like to read more about the organization and the cases they've solved, you can visit their website at www.unitedsearchcorps.org.

As always, any mistakes or inaccuracies are mine and mine alone.

Again, thank you so much for reading the twenty-third book in the series. It's a dream come true to continue to write these books for you. Thank you for sticking with Josie and her team.

Finally, I love hearing your thoughts and questions. You can get in touch with me through my website or any of the social media outlets below, as well as my Goodreads page. Also, I'd really appreciate it if you'd leave a review and recommend *The Couple's Secret*, or perhaps other books in the series, to other readers. Reviews and word-of-mouth recommendations go such a long way toward helping new readers discover my books. Thank you so much for your relentless enthusiasm and passion for Josie and the world of Denton, PA. I hope to see you next time!

Thanks,

Lisa Regan

www.lisaregan.com

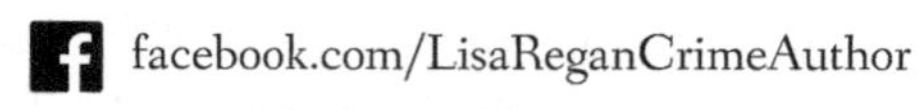

ACKNOWLEDGMENTS

Lovely readers: Your devotion to this series, especially now that we are so deep into it (Book 23!!!) is a gift that I treasure every single day. Your enthusiasm for the last book, *Husband Missing*, was astounding and humbling. Thank you so much for always showing up for me and for Josie. I know I say it at the end of every book but it always holds true: it is my privilege and pleasure to write these stories for all of you. You truly are the best readers in the world! Thank you to the wonderful members of my Reader Lounge. You never fail to make my day! Thank you to all the new readers who are just recently picking up the series, whether you're starting with *Vanishing Girls* or a book somewhere in the middle or toward the end. I really appreciate you taking a chance on Josie!

Thank you, as always, to my husband, Fred. Thank you for coming up with the junk removal company's name. Thank you so much for all of your excellent insight and knowledge, particularly about firearms and the different types of projectiles. Thank you as well for always being willing to sit down and help me brainstorm and keep me creatively charged. You are the best! Thank you to my daughter, Morgan, for your endless care and good humor and as usual, always knowing exactly the right thing to say!

Thank you to my rock star multimedia coordinator, friend and first reader, Maureen Downey, for being as encouraging with this book as you are with each one and never failing to remind me that yes, I can do this! Thank you to my first readers and friends: Katie Mettner, Dana Mason, Nancy S. Thompson, and Torese Hummel. I can always count on you for the most honest feedback and that is a treasure! Thank you to my very lovely, thorough and thoughtful beta readers: Greg Lavine and Brooke Busbee. Thank you as well to Charliene Moore for reading an early draft and for your incredible, insightful, excellent feedback for this book and for *Husband Missing*. I simply cannot thank you enough for the comprehensive, detailed, and astute feedback you provide so generously. I'm so grateful to have found you. Thank you to Matty Dalrymple and Jane Kelly for always being there for me whether it's to sprint, work out a plot point or just have a great lunch together!

Thank you to my grandmothers: Helen Conlen and Marilyn House; my parents: Donna House, Joyce Regan, the late Billy Regan, Rusty House, and Julie House; my brothers and sisters-in-law: Sean and Cassie House, Kevin and Christine Brock and Andy Brock; as well as my lovely sisters: Ava McKittrick and Melissia McKittrick. Thank you as well to all of the people who continue to proudly spread the word about my books even after all these years—Debbie Tralies, Jean and Dennis Regan, Tracy Dauphin, Jeanne Cassidy, the Regans, the Conlens, and the Houses. I am so thankful for you and your unwavering support! I am extremely grateful to all the awesome bloggers and reviewers who consistently read and review every Josie Quinn book. I'm also grateful for the reviewers and bloggers who chose to read *The Couple's Secret* as their first Josie Quinn book. Thanks for taking a chance on it!

Thank you, as always, to Chief Jason Jay for all your very detailed answers to my endless questions, no matter how bizarre a scenario I've concocted. Thank you for always getting back to me within minutes no matter what time of day or night I message! I am eternally grateful for your patience and generosity! Thank you to Stephanie Kelley, my fabulous law enforcement consultant, for having the patience of a saint and such a good sense of humor in walking me through those crazy scenarios. Your expertise is endless and fascinating and I can't tell you how grateful I am for it. You've saved many a book by zeroing in on the things I forgot, overlooked, or just plain got wrong. Thank you again to Leanne Kale Sparks for answering my legal questions in such detail, and for your willingness to talk me through any legal situation I plunge my characters into. Thank you to Joyce Prevot and Sara Miller for taking the time to answer all my questions related to managing type 1 diabetes. Thanks to Joyce and Ava for information about type 1 diabetes from a nursing perspective.

A very, very special thanks to Doug Bishop of United Search Corps for taking so much time to speak with me about finding and recovering vehicles (and remains) that have been submerged in water for years. I am in awe of you and your team. Thank you so much for sharing your fascinating experiences and all the unique aspects of the work you do. Most of all, thank you for working so hard to bring closure to families who have wished and hoped for it for so long—sometimes decades.

Thank you to Jenny Geras for making this process so smooth and being so patient with me. I'm so grateful for all of your insight and advice, which, as always, was spot-on. It was a delight working with you on this one! Finally, thank you to Lizzie O'Brien, Noelle Holten, Kim Nash, Liz Hatherell, and Jenny Page, as well as the entire team at Bookouture for all of your hard work, support and encouragement.

PUBLISHING TEAM

Turning a manuscript into a book requires the efforts of many people. The publishing team at Bookouture would like to acknowledge everyone who contributed to this publication.

Audio
Alba Proko
Melissa Tran
Sinead O'Connor

Commercial
Lauren Morrissette
Hannah Richmond
Imogen Allport

Cover design
The Brewster Project

Data and analysis
Mark Alder
Mohamed Bussuri

Editorial
Jenny Geras
Ria Clare

Copyeditor
Liz Hatherell

Proofreader
Jenny Page

Marketing
Alex Crow
Melanie Price
Occy Carr
Cíara Rosney
Martyna Młynarska

Operations and distribution
Marina Valles
Stephanie Straub
Joe Morris

Production
Hannah Snetsinger
Mandy Kullar
Ria Clare
Nadia Michael

Publicity
Kim Nash
Noelle Holten
Jess Readett
Sarah Hardy

Rights and contracts
Peta Nightingale
Richard King
Saidah Graham

Dear Reader,

We'd love your attention for one more page to tell you about the crisis in children's reading, and what we can all do.

Studies have shown that reading for fun is the **single biggest predictor of a child's future life chances** – more than family circumstance, parents' educational background or income. It improves academic results, mental health, wealth, communication skills, ambition and happiness.

The number of children reading for fun is in rapid decline. Young people have a lot of competition for their time, and a worryingly high number do not have a single book at home.

Hachette works extensively with schools, libraries and literacy charities, but here are some ways we can all raise more readers:

- Reading to children for just 10 minutes a day makes a difference
- Don't give up if children aren't regular readers – there will be books for them!

- Visit bookshops and libraries to get recommendations
- Encourage them to listen to audiobooks
- Support school libraries
- Give books as gifts

There's a lot more information about how to encourage children to read on our websites: **www.RaisingReaders.co.uk** and **www.JoinRaisingReaders.com**.

Thank you for reading.

www.ingramcontent.com/pod-product-compliance
Lightning Source LLC
Chambersburg PA
CBHW022329010925
31932CB00010B/314

* 9 7 8 1 8 0 5 5 0 1 4 2 8 *